INVISIBLY GRACE

INVISIBLY GRACE

AVERY MCDOUGALL

Published by
Forty South Publishing Pty Ltd, Hobart, Tasmania
fortysouth.com.au

Printed by
McPherson's Printing Group, Melbourne, Victoria
mcphersonsprinting.com.au

Cover design
Bianca Jagoe

References for the statement with the dedication opposite:
Ogdie A, Nowell W, Applegate E, *et al.*, THU0292 Diagnostic
experiences of patients with psoriatic arthritis: misdiagnosis is
common. *Annals of the Rheumatic Diseases* 2018;77:364-365.
Ogdie A, Nowell W, Reynolds R, *et al.*, FRI0180 Diagnosis journey
of patients with ankylosing spondylitis in the United States.
Annals of the Rheumatic Diseases 2018;77:631-632.
Seitz M. [Autoimmune diseases: frequent misdiagnosis]. *Schweiz
Med Wochenschr.* 1997 Mar 1;127(9):349-54. German. PMID:
9132933.

For my beloved husband

Thanks for telling me to shut up
every time I said you should get out while you still can.

Studies show it takes between four and ten years to get diagnosed with an autoimmune disease, and almost everyone gets a misdiagnosis first. Depending on the condition, over twenty-five percent of people reported a misdiagnosis of psychosomatic or 'it's all in your head'.

Thanks for sticking it out with me
and never once suggesting I was making it up.

CHAPTER ONE
New School

At least it's a Monday. That's the thought I try to comfort myself with as we pull into the parking lot of Riverview High. Logic dictates that your first day of a new school should be the first day of the school year, right? Like, I don't think I'm being ridiculous when I say it is a little unfair to expect your kid to rock up to a brand new school halfway through the third term of grade ten. But that's what's happening to me. I'm pretty sure that I'm going to have even less social capital than I had at my last school.

At least we found a school that my younger sister and I can both attend, even when I go into year eleven. Apparently, in Tasmania, grades eleven and twelve are their own separate school usually. My sister Ivy could make friends with someone who didn't speak the same language as her in under two hours. She had all these teary goodbyes when we left, and, no word of a lie, six farewell parties. I, on the other hand, had a weird 'promise to stay in touch' conversation with Abbie Lightfoot, who was my best friend on paper; in reality, we were more like two weirdos who formed a tentative alliance because we had no options. Like prison friends. I know that neither of us is honouring that promise to stay in touch, and I'm not even sad about it.

Oh, the other awesome thing about my brand-new school? The uniform is red. Not the usual burgundy or maroon or whatever you might see at other schools. No, Riverview High has the kind of red you could use to colour in a picture of Santa Claus. I can't imagine it looking good on anyone. Despite our shared, watered-down Asian heritage, I look yellow enough to be mistaken for someone with liver failure, while Ivy is almost pulling it off. Almost. Of course, she's not complaining, because she's perfect and I should aspire to be more like her. That's a direct quote from way too many adults in my life. It's a good thing I love the kid to death or I might have to hate her a little bit.

There's one good thing about this whole 'new school' thing. It's not, as my mother says, the opportunity to make new friends. It's not because they have a really good art program, which is what Dad tries to sell me on. The best thing about this new beginning is that nobody knows me, so no-one will know what's wrong with me. I will not be Sick Girl™. Mum says that I'm being 'short-sighted and unfair to my new peers'. She thinks I won't be able to keep it a secret forever and that I shouldn't be ashamed of who I am. Dad is scared for me, because at my old school if something went wrong, everyone knew what to do. What if something happens? Ivy is, as always, on my side. She really is the best. Secretly, I know she agrees with our parents, but she'll never say that to them. I don't know if it's because she's my sister, or if she knows what kids can be like, or if she thinks I deserve the chance to be normal. But I think she gets it, even if she's not entirely on board. But it's grade eleven, which is kind of important, and they're moving me mid-year, so I got to use the guilt to make them agree to it. The teachers will know, of course, because they have to. I'll get to keep my secret identity under wraps. Like the worst superhero ever: Sick Girl, her superpower is being in incredible amounts of pain and vomiting quietly.

Don't you want to be just like her?

'Are you sure about this?' Dad asks for, I shit you not, the thirtieth time this morning. We're sitting in the school carpark and I'm admittedly struggling a little to get myself out of the car. His face is a mixture of sympathy and dubiousness. 'Your knee braces are in the boot. And the emergency walking stick.'

'She's fine,' Ivy replies, exasperated and rolling her eyes. 'She's Grace goddamn Turing. She can do anything.'

'Damn straight,' I tell her, finally getting out of the car carefully. I subluxed my knee two days ago when we were moving so it's still not as stable as I would like. Ivy and I do our weird version of a secret handshake that is actually Auslan for 'everything is amazing'.

'You could use your knee braces,' Dad points out. 'If you weren't so determined to be you.'

'Exactly,' I reply with a sigh. 'I'm determined to be *me*.'

'Fine. I had to ask,' Dad said. I give him a look. 'Last time I'll ask, I promise. I swear on Netflix.'

'That's a pretty serious swear,' Ivy remarks. 'I like it. Want me to come find you at lunch?'

That's how great my baby sister is. She's willing to give up on the friends she'll have already made in four hours to hang out with her weird, unpopular sister. And she genuinely will not care.

'No, you'll cramp my style,' I tease her. Because I'm meant to be the big sister.

'Suit yourself. Let's get this show on the road,' Ivy says with a shrug and a grin.

The office lady has clearly read my file because the look she gives me when we arrive is not the same look she gives Ivy. I kind of want to slap that look off her face, but I smile at her instead and Ivy looks vaguely amused. She was probably hoping I'd slap the office lady.

'We've got buddies coming to meet you,' she tells us.

Buddies. Like we're in primary school. I do not grind my teeth.

'Do we get a nap break, too?' I whisper to Ivy. She laughs and we get curious looks from the adults.

'Ah, Lydia,' the office lady greets a girl who arrives. She's basically another version of Ivy, I can tell.

'Hi, Mrs Gruber,' Lydia says. 'I'm here for … Ivy.' She looks at us, wondering which sister she'll get. Ivy is prettier, and she's about to overtake me in height. You can't really tell there are two years between us unless you count the cold, dead look in my eyes that clearly denotes my world-weary extra days on the planet.

I'm joking.

Mostly.

'That's me,' Ivy says, smiling and stepping forward. She gives me an anxious look over her shoulder.

'You got this,' I tell her, grinning, and give her the secret handshake again. She nods, smiles back, and tosses it back.

'Have fun,' she tells me, and then she's gone.

'Shouldn't be too much longer,' Mrs Gruber says. 'How are you fee –, liking Launceston?'

'It's great,' I say. I've been in town literally fifty-six hours. 'I feel fine,' I add because that's what she was going to ask. It's what they always ask.

'Grace is a tough cookie,' Dad says, and I wrinkle my nose at him. He grins back because he only said it to annoy me. 'And Launceston is nice. It's quieter than we're used to.'

'It's a lovely place to live,' Mrs Gruber says. 'It's a real community, you know?'

We did know. We had strangers knocking on our door bringing us homemade cookies when we moved in. It was weird. We did not like it. Mum threw out the cookies in case they were laced with something. This neighbourly thing was not something that happened in Sydney.

'It seems that way,' Dad replies. 'Doesn't it, Grace?'

'Yep,' I say. Please, Jesus, let my 'buddy' arrive in the next three minutes. I'll actually read the Bible or something if You can make this happen for me, Big Guy.

'It's a big change to happen part way through grade eleven, isn't it?' Mrs Gruber asks me, sympathetically. 'But I'm sure you'll make new friends, a pretty girl like you.'

Oh, it's on, Mrs Gruber. Come around from behind the damn perspex so I can slap you.

'Ah,' Dad intervenes, placing a hand on my arm to restrain me and shifting forward in his seat as if I'll actually leap over the desk and go through the perspex. 'That's, uh, very kind of you.'

He's struggling to find the words to make me calm down and shut her up, and to do both politely. Which is why I think we're all grateful for the door being opened way too hard and a guy who looks way too attractive to be sixteen appears. His uniform is, I'll admit, a disgrace. But his face is a work of art: curly strawberry blond hair, blue eyes, adorable freckles, and the kind of smile that looks like he's a little embarrassed about his face. I know instinctively that we are not going to be friends. People who look like that are not friends with people who look like me.

'Hi, I'm here for … her, I guess,' he says, grinning and giving a little semi-embarrassed shrug.

'Liam,' Mrs Gruber says as if she's addressing her son. He's a golden boy. Everyone probably says his name like that. 'Lovely to see you again. This is Grace Turing. You're in good hands, Grace.'

Liam doesn't say anything, and I get the feeling he has definitely forgotten the woman's name. Dad gives me a look that warns me – well, begs me, if we're being honest –to be nice. I throw him a bone.

'Thanks, Mrs Gruber,' I say deliberately. 'See you, Dad.'

'Bye, Mrs Gruber,' Liam says. 'Come on, Grace.'

'I'll be here after school,' Dad promises.

'So will the bus,' I say.

'Grace,' he says, his voice full of warning.

'Fine,' I reply. 'Bye.'

'Have a good day,' he tells me as the door closes behind me. I sigh as I follow Liam.

'Parents, huh? They love to worry,' he says. 'I'm Liam, by the way. Liam Granger. I'm the SRC rep for our class.'

'Grace Turing,' I reply. 'New girl. Obviously.'

'Shitty time to be changing schools,' Liam says, stating the obvious that I feel like everyone is going to state.

'Something like that,' I agree. 'Any other words of wisdom before we arrive? Like, potentially reminding me of the teacher's name?'

'Miss Williams. She's alright. She's new this year, so try not to torture her too much.'

'Right.'

'You probably don't have to be nervous. Everyone's pretty nice,' Liam offers. I stare at him blankly. Of course, he thinks that. He has that face. No one is going to be mean to that face.

'Sure,' I say, poorly masking my sarcasm. 'Launceston is full of super nice people, so Riverview High is going to be delightful.'

'You sound like you're being sarcastic, but it's true,' he says with a grin. 'Well, mostly. Here we are.' He opens the door for me and ushers me through like he's a gentleman. Ivy would probably be swooning about now. Old Grace might have swooned a little, too. But New Grace is not a swooner. New Grace's default is a little cranky. You try being in this much pain all the time and see if you're Mother Teresa.

'Thanks,' I say, and walk onto the stage that is the front of the classroom. Twenty-two faces staring at me with varying degrees of curiosity. Miss Williams is smiling the kind vaguely pitying smile that adults always give me when they find out. I press my lips together for a moment to suppress the irritation. Liam takes his seat in the middle of the room and gives me an encouraging smile.

'Grace, welcome,' Miss Williams says. '10W, how about we welcome her?'

'Hi, Grace,' they chorus like they're in AA.

'Hi, 10W,' I parrot back.

'Would you like to introduce yourself?' Miss Williams asks me. 'Maybe a little something about who you are or what you enjoy?'

No, Miss Williams, I would not like to introduce myself. I am not entertainment.

'Uh … I'm into art and history. I'm allergic to nuts and if I could only eat one food for the rest of my life without consequences it'd probably be lasagne?'

There are some chuckles and nods of approval. There's one black kid in the back who is kind of smirking at me, but other than that it seems like I've been suitably vanilla. I say vanilla, but I kid you not, the kid in the back is the only other non-Caucasian in the room. My last school was a freaking rainbow and I feel so … I stick out like a sore thumb, to put it mildly, and so does he.

'Anything else?' Miss Williams asks and I know exactly what she's really asking. It's her way of saying *are you sure that you don't want to share the thing you hate the most about yourself with everyone?* No, Miss Williams, I'm good, thanks.

'Nope,' I say. 'I'm shy.'

The smirking kid is now hiding his face with his hands trying not to laugh. Okay, I might be making a friend.

'I doubt that, somehow,' Miss Williams says, but she's amused by me. 'Take a seat.' She indicates the only spare desk, which is in the back row one seat away from my potential new friend. 'Shall we go around the room and say our names and something about us to introduce ourselves to Grace?'

Please God, no. Let it end.

'Amber? Would you like to start?' Miss Williams asks. Amber stands up and turns to me.

'I'm Amber, and I'm the netball captain,' she says, adjusting her glasses on her nose slightly. She sits, and the girl next to her stands.

'Hi, I'm Mackenzie, but everyone calls me Kenzi. I'm a singer.'

'I'm Caleb. I like football.' He's almost more attractive than Liam. I'm seriously concerned about the water in Launceston.

'I'm Ryan. I like math and science.'

'Hi, I'm Elsa, I like reading fantasy.' Okay, she looks like a bitch, but I can get behind the reading. It's also at this point where I wonder why we're doing this because I am not going to remember everyone's names.

'Graham. Football captain.'

'Bonjour, I'm Emmanuelle, and I'm half French.' Okay, her, I'll remember. She's stunning, but also has an obnoxious, probably fake, French accent.

'Hello, I'm Jenna,' says a girl who might be more nervous than I am. She's the one sitting between the smirking kid and me. 'And I ... um ... I like lasagne, too.' There are some snickers, despite Liam telling me how nice everyone is. Jenna's a little overweight, okay, but seriously, at least she made an effort to connect with me.

'Idiots,' the smirking kid mutters under his breath. I think Jenna glares at him, but I can't really see from this angle. She stares at her desk as her cheeks pink.

'That's enough,' Miss Williams says, cutting through the noise. Then she nods at smirking kid.

'I'm Daniel,' he says, standing up. 'I like killing things on the internet.' He sits back down kind of like falling directionally into a chair. He catches my eyes and raises his eyebrow again as if he's throwing down some kind of gauntlet. I have no idea why, but I smirk back. I miss the entire next two people's introductions before I turn my attention back to in time to hear a guy named Morgan introducing himself.

'And that's us done for the morning,' Miss Williams says, smiling. 'Have fun with Mr Simmons.'

There are some groans and I look over at Jenna in question.

'Math,' she says.

'And Mr Simmons has a stick up his ass,' Daniel mutters to me as he brushes past.

'Language,' Jenna sighs. 'Sorry about him.'

'Is he right?' I ask.

She sighs again, and I take that as a yes. We move as a kind of swarm in the direction of the next classroom, but some of us veer off in a different direction.

'We're in room sixteen now, remember?' Liam calls after them.

'Why are they moving us now?' Amber complains. 'We've been in twenty-five all year.'

This is, I assume, my fault. I say nothing and hope none of them are smart enough or suspicious enough to put the new kid and new classroom together and get causation. Accessibility can be kind of an issue on a bad day for me and room twenty-five is both upstairs and a building over.

'Not ours to wonder why,' Liam shrugs. 'We just do what we're told.'

'Theirs not to reason why,' I correct, under my breath.

'What was that?' Amber asks me.

I wish I had some control over my mouth.

'The quote. It's ... it was misquoted in a movie or something and now everyone gets it wrong,' I say.

'What is it, then?' Liam asks, seemingly genuinely curious, while all of my brand-new peers give me the 'you are definitely a freak' look. Which I deserve by sixteen-year-old standards.

'Theirs not to make reply, theirs not to reason why, theirs but to do and die,' I quote. 'Tennyson's "Charge of the Light Brigade".'

'So, you're a nerd, then,' the French girl says dismissively without the accent. Emmanuelle, I remind myself.

'Seems that way, doesn't it?' I reply. I do not say: 'and you're not as French as you pretend to be'. I am proud of my restraint. Daniel is smirking at me again.

'You're into poetry?' Liam asks. 'That's cool.'

No, Liam, it is decidedly not cool.

'I'm not, really,' I reply. 'I'm just good at trivia.'

'Cool,' Liam says again. I wonder, not for the first time, if creating a human is a bit like creating a character for a game. You have a set amount of stat points to put in these different areas, and whoever made Liam put too many in 'pretty' and not enough in 'vocabulary'. And whoever made me put too many in 'intelligence' and not enough in 'constitution'.

'Did you know that a pig can orgasm for thirty minutes?' Daniel asks me.

'Myth,' I reply. 'No one has measured it or knows what a pig is experiencing.'

'Well, you're no fun,' he says.

'I get that a lot,' I reply with a slight smile and his grin widens, too.

'Hey, be nice,' Liam says. 'Grace is new. Maybe give her a day before you start being a dick to her.'

'Why pretend?' Daniel asks. 'Surely it's better to let her know where she stands from the beginning?'

'Is it so hard for you to be a decent human being?' Liam argues.

'I never thought I'd be glad to arrive at math class,' Amber mutters.

'Sorry about him,' Liam tells me.

'And I'm sorry about him,' Daniel says, rolling his eyes.

'I'm sorry about both of you,' Amber hisses before taking her seat. I gravitate towards the back of the room again, but Mr Simmons calls me back.

'Grace Turing, isn't it? I'm Mr Simmons,' he asks like he doesn't already know.

'Yes,' I say.

'You're not a descendant of Alan Turing, are you?' he asks, little nerd eyes bright with curiosity.

I blink. 'You do know that there are no direct descendants of Alan Turing, right? He was gay. That's literally why he died.'

I hear some snickers and I know that Daniel is one of them. Mr Simmons is less amused.

'A simple 'no' would have sufficed,' Mr Simmons says, his voice tight and his eyes flat.

The irony here is that I am distantly related to Alan Turing, I just hate the question. I'm quite proud of my heritage. I live to be contrary.

'Sorry,' I say, not meaning it at all. I think he knows that based on the look of derision he gives me.

'Take a seat, Grace,' he sighs. 'Okay, class. Today we're going back over the polynomials we talked about last week.'

I admit to being relieved that we're doing something my last school did earlier. I'm a little overwhelmed, if we're being honest, with the whole first-day thing and I need a little time to adjust. I wonder how Ivy's doing. I shouldn't worry, because she's Ivy. But she's also my favourite person, so worrying is part of the agenda.

'Do you know what we're doing?' Jenna leans over to ask me. 'They're a bit intense.'

'I've got it,' I say with a smile and start copying down the questions from the whiteboard. 'Thank you, though.'

She smiles back, nervous, I think. I think that she is the me of my last school. There's nothing wrong with her, she's just a little different. And it's enough to make her a target. I should probably avoid her if we're being mercenary and logical. It's not who I want to be, though. I focus on math.

Math is easier than people.

Lunch is … well, it's what I expected. Everyone already has their own groups and habits. I get a couple of half-hearted invitations to join them. Emmanuelle looks disgusted when Amber asks me to join them. Liam is awkward, and the guys jostle each other and smirk. Daniel, who I might actually want to have lunch with, disappears with what could be actual magic. Jenna lingers, shuffling from foot to foot. I almost regret telling Ivy not to find me. But that wouldn't be fair on her. Maybe I could go for a walk after I've eaten and see if I can spot her and make sure she's happy. In the time it takes me to have that thought, Jenna is gone, too, and I'm holding my sandwiches and apple while standing alone in the locker room. I should have joined someone. Hesitation gets you killed, Mum always said. I think she heard it in a war movie and made it a mantra. Seems she was right, yet again, because I hesitated and now I am slightly socially dead. Great work with your social skills there, Grace.

I take my lunch and my sketchpad out to the oval and sit under a tree. There are guys playing some variation of football that seems to have little regard for the rules. There are little picnics of girls dotted around the outskirts watching them. But the reason I picked this spot was not for the human view, but the natural one. The school backs on to a nature reserve, and I angle myself towards it and away from the school. I've always liked birds, and there is an abundance of them perched in trees, singing to each other, fluttering from branch to branch. There's something so innocent and free about them. I wonder if being a bird is easier than being a person. I wonder what flight feels like. I wonder if their joints can hurt with arthritis, and if their feathers can feel painful against their skin, and if the freedom to fall asleep whenever they want makes life easier. I start drawing and my mind stops spinning on what ifs and thought spirals and goes to the simple act of pencil on paper.

I know that I'm not supposed to have medication in my bag. That I'm meant to go to the office each lunchtime to collect it. But that seems like a great way to get found out. Instead, I wear them in my necklace. I slip out the two white tablets and take them. Could I do this if I sat with Amber and the popular girls? Could I do it just in front of Jenna? For the first time, I wonder if keeping this secret will have the same effect as not keeping it. I consider going to the office for a muscle relaxant to get me through the last few hours of the day. But the last period is history, and I kind of need my brain for that. I close my eyes, feel the warmth of the sun, and listen to the birds call underneath and above and between the human voices.

…

Dad is waiting for us in the car park after school. He's not even being casual and waiting in the car. He's leaning against the car and looking worried. I try not to sigh. Someone bounces up to me and links my arm through theirs. It takes a second to realise it's Ivy. She is grinning happily and I know that her first day of school was very different from my first day of school. It takes her about half a second to see the pinched expression that indicates my pain levels are a little higher than baseline. She takes my backpack from me before I can protest. Her arm is linked back through mine again before she speaks.

'Gray! How was your day?'

'It was good,' I lie, smiling. 'I think I started making friends. What about you?' I squeeze her arm, pulling her closer. I miss the days when it was safe for her to just launch herself on me.

'Oh, you know,' Ivy replies, looking coy.

I roll my eyes. 'I do.'

'Lydia is super nice, and her friends are so cool! Mei does martial arts, which is so badass. She invited me to come to a class to try it out.'

'Is it not a little stereotypical for an Asian girl to do martial arts?'

'Don't be a bitch, Gray. She's nice. Be nice to her. Or she'll kick your ass.'

'Na, you'll protect me,' I reply, and she beams.

'Good first day?' Dad asks when we're close enough.

'Yes,' Ivy says.

'Of course,' I say.

'Excellent.' I visibly see him relax a little. 'No problems with ... anything?'

'I have a fair bit of English Lit to catch up on, but I've done the maths already, and history is World War II and the Holocaust. So,' I shrug.

'So you could basically teach it then, huh?' Dad grins. He loves my inner history nerd.

'I'm going to try and find my copy of *The Nazi Doctors* to bring in. I think Miss Williams will find it interesting.'

'Such a nerd,' Ivy sighs. 'I thought you were trying to make friends with people your age. But, no, you're buddying up to teachers.'

'Ew, can we never use the word "buddy" again?' I ask.

Ivy laughs and I smile. Dad rolls his eyes.

'Celebratory Viennetta for dessert?' he asks.

'Yes!' we chorus.

Mum gets home so late that we're already eating dessert. She kicks off her heels in the hallway, leaving them scattered. Dad will pair them by the door later. Her pantyhose are removed somewhere between there and her bedroom. She throws them through the door with her jacket and collapses next to Dad on the couch.

'I'm home,' she sighs.

'We noticed,' I say.

'Big day?' Dad asks.

'You seem tired,' Ivy adds.

'Talk about the Spanish Inquisition,' Mum says. 'Do I get some ice cream, too?'

'Did you have a good day?' Dad asks. 'It's a celebratory Viennetta: you can't have it if you aren't celebrating.'

I roll my eyes as Mum smiles at Dad like he hung the moon. In my less angsty moments, I think that if I ever get married, I want it to be to someone who smiles at me like my mum smiles at my dad.

'If nothing else, I can celebrate you,' she says, looking at us.

'Gross,' I say.

'I love you, too,' Ivy says.

'You girls had a good first day then?' she asks. She's worried because she's done this to us. She packed us up and moved us to a new place because she got a new job that she felt she'd be stupid to turn down. And she would be, of course, but it doesn't change the tiny bit of resentment from taking root in my chest. Even if the way Tasmania seemed safer in the pandemic made them think it might be safer for my health.

'It was fine,' I say, as Ivy says: 'It was great.'

'Celebratory Viennetta it is,' Mum smiles. Dad goes and gets it for her while Ivy starts giving her a summary of all the things that happened. Mum looks at me out of the corner of her eye, and I know she wants to ask me questions and see if I'm okay. She wants to know if I took my medication when I was supposed to. She wants to know if I'm making friends. But sometimes it seems like Mum and I are on separate islands, with Ivy and Dad bridges across. So she doesn't ask and I don't tell her. I smile at her, though, and perhaps that's enough.

CHAPTER TWO
New Doctor

'Did you know that if a sumo wrestler makes your baby cry it's good luck?'

I have literally no idea where Daniel Perkins came from, but he's suddenly standing beside me and asking me questions. I place my hand over my racing heart.

'Shit, son. Give a girl some warning,' I say. He didn't speak to me in homeroom and we only shared one other class today, so, I'm not sure why he's speaking to me now. We've nodded and smiled at each other a few times, and made the odd joke, but nothing to justify him hunting me down at lunch on my third day at school.

He grins, expectant. 'Did you?'

'I ... Did you spend last night googling random trivia facts?' I ask, confusion lacing my tone. I fight the urge to smile.

'I asked you first,' he replies. 'You didn't, did you?'

I have no idea what is actually happening right now. I feel torn, because I want to stay and have a weird trivia off with this smirking idiot, but I'm also meant to be heading to the office to sign out to go to the doctor.

'I did not,' I admit, losing the battle not to smile back. 'Did you know that tug-of-war used to be an Olympic sport?'

'You're shitting me,' he says, eyes widening.

'Early 1900s,' I say. 'I shit you not.'

'Huh.'

'So, did you stay up all night looking for weird trivia to impress me?' I ask him, teasing. 'Or is this just a drive-by general knowledge drop?'

'All night might be an overstatement.'

Is it my imagination or is he kind of nervous all of a sudden?

'You went down the rabbit hole,' I grin. 'It's weirdly addictive, isn't it?'

He shakes his head. 'I thought I'd quickly find something weird. And I wanted to check the pig orgasm thing. My mum was kind of freaked out to find me on Wikipedia instead of Fortnite at eleven last night.'

I laugh and he grins back. It's easy. And then it's not. He frowns.

'Wait, where are you going?'

'Uh, the office.'

'Why? Are you sick or something?'

Yes, I am. I'm definitely sick or something.

'Oh, I just have an appointment.'

'So you are sick.'

'Na, I'm just skiving off to catch a movie,' I lie.

He doesn't laugh.

We reach the office, and he looks at me like he's trying to figure me out.

'Gray!'

Ivy's voice saves me, and I turn to see her jogging towards me. Daniel gives her a curious look.

'Hey, Ivy,' I smile. 'Miss me already?'

'You know it,' she grins. 'Tell Dad I'll catch the bus home tonight, okay? Lydia lives really close to us so I can just follow her. Save him doubling back.'

'This town is the size of a postage stamp. Everyone is really close.'

'So you must be Grace's sister,' Daniel decides, considering her.

'This is Daniel,' I introduce him and Ivy raises her eyebrows.

'You said you weren't making friends,' Ivy accuses me. 'This is clearly a friend.'

I sigh heavily. 'I didn't say I wasn't making friends. I said I hadn't exactly been popular.'

'That is also not strictly true,' Daniel points out. 'You've just not swooned at Granger's feet yet, so when you do, you'll be popular.

Except with Emmanuelle, but I'm going to go with you don't want to be friends with her.'

'There's a boy?' Ivy asks.

'No,' I say. 'There's no boy. And even if there was a boy, I don't swoon.'

'You could swoon,' Ivy says.

I give her a hard look.

She relents. 'Okay, but you could fall and make it look like you swooned.'

'Only for entertainment purposes,' I say, my voice is a little strained. I don't like how close she is to saying I'm going to fall because I'm sick.

'I'm a boy,' Daniel points out.

'You're … different,' I say. I can tell he wants to ask if that's a good thing or a bad thing, but Ivy gets there first.

'Are you Gray's boyfriend?' Ivy asks much to my mortification.

'Jesus, Ivy. No. We've been at school for two days!' I hiss.

'Not yet,' Daniel says, sounding annoyingly confident.

I shake my head. 'Nope,' I say. 'So much nope. Solid nope.'

'I think the lady doth protest too much,' Daniel laughs, teasing me. I think he's going to touch me. I lean away slightly.

'I like him,' Ivy decides. 'I'm an excellent judge of character.'

'I like you, too,' Daniel agreed.

'You like me,' I remind her. 'Making you a terrible judge of character. Go hassle Lydia, or get Mei to teach you to kick something.'

She gives our secret handshake and I return it.

'Bye, Danny, it was nice to meet you,' she calls over her shoulder before she jogs back the way she came. She's just given him a nickname and I'm about to apologise but Daniel has a strange expression and I find myself not wanting to talk.

'What was that?' Daniel asks. 'The hand thing.'

'It's a secret handshake,' I say. 'If I tell you, it stops being secret.'

'You're really weird, Grace Turing, you know that?'

'You say that like it's a bad thing,' I reply. 'I have to go. I don't want to be late.'

'It's an excellent thing,' he replies. 'See you tomorrow?'

'That's how school works,' I say. I go into the office, but I catch his reflection looking at me in the reception desk perspex for a moment. I wonder what he's thinking. But he's gone by the time I go out the other door, which is a good thing.

…

'You ready?' Dad asks when I get in the car.

'Yeah,' I say.

'Did something happen?' Dad asks. He's too perceptive sometimes.

'Kind of,' I say. 'It was weird. I think I made a friend.'

'That's good, isn't it?'

'I guess.'

'Wow, such enthusiasm.'

He's teasing me, so I roll my eyes. 'I'm just thinking about the appointment. Ivy said she'll catch the bus home tonight. Her friend Lydia lives close.'

'Good for Ivy,' Dad says. 'She could use some more independence.'

'Does this mean we get to catch the bus home?' I ask hopefully.

'Are you going to tell everyone about your health?'

'Blackmail doesn't suit you, Dad.'

'I just worry about you, Grace,' he says.

I can hear how tired he is with it. The worrying. I want to tell him not to worry about me, but it's a stupid thing to say. He's my father, so he's going to worry no matter what I say. But he's also right, he does have some legitimate reasons to worry.

'I'm sorry,' I say.

'It's not your fault.' He sighs the words out like they take his strength with them.

'I know,' I say. 'But I'm still sorry.'

…

Dr Xavier Rai is short, slightly overweight, and doesn't have an accent. He also seems to have a permanent scowl.

'Your bloods don't show any significant rheumatoid factor,' he says. Then he gives me 'the look' I hate most in the entire world. It's the look that says: *are you sure you're not faking it?*

'I'm aware,' I reply. 'But you'll find in the notes my last doctor sent over –'

'I've read them. Have you considered therapy?' he asks Dad. 'Some people with fibromyalgia find it the most effective treatment?'

I grind my teeth and my knuckles go white on the arms of my chair.

'She is not mentally unwell,' Dad argues, stepping up to the plate. 'As you can see, she's tried extensive tests and treatments, but nothing has been conclusive and nothing has helped.'

'Which is why I'm suggesting a psychological pathway,' Dr Rai replies. 'She's very young to be in so much pain.'

'I am in the room,' I snap. 'If you could talk *to* me instead of *about* me, that would be considered polite.'

It's the wrong thing to say judging by the expression on the doctor's face. But I can't believe I'm having to go through this again. Except, I can.

I sigh, relenting a little. 'Look, I'm not an idiot. All pain is neurological and psychological. All pain is only experienced in the brain. Everything is neural impulses. I get it. I know that when I'm more anxious or upset that my pain is worse. But I am telling you that I'm in pain all the time, and you're suggesting therapy. You can see why I'm a little upset by that, right?'

'Yes, but –'

'No,' Dad says, interrupting. 'No buts. Listen to her. Listen to me. She's not faking it. She couldn't fake it. Not like this. Do you want me to send you videos of her vomiting because she has a migraine so intense the pain is killing her? Want to watch her struggle out of bed on bad days? Should I video her sobbing because she feels trapped in her body? Look at the results, read the file, test whatever you want. But you aren't brushing her off because you can't be bothered.'

I stare at Dad with tears in my eyes. I have never seen him like this before. He's angry, and he's fierce, and he's all about protecting me. I remember being a kid and thinking about Dad like he was a superhero. He'd pick us up and throw us into the air. He could kick a ball further and run faster and I would have bet my favourite doll on him in a fight against anyone. Then I grew up and he was just a guy who loved me. But right now, he's a superhero again. He's definitely earning that No. #1 Dad mug we got him for Father's Day last year.

Dr Rai is looking back at his screen, but I know Dad got to him. He's remembering I'm human behind all those numbers and graphs.

'There's a decent rheumatologist in Launceston,' he says finally. 'I'll get you a referral. It might take you a while to get in, though. In the meantime, we'll get you some more blood tests and I'll do some research. I'm not saying we should rule out psychotherapy, but there is a lot about this kind of weird autoimmune type stuff that we still don't know.'

There are actual tears on my cheeks now. I wipe them away quickly and I wonder who cut an onion nearby.

'Thank you,' Dad says. 'When should we come back?'

'Next week,' Dr Rai says. Then he looks at me again, and I think he sees me differently. 'Do you have any questions, Grace?'

'I need a repeat for five milligram diazepam,' I say. 'I only take it when I need it for pain. No more than one a day, and never more than three a week.'

Dr Rai smiles at me. 'You've got that spiel down.'

I level my gaze at him. 'I am well aware that I'm sixteen years old and the last thing I need to add to the mix is an increased tolerance to drugs I might need for the rest of my life.'

He nods. I think he's getting it. Dad reaches over and takes my hand.

'We'll see you next week,' Dad says, standing up. I stand with him, leaning against him like I'm younger than I am.

'It was nice to meet you,' Dr Rai says, extending his hand to for us to shake. We take it and then leave.

We make another appointment for next week.

We take the referral.

We collect the prescription.

We sit in the car in silence for a minute in the parking lot.

'You did well, Gracie,' Dad says, using my childhood nickname and squeezing my hand tightly before letting it go.

'Dad?' I say.

'Yeah?'

'You're my hero,' I tell him.

He reaches across the console and drags me over it, holding me tight. It's probably the worst, most uncomfortable hug I've ever received in my life but I hold him back just as tightly. I might have been given a faulty body, but I really lucked out in the family department.

...

I can hear them arguing about the doctor from my bedroom. Mum wants to send me to therapy. Dad wants to send me to the rheumatologist first. We tried everything already, Mum thinks, except therapy. Maybe it would help. Maybe we should try it. Maybe men should be less inclined to dismiss therapy off the bat. Maybe she should trust her daughter a bit more.

'Sam, you aren't here. You haven't seen her at her worst,' Dad says.

'This is not about me being a working mother, Brett. This is about getting our daughter the help she needs!'

'She needs pain management,' he argues. 'If she wants to go to therapy, fine, she can go. But I'm not going to let them delay treating her for six months while she sees a psychologist.'

'What if they're right?' Mum asks. 'What if it's in her head?'

The pause that follows breaks my heart in ways I didn't know it could shatter. I curl up tighter in my bed, dragging the blankets up and over my head.

'You don't know what you're talking about, Samara.'

A door shuts in a way that is almost a slam. We're meant to be asleep, after all. I hear Dad walk all the way out of the house. My bedroom is right beside the driveway, so I hear him get in the car, too. But he doesn't turn it on. He just sits there. Mum's gone silent, too.

What if they get divorced and it's all my fault?

What if Ivy gets caught in this?

What if Dad leaves? Could I do it without him?

What if Mum doesn't want me?

What if Ivy and I get separated?
What if?
What if?
What if?
What if … what if they're right?
Dr Rai and Mum, I mean.
What if it's all in my head?

CHAPTER THREE
Cracks

It's only been two weeks, but I'm pretty sure that Mr Holt, the PE teacher, hates me. He has this way of talking to me that makes it clear that he assumes I can't do anything. Which, of course, makes me say I can do everything. It's a real problem that I could probably use the proposed psychotherapy for.

Today, we're doing the most dreaded PE lesson of all time: the Beep Test. I'm pretty sure every kid in Australia groans in unison when it is announced. It's probably the worst product of French Canada ever. But more to the point, I should absolutely not do the Beep Test. I know this. But Mr Holt asks if I'm sure I don't want to sit this one out, and my mouth operates before my brain does. I stand on the starting line and I know that this is a bad idea.

'He gave you an out,' Daniel says. 'What the hell are you doing? Do you actually like this form of torture?'

'I'm insane,' I reply. 'But he dared me.'

'Christ,' Daniel says. 'Did you know the Hill's Hoist was invented in 1945?'

'Too easy,' I reply. 'He was a mechanic in Adelaide.'

The first beep sounds and we dutifully jog to the other end of the basketball court.

'Did you know that Superman was written by two Jewish guys who were inspired by Jesus as the "Chosen One" lore?' I ask.

'Huh,' Daniel says.

Beep.

'A guy named Peter did 12,700 skips in an hour,' Daniel says.

'What are you guys talking about?' Liam asks Daniel.

'Spotify trivia,' I say. 'Weak sauce. And it was 12,702.'

'You're insane,' Liam says.

'Right?' Jenna agrees from my other side.

Beep.

'Longest crochet chain was 130 kilometres long,' I say. 'France, 2009.'

'Crochet? Seriously?' Daniel asks.

Beep.

'I like crochet. I can't actually do it, but it looks fun.'

'You're such a weirdo,' Jenna huffs.

'Right?' Daniel agrees in a way that could be mimicking Jenna.

Beep. Jenna waves off and goes and sits in the stands. She could have gone for longer, I think. But she's not competitive and I think she might feel a little self-conscious about her fitness because of her size.

'Okay,' Daniel says. 'A pregnant goldfish is called a twit.'

'You're shitting me,' I say.

Beep.

'Nope.'

'A goldfish has a three-second memory,' Liam suggests.

'Bullshit,' Daniel calls as I say: 'False.'

Beep.

'Five months,' I huff. 'Actually.'

'Huh,' Liam says as we approach the line.

And that's when my knee subluxates. I feel the grinding of a bone going in and out of joint; hear the subtle pop.

I go down.

Hard.

I emit a strangled groan as I look at my traitorous knee in frustration. Mr Holt is by my side in an instant, giving me a very clear 'what did I just say' look. *You think you can do these things, but you just can't, Nemo.* Daniel is crouching beside me, and Liam lingers as well.

'Can you stand?' Holt snaps at me.

'Maybe,' I say. I look at Daniel. 'Give me a hand?'

'Move it,' Holt says to the boys, dismissing them before they can help. 'Jenna, hit pause.'

When they're out of hearing, Holt's scowl deepens.

'You shouldn't have done this,' he says. 'You know your body better than this, I'm told.'

Condescending dickwad.

'Help me up,' I mutter. 'Arms under mine, I'll go up on my left leg. It's just a minor subluxation.'

He does as I ask. If I put any weight on my knee like this, it is going to give out and hurt more. I curse internally.

'I need to put it back in properly before I can put weight on it,' I say. 'Can you … distract them?'

He gives me a look of disdain. He definitely hates me.

'Do you need help? Should I get the nurse?'

'I've got this,' I say. 'I'll limp to the office after and get something to help with the pain, a heat pack, and strap it.'

'Jenna,' Holt calls. 'Help Turing to the office.'

Ah, the surname. Confirmation of hate. I'm not fond of him either. He strides over to the waiting class and starts talking to them about how they'll restart in a moment.

'What happened?' someone asks.

'She probably faked it,' someone says. Emmanuelle, that faux-French bitch.

'It's a decent fake,' Jenna says. I meet her eyes.

'Look away for a minute,' I tell her. She thinks I'm insane. But she does what I ask. I turn away from the class, lean down, and push my knee back in. There is an audible pop, but it's muffled by the class talking. Jenna turns to look at me in shock and takes in how pale I am and how pinched my expression is.

'Got it,' I say. 'Let's get out of here.'

She stands awkwardly looking at me. 'What do I … do?'

'Hold your arm out, like this,' I say, holding my arm firm at a right angle just out from my body. She does it, and I place my hand on top of hers, lining up our forearms like we're entering a regency dance hall.

'Are you okay?' she asks. The tone of her voice makes it clear that she's not sure if I'm faking this or not, despite my expression. The beeps start up again as we reach the door to the gym.

'Sure,' I say, with a smile. 'My knee is just a little dodgy sometimes. Besides, who'd want to actually do the Beep Test?'

She grins, relieved. She's leaning towards faking it. She thinks we're allies against the oppression that is PE. I hate it, because I know that everyone is going to believe I faked this. If they knew about me, they'd know I wasn't. But they're all going to say that I am an attention-seeking faker, because Holt gave me an out and I didn't take it. But the alternative is that they know, and I don't want that. Then I'd be Sick Girl.

'I swear, it's a form of torture,' Jenna says. 'They probably make prisoners in Guantanamo Bay do it.'

'I'd cave,' I laugh.

'Right?'

...

The school nurse is really just the accountant who knows advanced first aid. Apparently, there's a service they can call to get a nurse in, but after they send Jenna away, I tell her I don't need it.

'Are you sure?' Mrs Easton asks.

'Heat pack, painkillers, and some RockTape and I'll be right as rain,' I promise.

'Want me to help you tape it?' she asks.

'At this point, I'm an expert,' I reply, taking the tape and scissors from her. 'Give me half an hour.'

'You really should wear the brace.'

I know, I think. *But it's going to be hard to explain to everyone where it came from.*

'I've got this,' I say.

'Okay,' she says, clearly still not believing me. She hesitates. 'You don't have to do this alone, you know.'

She's giving me the I-swear-this-isn't-pity-it's-empathy look.

'I appreciate your support,' I say.

'Can I ask you a question?'

I hold back the smart arse 'you just did', and nod.

'Why don't you want to tell anyone?'

'I just want to be normal.'

She considers this for a moment.

'Normal is overrated,' she says. 'But I take your point.'

Then she does something so unexpected that my jaw literally drops. She lifts her left pant leg up to her knee, revealing a navy-blue prosthetic.

'I was eighteen,' she tells me. 'It was a car accident I don't want to talk about. Afterward … everything was different. Every*one* was different. It felt like I grew an extra head instead of lost part of a leg.'

She smiles like it's meant to be a joke, and it kind of is. I grin back.

'I can relate,' I say. 'I mean, I haven't –'

'I know what you mean,' she says, interrupting me. But it's a nice interruption. She's on my team, that's what she wants me to know. She doesn't think I'm judging her or comparing. She just gets it.

'I want to be Grace Turing,' I say. 'Because she's smart and loves art and eats too many Minties in a sitting. Not, you know, Sick Girl who doesn't look sick.'

'I get it,' Mrs Easton says. She might be in her fifties, but she's a pretty great person. 'Can I make a suggestion?'

'If you ask me to try yoga, I might have to kill you,' I say.

She laughs. 'God, no. You've got what they call an "invisible illness". But it seems to me that isn't very invisible if you know where to look. Like today.'

I wince.

'My suggestion is that you make a plan of what you want to tell people. How you want people to treat you. You don't ever have to use it, but I think it might help.'

'I'll think about it,' I say. She doesn't make me tell her that she's right, and I like her more for that.

'I'll check on you in half an hour,' she promises before leaving me alone in the room.

I take the pills.

I tape my knee.

I place the heat pack on it and lay back on the bed, staring at the ceiling.

I think about Daniel and how he lets Ivy call him Danny.

I think about Dr Rai and the new tests he ordered even though I don't think he believes me.

I think about Dad sitting in the car at night even though he hasn't done it again.

I think about Ivy taking my backpack every day after school and pretending it's normal.

I think about Jenna and how she thinks I'm faking.

I think about Holt hating me because I'm not healthy and I don't want to advertise it.

I think about the look on Daniel's face when I left and how I'm pretty sure he thinks I faked it to get out of the Beep Test.

I close my eyes and pretend to be sleeping when Mrs Easton checks on me.

I'm not ready to face everyone yet. I don't even want to be Grace Turing right now.

I just want to not exist for a couple of hours.

...

The next morning, I'm really aware that not going back to class yesterday was a mistake. I know it because of the sick feeling in my stomach when I wake up. I know it when I'm still limping, and they're all going to call me dramatic. I know it when I'm in the car with Dad and Ivy praying for a pipe to burst or something that cancels class for the day.

'It'll be fine,' Ivy says. 'You're Grace goddamn Turing. Take no shit, leave no prisoners.'

'I love you,' I tell her. 'But you and I have a very different understanding on how the world works.'

Dad says nothing. He says nothing very loudly. While he's saying nothing, he manages to communicate very clearly that he thinks that I could fix this problem by coming clean.

'How can I tell them I'm sick when I can't even get a doctor to believe me?' I ask when I get sick of his saying nothing very loudly thing.

'Grace,' he begins, but he catches himself.

'We're teenagers. We're not the world's most understanding group,' Ivy adds.

'I know that you think I'm doing the wrong thing, but it's my mistake to make.'

'I just want what is best for you. Both of you,' Dad sighs.

'We know,' I say.

We sit in silence in the car park for a moment.

'Is this helping?' Dad asks. 'Delaying the inevitable moment when you're going to have to go in?'

'Bye, Dad,' Ivy says with a roll of her eyes. She gets out of the car, but I sit there, lingering.

'Grace,' Dad says, with something like caution in his tone.

Ivy is less subtle. She yanks open the car door. 'Gray, get out of the car.'

I consider saying that she's not the boss of me as I scowl. But I'm on the wrong side of this battle. So I get out of the car. Dad pulls out of the car park as soon as the door is closed, like he's scared I'll get back in.

'I love you, but this is a rip off the band-aid moment,' Ivy says. Lydia and Mei are calling her over, so she gives me our secret handshake and jogs off after them. I wish that she could have stayed for a little longer. It's not like I can spend the day hiding in the car park. I sigh as I limp toward the locker room.

Daniel Perkins walks right past me. It stops me short for a moment: the feeling in my chest and the burning in my cheeks. I keep walking, and thirty seconds later I realise that the emotion I'm feeling is shame. I try to pretend he didn't see me because his headphones were on and he was looking at the ground. It doesn't work. Amber and Kenzi snicker. Liam and some of the football team look at me, and I can't hear what they say, but I know anyway.

'Like they've never faked being sick to get out of a math test,' Jenna says, coming alongside me. I try to smile gratefully, but I have pins and needles dancing over my skin with the injustice of it all. I want to scream, tell everyone that I'm not faking it. I want to go home. I self-consciously adjust my brace.

'Right,' I say, because Jenna's waiting for me to say something. 'How are you?'

'I'm good. You missed a math test. Mr Simmons was annoyed.'

'When isn't he annoyed?'

Jenna laughs. 'You make an excellent point.'

'How's your knee?' Emmanuelle asks in a condescending voice that makes me feel like hating her is justified.

'It hurts.'

'Right. I'm sure it does.'

I kind of want to punch her, so when Jenna says: 'Shut up, Emm, no one asked for your opinion.' I have the urge to cheer.

'Stick together then, losers,' she says with a toss of her hair. A serious hair toss. Who actually tosses their hair? If I tried that I'd probably sprain my neck. She stalks off towards the group of footballers.

'She's such a bitch,' Jenna says. 'Hey, I, uh … I was wondering if you play chess?'

'A little, I suppose,' I reply, unsure. 'I mean, I've played it a few times but I'm not good or anything.'

'Oh, okay. I just … I play chess. You can play it in the library at lunchtime.' She's looking at the ground instead of me. She reminds me of me, and of Abbie Lightfoot, and the awkward unpopular girl in every movie ever who is secretly nice.

'I'm assuming there's a question in there somewhere,' I say, kindly, smiling, trying not to spook her.

She smiles at me, nervous, but she meets my eyes. 'Wanna play at lunch?'

'Are you going to go easy on me?' I ask.

'Only if you're a sore loser,' she says, more confident now.

I laugh. It feels good. Everyone hates me and Daniel thinks I'm a loser, but Jenna Harrington wants to hang out with me and she's making me laugh.

'I'm probably not going to give you any competition, but let's do it,' I say.

She beams.

I swap my books out while she lingers.

I ignore the looks and comments.

'Are you sure you're okay?' Jenna asks as we limp to home-room.

'I'll probably be fine tomorrow,' I reply. 'But it's kinda painful.'

'What … what happened? I wasn't sure if you … well, I mean, everyone kind of assumes that you're faking it.'

The warm feeling leaves my chest and I try not to grind my teeth.

'It was nothing,' I say. 'I just fell. I have … weak knees sometimes.'

'Sounds like you're swooning.'

I start, because the voice comes out of nowhere. Liam is beside me, grinning.

'Were you swooning over me? I am very swoon-worthy,' he adds. 'I'd understand if you did.'

'You're an idiot,' I tell him. 'But whatever keeps you warm at night.'

'Excellent,' he says. 'Do you want me to carry your books for you?'

I stare at him for a minute. I'm not entirely sure what's happening. I look at Jenna, who looks equally shocked.

'Definitely not,' I say. 'You're being weird.'

'Can't say I didn't try,' he shrugs. 'So, did you sprain it or what?'

'Something like that,' I say vaguely.

'Right. Completely unrelated to the Beep Test,' Liam says.

I try my Dad's trick of saying nothing loudly. It works, I think, because he goes away without saying anything else.

'Liam Granger just offered to carry your books,' Jenna says.

'So I didn't imagine that, then,' I reply. 'Isn't he dating Amber or something?'

'Amber wishes,' Jenna scoffs. 'He likes you.'

'He does not like me. I mean, he tolerates me. But he doesn't like me, like me, or whatever,' I reply. 'He's just fatally nice. I think the world is nice to him. He has that face.'

'He does have that face,' Jenna agrees. 'And you don't want him carrying your books? Are you insane? Are you a lesbian?'

'Those are my only options? I don't think my sanity or lack thereof has anything to do with this. It was weird. He … I don't actually want to talk about it. How long have you been playing chess for?'

My non-sequitur makes her pause for a minute, but she goes with it.

'Forever. My mother is chess mad. She's really good at it. I'm barely okay, but she keeps hoping I'll get better. She won chess competitions and stuff in high school so I think she was hoping to relive her glory days through me.'

'Ah, I know how that goes. My mother made me sign up for drama. I can barely act like a normal teenager on a school day.'

We laugh, and it's back to normal.

I tell myself that it's enough and that I can have this much. But in class when I look past Jenna to Daniel, who is studiously not looking at me, I feel the hollow thing inside of me ache. I want to go up to him and say 'I thought we were friends.' But what would be the point of that?

So I don't.

I don't talk to him.

I try not to look at him.

I play chess with Jenna (who really is bad at chess given how long she's been playing).

I survive the day.

It's enough. It's enough. It's enough.

It isn't quite enough.

CHAPTER FOUR
New Meds

'Your blood test showed some rheumatoid factors this, as well as increased inflammatory markers, low iron, and your RAST – your blood allergy marker – results are certainly compelling,' Dr Rai tells us.

There's a part of me that could cry with relief. There's actually something wrong.

'What does that mean?' Dad asks.

Dr Rai sighs and leans back in his chair. 'It means that something is probably going on, but there's not enough information to point to anything specific.'

I consider crying for a different reason.

'So, what next?' Dad asks.

'Well, these results and Grace's pain levels seem to me to indicate something we should try to treat. There's been some research into some antidepressants and anti-anxiety medications that work on the brain in ways that can also modify pain responses. They've been used to treat chronic fibromyalgia and other nerve and neurological pain conditions with some success. I suggest we start Grace on two of them and see how we go.'

'I'm not depressed. Well, I'm a normal, reasonable level of depressed,' I say. 'I'm not saying you're lying to me, but if this is a convoluted way to get me into therapy-'

'It's not,' Dr Rai interrupts, and he smiles like he's proud of me for asking the question. I still don't like him, but at least he's trying.

'Okay,' I say, and smile back. 'Let's give it a go.'

'What drugs?' Dad asks. 'What are the side effects?'

'I think we'll start with pregabalin and amitriptyline. Pregabalin was originally designed for people with epilepsy, which acts as an inhibitor for some neurotransmitters. Because of this, it can make you a little drowsy, which is why it is best to take it at bedtime. It can also cause some weight fluctuation and suicide ideation, like most drugs in that class.'

I nod, thinking it through. 'Alright. And the other one? Ami... something?'

'Amitriptyline,' Dr Rai repeats. 'It's another that should be taken at bedtime as it can make you drowsy. It has been used to treat anxiety, migraines, and some other mental illnesses. You might get a bit of a dry mouth and have some constipation issues, but generally speaking, most people don't have much of a reaction to it.'

'You said there were other options?' Dad asks.

'I did. But I see no reason why these two shouldn't be used to start with. We can evaluate and change doses as we go,' Dr Rai explains. 'Most of these drugs are used in combinations to try and treat different aspects of the neurological symptoms. I think these two are a good starting point, besides which, you've said that Grace suffers some insomnia, and both of these drugs will help her get to sleep a bit easier hopefully.'

'Thank you,' I say. 'I'll do it.'

'Grace,' Dad says in his warning voice. 'I'm not sure we should just rush into taking drugs if we don't even have a diagnosis.'

'Mr Turing, in cases like your daughter's, we might never have a diagnosis. You wanted me to take this seriously, so I've done the research. Treating the symptoms is the only answer I have for you right now.'

We might never have a diagnosis.

Never.

Have.

A.

Diagnosis.

I might just be freaky Sick Girl for the rest of my life, never able to really say why or what it's called. I'll just name symptoms, like fibro and rheumatoid arthritis and nerve pain and knee subluxations. I feel sick with the weight of it.

Dad sighs heavily. 'We try the drugs,' he agrees reluctantly. He looks at me. 'Are you sure?'

No. 'Yes, I'm sure,' I say. 'It's hope.'

'No promises,' Dr Rai warns. 'But it might help.'

'I'll take 'might' at this point,' I reply, and he smiles at me, but I can see the sadness in it. Imagine how sad he'd be if he could watch me at school this week. I'd stopped limping, but Daniel bloody Perkins still isn't looking at me, and I'm playing chess in the library every lunchtime with Jenna, and Liam is back to standing around letting people talk shit about me without even coming over to apologise for them. Imagine if he could see Mum and Dad arguing about me and my health. Imagine if he could see me trying to hide how bad it is sometimes because I'm trying to spare my family the pain of seeing me.

'Start out at these doses,' he says, sliding me the prescriptions. 'After one week, double them, and then after the third week, add an extra tablet of the amitriptyline, but we'll leave the pregabalin at the second dose to start with.'

'Got it,' I reply. 'Double them after a week, and then a week later add a third amitriptyline.'

'And come back and see me earlier if you need to, but let's give it three weeks to start working,' Dr Rai says. 'Watch out for those side effects, and see if you can notice a difference.'

'Thank you, Dr Rai,' I say, standing. Dad stands with me.

'Thank you,' Dad adds, but he is clearly a lot more worried about the medication thing than I am. I can live with a few side effects if it means I can play at being a Real Girl™ again.

...

I stand in the kitchen at nine pm and take the pills. Ivy watches me from the counter where she's eating ice cream from the container. She's not meant to be eating ice cream, but it's not like I'm going to tell on her. Dad is watching the late news, and Mum is locked in the study theoretically working but probably playing mahjong online.

'What's that one?' Ivy asks, pointing to the capsule.

'Pregabalin,' I reply. 'It's going to make me fat and suicidal.'

She snorts a laugh. 'And the other one?'

'Amitriptyline, which will make me constipated and thirsty.'

'Delightful,' she says before putting another spoon of ice cream in her mouth. Mum used to say that butter wouldn't melt in Ivy's mouth, and I think about that sometimes when she's eating ice cream.

'Yup.'

'Do you think it'll really help?' Ivy asks. Her dark eyes are hopeful and serious. She looks way older than fourteen.

'I don't know. I hope so. Dr Rai seems to think they might. But he also said they aren't the only options if these ones don't work. It's better than nothing.'

'Dr Rai also said it was all in your head,' she points out. 'Do we trust Dr Rai?'

'I can't live like this, Ivy. I can't. I hurt every day, all the time. Sometimes getting out of bed makes me want to cry. I'm so tired by the end of the day that I can barely get through my homework. God, I can barely get through school! Mr Simmons might actually kill me if I space out in another science lesson,' I explain. I don't realise I'm crying until my cheeks are wet. I push at them quickly and too hard. 'I don't know what else to do.'

Ivy slides off the stool and comes over to wrap me in her arms. 'I love you, Gray. I'm sorry this is happening to you.'

I hug her so tightly that I'm surprised she doesn't complain. 'I love you, too, little sister.'

'I'm scared for you,' she admits. 'Because I don't think I could do what you're doing. I think I'd have given up.'

'I wouldn't have let you,' I say as my tears are wiped away by her hair.

'And I'm not going to let you,' she promises. She pulls back to look at me. 'Is Danny talking to you again, yet?'

I huff a little cry and wipe my cheeks again, stepping clear of the embrace. 'No, he's not. He may never speak to me again. And stop calling him "Danny", it's weird.'

'He will,' Ivy promises. 'He watches you sometimes.'

I blink, confused. 'He what?'

'He watches you,' she repeats. 'Like, at recess, when you go and sit near the oval to watch the birds. He sits up against the science block and looks at you.'

'No, he doesn't.'

'Gray, would I lie to you?'

'I don't think you're lying so much as you're delusional.'

'Look for yourself,' she shrugs. 'He was really nervous when I asked him what he was doing yesterday.'

I stare at her. 'You spoke to him? About me?' I don't know whether to be thankful or mortified. 'Why?'

'Because you're my favourite person and he made you sad.'

'Please tell me you didn't say that to him.' I hold my breath a little.

Ivy rolls her eyes. 'Of course, I didn't, I'm not an idiot,' she says, going back to her ice cream.

'What did you say?' I ask.

'I asked why he didn't go and talk to you if he was going to stare at you all the time like a creeper.'

'Ivy!'

'What? He asked if you were okay, and I said you were mostly fine but that he should ask you himself when he saw you in class. He looked at the ground and muttered something about it being weird or something. I said that you really do have weak knees that semi-dislocate sometimes –'

'Ivy!'

'– and he looked really upset by that, but then the bell went so I left.'

'Why would you tell him about my knees?'

'Because you wouldn't and you were sad,' Ivy argued. 'I get not wanting everyone to know, but you like Danny – Daniel, sorry, whatever – and I figured that a tiny bit of information wouldn't be a bad thing.'

'Christ, Ivy. It's none of your business who I tell what to. My social life isn't your concern. And, you knew I wanted to keep my health shit a secret. I can't ... it's not okay,' I fume. And I do fume. I'm furious and embarrassed and scared. 'You're my sister and I don't understand why you'd do this to me.'

Shock, hurt, and confusion dance across her face. 'I was trying to help,' she protests.

'Well, in future, don't,' I say, before stalking out of the kitchen and down the hall to my bedroom. I regret it almost as soon as I shut the door to my room. I want to comfort her and tell her it's okay and that I forgive her. But dread and betrayal have settled in my stomach again, and I don't want to go to school tomorrow and see Daniel because ... because of all the 'what ifs'.

What if he's different, and what if he's not?

What if he's my friend again?

What if he tells people?

What if he thinks I'm even more of a freak now?

What if nothing changes and he still can't look at me?

I curl up on my bed and hope the medication I just took will knock me out because if it doesn't, I can't see myself getting a lot of sleep tonight.

...

Friday morning arrives, and despite sleeping for a solid eight hours, I'm still so tired. Dad nudges me out of bed gently and uses his soothing-the-sick-daughter voice. Ivy keeps darting glances at me, and I'm too tired to figure out if it's because I'm so out of it or if she wants to apologise about last night. We never fight, not really. We don't know how to do this part very well. I fall asleep in the shower for a bit, which is weird, but Ivy gets me out. Dad gets me to the car.

'Do you ... do you want to take the day off?' Dad asks when we're already on our way.

I blink slowly. 'But I'm up and dressed and we're almost there.'

'I know, but you're ... I'm sure it's just the side effects,' he finishes. 'It might be better in a day or two.' He glances meaningfully at Ivy.

'You do seem a little ... off,' Ivy says carefully.

'Let me try,' I say. I suddenly feel like crying and I'm desperate to go to school even though I also want to stay in bed all day and maybe take up homeschooling myself. Meds and people and pain and ...

That's when it clicks.

My eyes widen, and I suddenly feel very awake.

'It's not as bad today,' I say. 'I'm still keen for the chiropractor this afternoon because I'm stiff. But it's not as bad today.'

'What?' Dad asks. 'Dr Rai said it would take at least a week and more likely two for things to change.'

'It's not gone,' I say. I hesitate. It's hard to explain to someone else. 'It's like it's further away.'

'Well, your brain is further away,' Ivy offers, with a small smile.

I smile back.

Her smile widens.

'It could be a placebo effect,' Dad says, warning in his voice. 'We can't celebrate yet. And I'm worried about how spaced out you seem.'

'Maybe I'm just too tired to connect,' I allow. 'I'd kind of like to sleep for a month, but I think I'll be okay. I'll call you if I need you to come get me. But I should try.'

'School might wake her up,' Ivy offers.

I snort a laugh and Dad rolls his eyes.

'I have art today.'

'That's the opposite of reassuring. You've gone to school with a fever before because you didn't want to miss art,' Dad says dryly.

'I also have math,' I point out. 'And Mr Simmons hates me.'

'He does,' Ivy agrees. 'He said that I was surprisingly pleasant the other day.'

'That doesn't mean he hates Grace,' Dad argues.

'Dad, we love you, but you're a bit dense sometimes,' I say.

Ivy laughs and Dad sighs.

'Fine,' he says. 'Go to school. Call me if you need me.' He's pulling into the carpark. 'And I mean it, you call me, Grace.'

'I'll be fine,' I promise.

'Grace,' he warns as he parks. 'I'm serious.'

'I swear I'll call you if I need you,' I sigh. 'I'm old enough to make this call, Dad. Thank you for caring.'

'I can check on her at lunch,' Ivy begins.

'No, thank you,' I tell her.

She flinches.

I sigh.

'Sorry,' she says in a small voice. 'I just wanted to help.'

'And I love you for it,' I tell her. 'But I'm old enough and ugly enough to manage my shit.'

'You aren't ugly,' Dad sighs. 'I wish you wouldn't say that.'

'It's a saying,' I say while rolling my eyes dramatically. 'Stop stalling. You just don't want to go to work. I see you.'

Dad laughs as we get out of the car. He pulls away and we watch him go for a moment.

'I am sorry,' Ivy says.

I smile and give her our secret handshake. Everything is amazing.

She returns it and then wraps me in a tight hug that would have made me wince normally.

'I love you, Gray.'

'I love you too, little sister. Now, get out of here before I have to hear your friends squeal with joy at your arrival.'

She laughs at me, with me, and then she bounces off to join her friends. I can see Mei having a conversation involving a lot of hand gestures with a boy in her class whose name I can't remember. His face lights up as much as Mei's when Ivy joins them, and I make a mental note to find out the guy's name. Boys' faces aren't meant to light up at my little sister. But she's not twelve anymore.

'I know where he lives,' Daniel says, making me jump out of my skin because I had no idea he was there. He grins at my jump. 'Nathan Ogilvie.' He nods at the boy. 'You were plotting his tragic demise, right?'

'I ... no,' I say, pressing my lips together.

'It's okay if you were,' he tells me. 'Your sister is ... special.'

'This better not be where you say you have a crush on her because I really hadn't planned on murdering anyone today,' I tell him, narrowing my eyes.

'Are you jealous?' he asks. 'You're still my favourite Turing sister.' He slings an arm around my shoulders.

I step out of it and try to figure him out. 'What are you doing?' I ask in the end.

He looks away and sighs heavily before turning back to me. 'I'm sorry,' he says. 'I was a dick.'

'Okay?'

'I thought ... it doesn't matter. I should have asked you and I didn't. And my mother ... it doesn't matter,' he says. I don't recognise this version of Daniel Perkins. But I want to.

'You're saying 'it doesn't matter' a lot, which usually means something does matter,' I say. 'But I won't ask you about it if you don't want me to.'

'Thanks,' he says, and he looks more like himself again. Then he grins. 'I like how much you love your sister. I'm an only child.'

'I'm told we're the exception,' I say, walking towards the locker room. He follows me.

'Probably,' he says. 'But it must be nice to have someone who gets what your family is like.'

I look at him, and the different Daniel Perkins is showing again. He doesn't want me to ask about it, I remind myself. So I don't. 'Did you know that ducks have a corkscrew penis?' I say instead.

He chokes on his tongue and nearly falls over, and I grin.

'Christ, Turing. Where the hell did that come from?' he says.

I laugh. 'You missed me,' I tell him. 'Also, I'm surprised you didn't know that one from your animal trivia addiction.'

'I blame you for that,' he says. 'Seriously though, can we go back to the duck penis? I have questions.'

'Wikipedia them,' I say. 'Maybe turn Google image search off, though. There are things you can't unsee.'

'Now I have to see it,' he says, pulling out his phone. He lingers while I open my locker and change out my books, stowing my backpack. I try not to smile in anticipation of his reaction.

'Hey, Grace,' Jenna says as I close my locker. She's looking at Daniel suspiciously.

'Hey, Jenna. How are you?' I ask.

'I'm okay. You disappeared yesterday afternoon,' she says.

'Doctor's appointment,' I say. 'Nothing exciting.'

'Holy frickin' shit, Batman,' Daniel exclaims. 'What am I looking at?'

'A duck penis?' I suggest helpfully.

'A what now?' Jenna asks.

'You don't want to look,' I tell her.

'Okay, so my first question is, what does a duck vagina look like?' Daniel asks.

I snicker and Jenna looks mildly disgusted.

'Weird trivia,' I explain. 'A duck has a corkscrew penis.'

'Ducks have nightmare penises,' Daniel corrects. 'Penii? Penises? Whatever.'

'Both, technically. I think.'

'I'm sorry, why are you talking about penises?' Liam asks, the football team lingering around us.

'Look at it,' Daniel says, offering his phone to them. Apparently, weird animal penises break down social boundaries, because there's no way they'd all be talking otherwise.

'What the hell?' Graham asks.

'That's insane,' Caleb says.

'How did you even start talking about this?' Liam asks me.

'She's a fucking weirdo,' Caleb says. 'Of course, she's talking about penises. Probably desperate to see one in the flesh.'

'Don't be disgusting,' Jenna says.

'Shut up, Caleb. No one cares about your opinion unless you've got a football in your hand,' Daniel says.

Liam says nothing, and I like him less for it.

'It's just random weird trivia,' I say with a shrug.

'What does a duck vagina look like?' Graham asks.

'That's what I wanted to know,' Daniel says with a sage nod.

'Did you guys know that whacking off killer whales was a legit job?' Ryan asks. I hadn't even noticed him join the group. My theory about animal penises and social boundaries is clearly correct, because I don't think I've ever seen any of the jocks be friendly to Ryan the Math Nerd before, but a newcomer would think they were all friends.

I turn to Jenna to ask if she wanted to walk to class, but she's already gone. Without doing her ritual of confirming our lunchtime chess game. But that could be because I'm suddenly so tired again that someone could spill hot coffee on me and I might not notice. I leave the group of guys and wander to homeroom.

. . .

Somehow, it is recess, and I have missed English completely despite being here the whole time. I have no notes, but there's a homework assignment written on the board, so I copy it down and hope I'll be able to figure it out later. I consider sitting in my usual spot near the oval, but I'm genuinely concerned I won't hear the bell. I'm too tired. I consider calling Dad, but that seems like too much work, too. And it's art. I don't want to miss it. My lino cutting is coming along nicely and I want to finish it today. So I eat recess outside the art block. Or, more accurately, I sit outside the art block with my recess in my lap, not eating, because that seems like work, too.

Okay, I'll admit it. Dad was right. I shouldn't be here. I close my eyes and feel the warmth of the spring sun.

'Grace?'

I open my eyes to find a concerned Mrs Connors, the art teacher, looking at me.

'Are you okay?'

'I'm fine,' I say, serenely. I feel very serene.

'You aren't eating,' she says.

I sigh. 'I'm fine,' I repeat. 'I'm just not hungry.'

'Are you sick?'

'No.'

'You look a little out of it. Were you asleep?'

'I'm just a little tired,' I say. 'I have new meds.'

'There you are,' Daniel says, coming over. 'You weren't bird-watching.'

'Has she been like this all day?' Mrs Connors asks him. 'She seems a little out of it.'

'Yeah, she has, now you mention it,' Daniel says, frowning a little. He squats down to my level.

'I'm okay,' I tell them. 'I'm just tired.'

Mrs Connors frowns and chews her lip. 'New medication,' she muses, aloud. 'I think we might need to call your mother.' Then she looks at Daniel and winces.

'It's a secret,' I say.

'Sorry, I'm just worried,' she says.

'It's my dad you have to call. Mum isn't good with this stuff,' I sigh. 'I wanted to finish my lino cutting. You aren't going to let me play with sharp tools today, are you?'

Mrs Connors smiles and suppresses a laugh. 'No, I'm not. You'll stay with her?' she asks Daniel. 'Maybe we should get her to the office?'

'I can walk,' I say. 'I'm fine.'

'You don't seem fine, Turing,' Daniel tells me. 'Sick bay time.' He stands and offers a hand to help me up.

'I really am okay,' I protest as I take his hand, standing. 'I'm just really tired.'

'Tell them I've called her father,' Mrs Connors tells Daniel.

'I'm right here,' I say.

'I will,' Daniel promises. 'Let's go.'

I scowl. 'I should get a say.'

'Which dwarf are you? Sleepy? Grumpy? Dopey? Pick one,' Daniel tells me. 'And only one.'

I try to scowl more but I laugh instead. 'Idiot,' I say.

He grins. 'I know. Come on.'

'Look after yourself, Grace,' Mrs Connors says. 'I'll see you next week.'

'Bye,' I say, and let Daniel lead me away. He doesn't keep holding my hand, but he stands so close I can feel the warmth of him.

'I'll tell your sister,' he says as we walk. 'She was kind of worried when you weren't birdwatching, too.'

'I like birds,' I say. 'I'm a bit weirded out that I'm not allowed to change my routine without causing concern. How do you know about the birds?'

'Because I do,' Daniel says after a moment.

'Ivy isn't meant to talk to you,' I say. 'She promised she wouldn't do it again.'

'I talked to her. Why can't she talk to me?' He's frowning.

'I don't ... Don't be offended.'

'I'm a little offended.'

'It's not about you. It's about me.'

'Uh-huh. That's a break-up line. You have to agree to go out with me before you can break up with me.'

'I'm not ... She told you a secret. She's meant to be on my side,' I say in the end.

'Why is it a secret?' he asks. 'And ... a new medication that makes you this drowsy? You're basically a zombie.'

I laugh. 'If I become a real zombie, you've got permission to brain me.'

'You don't have permission to brain me,' Daniel smirks. 'You'll probably pretend you thought I'd turned and whack me early.'

'Maybe.'

'Grace?'

'Yeah.'

'Why is it a secret? It's not just your knees, is it?'

Silence drags out between us. He's waiting for me to speak. He wants me to spill all of my secrets on the asphalt.

'Because it is,' I say. 'It doesn't matter.' The words are like some kind of code he understands immediately.

'Of course, it doesn't,' he replies. 'Did you know there are two ATMs in Antarctica?'

'What? How? Why? Who services them? What currency is in them?' I ask and pretend the surge of feeling in my chest isn't a form of love.

He grins. 'One of them is there for parts,' he says. 'American dollars. And they get serviced every two years.' He looks smug and happy.

'I mean, I suppose they'd have to be ATMs,' I say. 'There are people, and they can't do nothing but work. They'd be general stores and probably a coffee shop or something. I kind of, I mean, I haven't really thought about it before. But, if I had thought about it, I'd think it was like the *Enterprise*, so something.'

'As in, Star Trek?' he asks.

'Yeah. Like, they work and have rec rooms and a cafeteria. But not, shops or anything.' I felt dreamy and vague, and kind of warm.

'Huh,' he says. He's still grinning.

'What's with your face?' I ask.

'Nothing.'

'Liar.'

'I'm just … this is the first time you've been so excited by one of my facts,' he says. 'It's … I'm … proud of myself.'

'Smug bastard,' I say.

'Definitely.'

'Don't let it go to your head.'

'Too late.'

We're at the office.

'You don't have to come in,' I say.

He rolls his eyes. 'Shut up and do as you're told.'

I sigh, too tired to argue.

'See, if you can't argue, you're too tired to be here,' Daniel says as he opens the door. 'Hi, Mrs Gruber. I've got a patient. Mrs Connors sent us up, and she's already called Mr Turing.'

'Daniel,' Mrs Gruber says with a purse of her lips. She doesn't like him. I kind of want to slap her again because I have a feeling she doesn't like him for the same reasons she likes Liam. Gossip. 'Grace! Are you okay, pet?'

'I'm just tired,' I say, making a fist. Daniel notices it, and I know because he smirks a little.

'Do you have a fever, cough or cold?'

'No, I don't think so,' I reply but she comes out and tests my temp anyway with a forehead scanner.

'Well, let's get you settled. I've got it from here, Daniel,' she says.

'I'd rather he stayed,' I say, more because I want to be contrary than any other reason. They're both kind of surprised.

'I suppose that's fine as long as you both mask up,' Mrs Gruber says slowly. 'Mrs Connors sent you, you say?'

'Yep,' Daniel says. 'You can call her, if you like.' He hands me mask that was proffered by Mrs Gruber before putting one on himself.

'I will,' Mrs Gruber promises. 'I'll send Mrs Easton in shortly.'

'Thanks,' I say, adjusting my mask.

'You'd rather I stay, huh?' he asks when the door on the sick bay is closed.

'I'd rather piss off Mrs Gruber,' I reply. 'If she calls me "pet" again, I'll need someone to hold me back.'

He laughs with his head thrown back. I've never seen him do that before. It's another version of him I haven't seen. I wish I could have seen his smile under the mask.

'Clearly, you're not a fan either,' I say.

'Have you ever watched *Die Hard*?' he asks me.

'Uh, no?'

'Seriously? Bruce Willis? Alan Rickman? Best Christmas movie of all time?'

He seems a little offended.

'No,' I say. 'I'm not really a Christmas person. Or a Christmas movie person.'

'Grace? I'm about to ask you to do something for me.'

'Okay.'

'I'm serious, it's very important.'

'Mm-hmm.'

'You need to watch *Die Hard*.'

'Right.'

'Because if you don't watch it, we can't be friends anymore,' he says, seriously. 'Also if you watch and don't like it.'

The mask hides my smile.

'I'm serious,' he says.

'I can tell.'

'Promise me.'

'I promise,' I say. 'I will watch it over the weekend. Now, what does *Die Hard* have to do with anything?'

'The villain's last name is Gruber,' he says, grinning.

'Ah,' I say. 'That makes sense.'

'Right? She's clearly related to him.'

'Obviously. You're kind of a ridiculous person, did you know that?' I ask him.

'You're the first to say it,' he says. 'But I've had a suspicion. I think you make me weirder.'

'I'm going to take that as a compliment,' I tell him.

'You should,' he says. 'Now shut up and rest. Though it is tempting to keep talking. I feel like you're not going to remember this tomorrow. I'll be sure to tell Ivy you promised to watch *Die Hard* this weekend, just in case.'

'She'll say that you should offer to watch it with me,' I sigh. 'She keeps calling you Danny.'

'She likes me, huh?' His eyes light up.

'She likes everyone. It's her worst quality.'

'I like her, too. She cares about you. You could call me Danny, too.'

'It's weird,' I say. 'You're not a Danny. You're a Daniel.'

'That's a weird distinction.'

'It is what it is. Don't talk to my sister.'

'I'm going to,' he says. 'I have to tell her you've gone home and that you're okay.'

'She wants to believe in a world where wishing makes things true and you actually want to go out with me instead of just being a teasing prick,' I sigh. Then I realise what I've said. 'That didn't come out like I meant it.'

'I am a teasing prick,' he admits.

'Exactly,' I say. 'Don't make her think you like me.'

'Okay,' he says.

'I'm serious. She doesn't understand what it's like to not be pretty, sweet, kind, and loved by everyone.'

'Grace,' Daniel says, his voice weird. 'I feel like you're trying to tell me something about you. Is the idea of dating me so horrific?'

'No. I don't know. I haven't actually thought about it. Dating isn't on my radar. One day, Ivy's going to figure out that her big sister is an asshole and not as pretty as she thinks I am.'

'Are you trying to delay that or make it happen faster?'

'Both.'

'That makes no sense.'

'I never said it did.' My eyes are closed. When did that happen?

'Grace?'

'Mmm?'

'Are you awake?'

'Mmm.'

There's a long pause.

'You're prettier than you think you are,' he whispers.

I'm pretty sure that I'm not meant to hear it, so I keep my eyes closed as he leaves the room. I wonder if I'll remember this later, or if he's right, and I'm too tired to remember anything.

…

The next thing I know, Dad is shaking me awake and sighing a lot.

'We're going to see Dr Rai tomorrow,' he says when he gets me in the car.

'Give me the weekend,' I say. 'We don't have to be anywhere, and it might take a couple of days for the side effects to balance out.'

'Grace, I'm worried.'

'Please.'

'Fine,' he sighs. 'But if I can't rouse you, I'm taking you to the emergency room. I know how you love that.'

'Deal,' I say. I close my eyes and sleep for the car ride home.

CHAPTER FIVE
Side Effects

I sleep for most of the weekend. Dad wants me to stop taking the medication, or at least stop taking one of them. Mum argues that we should follow the doctor's advice. Ivy makes sure I stay awake all the way through *Die Hard*.

'Danny made me promise,' she says. 'It was actually a pretty good movie.'

'Don't call him 'Danny',' I say. 'And he was right, I do love it. Smug bastard's going to love this.'

'Who is Danny?' Mum asks meaningfully. She clearly has an opinion on who he is, and it irritates me a bit.

'A guy in my class,' I say. 'He's into weird trivia, too.'

'He's into Grace,' Ivy mutters.

'He is not into me,' I say. 'We've talked about this. He's just a teasing prick.'

'Grace, is that a nice thing to say about a friend?' Mum asks.

'Yes,' I reply, deadpan. 'He calls me a weirdo all the time.'

'Friendship has changed since I was in high school,' Mum sighs.

'You're very old,' I say. 'Do you miss the dinosaur you rode to school on?'

She throws a pillow at me while Ivy laughs.

'There are more *Die Hard* movies, you know,' Mum says.

'Marathon time?' Ivy asks, hopefully. 'I want to see John and Holly be a family with their kids.'

'So naïve,' I say. 'They're action movies. More movies means no happily ever after.'

'I'll get snacks,' Ivy says. 'You'll watch it with us, right?' she asks Mum.

'Of course, I will,' Mum says, pleased to join us. It makes me feel worse for not being as nice to her as Ivy is.

'Tell me about Danny,' Mum says when Ivy is gone.

I sigh. 'His name is Daniel, and he's just a friend, Mum. We have a similar sense of humour.'

'Hmm, I'm not sure you should be hanging out with people who have the same sense of humour as you,' Mum teases me a little. 'That can only end badly.'

'Right?' I say, smiling. 'But it's ... nice to have a friend.'

'What about Abbie? You were friends with her?'

'We were like prison friends,' I say. 'I'm out of that prison, so we're not still friends.'

'Does she think that's the case?' Mum asks. 'Sometimes, that is how friendships go, but ...'

'She hasn't emailed me either,' I say. 'It's fine. Anyway, *Die Hard* movies. How many are there?'

'Five,' Mum says. 'We're not getting through all of them today. And some of them aren't very good.'

'Do you want to see if Dad wants to join us as well?' I ask.

She beams. 'What a good idea.' She's thinking about family time and togetherness, and I'm thinking about a buffer between Mum and me if I get cranky.

'Wake me up if I fall asleep,' I say. 'I want to enjoy this.'

'Deal,' she says and goes to get Dad.

It's nice, in the end. Family movie weekend. We'll do it again, I hope, but I can't remember the last time all four of us sat down and paid attention to a movie together. It's really nice.

By Monday morning, I'm a manageable level of sleepy. Dad still wants me to go and see Dr Rai again, and I concede to making an appointment for this week to chat about the side effects. But until then, I'm taking the pills. Because I want this to work. I need it to. And I need to give it time to work. The pain still feels like it did when I started taking them; like it is just that little bit further away from me. It still hurts, it's just not as pointy.

Jenna finds me at my locker on Monday morning, and she looks really uncomfortable.

'Hey, what's up?' I ask as I shut my locker.

'You and Daniel,' she says. 'Are you … friends?'

I pause. 'Good morning, my weekend was fine, how was yours?'

She huffs a self-conscious laugh. 'Sorry. I just … I don't know.'

'We're friends, I think,' I say. 'Why?'

Jenna presses her lips together tightly and can't meet my eyes.

'Do you,' I pause and look around, making sure no one is going to overhear. I lower my voice anyway. 'Do you like him?'

She makes a strangled sound in the back of her throat. 'God, no. The opposite, actually. He's … I don't like him at all.'

'Ah,' I say as if I understand. But I don't really. I don't speak 'high school'. 'Does this … is this a thing?' I want to say *are you asking me to choose* like this is some kind of high school friendship divorce scenario. But I don't, because I don't want to assume that Jenna is that petty, and I don't want to be caught in the drama.

She sighs. 'I don't know. It … it might be. He's been kind of a dick to me forever, and you and I are friends, I think. Or maybe I was just your backup friend for when he wasn't talking to you?'

Christ. 'Jenna, I have a question that is going to sound really blunt, so I apologise in advance, but I'm not trying to be a bitch.'

'Okay.' She's worried. She should be.

'Are you … did you see a psychologist or something between Friday morning and now?'

She looks at me in shock for a moment, and then she laughs.

I wait it out, unsure.

'My mother's a therapist,' she says, grinning.

'Ah,' I say. 'That would explain it. I mean, I'm not trying to invalidate your feelings or whatever. I've just never had a conversation like this before.'

'I figured. I can be a bit … therapy-sounding. It probably doesn't help the whole popularity thing,' she admits.

'Well, first of all, there's a show on Netflix called *Sex Education* and you're going to love it. Second: you aren't a backup friend. You're a legit friend like Daniel is.'

'Okay,' she says.

'But, in the short time I have been attending Riverview High, I have to say that I don't think Daniel is a dick to you. He probably was in the past, or maybe he is now and I can't see it.'

She frowns. 'Give me an example of him not being a dick to me.'

'My first day. You agreed with me about liking lasagne and he called them idiots for laughing.'

She blinks, surprised, and stares at me. 'Huh,' she says.

I nod. 'I'm not into the whole choosing thing, to be honest. And he's been a pretty good friend to me, but so have you.'

'That's fair. I think I need to think about this,' she says. 'Like, you're right, he was on my side. Maybe I'm letting the past dictate the present.'

'That is the most therapy-sounding thing I've ever heard someone say in real life,' I reply with a grin, and she laughs again.

'Yeah, yeah, I get it. Therapist-in-training over here.'

'Now, I would offer to play chess with you at lunch, but my brain is basically empty because I'm too tired to function. Do you want to watch some birds with me instead?' I ask.

'You're the only teenager I know who watches birds for fun,' Jenna replies. 'So maybe don't throw stones in glass houses.'

I grin, and we're friends again, better friends, even. Maybe I'm not so bad at high school after all.

...

Daniel joins us halfway to homeroom. Jenna looks a little uncomfortable, but she stays, so I give her a supportive smile.

'Did you watch it?' he asks.

I roll my eyes. 'Good morning, Daniel. I had a lovely weekend, how was yours?'

Jenna laughs and Daniel grins.

'Whatever,' he says. 'Did you watch it?'

'What was she meant to watch?' Jenna asks.

'The best Christmas movie of all time.'

'Ah,' Jenna says knowingly. '*Die Hard.* Of course.'

'You say that like it's not a great movie, Harrington.'

'It's an eighties action flick,' Jenna replies. 'It is what it is.'

'You're breaking my heart here,' Daniel sighs. 'It was genre-redefining. It was Bruce Willis at his best.'

'Personally, I don't think you can go past the *"so this is what a TV dinner feels like"* line,' I say. 'But the *"now I have a machine gun ho-ho-ho"* shirt had me laughing until I cried.'

'Oh my god,' Jenna says. 'He's converted you.'

'Yes!' Daniel says, actually pumping his fist in the air. 'What did Ivy think?'

'Ivy wanted there to be a happily ever after for John and Holly,' I sigh. 'We're watching number four tonight, and she's still holding out hope.'

'Is Ivy your … sister?' Jenna asks.

I nod. 'Yep. And I'm pretty sure the happy ending thing actually defines her as a person.'

'So, nothing like Grace,' Daniel grins.

I scowl as Jenna laughs.

'Wait. Jenna. Has anyone ever called Daniel "Danny" before?' I ask.

'Don't answer that,' Daniel says.

'Yes,' Jenna replies without hesitation.

'Oh god,' Daniel says.

'His mother,' she begins.

'Well, that makes sense,' I say.

'And when we were in, what, grade seven? He tried to get everyone to call him that,' Jenna muses. 'It was kind of sweet.'

'That is the least complimentary thing anyone has ever said about me,' Daniel says, disgusted. 'Sweet.'

I laugh. 'I knew it. You're not a Danny at all.'

'I blame you,' Daniel says to Jenna.

She shrugs and grins. 'Well, I owe you,' she tells him. 'Were you really going to call him Danny?'

I pull a face at the thought. 'I could be convinced to go with Dan. But, I don't know, you're a Daniel. It is what it is, friend.'

'A real friend would call me whatever I wanted,' he complains.

'A real friend tells it like it is,' I reply. 'Which might be why I have no friends.'

'I'm right here,' Daniel says. 'Rude. We should leave, right? Clearly, we don't exist.'

'You might be right,' Jenna agrees.

I do what I do when I know I need to change the subject. 'Did you know that people were still getting guillotined in France when the first *Star Wars* movie came out?' I found that one last night specifically for Daniel.

'No,' Jenna says, aghast.

'Wait, Episode One or Episode Four,' he asks.

'The one with Luke and Leia,' I say. I can't remember.

'No shit,' he says thoughtfully.

'I shit you not,' I reply.

'What year did it come out?' Jenna asks.

I shrug because I can't remember.

I'd normally remember.

Why can't I remember? 'I think the late seventies, early eighties?'

'I feel like you should know that before you drop that little fact,' Daniel says.

'I feel like you should just be suitably impressed my brain holds so much weird shit,' I reply.

'I'm impressed,' Jenna says. 'I'd be even more impressed, though, if you could make it through a science class without pissing Mr Simmons off.'

'Jenna, you ask the impossible. Her face pisses Mr Simmons off since the Turing thing.'

'I regret nothing,' I say. 'You wanna know something weird?'

'Always,' says Daniel.

'Maybe,' says Jenna.

'I am distantly related to Alan Turing, I just really hate that question.'

They dissolve into laughter and I join them. They think I'm ridiculous. Daniel thinks I should get a shirt printed and Jenna wonders why I decided to piss off a teacher of two core subjects on my first day. I tell them that I couldn't help myself, and Jenna despairs of me. Daniel thinks this is even funnier.

'Riverview High was definitely less fun without you,' Daniel says.

'It was also quieter,' Jenna adds, but there is something melancholy in her voice.

'Well, now you're stuck with me. Unless Mum decides to take another job on short notice and drags us across the country again.'

'It's cute how you think you're allowed to just abandon us,'

Daniel tells me. He leans back in his seat to talk to Jenna. 'Right? You want to keep her, too?'

'Maybe,' Jenna says. She gives me a small smile.

'That's Jenna for yes,' Daniel says. 'Girl is timid like a mouse. Definitely a Hufflepuff.'

'Don't mock Hufflepuff!'

'No one wants to be in Hufflepuff except people in Hufflepuff.'

'Says the Slytherin,' Jenna says.

'I'm not a Slytherin!'

'Well, you're sure as shit not a Gryffindor.'

'I don't know,' I cut in, teasing. 'Gryffindors are not known for their intelligence.'

'Gryffindors are jocks,' Daniel argues. He points to the football team. 'Look at them all. All brawn, and not enough brains to figure out they should be scared.'

'Hey, Hermione was a Gryffindor,' Graham argues, overhearing us. 'She was smart.'

'Whatever,' Daniel replies. 'Turing is clearly a Ravenclaw.'

'She's Slytherin,' Kenzi says. 'She's too slow to be a Ravenclaw. But then, books hardly require physical skills, do they?'

'Shut up, Kenzi, if I wanted you to speak I'd wave a Schmacko over your nose,' Daniel says.

'Be nice to the house elves,' I say. 'But make sure you don't give her any clothing, she's too stupid to survive in the wild.'

Kenzi sputters while half the class laughs.

'You're a grade-A bitch, Grace,' Amber snaps. 'Definitely a Slytherin.'

'Slytherins aren't evil. They are just proud and like leadership roles,' Elsa says. 'I'm not saying Grace isn't a Slytherin, but there are bitches in every house.'

'What house are you in?' I ask Elsa.

'Hufflepuff,' she says proudly. Jenna and Elsa share a nod and smile of alliance. 'You're a Ravenclaw, right?'

I go to answer that she's wrong, but I pause. Old Grace was a Gryffindor. In the time before I was Sick Girl, I was fearless and caring and bold. I didn't care what people thought and I would always do what I considered the right thing. But that was almost two years ago. 'I don't think I know anymore,' I say in the end. 'Maybe.'

There is a strange pause in the conversation.

I think about spouting a weird fact. Like that 'Dumbledore' is actually Old English for 'bee', or that J.K. Rowling made up the house names on the back of an airplane vom bag.

'Well, I'm a Slytherin,' Daniel announces. 'Because I'm awesome and you should all listen to me.'

The pause breaks and everyone goes back to calling out what house they're in, or their original conversations. Things move on around me, but I can't join in. I'm stuck in my head wondering who I'll be if I'm Sick Girl for the rest of my life. Hogwarts wasn't exactly designed for people with disabilities. All those stairs. Can you be brave with a walking stick? Adventurous when going for a walk up a hill makes you cry? Smart when the medication you take to cope makes you a zombie? A leader when you struggle to get out of bed sometimes? Chivalrous when you're the one who needs the doors opened for you? Loyal when your body betrays you?

Jenna tries to get my attention and Daniel talks at me as we walk to math. I'm monosyllabic, which is a wonderful word and my mother's greatest fear for me. I'm stuck in my head and Mr Simmons yells at me for failing to pay attention. By the time class is over, I'm too tired to do much more than sit at the oval and stare at birds. Daniel and Jenna sit with me. Daniel keeps talking, but mostly to Jenna. Which makes her nervous, I think, but she engages. They both look at me strangely. When the bell goes, Daniel catches my wrist and holds me back, letting Jenna take a few steps away from us.

'Do you need to go to the office?' he whispers.

'I'm fine,' I say.

'You say that when you're not fine,' he points out. 'What about Ivy?'

'I'm fine, I promise,' I say, forcing a smile. 'Did you know "Dumbledore" is an Old English word for 'bee'?'

'You're not fooling me, Turing,' he says.

'It doesn't matter.'

Those magical code words that keep our secrets to ourselves.

'Okay,' he says. 'Jenna, wait up! I just had to tie my shoe.'

She stops and he gives me a look that tells me to get my shit together. We catch up to her and I force myself back into the real world.

'Why are you even doing home ec?' Jenna asks Daniel. 'You're the only guy in our class.'

'I like cooking. Besides, I'm more likely to need to know how to make a cake than a toilet roll holder,' Daniel replies.

'He's going to be forever alone, he'll need to know how to cook for himself,' I tease.

'Nah, I'm going to marry you. You can cook, right?' Daniel says, clearly joking.

'That's some nightmare fuel,' I say. 'Ivy's a better cook than me.'

'I do like Ivy,' Daniel says, thoughtfully.

I punch him in the arm.

'You did deserve that,' Jenna says.

'I know,' he sighs. 'Will you marry me instead? Your cinnamon tea cake last week looked so good.'

'Piss off,' Jenna says.

'You girls can be real bitches sometimes,' Daniel complains.

We all laugh and everything is normal.

I'm normal.

I'm normal. I'm normal. I'm normal.

Normal becomes a weird word really fast.

...

By Thursday, I'm still feeling vague but I have a doctor's appointment that afternoon. But my pain levels have gone down. I mean, really down. Ivy and I had a dance party in the lounge room to celebrate her getting an A in history. I should have been able to dance way less. I should be feeling like absolute shit today (worth it, though). Instead of feeling sore and stiff and hating life, I just feel the same tired that I've felt every day since I started taking the new meds.

Ivy calls me 'Zom-Gray' and thinks it is kind of funny that her previously organised sister forgot her lunch yesterday but took an extra sports shirt. We didn't even have sport yesterday. I have no idea how that happened.

Mum calls it a miracle that I'm not in pain. I agree with her. She thinks Dad is being dramatic and we should see how this plays out. It's only been a week, after all.

Dad stomps around and says it isn't a miracle, it's a bloody problem. The doctor is a quack and he misses his daughter. I tell him I'm right here. He tells me that while he appreciates my physical presence, my brain is the best thing about me. I think it's a compliment.

Mr Simmons thinks that I'm being deliberately disobedient and disrespectful, and a bunch of other d-words I didn't really pay attention to. Spittle flew from his mouth. Jenna was disgusted. Daniel was pissed at him for me. I think that Mr Simmons enjoys me being a space cadet because it gives him a reason to yell at me. Who am I to deprive him of that?

...

We talk to Dr Rai.

I stop taking the pregabalin.

My brain comes back.

The pain comes back.

We start having a new argument.

'Are you sure about this?' Mum asks on day five of no pregabalin. I went for a walk yesterday and now I'm struggling to get out of bed. It's sport day, so I'm going to need a note to excuse me. Which will make the knee incident fresh in everyone's minds. It hurts. I'm sick of it. There's just one problem.

'Dad's right. I was a zombie,' I say. 'I need my brain, Mum. I like trivia and history. I like not getting yelled at.'

'Who yelled at you?' Mum asks, her tone sharp and her eyes narrowed.

I win the battle not to roll my eyes. 'Mum, it's fine.'

'It's not fine,' she says. 'You've got a disability and a teacher is belittling you!'

This is why kids should be allowed to choose their mothers before they log into a womb. She's great, but she gets a bit social-justice-warrior-ish. I blame her job – she does marketing for not-for-profits. And she's awesome at it.

'I'm not your project,' I say.

'You're my daughter. Which makes you the definition of my project.'

'It's not a problem. I don't want to make it a problem.' My argument is ruined when a wince while reaching for a piece of fruit.

'Grace,' she says, and her voice is full of sympathy.

'Don't,' I snap.

She winces and sighs. 'I love you,' she says. 'It's hard for me.'

'Well, try being me. I hate this and I hate sympathy. I'm fine.'

She sighs heavily, and I think that she's thinking that I should be more like Ivy. Easy going. Sweet. Tolerant. Even before I got sick I wasn't Ivy.

'You can let people help you,' she says.

'I know. But I've got this.'

'You argued to keep taking it,' Mum reminds me. 'You said you didn't mind the fog because it hurt less.'

'And then the fog left and I realised that I missed my brain,' I reply. 'I couldn't remember things and I couldn't focus at school. I liked the less pain part, but I don't like being a zombie.'

'In hindsight,' Mum points out. 'You didn't mind at the time.'

'And you don't think that's a problem?' I ask. 'That your daughter was over-medicated to the point of not caring she was a zombie? Didn't you go on some long rant about that happening in nursing homes the other day?'

I can tell that she wants to say, 'that's different'. I see it forming in her brain. I see the look in her eyes. She's holding the argument inside, playing it out.

'I just want you to be okay,' she says eventually.

I smile. 'I know.'

'I love you.'

'I know that, too.'

'Grace.'

'I love you, too, Mum. I understand your point of view. But, I think I'd rather be in pain than disappear like that. It's shitty either way, so I'm picking the one I think is less shit.'

Mum looks at me strangely. 'When did you get so grown up?' she asks.

I laugh. 'I'm sixteen. I think it happens as time passes, you know, like literally everything else.'

She hugs me, tighter than I'd like, but I don't complain. I hug her back.

'I'm proud of you,' she says.

'For what?' I ask, confused.

'For being you.'

...

The last class of the day is speech and drama with Ms Oakley. She's basically a raven-haired, slightly older version of Miss Frizzle from the *Magic School Bus*. She's always asking us to 'feel' the characters and telling us to 'express ourselves physically'. I think that we all think she's a couple of raisins short of a fruitcake, but we all like her. If it was allowed, I think she'd want us all to call her 'Winnie' instead.

Today, we're meant to be rehearsing for the qualifiers before the state competition. I have no idea how I ended up in drama, to be honest, because it really isn't my thing. But Riverview High doesn't have a Spanish class and I'm not picking up German this late in the game. It's not so bad, really. But I so do not feel up to pulling myself together. I'm still tired, but it's a different kind of tired. It's exhausted tired. It's 'I've already survived a whole day and I'm paying for yesterday's activities, and can I please go home now' tired.

'Grace,' Ms. Oakley says making too much eye contact. 'Are you not feeling the role of Nora?'

I blink. 'I ... It's not Nora. I mean, I can't decide if she's plastic or if she's actually a real woman underneath. Which, even if she is plastic, is it actually her fault that she is because the patriarchy is balls.'

'Yes, yes. Excellent! Excellent character exploration,' Ms Oakley says, basically clapping her hands with glee. '*A Doll's House* is a marvellous play and a wonderful lens through which to view society.'

'Right,' I agree.

'Yeah, Helmer's a dick,' Daniel says. He gives me a strange look. 'But Nora is definitely a real person under all that. I wonder who she is after the door closes, you know?'

'So insightful, Daniel,' Ms Oakley says as she makes heart eyes at him. She is the only teacher who likes him. I think it's because, in her words, he is so 'free of inhibitions' and 'transparently honest'.

'So, Grace, what's wrong if not Nora?'

I hesitate.

'She's just tired,' Daniel says, still looking at me strangely.

Ms Oakley frowns. 'You don't seem as ... vague as you have recently. Is everything okay?'

'I'm fine,' I say. 'Sorry, Daniel's right. I'll get it together.'

'I would hate to see you not make it to state. You're both talented enough, and you've chosen excellent material.'

Daniel and I exchange a look that communicates our mutual, total lack of desire to go to state to each other. We'll probably call in sick on the day of qualifiers.

'Sorry, Ms Oakley,' I say.

'Don't apologise to me, dear, apologise to Daniel. And Nora. She deserves your all,' she says dramatically before swanning off.

We watch her go in wonder.

'She is the weirdest person I have ever met,' I say.

'Isn't it awesome?' Daniel asks. 'I want to be that weird when I grow up.'

'You'll get there,' I say.

'You say that like it's not a compliment.'

'Did you know that Ibsen was going to be a pharmacist?'

'I did not.'

'Did you know that he failed to get into university multiple times?'

'These are not at the level of trivia I have come to expect from you, Turing. You disappoint me.'

I roll my eyes. 'He's a playwright who died in 1900. I have limited material to work with. Come on, let's get this show back on the road.' I stand up too quickly, though, because the net of pain around my muscles tightens. I hiss with pain and slowly lower myself back down into the chair.

Daniel gives me the strange look again. 'You're not okay.'

'I'm fine,' I say. 'I'm always fine.'

He looks at me like he wants to say things. He checks around to make sure no one is in earshot. And no one is. Everyone else is actually rehearsing their competition pieces.

'This is part of the secret, right? You changed meds again?'

'You aren't meant to notice this stuff,' I sigh.

For an invisible illness, it's doing a shit job of staying under the radar. But I guess that's kind of the point. It's not invisible if you know where to look.

'I care,' he shrugs, trying to play it off. But I can tell this means something to him. I mean something to him. We're friends, I remind myself. It's just friend stuff. I wish Jenna was here so I could spin the conversation away from this, but she's in horticulture instead of drama. I'd have picked it over drama but I have a black thumb and that much direct sunlight screws with me.

'It's not a big deal,' I say. 'Just give me a sec to regroup.'

'You've been in Launceston over a month, Grace. I know when you're lying.'

'We all have secrets,' I say, giving him a meaningful look. He is always sloppy on the uniform front, but it's never actually dirty. It is today. Which means he probably didn't go home last night, or something else is going on. He's also been a little distracted.

He sighs and looks away.

'Exactly,' I say. 'So. It doesn't matter?'

The question lingers.

'Grace, I want –'

'Are you going to tell me yours?' I ask, cutting him off. 'Or are we going to agree that it doesn't matter?'

He hesitates.

'It doesn't matter,' he says, but he's not happy about it.

'It doesn't matter,' I agree, but I find myself wanting to tell him. Wanting to say that I'm in so much pain I nearly threw up at lunch. The diazepam I took is only taking the edge off. I need a nap so badly I could cry.

'*We have been married now eight years. Does it not occur to you that this is the first time we two, you and I, husband and wife, have had a serious conversation?*' I say as Nora.

'*What do you mean by serious?*' he replies as Helmer after a moment.

'*In all these eight years – longer than that – from the very beginning of our acquaintance, we have never exchanged a word on any serious subject.*'

'*Was it likely that I would be continually and forever telling you about worries –,*' he cuts himself off from Helmer's words. 'Is this ... are you trying to tell me something?' he asks, tilting his head.

'It's a play,' I deadpan. 'It's all about telling people something.'

'You know what I mean.'

'I really don't.'

'Don't be dense, it doesn't suit you, Turing. Just tell the truth and I'll leave it. We'll go back to "it doesn't matter".' He's upset and it takes me a minute to process what's happening.

'Daniel Perkins, you are not Helmer and I am not Nora,' I begin.

'I'm serious –'

'We are not married and I am not breaking up with you.'

'Obviously,' he sighs as if I exhaust him. 'I meant, is that what you want – the never having a serious conversation thing?'

'We –,' I pause, thinking. I had been about to say we'd had a serious conversation. But we haven't.

'Figure it out,' Daniel tells me. '*Was it likely that I would be continually and forever telling you about worries that you could not help me to bear?*' He's Helmer again.

I say my line, but I'm not thinking about Nora and Helmer anymore. I'm wondering if I'm doing the right thing by keeping my secret. By keeping it from Jenna and Daniel who are my friends. Especially from Daniel, because he knows enough to be worried. But I don't have the words or a diagnosis or evidence to show them. I'm scared they'll treat me differently. I'm scared they'll say I'm doing it for the attention.

'Grace? It's your line,' Daniel says when I drift a little too far off course. '*How unreasonable and how ungrateful you are, Nora! Have you not been happy here?*' he repeats.

'*No, I have never been happy. I thought I was, but it has never really been so,*' I say as Nora.

Maybe Daniel is right, and we've picked a scene that is a little too close to home. I thought I was happy before I got sick and maybe I was. I don't think I'd been happy for a long time. Yet despite everything else, I think I could be happy here – not just Launceston, but Riverview High. My chest is tight with the thought of it, but I don't say anything. I just keep acting the part of Nora, enjoying Daniel's dramatics, and waiting for the day to be over. The next diazepam, the one I can't take without going a little loopy, is waiting for me in the car after school. I'm hanging out for it.

But if I'm honest, I'm also weirdly okay with being in drama, laughing at Daniel – who's being an idiot just to make me laugh. He keeps me present even when the pain threatens to shut me down again.

...

If I ever tell him the truth, it'll come with a thank you.

CHAPTER SIX
Infection Protocol

It starts at recess.

That's not entirely true. I woke up feeling a little strange. But the amitriptyline is meant to make you a bit constipated, so I figured that was what it was. I figure out that it probably isn't that at recess. I'm tempted to ask Dr Google what he thinks about the situation, but that never ends well.

'You look a little pale,' Jenna whispers to me as we walk towards the locker room before the bell. Daniel has stopped to tie his shoelace. Again. I'm tempted to suggest those silicone laces that you don't need to tie … except I know that's not why he's stopping.

'I'm okay,' I reply with a smile.

Her eyes track to my hand over my stomach. 'That time of the month?' she asks sympathetically.

'No,' I reply with a frown. 'It's not that.'

'But it is something?' she asks, concerned. 'I mean, you've been spaced out on meds, and I know you get a little … whatever, sometimes. But you don't look great, Grace.'

'What a compliment,' I tease. Daniel catches up to us, so I say: 'I bet you agree with Jenna.'

'Rarely,' Daniel grins.

'Shut up,' Jenna sighs. I like that they're friends now.

'What did you say?' he asks her.

'I said that Grace didn't look great.'

'The audacity!' Daniel gasps mockingly. 'Turing always looks great.'

'You know what I mean,' Jenna says, narrowing her eyes at him, and then me.

I catch a hint of concern in Daniel's eyes. I think he wants to ask me about last week when he told me to think about if we're serious friends or not. I've thought about it a lot and I'm a little scared of the answer. So, I haven't said anything.

'I'm fine,' I say again. The spasm hits and I'm nearly doubled over with the pain. It's sharp and distinctly on the left-hand side, which rules out my appendix and gallbladder. Kidney pain is higher, and on the back. My period was last week, so it's not that.

'Grace,' Daniel begins, but he stops.

I straighten back up. Mostly. 'It's fine,' I repeat. Then I dry-heave and drop to one knee as it spasms again.

'It's not fucking fine,' Daniel says, finally. He's angry. Why is he angry?

'Grace,' Jenna says, kneeling beside me. Her hand hovers as if to touch me.

'Don't,' I say. 'I can't –'

'Don't what?' Daniel snaps. 'If you say "it doesn't matter" right now, I'll never speak to you again.'

'– touch me. Please don't touch me,' I finish, gasping. I look up. Jenna looks terrified. Daniel is a mix of angry and worried. 'Hurts. Get Ivy,' I manage. 'And Mrs Easton.'

'Who's Mrs Easton?' Jenna asks.

'Accountant slash nurse,' I say. It ebbs a little and I manage to get on my feet again.

Daniel hesitates.

'Please. I need … I need her.'

'You take her to the office,' Daniel instructs Jenna.

'I don't know,' Jenna starts to say, but Daniel interrupts her.

'Jenna, you take her to the office. Or as close as you can. I'll get help.'

Ivy meets us before we make it to the office. The pain has me almost shuffling, and while Jenna is letting me use her arm as a crutch, I can tell that she's freaking out. She's scared of touching me.

'Oh, Gray,' Ivy says, her beautiful eyes look on the brink of tears and I wish I could hug her.

I swallow down and try to straighten up again. It's not entirely successful.

'What's happening?' she asks. Then she looks at Jenna. 'I've got her from here.'

'Are you sure?' Jenna asks.

I can see that she wants to go. My random, sudden onset pain is making her really uncomfortable. I don't think we'll be friends after this. I feel like throwing up.

'Ivy's got me,' I say and Ivy nods.

Jenna leaves.

'I leave you alone for two hours,' Ivy teases me, gently. She knows the sympathy just makes me angry, but I'd consider taking it right now.

'Don't know,' I say to her unasked question. 'Maybe an amitriptyline side effect?'

She nods. 'Phone,' she says, extending her hand for it.

'Locker,' I say. I dig the keys from my pocket and hand them to her. 'Seventy-eight.'

She pockets the keys and slips under my arm, holding me tight to her side as she helps me walk. I cry out when she straightens me too much, and she adjusts.

'I've got you,' Ivy tells me. 'Daniel looked like he was about to have a stroke.'

'I think Jenna will have a stroke,' I reply. 'I should have said it was period pain.'

'It's definitely not, then?'

'Pretty damn sure,' I hiss as the spasm hits again. I dry heave and Ivy struggles to suppress her sympathetic gag reflex. 'Sorry.'

'You aren't doing it on purpose.'

'Still.'

'Gray, shut up and keep walking. We're almost there.'

Daniel and Mrs Easton jog towards us before we hit the last turn to the office.

'Thank god,' Ivy sighs.

'Grace!' Mrs Easton exclaims as she rushes forward. She takes the other side. 'What's happening?'

'Don't straighten her up,' Ivy says quickly. 'It makes the pain sharper. Lower abdominal pain, left-hand side. Constant with irregular spasms that make it worse. No COVID symptoms'

'Do we know why?' Mrs Easton asks.

'She thinks it's a side effect from her new meds,' Ivy answers for me. 'Out of ten?' she asks me.

'Eight,' I say.

Ivy nods. 'She'll dry heave, but she won't vomit.'

'Fu– eff me,' Daniel says. 'What the hell is happening?'

'Ambulance time?' Mrs Easton asks me.

'Um,' I say. 'Maybe –'

'Yes,' Ivy answers for me. 'That means yes, but I hate the hospital so don't send me.'

'Is that right?' Mrs Easton asks. I can tell she's smiling but my eyes are closed with another spasm.

'Ugh, gang up on me then,' I mutter. It hurts so much that I'm now Lamaze breathing.

'I need to go get her bag and phone so we can call Dad,' Ivy says. 'Can you get her to the office from here?'

'I'll go,' Daniel says. He looks at me. 'If that's okay? I figure you'd rather have Ivy with you.'

'Thank you,' I say.

Ivy tosses him the keys. 'Thanks, Danny.'

'Anything for you, kiddo,' Daniel says with a wink.

'I can't punch you now,' I say. 'But I'll do it later.'

'So, she's not dying then,' Daniel says with a roll of his eyes. He's pretending he's not as relieved as he is. 'I'll be right back.'

We're alone in the sick room. Mrs Easton is making phone calls and Daniel isn't back yet.

'You owe him an explanation,' Ivy says. 'He really cares about you.'

I sigh.

'You should have seen him,' she continues.

'Later,' I say. 'I can't … I don't …'

The door opens before I finish my sentence. Daniel steps in and hands my bag to Ivy.

'I should go to class,' Daniel says, but he doesn't move. 'You're …'

'I should probably head back, too,' Ivy says.

Daniel looks at her. 'You're not going to stay? They're calling an *ambulance*.'

Ivy and I share a little smile which makes him look more incredulous and confused.

Ivy's right, I owe him.

'A day in the life, huh?' I say. I don't have to like that I owe him.

'Something like that,' Ivy replies, sounding way older than fourteen.

'I'm going to be fine,' I tell Daniel. 'It's probably nothing.'

'For fuck's sake, Grace,' Daniel says. 'They've called a fucking ambulance and you can't stand upright.'

'That's an accurate description of the facts,' I snap.

'Gray,' Ivy scolds me. 'Be nice. Sorry, she's bitchier in pain. And she hates the worry thing.'

'Great. You can't even admit that things aren't fine. I guess that answers that question,' Daniel snaps. 'I'm so fucking worried about you and you don't give a shit.'

Ivy glares at me, then tilts her head. She doesn't have to say the words for me to very clearly hear that she thinks I should talk to him. Daniel turns to leave.

'I'm sorry,' I say.

He stops, his back still to me. 'You're gonna have to do a little better than that,' he says.

I wonder if I've lost him, too. Grace Turing, now billed as 'Sick Girl: Forever Alone'. Mrs Easton opens the door and steps inside.

'They're on their way,' she says. 'About twenty minutes.'

'Damn,' Ivy says. 'That's a benefit to Launceston we didn't think of. Ambulance wait times are much more manageable.'

'You've got dance this period, right?' I ask Ivy.

She nods. She loves dance. She lives for dance. She wants to stay and be a good sister, but she also wants to go.

'Go,' I say. 'Have fun, Tiny Dancer.'

'Love you,' Ivy says, and presses a kiss to my forehead. We do our secret handshake, and then she's gone. I smile after her until another spasm hits and I curl up into a ball.

'I've got her,' Mrs Easton tells Daniel. 'You can go back to class if you like.' The 'if you like' was polite, but she clearly thought he should go back to class. Daniel was still angry, and part of me wanted to stop him. Make up. But I can barely sit up right now. How could I tell him everything I needed to say like this?

'I'll be okay,' I tell him. 'Thank you for helping me. I'll … I'll talk to you soon.'

He gives me a dark look that doesn't entirely hide how worried he is.

'I promise,' I add.

'It matters, Turing,' Daniel said. 'It matters a fu– freaking lot.'

Mrs Easton looks a little amused, but she doesn't say anything.

'It matters,' I agree. It's a peace offering and his nod indicates his acceptance. The tiny quirk at the corner of his mouth is his concession.

'You'll be okay?' he asks.

'Probably,' I say, slightly teasing.

'I'll leave if you can tell me something weird,' he says.

I smile, pleased. He's figured me out. It's a weird, nice feeling. But it hurts, too, and the pain is distracting.

'Coca-Cola made Santa red?'

'Too easy,' he says. 'Try again.'

I wince and dry heave with a spasm.

'Cute trick,' he dead pans. 'Try again.'

'It wasn't a trick,' I hiss. 'It fucking hurts.'

He raises his eyebrows. 'Grace. Either you convince me you don't need a friend with you until the ambulance arrives or Mrs Easton has to forcibly drag me out of this room.'

'Ivy left,' I point out.

'I don't care,' Daniel replies.

I sigh. It's hard to think. He knows it. That's why he's playing this dumb game. 'Oh! I've got one. Crocodile shit used to be used as a contraceptive in Ancient Egypt.'

'What?' Mrs Easton says, eyes wide.

'You're shitting me. Pun intended,' Daniel says, gleefully. 'That's amazing. Tell me more. Did they eat it, or?'

'Mixed it with honey into a paste and used it as spermicide.'

'They stuck it in their – up themselves?' Daniel asks. This is possibly the best thing he has ever heard in his life. I'm happy for him.

'Yes. Before sex,' I say.

'And Egyptian dudes were down with this?' Daniel asks.

'Obviously. Have I proved I'm fine?' I ask, my voice tight with pain again.

Daniel hesitates, chewing his lip.

'I don't think there's a weirder fact out there,' Mrs Easton says. 'I think she's fine.'

'You clearly don't know Grace,' Daniel says. 'She's always saying the weirdest sh– stuff.'

'I think you get a pass on swearing today,' Mrs Easton offers. 'Your girlfriend did collapse in agony.'

'Not his girlfriend,' I say.

'You don't always have to correct them,' Daniel replied. 'You'll hurt my feelings.'

I roll my eyes. 'Will you correct them, then?'

'Of course not,' he says. 'That wouldn't be any fun.'

'Go,' I say. 'Find Ivy after school if you really want an update.'

'I'm allowed to talk to Ivy now?' he asks. 'Because this opens up a whole new –'

'Daniel Perkins. Leave. I'm in pain and want to cry about it,' I tell him. 'And, for today, you may talk to my sister. Don't make it weird.'

'Again, you're no fun,' he says. 'I'm going. But I'm worried and you agreed that it matters – so don't forget. You owe me.'

'Go,' I say again, and he does.

'I'm sorry about the boyfriend thing,' Mrs Easton says.

I shrug. 'It's not an issue.'

'He does seem like your boyfriend though,' she continues. 'I think Mrs Gruber was surprised he didn't leap through the perspex to get to my office.'

I consider saying something about Mrs Gruber, but I hold my tongue. 'We're friends,' I say. 'Possibly ... I don't know.'

'Being a teenager is complicated,' Mrs Easton says wistfully. She's gotta be heading toward retirement. 'Everything was complicated and emotional.'

'Yep.'

'Your sister is wonderful,' she says. 'She knew all of the important information.'

'That's Ivy,' I smile. 'She's great. She's had practice.'

'Can I ask you a question?'

'Didn't you already? Sorry. Pain. Snappy. No filter.' I dry heave again.

She laughs before sobering. 'It's worse than you let on, isn't it? And worse than the file says?'

I roll my lips inward.

'I thought so,' she says.

'Will you tell anyone?' I ask, nervous.

'No,' she sighs.

'They'll probably assign me a carer or something and make a big deal out of it if you do. That's what happened at my old school,' I say. 'Everyone knew and treated me weird.'

'I know,' Mrs Easton said. 'They considered doing it here, too. But the title of 'school nurse' does carry a touch of weight despite my lack of qualifications.' Her lips are pressed into a small smile.

'Thank you.' The words are breath and I close my eyes.

'I can't leave because of the protocol for calling an ambulance, but you can pretend I'm not here,' she says. 'Do you want any pain relief? I noticed we have some oxycodone here for you, as well as some diazepam.'

'No. If I take something before they see me it can warp the symptoms.'

'Not your first rodeo, huh?'

'Just another Wednesday,' I smile. Then I dry-heave again.

'Uh-huh,' Mrs Easton says, a little sarcastic. But she's not pitying me or sympathetic.

I consider proposing marriage.

'I appreciate you,' I tell her. 'Just so you know.'

She laughs a little, but my eyes are closed so I can't see her expression. I curl tighter.

'It's getting worse, isn't it?'

'Yes.'

'Changing?'

'No.'

'Just rest. I've called your father, should I call your mum, too?'

I hesitate. It's been a long time since I've needed her when I'm sick, or wanted her. But it hurts so much and it's different and –

'Yes, please.'

'Okay,' Mrs Easton says. Her voice is soothing, and there's an implied 'sweetheart' that is kind of reassuring instead of condescending.

I stay curled up with my eyes closed until the ambulance arrives.

...

'Bloods came back clean. Well, her white cell count was a little high,' a doctor muses.

'Normal high?' Dad asks.

The doctor looks confused. He hasn't read my file, clearly. Dad's livid. I'm exhausted.

'Are you sexually active?' the doctor asks.

'No,' I say. 'It's not my period, either.' Aside from the fact there's not exactly a line of willing candidates, I've never been terribly interested in sex. And, of course, this much pain and an optional physical activity? I'll pass.

'What about recreational drugs?' The doctor looks at Dad for a moment. 'If you'd prefer, your father could leave the –'

'No,' I say. 'No drugs and no leaving.' I dry heave. I whimper. I dry heave again and wonder if I'm about to vomit.

'Bag,' I tell Dad, and there's one on my bed in a heartbeat.

'Is there a reason you can't give her pain relief? We've been here for over an hour,' Dad argues. 'Finish the damn tests and get her a painkiller!'

'Mr Turing, we understand your conc –'

Dad scoffs.

'– ern, but we do have procedure. Grace will go for an ultrasound soon, and after that, we'll organise some pain relief. I can offer you some paracetamol?'

'Sure, give a starving man a grain of rice,' Dad says, disgusted.

I actually vomit from the pain. Hello, pain level nine. I want to start a cheer squad for Dad, though. He's being Hero Dad again. But I'm more focussed on the vomiting.

'Are you nauseous?' the doctor asks.

'She just threw up,' Dad mutters.

'No,' I reply. 'It's just the pain.'

'What would you score your pain out of ten right now? Ten being the worst pain you could possibly imagine.'

'Nine,' I say.

'She's a sixteen-year-old girl with chronic pain – nine means an eleven for a normal person. She says ten is when she passes out,' Dad supplies.

'And we have all your medications listed here?' the doctor asks, his voice flat and uninterested. I'm not a fan of sympathy or pity, but some concern would be nice, doc.

'Yes,' Dad says.

'When was your last bowel movement?'

'Two days ago,' I say.

'I'm reluctant to give you anything stronger as it might compound your constipation problem, which still might be the cause,' the doctor says.

Dad hands me some water, which I gargle before spitting in the bag. Dad takes it away and hands me a piece of chewing gum.

'She's vomiting from pain. Be reasonable,' Dad snaps.

'Can you hold out until after the ultrasound?' he asks.

I want to say no.

I want to cry at the unfairness of it all.

I want to beg for an opiate.

'I'll try,' I say.

The doctor thanks me and leaves.

Dad runs his hands through his hair. 'You don't always have to be a warrior. You don't have to prove how tough you are.'

'I know,' I say, trying to smile. 'Thank you for having my back.'

'Do you need anything else?'

I shake my head. 'It just hurts.'

'Distraction time, or leave you alone?'

'Leave me alone,' I say, closing my eyes and being grateful that he's not going to take offense.

'I love you,' he says. He strokes my hair. 'Mum's on the way.'

'Thank you.'

...

'They're officially saying it's diverticulitis,' I tell Ivy on the phone at lunch the next day. She's calling to check in even though she's not meant to use her phone at school. I know that Daniel has been seeking her out for updates, and may even be sitting beside her right now. He hasn't messaged me and I haven't messaged him, so everything is just kind of weird between us. The next conversation we have kind of needs to be an IRL situation.

'Diver–what now?'

'Diverticulitis,' I repeat. 'Little pockets that form in your intestines, and –'

'Nope!' Ivy cuts me off. 'It already sounds too gross.'

I laugh. 'Well, it's a minor infection. But it is hard to find on a scan or anything, so they're doing bloods again and keeping me until tomorrow at this stage.'

'Eww, no,' Ivy complains for me. 'Hospitals are the worst. And hospital food is nasty! Do you want me to bring you food?'

'If someone would bring me real food, and, like, a packet of snakes, they would be my actual hero. I would organise a parade,' I tell her. 'God, and some lemonade.'

She laughs. 'I'll keep that in mind. But you're okay?'

'I'm going to be fine,' I say. 'It can recur, but it's going to be a couple of extra shitty days periodically. Not a big deal in the scheme of things.'

'Okay,' she says, reassured. 'I love you but I have to go and repeat this conversation to Danny.'

'Don't call him Danny.'

'Bye, Gray.'

'Bye, little sister, I love you.'

...

'You have visitors,' Emily, my favourite nurse so far, says. She gave me the wifi password for the ward which you aren't supposed to give to patients. Which is rude, because what else do we have to do in hospital? Wifi is a basic human right. Anyway, she saved my life. All hail Emily, goddess of wifi.

I glance at the time, confused. 'Uh … I shouldn't?' I say. Dad is bringing Ivy before dinner, and Mum is stopping by after dinner with dessert (thank you, Jesus). It's 3:30 pm, and I don't know anyone in Launceston that would visit me.

'Do you not want to see them?' Emily asks. 'Because I have a feeling that I'll have a hard time stopping them.'

'Call security,' Daniel announces, walking in. He sits on the edge of my bed. 'Jenna's out in the hall. Reckon you can make it out there?'

'I'll get you a wheelchair,' Emily says. 'Protocol. And mask up while you're out of this room.'

I stare at them. 'What ... uh ... hi?'

'Am I calling security? They do look a little dodgy,' Emily teases me.

Daniel grins. 'Security and I are good mates,' he tells her. 'But Grace likes me, don't you, Grace?'

'I –'

'See?' Daniel says. 'Speechless with joy.'

Emily goes and gets the wheelchair while Daniel inspects me.

'I know I'm not exactly giving you options, but this is okay, isn't it?'

I smile and nod. 'I'm just ... surprised.'

Emily comes back with the wheelchair and makes Daniel promise I won't get out of it – like he gets a say. I put on the stupid paper mask that makes my face itch and let Daniel wheel me out of the room and into a kind of foyer just outside of the ward. Jenna is sitting on the edge of an ugly and uncomfortable hallway chair and looking nervous.

'If you'd prefer us not to be here ...' Jenna says.

'I feel like I should have expected you both, but I didn't,' I say.

Daniel parks me adjacent to the chair closest to Jenna and takes a seat. He looks relaxed, like this was a completely normal place to be.

'So, Turing, I've seen some excellent ways to get out of a maths test, but full hospital is next level,' Daniel tells me. He digs into his backpack and tosses me a bag of milk bottle lollies. The good, old-style milk bottles with a soft shell and foamy centres. 'Ivy said they're your favourite.'

I stare at them.

'I brought you homework,' Jenna says, placing a stack of paper on my desk. 'Less awesome than lollies, I know.'

'Are they ... did I get the wrong ones?' Daniel asks. 'I could go downstairs and get you snakes, which was my backup plan.'

I shake my head. 'No, they're, uh, they're great. Where did you find them? I clearly haven't figured out where the best candy in Launceston is yet.'

Daniel grins, relieved. Happy. 'There's a shop near the theatre in town. They have them there. And Dr Pepper and candy corn. Candy corn, Turing. It's magical.'

'It's gross,' Jenna replies. 'They look like rotting teeth and taste like sweetened honey.'

'They're amazing.'

'They're weirdly addictive,' Jenna concedes. She's smiling and then she remembers where we are, and the smile leaves.

'So, how is hashtag hospital life?' Daniel asks. 'Breakfast in bed? Turn-down service?'

'No sleep and frickin' cold,' I say, grinning. 'It's the dream, y'all. Straight Gucci.'

'Yeah, but the drugs must be a decent compensation,' Daniel says. 'Wanna hook me up while I'm here? I hear oxy makes you pretty chill.'

'Daniel,' Jenna hisses.

'Sorry, bud,' I reply. 'Get your own weird infection for drugs.'

'Yeah, Ivy said it was diver–whatever,' Daniel replies. 'Something about your intestines that made her gag?'

I laugh, but that hurts a little, so I place my hand on my stomach. Daniel tracks the movement, but then looks back to my face. Jenna's eyes linger. 'Yeah. So, little pockets get made in your large intestine or colon, and then –'

'Can we not?' Jenna asks, making a face.

'I wanna know!' Daniel says. 'Cover your ears.'

'I can tell you later,' I say. Jenna's uncomfortable and I don't want to make it worse.

Daniel sulks. 'Fine. But you owe me.'

'I'll send you the Better Health page,' I say.

'No, I want you to tell me,' he says. 'You're way more interesting than a website.'

'You are clearly on the wrong websites,' I say. A thought occurs to me alongside anxiety. 'Wait, you brought my homework?'

'Uh, yes,' Jenna says, nervous. 'Should I not have?'

'No, it's just … does … does everyone know that I'm in hospital?' I ask. My heart is pounding, my brain is racing, and I'm trying not to hyperventilate.

'No,' Daniel answers for her. Jenna looks like a stunned mullet. 'We were subtle.'

'I don't understand why you can't say you're in hospital, though,' Jenna sighs. 'It's weird.'

'I know,' I agree. 'But, people … teenagers don't get it. It makes things weird.'

'Weirder than you are already? That's some next level weird, Turing,' Daniel says, cutting through the awkwardness easily.

I smile and I thank my mother for the diluted Asian skin that doesn't blush easily. I'm … happy. I'm frustrated and I hate hospital and the diverticulitis thing is easing but still painful, and I'm happy. It's, as Daniel said, next level weird.

'Are you … are you like … really sick?' Jenna asks. 'Like, cancer sick?'

'I don't really know how to answer that,' I reply. Because I don't. 'It's not cancer. It's a weird, undiagnosed, atypical autoimmune disease thing.'

'What does that mean?' Daniel asks, tilting his head to inspect me. I don't often see Daniel look this serious. It's unnerving, but I also feel … safe to tell him. Like, it won't change our friendship if I say this. I'm less sure about Jenna because she looks like she sat on an echidna. But Ivy's right, I do owe Daniel this. And if Jenna is going to be my friend, she needs to know it, too. Ugh, I hate it when my parents are right.

'It means that no one knows what's wrong with me. So far, it's just fibromyalgia and rheumatoid arthritis, but there's suspicions of Hashimoto's or Lyme disease or Ehler-Danlos, or something. Probably not actually lupus, because it's never lupus.' The lupus joke falls flat; clearly they aren't obsessed with medical television shows like my mother was when this started. Because watching *House* was going to give her the magical answer to fix her daughter.

They stare at me.

'Mostly, it's pain,' I say, trying to explain it. 'Like, I'm always in pain. Sometimes it's horrific, but mostly I just ... manage. And I have to be careful about getting sick, because my immune system is pathetic, and if I catch anything, I'm down for the count.'

The silence continues.

I swallow thickly and wonder if I've just made a mistake. I wish Ivy were here, she'd know what to say.

'I mean, at least it's not cancer?' Jenna says.

I close my eyes and sigh. 'I wish it were cancer. Then there would be a treatment plan or something. I could say *'hey, I can't do that because I have cancer'*, and people would know what was going on. There's no treatment, really, because there's not even a real diagnosis. I'm just ... stuck in pain limbo forever.'

'Well, no wonder you're such a bitch sometimes,' Daniel says, and instantly the tension is gone. 'If I were in that much pain I'd just say eff it and stay home forever. You're metal AF.'

I laugh, and Jenna tries a smile.

'How do we ... help you?' Jenna asks.

'I– I ... I don't know. Can we ... it's hard enough telling you about it without ...,' I trail off.

Jenna looks like she'd leave if she could.

'Meanwhile at school, Emmanuelle made a play for Liam and got shot down,' Daniel says, changing the subject easily. He always dramatically pronounces Emmy's name with hand gestures. 'I think Liam didn't even notice. It was hilarious.'

'Seriously?' I ask. 'Because she's not exactly subtle.'

'Yep. And Caleb was talking shit about you faking being sick, so he and Elsa argued. Apparently, Elsa likes you now,' Daniel said. 'She even asked if you were okay.'

'She did,' Jenna agreed. 'I didn't know what to say, though.'

'I said you were on an urgent spy mission,' Daniel says. 'Top secret.'

I laugh. 'Excellent. Oh, next time, can we say I've gone off to combat zombies?'

'Yes, I like it,' Daniel says. 'Let's go full *Die Hard*. You can go to fight terrorists in a skyscraper. We'll talk up the helicopter scene.'

'How about an archaeological dig and the curse of a mummy?' Jenna suggests. She's hesitant but she's trying, so I beam at her.

'Yes! I love that,' I reply.

They leave half an hour later. Daniel wheels me back into my room and stands by my bed for a moment, watching me transfer carefully. I'm not sure I understand his expression, so I wait for him to speak.

'I have questions,' he says. 'But they're probably longer than Jenna waiting in the hall.'

'I'd have told you,' I say, because that seems important. 'Even if I didn't end up in hospital, I mean. Not just because Ivy was nagging me to do it. She likes you.'

He blows out a sigh, nodding. 'Thanks. Do you know when you're back at school?'

'I'm arguing for tomorrow, but I have a feeling it's going to be Monday,' I say.

He rolls his eyes. 'Seriously, Turing. You have a free pass to take it easy. Why are you working so hard?'

'Because it's the only choice I have,' I reply. His eyes meet mine and we're serious again. Serious and intense. I want to look away, but I don't.

Was it likely that I would be continually and forever telling you about worries that you could not help me to bear?

'I get that,' he says. 'I'll … I'll message you.'

'I'll send you the website,' I say.

'Nope,' he says. 'I told you, you have to tell me. I want the Grace Turing version with weird facts and gross details.'

'Deal,' I tell him. For a moment, I think he might do something. Something affectionate. Like … I don't even want to think about it. But I do anyway. I think about him kissing my cheek. About him hugging me. I wonder what I'd do if he did.

'See you, Turing. Try not to die before I see you next,' he says, and pounds his chest twice before throwing up a peace sign.

'Dork,' I tell him, but I return the gesture.

'Now I've got a secret Turing handshake, too,' he gloats. 'Imma show Ivy.'

'Stop hanging out with my sister,' I say.

'Bye!'

I smile after he leaves like an idiot.

...

'You said you didn't have friends,' Emily the nurse says as she comes in to do yet another set of obs.

'I was wrong,' I reply. 'Turns out that happens sometimes. Well, I have one friend. I don't know how Jenna is taking it.'

'I might have overheard you explaining that your health is a little more complicated than the average bear's.'

'Yeah, well. It was time, I guess. I never know how to talk about it to people who don't already kind of understand weird health stuff,' I sigh.

'Have you heard of Spoon Theory?' Emily asks. 'I think you might get a lot out of it. A woman with lupus invented it as a way to talk about her life to a healthy friend. The community around it is really supportive, too.'

'I hadn't, thanks,' I say. 'I just ... I'm scared of being Sick Girl again. That's all people see when they find out.'

'Yeah, but you're not Sick Girl, you're Grace Turing. You have a disease, yes, but that's just a thing about you. It isn't who you are,' Emily says. 'You choose what defines you, not anyone else.'

'You clearly haven't been to high school in a while.'

Emily sighs. 'High school sucks, no one is saying otherwise. But don't let being sick be the most interesting thing about you. You do have a choice in that. Just, think about it.'

She leaves without saying anything else, and I do think about it. I think about it a lot. I think about the way that people introduced themselves on the first day of school. I think about the way I think of myself. I think about Mrs Easton, and how she kind of said that I might be putting the Sick Girl thing in front, not other people. I think about my last school, and how weird everything got.

I don't know what any of it means, but I think about it.

CHAPTER SEVEN
Radio Contact

FRIDAY
11:02 am
> Well school is boring as shit
> There's no weird facts and I think Mr Simmons may not fully understand the math he's teaching
>> < I dare you to ask him
> I would if grandma didn't have her heart set on me graduating
> If I had a grandma
11:05 am
> Turing
> What can possibly be more interesting than this conversation
> Hospital is boring as shit
11:09 am
>> < You're kind of needy. Did you know? Because I didn't.
> Oh, I see Ivy. Maybe I'll go talk to her
>> < I know what you're doing.
>> < And it's working. Marconi won the Nobel Prize for his work on wireless radio transmission. He shared it with a physicist no one remembers.
> Why yes, Ivy, your sister is kind of boring sometimes.
>> < Asshole
>> < The first text message was sent in 1992.
>> < Vodaphone network, text read 'Merry Christmas'.
> Now you mention it, Grace does have beautiful eyes.
>> < Stfu
>> < More people in the world own mobile phones than people who own a toilet.

> Okay, but recess is nearly over.

    < The Hungarian title for Die Hard is Give Your Life Expensive

> Seriously? I love it. Yessssss. This is the good shit.
> Okay. I forgive you for your shitty trivia.

    < Uh-huh. Go learn some stuff.

11:33 am

    < Wait. I'm the one in hospital. You should be entertaining me! Not the other way around!

1:15 pm

> Entertaining me is entertaining you
> Elsa is being really intense about if I know where you are. She didn't believe the ninja thing. I'm trying zombies.

    < Zombies are much more believable

> Right?
> Didn't work.
> Apparently we're dating now. Did you know? Liam is glaring at me about it.

    < Liam is asking about me?

> Wow. I say we're dating and you're already looking for the next guy. You wound me Turing

    < Daniel. You're an idiot.

> Because I'm the perfect man?
> You're right.
> You should be so lucky.
> Should I give Liam your number?

    < NO

> Okay then.

    < You're not denying the dating thing are you?

> I can neither confirm nor deny those allegations
> You're breaking Ivy's heart

    < Christ. I need another diazepam.

> Not getting better?

    < No, you're making me crazy!

> Rude.

    < You started it.

1:26 pm

      < Daniel?

1:40 pm

      < I'm sorry

      < I don't know what I said but I'm sorry

2:09 pm

      < Okay so lunch is over and I've definitely upset you. What did I say?

2:41 pm

      < Richard Gere, Arnie Schwarz, Stallone, Han Solo, and Burt Reynolds were all offered the role of John McClane

      < It's based on a book called Nothing Lasts Forever from the sixties

      < You know the part where McClane is in the elevator shaft and he misses the first vent? Yeah, he was meant to catch it. The falling was accidental but they kept it because great footage. Like the Mission Impossible Tom Cruise ankle break.

3:22 pm

> The crazy thing is a sore point. It's my 'it doesn't matter' thing.

> And if radio silence gets me Die Hard facts I'm going to do it more often.

      < Do you want to tell me about it?

> Not yet.

> In person. Maybe. I don't know how to talk about it.

      < Because I did?

> That's fair.

3:36 pm

> It's my mother. She has bipolar. It's bad sometimes. Hospital bad. Out of nowhere. I come home and she's repainting the walls lime green because she's up. When she's down it's worse.

> I've only ever told therapists before.

> She's a good mother though. I love her. And she's fine when she's on her meds.

> Say something

< Well, as much as you're an asshole, she raised
     you. And I don't hate you. So I figure she's a
     pretty good person. Diagnoses aren't people,
     you know?

> Exactly

> Thanks for not apologising.

          < Np

          < If you want to talk about it, I'm here.

> Are you still in hospital? Want a visit?

          < I'm home now. I'm mostly just basking in the comfort
             of my own bed.

> Hmmm. Grace on a bed... What are you wearing?

          < Shut up

> I'm just saying

          < I'm just saying shut up. I already owe you one punch

> You're lucky I like your violent streak, Turing

          < You're lucky I like you at all.

> lol

5:30 pm

          < I haven't heard from Jenna.

> She hasn't spoken to me either

SATURDAY
11:58 am

          < And the family Die Hard marathon continues. He
             just drove a car into a helicopter

> Ah, you've entered the modern era of Die Hard. It's all down
   here from there

          < I don't know. Justin Long is kind of adorable. And
             the plot is kind of interesting though perhaps a little
             ridiculous.

> It goes, in order of awesome: Die Hard 1, 3, 4, 2, 5.

          < Yeah 2 was a bit flat. Samuel L Jackson was
             amazing

> He's always amazing. Samuel L Jackson swearing is my favourite

          < lol

4:59 pm

< Am I being paranoid about Jenna? She hasn't responded to my message.

> It'll be fine

< I'm not so sure. I think she doesn't get the whole sick thing. I think I scared her off.

> She just needs time. Or she's not worth your time. Besides, you still have me.

< Yes, you truly meet all of my needs in the friendship department. Shall we discuss my menstrual cycle? The ordeal of trying to find a bra that's comfortable?

> I'm definitely here for one of those.

< Great. So, my cramps are hell at the moment because of my polycystic ovaries. Have you tried a menstrual cup?

> I'll message Jenna.

SUNDAY
9:23 am

< Yippee ki yay means 'here eat this' in Urdu

10:46 am

> You probably should have saved that one for a special occasion because I'm losing my mind rn

< lol

< So easy to please

> Very easy. Easy is my middle name.

< Have you heard from Jenna?

< The trivia was a bribe

> And here I thought we were flirting

> She hasn't replied

> She's seen it though

< Sigh

> How are you feeling?

< All g. Back to normal

> Define normal

< Pain is sitting at a workable 5/10. Stiff back from hospital bed. Stomach tender but okay.

> I just googled the pain scale. How is 5/10 good? That's constant and hard to ignore.

< It's normal for me. It is what it is

> And that's it, you just walk around in agony all the time?

< Did we not have this conversation in the hospital? Yes. I am always always in pain. Sometimes it is worse. It's never gone. Welcome to my life. What did you expect?

> I don't know. Less pain? How do you cope?

< I just do. There's not another option, is there?

> And they can't give you anything?

< Remember Grace Turing: Zombie Edition?

> Well that's a solid no then.

> Where does it hurt? Or is that a stupid question?

< Everywhere. But mostly neck, back, shoulders, hips

> And your knees?

< Only when they subluxate.

> Fuck. I just googled a video of a knee subluxing.

> Wow

> You're amazing.

< Yep, I'm a medical marvel

> You know what I mean, Grace. Don't be dense.

< I'm deflecting, don't you be dense

> Fine.

< Fine.

7:18 pm

> Slugs have five nostrils.

< A shrimp's heart is in his head

> Are you going to school tomorrow?

< Yeah

> Good. See you there.

< Yep

9:56 pm

> Elephants are the only animals that can't jump

10:05 pm

>   <   Nearly 3% of ice in Antarctica is penguin piss

> Why do you always win the trivia off?

>   <   Because I'm amazing

> You know the trivia thing is an apology, right?

>   <   I do

> We're good then?

>   <   We're good

>   <   Go to bed

>   <   After you find me a weird fact for tomorrow

> Back at you

> Night Turing

>   <   Night Perkins

CHAPTER EIGHT
White Flags

Dad looks at us with narrowed eyes, suspicious. In his defence, it's Monday morning and we're both ready on time and seemingly looking forward to school.

'Are you planning on wagging?' he asks. 'Are you on drugs now? Is there a dealer at your school?'

'Dad,' Ivy complains, stretching the word into syllables. 'Don't be weird.'

'Me weird? You're weird. Grace has been messaging a boy all weekend and you're ready to go to school on time on a Monday for the first time in the history of Mondays,' Dad replies.

'I don't think drugs are a realistic thing to worry about,' I sigh. 'The doctor gives me the good stuff anyway. Hey, maybe I could sell my supply.'

'Grace,' Dad says, and gives me *the look*.

'I'm joking. And he's just a friend.'

'And I'm not reassured.'

'Can you just drive us to school, please?' Ivy asks.

Dad's eyes narrow again, but he sighs and gives up. 'It is my job as the Dad Taxi.'

'And we appreciate it,' I say. 'But we could catch the bus.'

'We've talked about this,' Dad says. 'It's not going to happen unless you tell people about your health concerns.'

'I have,' I say. Dad stops halfway out the door with his keys in his hands. He turns back to look at me.

'You have?'

'I told Daniel and Jenna. They visited me in hospital.' I give Ivy a look to remind her that she's a traitor, but she just smiles at me, pleased with her work.

'You didn't mention that earlier,' Dad says. 'Why not?'

'I wasn't ready to tell you. It's weird. I'm ... I'm making friends. Well. Friend. I think ... I think Jenna didn't take the sick thing too well.'

'Well then she's an idiot,' Ivy says, crossing her arms defensively. 'You're amazing. And the fact you're sick makes you even more amazing.'

I give her our secret 'everything is amazing' handshake and she returns it. Ivy's the only person who gets to say the sick and amazing thing – I'm so not here to be disabled inspo–porn.

'I love you, little sister. You're way too good for us. I feel sorry for your birth parents, they obviously got the shittiest kid in the switch.'

'Hey! You're both definitely ours,' Dad says, but he grins.

Ivy sighs. 'You guys needed me more. They were probably both nice, sane people.' Her lips twitch in a smile.

'The point is,' I say. 'That I told people. That was the deal. I tell people, I can catch the bus instead of the Dad Taxi.'

'Grace, I just don't think it's a good idea.' His voice makes it clear that he never intended to let me catch the bus.

Tears prick at my eyes. I shouldn't have said anything. I've ruined a perfectly good morning. It's so unfair.

'What do you want, Dad? You want me wrapped up in cotton wool? Should I get a giant hamster ball to live in? I'm sick, I get it. You think I ever forget? Even for a fucking second? God, I'd kill to forget sometimes, to not hurt all the time. But you know what? I'm not just Sick Girl. I'm not just your daughter. I'm also a person who should be allowed some normal teenage shit sometimes.' I'm yelling at him, and crying, and I wish I could take back the last thirty seconds back. I wish I could make him understand. I wish I were healthy. I wish I were healthy. I wish I were –

'Sweetheart, I'm not sure you understand how hard it is for us. We're just trying to keep you safe,' Dad says. He's begging me to understand. 'Your pain belongs to all of us.'

'Screw you,' I say. 'And screw that.'

'Grace!' Dad shouts. 'Watch your language!'

'How about you check your privilege, Dad,' I spit back. 'Oh, healthy, normal adult with a job. Please, tell me all about *my* life and what *I* need.'

'Gray,' Ivy says quietly.

'No. It's a valid question, Dad. You tell me. How safe do you want me? What happens after high school? Do I get to go to college? What about university? Should I work? Should I just live in a granny flat out the back of your house for the rest of my life and never do anything different or normal?' My chest is heaving and everything hurts and I sink to the floor, hating myself.

'Gray,' Ivy says again, crouching down beside me. She hesitates to touch me. She looks up at Dad. 'She does have a point. I mean, so do you –'

'This isn't your fight, Ivy,' Dad snaps.

'Of course, it's her fight,' I argue. 'Because it isn't fair on her either. She's fourteen and runs around like my goddamn nursemaid. She can't do the normal teenage shit either because she's stuck with me. If my pain is yours, it's hers, too.'

Dad turns away from us and runs his hand through his hair. He's trying to get himself under control again.

Ivy takes my hand in hers. She digs in her pocket for tissues and offers them to me. Tears threaten in her eyes, too, but she holds it in.

A heaving sob wracks my body.

'Let's just go to school,' Dad says, turning back to us, his voice laced tight. 'We'll talk about this later.'

'Fine,' I say, and struggle to my feet. I'm not a pretty crier, but I don't care anymore.

'Do you want to wash your face first?' Ivy asks softly.

'No,' I say. 'I just want to go.'

The car ride is silent. Dad doesn't even turn the radio on. We all sit there in our angry, silent pain. Ivy sits in the front seat next to Dad. She keeps darting glances back at me. I pretend I don't notice. Dad doesn't look at anyone. The second the car is parked, Ivy and I are moving. I don't think the car is even properly stopped when we open our doors.

'Wait,' Dad says.

'No,' I say. 'Not right now.'

Ivy hesitates, nervous.

'I love you both,' Dad sighs. 'As long as you know that.'

'I love you,' I say. 'But I don't like you much right now.'

'That's fair,' Dad says with a nod. 'Bye, Ivy. I love you.'

'Love you, too, Dad,' Ivy says.

I turn my back and stalk towards the locker room with my head down. Ivy jogs to catch up.

'You okay?' she asks. 'Stupid question. You know what I mean.'

'It's … no. Maybe. I don't know,' I sigh, stopping. Tears threaten again. 'I really need to wash my face, don't I?'

Ivy smiles and links her arm through mine. 'You look like shit,' she says with a smile.

I laugh a little. 'I'm sorry. I ruined the vibe.'

'You did,' she admits. 'But you weren't all wrong, either. Dad's a little … overprotective of you. Because he loves you. I get that you missed the worst parts, but we thought you were going to die when you had golden staph. You almost did. We can't … we can't lose you, Gray. We won't. And this is Dad's way of trying to make sure we don't.'

'I'm not about to die immediately,' I argue. 'So he can probably take a chill pill. It's the bus, not a transcontinental flight to backpack around Afghanistan.'

'I know,' she laughs. 'But what if some sick bus kid sneezes on you and two weeks later we're at your funeral.'

'That's dramatic and ridiculous.'

'It's how we think,' Ivy said.

I sobered suddenly. 'You can't.'

'But we do.'

'Anyone could be hit by a bus tomorrow.'

'Well, you have multiple buses heading toward you,' Ivy shrugs. 'It's just how it is. And golden staph was only, what, four months ago?'

'I –'

'Just accept the bus thing,' Ivy says. 'I'll try and ask again for you. And you really shouldn't have said "screw you" to Dad.'

'Probably not,' I agree.

She's steering me into the bathroom when I hear someone call our names. We turn.

'The Turing Sisters! How are my two favourite ladies?' Daniel registers my face and his eyes widen. 'Who are we killing?'

I laugh and a weight lifts from my chest. 'No-one. Bad morning.'

'She telling me the truth, kiddo?' Daniel asks, doing the chest pound and peace thing to Ivy.

She returns it. 'Yep. Just parental drama. You know how it is. How was your weekend, Danny?'

'Don't call him "Danny",' I say. 'I'm going to wash my face, and when I come back, you better not be talking to each other.'

'Why is she so obsessed with keeping us apart?' Daniel asks dramatically. 'We're torn apart by tragic circumstances!'

Ivy giggles. Actually giggles. 'Grace isn't tragic,' she says. 'She's the best.'

'Of course she is,' Daniel agrees. 'But you do need to wash your face. You look like someone smacked you repeatedly with a wet fish.'

'You say the nicest things,' I say, dropping my bag at their feet and heading into the bathroom. I splash the water on my face, and then wet some paper towel to dab under my eyes. I can make out their conversation once the water has stopped running.

'She's really better?' Daniel asks.

'Yeah. Well, she's Grace-better.'

'I don't know how she does it. It's a lot to take in.'

'Don't say that to Gray. She hates that kind of sympathy,' Ivy warns him.

'What am I meant to say?' Daniel asks. 'I want to be ... supportive, or whatever. But it's so far out of my wheelhouse.'

'Just be you. You're her friend. Be a friend.'

'I –'

'Unless you want to be more than friends,' she adds, cutting him off.

'If only she'd have me,' Daniel says, dramatically.

I decide that my face is good enough. This conversation should be over.

'What did I say about when I came out?' I ask.

'Chill, Turing,' Daniel says. 'We're just talking like normal humans.' Ivy grins.

'And stop pretending you like me, she believes you,' I say.

'Gray, I love you, but you're an idiot sometimes,' Ivy tells me. 'Be nice to your friend. You going to be okay?' Her eyes hold this morning's argument in them.

'I'm okay,' I tell her. 'I promise. I'll … figure out how to make peace with the old man later. Or he'll buy me the giant zorb ball to live in. Either way.'

She rolls her eyes.

'Have a good day, little sister,' I say.

'Bye,' she says before heading away. I watch her go, catching her looking over her shoulder before she turns the corner that takes her out of my sight.

I sigh and slump.

Daniel raises his eyebrows. 'So, you're not as fine as you said, then.'

'I just don't want her to worry,' I sigh.

'It doesn't matter?' Daniel asks, something tight in his tone.

'No, it's – I just want a bit more freedom than I have,' I say. 'Dad's acting like I'm doing heroin on the side or something when all I want to do is literally ride the bus home.'

'Yeah, but you're … sick,' Daniel tries. 'What is the thing we're calling it?'

'Sick works. Disabled. Medical marvel. But, you know, I still don't want everyone knowing.'

'Why not?' Daniel asks.

I give him a dirty look and he rolls his eyes.

'I mean, I get there are reasons, but I want to know what yours are.'

'I got sick while I was at my last school. And the sicker I got, the weirder everyone got. I was never popular or anything, but no one wants to be friends with Sick Girl.'

'I want to be your friend,' Daniel says. 'You're Grace Turing.' He looks at the backpack dropped at my feet and picks it up without asking.

'Hey! Give it back!'

'Nope,' Daniel replies. He walks toward the locker room and I jog after him.

'Give me back my bag,' I say, trying to take it from him. He ducks away from me and pivots.

'Accept the new world order. I'm carrying your bag.'

'You aren't actually my boyfriend, and this isn't a bad teen rom com.'

'God, this would be a terrible rom com. It'd be *The Fault in Our Stars* or something equally tragic.'

'Daniel, please. I'm not an invalid,' I say, and desperation breaks in that last word, and Daniel hears it. He stops, and I stop. Something changed in the air between us as he turned to face me.

'I can't fix you,' he says. 'I can't ... This is all I can do to make your life a little better. Let me.'

I stare at him.

He stares back. I don't recognise the look in his eyes. But I hear the serious tone of his voice. This matters to him. I think about his mother, and how he can't help her either. How much it must suck to love someone broken when there's no fix. Him loving his mother. My family loving me. Him loving me – platonically. Caring about me. Him caring about me. He's collecting broken people without realising it. Suddenly, Daniel is different in my head. I see him differently. More clearly. He's more than I thought. Better. Stronger. Kinder.

'Okay,' I say. 'Male giraffes drink their mate's pee to figure out when they're ovulating.'

'That's disgusting. But smart. I'm glad I'm not a giraffe. Yet another sentence I thought I'd never say,' Daniel says, giving me a tight smile. He accepts my apology. 'Seahorses are the only animal where the guy carries the unborn kid.'

'I knew that,' I say. 'They mate for life and don't have a digestive system so they're basically always eating.'

'One day, Turing, I'm going to blow your mind with a fact.'

He turns back toward the locker room and I jog a step to walk beside him.

'I liked that Antarctic ATM one.'

'Don't offer me pity props.' He stops beside my locker and hands my bag to me.

'Are you going to carry my books, too?' I ask sarcastically.

He grins. 'Do you want me to?'

'No.'

'I don't mind.'

'I do.'

'It's settled then,' he says.

I have swapped all my books over, and I clutch them to my chest. 'Yes, it is.'

'Give me the books, Grace,' he says.

'You have your own books,' I reply.

'We're both going to the same place,' he points out.

I take a hesitant step back, the lock of my locker digging into my back.

'I'm going to carry your books,' he says.

I blink and consider my options.

'I'm stronger than you,' he says, taking a step towards me. He's in my personal space and I have nowhere to go.

'Uh,' I say, and try to slide sideways.

He moves with me, still grinning.

I try sliding down, he goes down, too.

We're crouched on the floor of the locker room and I wonder what people think we're doing.

'I'm going to win,' Daniel says. 'You should just give in. Don't fight it.'

'Well that doesn't sound like something a rapist would say at all.'

He laughs.

'I think Richard Gere would have been a better John McClane,' I say.

He gapes in shocked horror as I push his shoulder, and he lands on his ass. I'm up and sprinting for homeroom before he can recover.

'Hey!' he calls after me. 'That's fighting dirty!'

I laugh and don't stop running.

...

I'm winded when I hit homeroom, and slump into my seat. Daniel enters a few seconds later and sits in Jenna's chair.

'You fight dirty,' he repeats.

'You left me no choice,' I say.

He grins. 'You're such a weirdo. But you don't think the thing about Richard Gere, right?'

'Of course not,' I say. 'Bruce Willis or nothing.'

He shakes his head.

'Grace, you're back!' Elsa says, coming over to my desk. She looks between Daniel and I, suspicious.

'Yep,' I say. 'How are you?'

'Where were you?' Elsa asks.

The classroom is suddenly quiet and listening to our conversation.

I cut my eyes to Daniel. 'Fighting ninjas,' I say.

She rolls her eyes. 'Come on. Where were you? Were you sick?'

'Ninjas,' I repeat. 'Ninja zombies, even. It was intense. I'm glad to be back.'

'Whatever,' Elsa says, sulking, and goes back to her seat.

'You're such a bitch,' Caleb says to me, going over to console Elsa. 'God forbid you speak to someone who actually cares about you.'

'Do you have a football in your hand?' Daniel asks him. 'Because I think we've had this conversation.'

'Do you want to settle this the old-fashioned way?' Caleb asks him. 'Because I'm happy to make time.'

'Or we could all take a chill pill,' I say. 'And remember that it's my business where I was, and I don't owe you anything. It's personal.'

'Now you have girls defending you,' Caleb says to Daniel.

'Caleb,' Elsa says. 'Just leave them.'

'No, you were genuinely worried and she's being a bitch,' Caleb says.

'Drop it,' Elsa says. 'I won't make the mistake of caring again.'

'It's personal,' I repeat. 'I don't want to talk about it.'

'He knows though, doesn't he?' Liam says, stepping forward.

'He's my friend,' I say.

'He's right here and his name is Daniel,' Daniel says.

'And I'm not?' Liam asks, sounding a little hurt.

'You're not in the inner circle, no,' I say. 'Would you tell me your secrets?'

'Yes,' Liam says.

'Liar,' I say. 'I know literally nothing about you. So why do I owe you my secrets?'

Jenna enters the room, and I tune Liam's complaining out. She doesn't look at me. She looks at Daniel for a beat and they exchange a complicated non-verbal exchange. She sits in Daniel's seat. My eyes prick with tears again, and I stare at the desk.

'Do you know where she was?' Emmy asks Jenna, tossing her hair.

'No,' Jenna says.

My chest tightens.

'Jenna,' Daniel hisses.

'Leave her,' I say. 'It doesn't matter.'

But it does matter. It matters so much.

Miss Williams enters the room, and the chatter stops. She gives me a significant look that I feel like everyone can interpret.

'Glad to have you back with us, Grace,' she says.

'Glad to be back,' I lie.

An hour ago, it was the truth.

What a difference an hour can make.

I can feel Daniel beside me without looking at him. I can feel the possibility of reaching for his hand. I feel like he'd take it. An act of silent support. Of comfort. Of doing the little things that I think he knows make all the difference to someone with a chronic illness.

I tell myself it's enough.

...

It's Monday again and Jenna still hasn't spoken to me.

'She'll come around,' Daniel says at recess.

'And if she doesn't?' I ask. 'I like her. I miss her.'

'Then she doesn't, and you still have me. But it's not on you, it's on her.'

'Ivy had to speak to you,' I point out. 'After the knee thing.'

'Yes, let's refer to you popping your knee in and out of joint as a "thing". And I have Ma,' he reasons. 'I can try talking to her again?'

'No,' I say. 'You're right. If she won't play chess at lunch, I'll give up.'

...

I really don't want to give up. I'd given up on the bus. I'd given up on pregabalin. I'd given up on fitting in and trusting people easily. I'd given up on fighting my parents over stupid shit because Ivy was right, they care and they worry. It felt like I'd been waving a white flag all week, but I kept getting shelled.

I go to the library at lunch time. When Jenna sees me, she gets up and walks out. I hide in the stacks for the rest of lunch trying not to cry. I don't want Daniel to know how hurt I am because he'll take it personally, too. I wish that my pain was just mine, but it's not. So, instead of going to find him, I google Spoon Theory on my phone, because I wish I could talk to Nurse Emily.

Basically, being chronically ill is like having a dozen spoons and every activity you do costs spoons. You can't borrow more, or buy them. Having a shower and getting dressed is three spoons. So the first hour of your day uses a quarter of your spoons. Or you skip the shower, and it's only one spoon. Travel is spoons, being somewhere is spoons, cooking food is spoons, and eating food is spoons. It kind of feels like someone had written this thing exactly for me. Then, I start reading the comments. People who had lupus or other invisible illnesses. Friends and family of people who were 'spoonies' could understand them better now. I email the page to my parents and Ivy. I almost send it to Jenna, but I stop myself.

...

Art is my last class of the day, and that's when things hit a new level of shit.

'We're going to use the liquid frisket technique today,' Mrs Connors says. She holds up a couple of paintings. 'You put the frisket on before you apply the paint – and be sure not to use the sable brushes, though, as it will ruin them and your work.

We'll start with a sketch of an object with a split background.' She indicates what she means in the sample paintings. One of them is a pear sitting on a tiled bench with a pink backsplash. It's simple, but the vibrancy of the frisket is fascinating. I'm drawn to it.

I decide to draw a daffodil in a field.

I take out my art sketchbook and my number two pencil.

I rule a box and mark the background change.

I smile to myself as I begin to sketch the flower.

My hand jerks, drawing a hard line through the light sketching. I frown. Erase it. Try again.

And again.

And again.

And again.

I hold my hands out in front of me. They're shaking. Trembling.

I frown and press my lips together hard.

I blink back the tears.

I shake my hands out.

They still tremble. It's a new tremble. Distinct and not going away. Not like the subtle steroid induced tremble, or the stupid-amount-of-pain tremor. Actual tremors.

I try again and again and again.

'Are you okay, Grace?' Mrs Connors asks in a low voice. She looks at my hands and I fist them, placing them on my lap under the table.

'I'm fine,' I say.

'Grace,' she says, her voice heartbreakingly soft.

'I just need a minute,' I whisper.

'Go,' she says. 'Take your time.'

I nod, grateful, and bolt out the door.

Dr Rai had put me on duloxetine after the pregabalin, a week before I'd gone into hospital. He'd said that the side effects were similar to the others: constipation, fatigue, dizziness. And then he'd said that some people develop hand tremors with the mix of duloxetine and amitriptyline.

I sob, covering my mouth with my stupid, trembling hands to muffle the noise.

My white flag waves in the breeze.

It hurt less. I have more energy – more spoons. Nowhere near Real Girl Grace. But enough. It was enough.

Hand tremors and Real Girl.

Sick Girl and art.

Art was my favourite subject. It was home. It was safe. Even as I gave up sport and walking and lounge room dance parties with my sister, I still had art.

I know it's a choice, I do.

'*I just want you to be okay,*' Mum had said. She'd been willing to accept the zombie for my sanity.

Dad's fear of my pain, the way he wants to protect me from the world. The way his heart breaks for me every goddamn time.

Ivy's hopeful eyes when I dance with her. When I wake up and can function.

The look in Daniel's eyes every time he tries to steal my books or bag to carry for me.

It's not a choice, too.

And if it is, I've already made it. Sitting in the worst toilet block at Riverview High. Sobbing.

Because it isn't just about me. And it never was.

...

I don't go back to art.

I wander to the office with my head down. Mrs Gruber doesn't ask any questions, just opens the door to let me through to the sick bay. Mrs Easton comes in a few moments later. I'm sitting on the bed, staring at the floor, but I know it's her. Her rose perfume, the click of her heels.

'Grace?' she says. 'What's up?'

And I sob. I howl and sob and cry and she rubs my back and waits without speaking.

'It's not fair,' I manage eventually. 'It's not fair.'

'What isn't fair?' she asks.

'Everything,' I say.

'I know,' she soothes me. 'It's not. You just let out, sweetheart.'

I lean into her and cry harder.

I cry myself to sleep, in the end. Mrs Connors brought my stuff up to the office when I didn't come back. Ivy comes to find me when I'm not in the car park waiting for Dad. She wakes me up holding my hand.

'You okay?' she asks, beautiful eyes round with sympathy and sadness for me.

'No,' I say. 'I'm not okay at all.'

'What do you need?' she asks.

I sob once, and catch it, holding my breath. I shake my head.

I pull my hand out of hers so I can show her my hands. My trembling, traitorous hands.

She watches them.

'What's wrong with them?' she asks.

'I don't know,' I cry. But I'm pretty sure I do. I cover my face with them. I'm embarrassed and stupid and I'm going to make a spectacle of myself getting to the car and it's so unfair. It's all so fucking unfair.

'I love you,' Ivy says. A tear trickles down her cheek. 'You had art, didn't you?'

I nod.

'I'll go let Dad know,' she says. 'We'll wait until the buses go.'

She's fourteen. She's my little sister. What have I done to her that she can manage this situation so well? She's just a kid. She's meant to be just a kid.

I cry harder once she's gone.

...

I barely manage to keep it together in the car.

Dad asks what's wrong again and again, but I can't speak. I just cry.

When we get home, I shut myself in my room.

I look through my sketchbooks. The art I made on my wall. The linocut print I'd been so proud of. The oil painting that won the award. The twisting clay sculpture that had been shown in an art gallery. The half-finished sketch of Daniel's face. The sketch planning the next sculpture. The art supplies scattered across every surface of my room.

Mum knocks on the door when she gets home.

'Not yet,' I say. 'I just … not yet.'

'We're worried about you,' Mum says.

'Just leave it, please.'

I take the half finished works and screw them into balls. I find an empty shopping bag and shove them in. I hold my palomino pencils in my fist. I imagine them stabbing into my heart. I think it would make a great work of art, so I shove them in the bag, too.

Ivy knocks on my door.

'Go away,' I cry.

She comes in and sits beside me. She hugs me, even when I hit her, trying to get away.

'I'm not going anywhere, Gray. And you're not alone. We'll work it out.'

'We won't,' I say. 'It can't.'

'Dad's made an appointment for you to see Dr Rai in the morning.'

I nod. 'Okay.'

'Maybe don't throw all your art supplies away just yet, then?' She picks the pencils out. 'I got you these for your last birthday. They're stupid expensive for pencils.'

I laugh and cry and hug her back.

'I love you,' I say into her hair. 'I love you, I love you, I love you.'

'I know,' she soothes me. She strokes my hair. 'I love you, too.'

'It hurts so much,' I say.

I don't need to clarify.

'Stupid meat sack,' she says. 'This is why you can't have nice things.'

I laugh and cry again.

She leads me to bed and curls up beside me.

'I'm hashtag Team Grace five-ever,' she says.

'Gross.'

'Yeah, but you love me anyway,' she says.

'I do,' I say. 'I'm scared.'

Ivy says nothing.

'I'm so fucking scared, Ivy.' I'm crying again and holding her tight. 'I don't know if I can do this without art.'

'You're stronger than you think.'

'I don't know, anymore. I think maybe I'm hitting my limit.'

'You're not,' she says, firmly. 'And if you are, we'll smash the limit and get a better one.'

'I'm scared. I don't want to do this anymore.' The admission tears free of me with a sob.

Ivy holds me tighter and tighter and tighter and promises me that she's on my team and we can slay dragons together.

I fall asleep thinking that I've got the best sister in the world and holding onto her like a lifeline.

CHAPTER NINE

New Normal

Dr Rai is running his mandatory forty-five minutes late. Today, though, it feels more like two hours. I feel sick with anxiety and my mandatory mask is suffocating. Mum took Ivy to school and Dad is with me instead. I've had three messages from Daniel so far, but I haven't even read them. I can't. I can't do anything except keep my hands balled into fists in my lap.

'It's gonna be okay, Gracie,' Dad says, his voice soft and hopeful and sad.

'I know,' I say. 'It's fine. It doesn't matter.' The words remind me of Daniel and our code of normal.

'Grace,' Dad says. He covers one of my fists with his hand and holds it. 'If it's a side effect of the medication, we can try something else.'

'There's always going to be a side effect,' I say. 'No matter what drug I get put on.'

'Your hands, though,' he says. 'It's ... I know I complained about the zombie thing, but art is your thing. It's how you've coped this long.'

'I'll adapt,' I say. 'Or ... I can't do this, Dad. I can't be brave for you right now. I'm breaking apart and I can't –'

'Grace?' Dr Rai calls from the waiting room door.

I stand up, push at my cheeks to wipe the tears away and pretend everything is fine. Dad walks behind me.

'How are we today, Grace?' Dr Rai asks.

'I'm here, aren't I?' I say.

'That's a fair point,' Dr Rai replies, amused.

'So,' he says, once we're settled in his office. 'What brings you here today. I noticed you had a hospital admission just over a week ago.'

I hold out my hands for him.

'Ah,' Dr Rai says.

'I noticed it yesterday,' I say. 'I had art. I couldn't … I couldn't draw.' My voice breaks and I hate myself for showing him weakness. I hate that I have to explain it. I hate that I'm here at all.

'You said it might be a side effect of the medication?' Dad says. 'What do we do about it?'

'It's a deal with the devil, Dad,' I say. 'There's no magic pill out there.'

'You're being a little dramatic,' Dad says.

I narrow my eyes at him.

'Regardless, Grace is correct,' Dr Rai says before I can start a verbal war with my father. 'Side effects are going to be part of the deal. Which leads me to my first question: how is the pain?'

'Better,' I say. 'Well, not better. Just, you know, more manageable. I still don't have enough energy and it hurts all the time. It's less, though. It's working. And I still have my brain.'

'And the tremors – are they consistent or do they come and go?'

I screw my mouth up, thinking. 'I'm not sure. I think they're worse when I'm tired. But like I said, I only noticed them yesterday.'

'Well, they might settle down, or they might not. We'll have to wait and see,' Dr Rai says. 'But you're going to have to decide if you want to keep taking the medicine if they do. Unfortunately, we don't have a lot of other options for the undiagnosed pain condition. Tolerance and addiction are real concerns for you.'

'Grace's art is important to her,' Dad says. 'And her hands …'

'Have you heard the phrase work smarter not harder?' Dr Rai asks. 'Grace might have to get creative, but hand tremors don't mean she's not able to do any art ever again. Sculpture and clay could even be considered therapeutic.'

'But not the fine detail stuff,' I say on a sigh. He's right, I think. He's right, because it's not over. I can cope with this. I have options. I'll make it work.

'She's sixteen,' Dad says, and I think I hear disbelief in his tone.

'Grace is pretty resilient, it seems,' Dr Rai replies. 'I think you don't need to worry too much about her. Some people get sick, it is what it is. If I had a magic wand, I'd offer it to you.'

'I appreciate that,' I say dryly because he was clearly being a little sarcastic.

'But with regards to next steps, I suggest we give it some time and see if things settle down,' he says with a note of finality.

'Right,' I say.

'Grace, are you sure?' Dad asks. 'Yesterday was ... you weren't okay.'

'I'm not okay,' I say. 'But he's right, there's more than one way to do art, life is a little more manageable, and I can handle this deal with the devil. I'll get there.'

...

Afterward, we sit in the car outside school sipping chai lattes. It's almost recess, so there's no point in me going in now.

'I wish I could fix this for you,' Dad says. 'Your hands ... I can't imagine how upset you must be.'

'I don't want to talk about it,' I say.

'I think you should. It'd be good for you to process it.'

'Dad, I love you. Thank you for caring. I don't want to talk about it yet.'

'Grace.'

'Dad.'

'I'm here for you, you know? I love you. You're my favourite eldest daughter.'

'When I'm ready to talk about it, I'll let you know. But it's not just about me, is it? My pain is your pain; everyone's pain,' I say. 'This isn't just about me and what I'm prepared to live with. It's about what I'm prepared to make you live with.'

Dad looks like he's about to cry. I suddenly consider bailing out of this conversation. White ninja. Barry bolt. GTFO. I don't move. Because if my pain is his, then his pain should be mine.

'Grace, you are sixteen years old. This shouldn't be your life. You shouldn't ... don't worry about us. You need to do what's best for you. Be selfish,' Dad says.

I shake my head. 'That's not realistic.'

'You're just a kid.'

'I'm sixteen, Dad.'

'And you're acting like an adult. You don't have to always be mature about this. You're allowed to be selfish and angry – God knows I'm angry for you.'

'I know,' I say. 'Your life is at least fifty percent about me and my health.'

'You aren't meant to think about that,' Dad sighs. 'But you're Grace Turing: brilliant, beautiful, and brave.'

'That's some great alliteration,' I deadpan. But it's a front to stop me tearing up before I have to go into school.

Dad holds my hand again. 'I love you. I'm so proud of you.'

'Dad,' I say, trying to sound irritated instead of pleased. I'm pretty sure he sees right through me because he leans over and kisses my cheek.

'Have a good day,' he says.

'I will,' I say. The bell sounds for recess and my phone pings again.

'You know, one of these days, I'm going to have to meet this boy of yours.'

I roll my eyes. 'His name is Daniel and we're just friends.'

'That's not what Ivy says.'

'Ivy needs to mind her own business. He's just a flirt, he doesn't mean it.'

'He might, you know. You should think about that option. Do you like him?'

'Dad, I'm not having this conversation,' I say. I look down at my phone.

8:50 am

> **Where are you? Elsa said you bailed on art yesterday and you never bail on art.**

8:55 am

> **Ivy says you're at the doctor but she won't tell me why.**

8:56 am

> **Are you okay?**

11:00 am
> **Turing. Message me or appear. Either works.**

'You're smiling,' Dad says.

'I'm not,' I say, schooling my face back to neutral.

Dad laughs. 'I'll go home and clean the shotgun, shall I?'

'You don't even own a gun,' I say, rolling my eyes. 'Bye, Dad. See you after school.'

'Bye, Grace,' he says, smug grin in place.

...

I find Daniel lingering by my locker.

'Hi, stalker,' I say. 'You're so needy.'

There's a flash of relief when he sees me, but he covers it with a smirk. 'I spend all night finding the best, most ridiculous fact I can find, and then you don't even have the decency to show up for it,' he says.

'Impress me,' I say.

'Tell me about the doctor first,' he says. 'Are you okay?'

'It doesn –,' I stop myself and flatten my lips into a line, swallowing the words.

'Uh-huh,' Daniel says.

'I don't want to talk about it yet,' I say. 'It's shit.'

'Okay,' he says. 'Oral contraceptives work on gorillas the same way as they do on humans.'

I stare at him for a moment. 'That is frickin' weird.'

'Right?'

'Are you for real?'

'I shit you not.'

'Gorillas?'

'Yep.' He's gloating. He's earned it.

'Well, damn, Perkins.'

He laughs and I feel like I can pretend that my hands aren't shaking. I'll probably never be able to sketch him. I like the darkness of his skin and his broad nose and full lips. I like the way his eyes are so deep that in the right light they look completely black. The white of his teeth and the red of his mouth when he laughs. He's not handsome, he's not good-looking like Liam or built like Caleb. But the artist in me itches to draw him, and I only held off so long because it was kind of creepy.

I left it too late.

I shake myself mentally. You could sculpt him, I think. It won't be the same. But it's something.

'Earth to Grace,' Daniel says. 'Where are you, space girl?'

'I'm here,' I say.

'You were looking at me weird.'

'I am weird,' I say, because I'm obviously not telling him I was thinking about drawing his face. 'Looking at you normally would be weirder.'

'Ivy,' Daniel says, looking over my shoulder. 'Your sister is being weird.'

'Weird is normal for Grace,' Ivy says, coming to stand beside me.

'See?' I say.

Ivy does the chest pound and peace. Daniel does it. They look at me expectantly until I do it.

'Yes,' Daniel says, grinning. 'Day made.'

'How was the doctor?' Ivy asks. Her eyes track my hands and I ball them into fists self-consciously.

I sigh. 'I don't want to talk about it.'

'Ah,' Ivy says. 'Okay. Are you ... okay?'

'I will be,' I say and give her a brave smile.

She nods, nervous and unsure. I love her so much that I ache with it. She held me all night. She's my lifeline.

'I promise,' I add.

'I feel like I'm missing some critical information,' Daniel says. 'But feel free to keep having a conversation I'm not part of.'

I roll my eyes and Ivy frowns.

'You haven't told him?' she says. 'Why not?'

'Because I can't talk about it yet,' I snap. 'I don't want to talk about it and how fucking unfair it is and I don't want to have to be brave for another person!'

Ivy flinches and Daniel is shocked and I feel like the worst person to ever walk the earth.

'Sorry,' I say. 'I'm just … I'm –'

'No, you're right,' Ivy cuts in. 'I shouldn't have pushed. You don't have tell anyone anything you don't want to. Sorry.'

'I love you,' I say.

'I love you, too. I'll talk to you after school?' she says.

I nod, and she leaves quickly. I watch her go and hate myself.

'I'm an asshole,' I sigh.

'Yep,' Daniel agrees.

I glare at him.

He shrugs. 'If you wanted me to lie you should have led with that.'

I sigh.

'It's Ivy,' he says. 'She's special.'

I groan and bang my head against my locker. 'I know.'

'It's okay if you don't want to tell me what happened.'

'I'm the worst,' I say. 'Literally the worst.'

'Hey,' Daniel says. His hand catches my wrist and turns me to face him. 'You have a lot on your plate. You're allowed to be an asshole sometimes.'

'Ivy's special and I'm an asshole,' I say. 'Story of my fucking life.' I think I'm going to cry, because of course he thinks that. Everyone thinks that. It's true. I thought … I let myself believe that he'd have picked me if he could only have one Turing sister. He said I was his favourite, but I wasn't. I never was.

I feel bereft. Of art. Of friendship. Of Ivy.

I pull myself out of his grip and try to walk away, but he catches me again.

'Grace.' His voice is different. It's almost like he wants me to understand something he's not saying.

'Leave me alone,' I say. 'I can't do this right now.'

'I didn't mean it like that,' he says.

I pull my arm free again. 'And when I calm down, I'm sure I'll know that.' I stalk off and he lets me go.

I hide in the toilets until recess is over. I delay going to my locker to get the right books until the bell rings so I miss everyone. I get to class four minutes late. I hand Mr Simmons a note from Dad explaining I was at the doctor, and he sniffs imperiously before telling me to take a seat. Jenna is back in her old seat again, and Daniel is one seat away.

'Trouble in paradise?' Emmy sneers.

'You're here, so it clearly isn't paradise,' I mutter back. Not my best burn.

But it stings that she's right. Whatever tentative paradise I'd been building at Riverview High was shattered with Jenna's reaction and my bullshit towards Daniel.

I'm an idiot.

And Daniel doesn't have third period with me, so I was going to have to wait until lunch to clear the air. If he even wants to.

Was I always such a disaster or did getting sick make me worse?

...

Watching Daniel and Jenna walk off towards German together speaking in low voices rips at me.

'Are you really dating him?' Liam asks me.

'No,' I say. 'I'm really not.'

'Now, or?'

'We're just … friends. We were. We are. I don't know anymore.' I feel very melodramatic and more like a teenager than I have in weeks despite Dad's claims about my maturity.

'Well, with your attitude I'm not surprised,' Emmy says and flips her hair. 'Come on, Liam.'

'What happened?' Liam asks.

Emmy scowls at me.

'I was an asshole. I'm always an asshole.'

'Na, you're not,' Liam says. 'You're just yourself and you don't care about anyone's opinion.'

'Because she's a bitch,' Emmy mutters.

Liam looks at me like he wants to say something else, but he doesn't. He never does.

'We'll be late,' Graham calls from a little further down the hall. 'She's not worth it, Liam.'

I look at him and wonder if he'll defend me. Today, it almost looks like he will.

'I'm coming,' he says and lets Emmy link her arm through his and pull them down the hallway.

Liam is, I decide, the kind of person that I like least. He lacks the courage of his convictions; he never defends anyone. He coasts by on being good looking and uncontroversial.

I miss Daniel already. He'd have rolled his eyes and made a joke about 'sheeple'.

...

I know that I should go looking for Ivy, or at least Daniel, at lunch time. But I don't. Because, I realise, that I don't know where to look. They both always come to me and my spot on the oval. I know Daniel used to sit at the science block, but that was because of me, too. I've never even thought to find Ivy.

I'm so freaking selfish.

I hate myself.

Because I'm definitely the worst.

Grace Turing: Patron Saint of Assholes.

I decided to go to my spot on the oval because I'd feel stupid wandering around looking for them. But I feel bad for doing it. I almost don't want them to find me. It's stupid and complicated and so disgustingly typical of being a teenager. I'm almost proud of it. I wonder if Dad will appreciate my new teenage circumstances. He wanted me to be normal, after all.

Okay, being a sarcastic bitch in my head isn't helping.

I round the corner of the science block and I can see Daniel and Jenna sitting in my spot.

Jenna.

Is.

In.

My.

Spot.

I stop dead in my tracks. I don't know what's happening. But it can't be because she wants to speak to me. It can't. I didn't have Daniel down as cruel, but maybe he is. Maybe he's punishing me. Replacing me.

I know I deserve it, but it makes me feel sick and empty and hot.

Someone touches my hand, and it makes me flinch, but I know it's Ivy before I finish turning to look. I hadn't realised my hand was a fist, but she's covered it with hers. She's got beautiful, long fingers that I've always been jealous of.

'Hey,' she says, and then she chews her lip nervously. 'I'm sorry about this morning.'

I pull my hand free and wrap my arms around her tightly.

'*I'm* sorry,' I say. 'I shouldn't have been so harsh. I'm a dick, but I do love you, little sister.'

'I know.'

We step back from the hug.

'You know that it's very uncool to be this affectionate, right?' Ivy asks, a small smile teasing me.

'Yep. I am the most uncool,' I say. I look back over to Daniel and Jenna.

'Go on, they're probably waiting for you,' Ivy says.

'I don't know,' I reply. 'They might not be. I … Daniel and I …'

'It's your spot. They're waiting for you,' Ivy says with logical certainty. She pushes me when I don't move. 'Go.'

'Ivy –'

'Go!' She shoves me again, harder this time, and I stumble forward.

I look over my shoulder at her, but she's waving at someone. I turn back to the oval. Daniel. She's waving at Daniel.

'Ivy,' I hiss.

She does their secret handshake, ignoring me, and then walks away. I look back to Daniel and Jenna, and they're looking at me. I can't quite make the expression out from this distance, but I know that I'm meant to walk over there.

So, I do. Slowly. Like someone walking to their death.

Jenna smiles at me nervously and Daniel looks … determined. His jaw is set and his expression is a little flat.

'Hi,' I say.

'Hey,' Jenna says. She looks like she'll flinch at sudden noises.

'Turing,' Daniel says. 'What took you so long?'

I sit down feeling like the most awkward person to ever person.

'About this morning,' I begin.

'We're good. You don't always have to be fine,' Daniel says.

I open my mouth to argue.

'Jenna has something she'd like to say,' Daniel says, and gives Jenna one of the best parental '*do it*' looks that I've seen in my life.

'I'm sorry,' Jenna tells me. 'I was a bitch and you didn't deserve it.'

'Don't worry about it. If I could stop talking to me, I would,' I reply.

Daniel turns his look on me.

I shift uncomfortably.

'No, it wasn't okay,' she says, more forcefully this time. 'And I know that. I should have ...'

'It's how people normally react. Being sick makes people uncomfortable. Like I said, I'm proof teenagers aren't invincible,' I shrug. 'Coming back is unusual. I assume we have Daniel to thank for this reunion.'

'I – yeah. I want to pretend that ... Yeah,' Jenna finishes. She looks at Daniel. 'I'm glad he did, though.'

Daniel is looking at me expectantly. He's waiting for something. For me. I look away from him.

'Don't let him railroad you into something you don't want to do,' I say to the grass. I don't say: '*I'm not worth it*'. But I think it to the beat of my heart.

'Grace, stop it,' Daniel says. His voice is harsh, and it draws me back to his face. 'You're being ... not you. You're sulking like a child.'

'And?' I ask. I'm angry and it's stupid. I want to tell him I'm sorry and make up for this morning and he's giving me the gift of Jenna's friendship back. I want to tell him that I'm losing something important, and I want to cry and rage with the unfairness of it. I'm not being fair, and I know it.

'And you're better than this,' Daniel says. There's something he's not saying, and I can see it in his eyes. I wish I knew what it was.

And, damn it, I want to be better than this.

I turn back to Jenna.

'I missed you,' I say and smile.

'I missed you, too,' she replies, smiling back.

'And I have a harem again,' Daniel announces with a clap of his hands. 'I'm back to being the envy of every guy at Riverview High.'

'Shut up,' I say and throw some grass at him.

'Idiot,' Jenna says.

'Rude,' Daniel sighs. 'Do you wanna catch a movie tomorrow after school? There's a new Marvel movie.'

'There's always a new Marvel movie,' Jenna says.

'Sure,' I say. Then, I hesitate. 'I'll have to ask Dad.' I wonder if he'll let me go, but I think he should because it is a controlled environment with two people who know what's up. But he also won't let me catch the bus to school. So, who knows? Maybe he'll helicopter parent and sit in the back of the theatre just in case. God, I hope not.

'All g,' Daniel says. 'Do you think Ryan is going to break Miss Thompson today?'

Jenna snorts a laugh that is very unlike her. 'My money is still on Caleb and Graham. I understand the point of a debate series, but, really, it's one of those "when are we going to use this" things.'

'I've actually been enjoying them,' I say.

'Of course you are, Queen Contrary,' Jenna replies.

'I just mean that being able to discuss and understand multiple points of view will make us better people. You know, people that didn't vote for Trump or get their information from clickbait,' I say. 'And I thought the debate about mental health as disability was interesting.' I pause and cut my eyes to Daniel. He'd been on the negative for it, and I knew that it had to have been hard for him with his mother.

'You're such a nerd,' he tells me. 'But, sure, let's all be good citizens or whatever.'

'You can pretend you don't care all you like, Daniel Perkins. You aren't fooling me,' I tell him.

'I'm eighty percent sure he doesn't care,' Jenna sighs. 'He never tries.'

'Laziness and not caring are different,' I argue.

'Why not both?' Daniel asks. 'It's lunch. Can we stop talking about schoolwork now?'

...

The word 'EUTHANASIA' is written in capitals on the board when we walk in and something in my stomach twists. I make my way to my seat at the back of the class and stare at it.

'Grace?' Jenna whispers. 'Are you … having a … thing?'

I blink at her. 'What?'

'A … you know,' she says, gesturing at nothing with her hands.

'Can you use actual words?' I ask.

'She means the ninjas,' Daniel hisses from the other side of her.

'Oh,' I say, realisation dawning. 'No. No ninja attacks. I'm just thinking.'

Jenna looks at me like she doesn't quite believe me. I turn back to the board and stare at the word. I suddenly realise that this conversation could be the thing that outs my secret to the class. Because I'm not sure how objective I can be about this.

Euthanasia is one of those Old Grace/New Grace divides. Like being a Gryffindor or liking long walks on the beach. Before I got sick, I didn't really agree with euthanasia as an ethical thought experiment. But when you live in pain everyday, when you are sick and exhausted 24/7, euthanasia becomes less thought experiment and more a legitimate option you'd like to have on the table.

'So,' Miss Thompson says. 'Euthanasia. Who wants to define it?'

'The voluntary death of someone who is dying anyway,' Elsa offers.

'Putting an animal to sleep, but for people,' Liam adds.

'Yeah,' Miss Thompson says, with a nod. 'It can also be called 'assisted suicide' or 'voluntary assisted dying', and it is about relieving the pain and suffering of a person by ending a life with dignity.'

My stomach twists.

'Different countries have different laws about it,' Miss Thompson continues. 'Does anyone know the law for Australia?'

'It's not legal, right?' Emmy asks. 'I know it isn't in France, but it is in Belgium.'

'I thought it was legal here?' Ryan asks.

'It was legal briefly in the Northern Territory,' Miss Thompson confirms. 'And it has been legal in Victoria since 2019 and Western Australia since July this year, and we passed the law here in

Tasmania to take into effect in October 2022. Queensland is currently debating it.'

I swallowed thickly. I hadn't been aware it would be legal here so soon and there was a part of me that wanted to celebrate, and another part felt anxious and weird about it. It was real. It could be my future. Would it be my future if everything kept getting worse?

'Why is it only some states?' Elsa asks. 'It kind of seems like it should be a countrywide decision. Like gay marriage was.'

'It's still state by state,' Miss Thompson says. 'But I'm sure parliament will consider overturning it if they don't think the Victorian legislation is good enough.'

'Like, what?' Liam asks. 'What kind of problem would make it overturned?'

'You tell me,' Miss Thompson says. 'What do you think the pitfalls are?'

'Consent,' Elsa says. 'If you're too sick to make the call yourself, or if your family or whoever want to kill you for the inheritance. Elder abuse is a real issue.'

'Excellent,' Miss Thompson says.

'Yeah, but if you're too sick to make the call yourself, surely that means you should be eligible,' Liam argues. 'Nan was bedridden and miserable in a home for months before she died. She hated being alive.'

'Yeah, but what if medicine changes and we could make life a little better for them?' Ryan asks. 'Like, is death the only option here?'

'They're dying anyway,' Caleb shrugs. 'Kill 'em off and save the resources.'

I raise my eyebrows, mildly impressed by Caleb's suggestion. Even if he did say it in the most brutal way possible.

'We can't just go around killing off everyone over eighty,' Emmy argues.

'What about younger people?' Jenna asks. 'Is there an age requirement for euthanasia?'

I tense, bracing myself for impact.

'I don't like the idea of killing off kids,' Liam says.

'They're terminal, I suppose, but it feels ... wrong,' Elsa agrees.

'Older people who've lived a full life make euthanasia easier to think about, you know?'

'There's, like, potential, or something,' Graham says.

'I can't imagine good parents agreeing to kill their kid,' Kenzi says.

'So, what's the age threshold, then?' Ryan asks. 'Is it a pain limit, age limit, terminal diagnosis?'

There's an edge in Ryan's voice that makes me want to be friends with him. He's trying to sound noncommittally curious, but I hear his irritation at the double standard.

'I think it should be a combination,' Emmy says. 'Like, you don't want to kill a three-year-old off, but –'

'Hypocrites,' I snap. I don't realise I'm speaking until the class falls silent. 'Who gives a shit about how old someone is? You'd make a three-year-old spend a year in agony, dying slowly, and barely understanding why? But sure, let's kick all the old people off the planet!? This isn't about population control. It's about humanity and kindness.'

There is a weighted pause.

My stomach twists.

My cheeks burn.

'You're using judgmental language,' I add, talking to my desk. "Kill" and "murder". You don't say that when you put down a puppy, do you? You "put them to sleep". You do it *for* them, not *to* them.'

'It's an animal,' Liam says. 'It's different.'

'What's different? Shouldn't it be about the same things? Compassion, right? Easing pain and suffering?' I ask. 'Aren't we all just animals in the end?' I raise my eyes to look at Miss Thompson. Her face is an open book. She's heartbroken for me and clearly apologising because she didn't think it would be so personal for me. I look away again.

'There's too many ways it can go wrong,' Kenzi decides. 'It shouldn't be legal.'

'And then there's mental illness and impulsiveness,' Daniel says.

My heart twists. I know he's thinking about his mother and bipolar. If she got sick ... Even when she's not and she's in a depressive episode.

'Suicide and euthanasia aren't the same thing,' I say. 'You can't put them in the same category.'

'Can't you?' Graham asks. 'It's all death. Miss Thompson even said that it was called "assisted suicide". Seems pretty similar to me – it's all giving up.'

'And then there's the religion aspect,' Amber adds. 'God would view them both as the same, right? Right? God is in control of your lifespan, and checking out early is still checking out early, regardless of your reason.'

'Because he wants us to suffer,' I scoff. 'Do you take paracetemol when you get your period? Because that could be considered against his will, too. He cursed us, after all.'

'That's like saying masturbation is equivalent to abortion,' Kenzi scoffs. The boys break out in snickers.

'Maturity, gents,' Miss Thompson sighs. 'Show some, please.'

There are some muttered apologies.

'Kenzi is right. If you could guarantee a system where no one would abuse it, then euthanasia is viable. But you can't. There's too many ways it can be abused or go wrong,' Elsa says.

'I agree,' Liam says.

'Let's take a quick vote,' Miss Thompson says. 'If you agree that euthanasia should be legal, raise your hands.'

I raise my hand.

Jenna raises hers, and so does Ryan.

Three hands out of twenty-four.

Daniel won't look at me.

'There's too many ways it can go wrong,' Daniel says to his desk. I can hear the apology in his voice. I'm surprised at the size of the lump in my throat, and how hard it is to swallow around it.

'Let's separate into for and against,' Miss Thompson says. She shakes the box that she keeps our names in and starts drawing. It's her way of keeping it random. We divide in half, for and against. And then half again to work in teams to research and develop our arguments.

'You're Queen Contrary,' I whisper to myself. 'You can do this.'

'You're Grace Turing,' Jenna whispers.

I jolt, surprised that she heard me.

She smiles at me, encouraging. 'I'm pretty sure you can do literally anything.'

I smile back.

'Like Daniel said, you're metal AF.'

I take a deep breath and find my eyes meeting his over Jenna's head.

'He says a lot of things,' I say. I look away.

I haven't been so unproductive in humanities since I was 'Zom-Gray'.

I bolt from class before Miss Thompson finishes dismissing us, but she calls me back. I linger by her desk as we wait for the class to file out. Jenna gives me a smile of encouragement. Daniel clearly wants to talk to me, but I ignore him. It's easier.

'I didn't realise that this would be such a sensitive topic for you, Grace. I would have spoken to you about it beforehand if I had,' she tells me when we're alone.

'It's ... since I got sick,' I say. 'It's different when it's about you.'

Miss Thompson frowns. 'Is there something you're not telling us, Grace? We know about the chronic pain, but –'

'No,' I interrupt her. 'No, everything's ... fine. It's just, like you said, chronic pain. Daily. It's a lot.' I don't want to tell her everything. I don't want to tell her about how I think about killing myself to stop the pain at least once a week. That life is agony and I want to give up so often. She's my teacher, not my shrink. Not that I have a shrink. Huh. Maybe Dr Rai was right and I should consider therapy given the whole suicide thing. I wonder if there is a guide for that:

If you're in chronic pain and think about killing yourself more than three times a week. Or, if you've considered the overdose you'd take ...

'Grace?' Miss Thompson says. 'Are you listening?'

That'd be a no. 'Sorry,' I say. 'I was just ...' My eyes drift to the word still written on the board.

She smiles. 'Are you okay?'

'I'm fine,' I say. 'I'm always fine.'

'I'm very proud of you, you know,' she says.

I thank her, but it irritates me. Who is she to be proud of me? And proud of what? Showing up while disabled? I want to scream, cry ableism and inspo–porn. The reverence some people have for people like me is just as offensive as the attitudes of bigots.

'I'll see you tomorrow,' I say.

'Of course,' she says, dismissing me. 'But if you ever need to talk, I'm here for you.'

'Yep,' I say over my shoulder as I exit the classroom.

I stop short when I nearly run into Daniel, who's waiting for me.

'Grace,' he begins.

'I'm late,' I say and step around him.

'Grace, wait,' he says, he jogs a step to catch up.

My hips complain, but I power walk to the locker room. The sooner we're back among the masses, the harder this conversation will be to have.

'Can we talk, please?' he asks as I open my locker. 'I know that I upset you, but –'

'It's fine,' I lie, slamming the locker shut. 'It's a non-issue. It was just a class debate. Why would that be a problem?'

'It obviously is,' Daniel says. 'Or you wouldn't be slamming things.'

I turn to face him. 'It's fine,' I repeat. 'And if it's not fine, it'll be fine by tomorrow. Just … don't worry about it.'

'It wasn't about you,' he says. 'You know it wasn't, right?'

'Of course, I do.'

I shoulder my bag and head out of the locker room.

'Will you just listen?' he snaps. 'Christ.' He catches my wrist, pulling me back. 'I think I've earned that much from you, right?'

I look at his brown hand wrapped around my wrist so easily. My eyes follow his arm, up to his face. 'People are going to think we're breaking up,' I say.

'Who cares what people think?' Daniel asks. 'Because I sure as shit don't. I care about what *you* think.'

'I think you're being dramatic. I think you were thinking about –,' I stop and lower my voice. '– about your mother.'

I can't read his expression.

'I was,' he admits.

I nod. 'See? I get it. No hard feelings.'

'So why aren't you talking to me?'

'I'm late,' I say. 'I told you.'

'You saw the doctor this morning.'

'Because all I do is go to the doctor? You do know I have a physiotherapist and podiatrist, too, right? But maybe there's a family dinner or something non-illness related in my life.'

'That's not what I meant.'

'Let me go, Daniel.' I look meaningfully and where his hand is still holding my wrist. He drops it like it gave him an electric shock. 'Thank you. I have to go. I'll see you tomorrow. I'll … I'll ask Dad about the movies. He can be a little over-protective.'

'Okay,' he says. 'I'll … see you tomorrow.'

He sounds so sad I nearly go back and keep trying to reassure him. But Daniel Perkins has seen right through me since the day we met. He won't believe I'm fine until I am. It's his superpower.

…

Everyone is studiously not asking how my day was or how I'm feeling. Dad is having a forced conversation with Ivy about if Taylor Swift or Michael Jackson was the better musician. Yeah, because that's not half obvious as an attempt to mask the awkwardness. Mum's chiming in with Jimmy Barnes, but the argument is that he doesn't deserve a place in the discussion.

'Some friends are going to the movies after school tomorrow, can I go with them?' I ask when there's a lull.

Silence descends as they all stare at me.

'What?' I ask.

'You've never gone to the movies with friends before,' Mum says.

'Is it Daniel?' Dad asks in that annoying sing-song tone.

'Daniel and Jenna,' I say. 'It's not that weird. It's a thing teen-agers do.'

'Yeah, but not you,' Dad says.

'Ivy does it,' I say, defensive.

'Daniel is a really good guy,' Ivy says. 'And Jenna seems nice.'

'How would you be getting there?' Dad asks. 'Do they know about your health? What happens in an emergency?'

'It's the movies, Dad. And I've told you that they know,' I remind him. 'You were just saying this morning how you wanted me to do normal teenager things. Well, it's happening.'

'I don't know, Grace,' Dad sighs.

The last time we fought about my ability to do normal shit flashes through my mind.

'Dad, be reasonable,' Ivy says. 'Daniel's even gone and gotten me at school when things aren't okay. He's safe.'

'He's a sixteen-year-old boy,' Dad says. 'Safe is not the word I'd use.'

'Does he like you? Do you like him?' Mum asks conspiratorially.

I cover my face with my hands and groan.

'Ivy?' Mum asks. 'She tells you everything.'

'Well, he definitely likes her,' Ivy begins.

'No!' I shout. 'Nope, can we not? Can I go to the movies or not?'

'I –'

'I don't see a reason why not,' Mum says.

'Samara,' Dad hisses.

'Brett,' she replies. 'I know what you were doing at sixteen.'

'Exactly,' he says.

'She's way more mature than you were,' Mum continues. 'And than I was.'

'I'm just not sure,' Dad says. 'What if something happens?'

'Look, the new normal is me being sick. The new normal is this,' I hold up my trembling hands. 'But the new normal also involves me having real friends and being sixteen. I will make sure they have your number. I will be careful.'

'Let her go,' Mum says.

'Don't make me the mean parent,' Dad argues.

'Don't be the mean parent,' Ivy mutters.

'Ivy,' Dad snaps.

'She has a point,' Mum says.

'Sam,' Dad cautions.

'Please,' I say. 'I get it. But I'm asking.'

'Fine,' he sighs. 'I just … just, be careful. And I get to pick you up after.'

'It's the movies,' I say. 'Not rock-climbing.'

Dad rolls his eyes.

Mum tries not to laugh.

Ivy grins at me. 'Don't be difficult or he'll take it back,' she says.

'Listen to your sister,' Dad says.

'Always,' I grin.

...

I send a message to a group chat between Daniel, Jenna, and me.

7:41 pm

<   And we're on for tomorrow afternoon!

Jenna 7:42 pm

> Sweet. Looking forward to it.

Daniel 7:42 pm

> Nice.

I stare at my phone.

I wonder if I'm projecting something on Daniel's single word message. I open and scroll back through our private messages. He only ever sends one word when something is wrong or when it is in a stream of messages.

8:01 pm

<   If you put even a little bit of alcohol on a scorpion, it'll go mad and sting itself.

The three dots appear.

They disappear.

They appear.

They disappear.

I throw my phone on my bed and pull out some air-dry clay. I can't check my phone if my hands are covered in clay. It's solid logic.

Until my phone dings ten minutes later.

I curse loudly enough to bring Ivy in from the hallway.

'Hands?' she asks.

'No, phone,' I sigh. 'I think that I'm failing at the friendship thing. I've … I've been a real bitch to Daniel today.'

'Okay,' Ivy says, taking a seat on my bed.

'The three dots were tormenting me. So,' I raise my clay covered hands. 'Can't check my phone, not a problem.'

Ivy laughs. 'You know he'll forgive you.'

'I think he just messaged back,' I say.

'Want me to check it?'

I hesitate. 'Okay, but you can't say anything about it.'

'O-kay.'

'It might ... it might mention his mother,' I say. 'There was a debate at school today and things got ... tense.'

Ivy doesn't quite understand, I can tell by her expression. It's one of those moments that remind me she's only fourteen. But I know I can trust her.

'You aren't sexting, are you?' she asks. 'Because I feel like I should be warned about that.'

'Just check the damn phone.'

She stares at the screen for a full minute.

'Ivy!'

'Sorry,' she says.

'What did he say?'

'He said that he will try that out if you try eating worms because he just read that they taste like fried bacon. And this one species of beetle tastes like apples.'

I laugh with relief and enjoyment of the weirdness.

'That's amazing,' I say.

'That's really frickin' weird, Gray,' she corrects me.

'Can you tell him that more people die from bee stings than snake bites every year?'

'This is the weirdest foreplay ever,' Ivy says.

'It's an apology,' I tell her. 'Not foreplay.'

'Well then it is definitely the weirdest apology ever,' she says. 'You make no sense at all.'

'Just send the message and tell him I'll see him tomorrow.'

'So I should delete this confession of your undying love?'

'Ivy!'

'I'm *joking*, Gray. Jesus,' she says as she sends the message.

'What about you and that Nathan Ogilvie?' I ask. 'I see him

looking at you.'

Ivy rolls her eyes. 'He's a friend. Besides, I'm pretty sure Mei likes him.'

'Because that's ever stopped a love triangle from happening,' I reply.

'Gray, be serious,' she sighs.

'I'm very uncool,' I remind her. 'I get to ask these questions.'

'Very,' she sighs. 'I think I got all the cool genes. You shouldn't have left so many behind.'

'Since when am I capable of denying you anything?' I ask her.

My phone dings again.

'He says that he is actually sorry about today and he is on your side. But it wasn't just about his mother. What does that mean?' Ivy asked.

I frowned.

An actual apology meant serious business.

'I've got it from here,' I tell her, reaching for the hand towel I kept beside my desk to get the worst of the clay off. 'Night, Ivy.'

'Good night,' she says. She leaves but she gives me a strange look that I probably deserve.

8:15 pm
> I am actually sorry about today and I'm obviously on your side.
  But it wasn't just about Ma
8:16 pm
         < Okay?
8:17 pm
> It felt like agreeing meant giving you permission to take an early
  exit
8:17 pm
> Which is selfish I guess
8:18 pm
> Being friends with you is making me way too real Turing
8:18 pm
         < It won't be tomorrow. Or next week. But ... I don't
           know. I've kind of stopped hoping for a cure.

8:20 pm
> Why? Modern age of science etc
8:21 pm
        < I don't even have a real diagnosis. Maybe I'm wrong and the future will be different. It's Future Grace's problem.
8:22 pm
        < I guess I had a similar view on euthanasia before I got sick. I get it
8:22 pm
        < I'm sorry about being a bitch today anyway
8:23 pm
        < See you tomorrow?
8:24 pm
> All g. I'm assuming you got bad news at the dr
8:24 pm
> You don't have to tell me
8:25 pm
> But I'm here for you. #teamgrace
8:26 pm
> An ostrich's eye is bigger than its brain
8:27 pm
        < I knew that. Thanks. And that was way too easy
8:27 pm
        < A rhinoceros' horn is made of hair
8:28 pm
> A dolphin sleeps with one eye open
8:29 pm
        < A giraffe can clear its ear with its tongue
8:30 pm
> You win. Again. Night Turing.
8:31 pm
        < Night Perkins.

As I go to sleep that night, I think I'm kind of a fan of the new normal.

CHAPTER TEN
Friendship

It's strange to be on a bus with Daniel and Jenna. Daniel is sitting next to me, and Jenna is in front of us with a guy who has head-phones you can see from orbit. But, it's normal, too. Daniel is ranking the Marvel movies by awesomeness, and Jenna is arguing – secretly, I think, for the sake of it. Her eyes sparkle, now. Daniel brings out the best in her, I think. I wonder if there's something there, between them.

Jenna's sulking because Daniel is calling *Thor: Ragnarok* some kind of weird, canon fan fiction instead of a legitimate MCU movie. Daniel winks at me, delighted to have irritated her. Then, he frowns.

'Turing, have you been fighting the zombie hordes again?' he asks me.

I blink. 'What?'

'You're limping, you keep rubbing your knee, and you're paler than normal,' he says. 'You're also not talking.'

'Right? Grace not talking is always a sign something is up' Jenna says, turning back around. 'You look exhausted.'

I'm speechless for a moment.

'Do we need to reschedule?' Jenna asks. 'Because we can.'

'No. I'm …' I catch myself before I say I'm fine. I sigh in defeat. 'I didn't sleep well, my pain is a little high, and I don't want to take the next painkiller because it might make me dopey and I won't get to enjoy the movie.' I reach into my bag and remove my knee brace. I strap myself in and close my eyes for a moment of relief. Sometimes it feels so good to have that support in place and I'd been thinking about it since lunch time. 'It's fine,' I say, opening my eyes and reading their concerned expressions.

'Really. There's no magical day I'm not in pain.'

'But there are non-magical days when you're in less pain,' Jenna points out. 'And we've been at school all day. Maybe after school wasn't the best idea.'

Daniel flinches beside me.

'I'm sorry,' he says. 'I didn't –'

'No,' I say, my voice loud and awkward. 'It's fine. I want to do this!'

'Grace, it's okay,' Jenna says softly, and I hear my father in her voice. My mother. The pitying sympathy of everyone when they realise that I'm less than human. And that's how they make me feel: less than human.

'Exactly,' I reply. 'It is okay. We're going to the movies.'

'We don't have to do this today,' Daniel says, his voice quieter than I've ever heard him. My chest aches for him. He looks at me with his dark brown eyes, his mouth tugging down at the corners. I itch to drag him even though I know I can't. 'I can't … this weekend, I can't come. But –'

'Why not?' Jenna asks.

Daniel flinches again. 'It's … family stuff.' His eyes flick to mine, then away again.

His mother. It must be bad.

'So now you're into privacy,' Jenna says, rolling her eyes.

'We're going today so it doesn't matter,' I say.

It doesn't matter.

Daniel looks at me again with something serious and odd in his expression. 'If you aren't up to it –'

'We. Are. Going,' I say, with the kind of finality I'd expect an army general to use when giving an order.

Jenna looks meaningfully at my knee.

'It's fine,' I say. 'It's normal. Normal is shitty. Well, it was shitty.'

'Was?' Jenna asks. 'Is it not still shitty? Are you … I thought you … you can't get better, right?'

'Correct,' I say. 'But I have you guys. Having friends is new and it makes things less shitty.'

'Aw!' Jenna says. She reaches over the chair to squeeze my hand. 'Same.' She gives Daniel a meaningful look. 'Same, right?' she prompts him.

'Did I not mention my harem was the envy of every guy at Riverview High?' he asks, teasing. If he thinks I can't see through him the way he sees through me, he's dead wrong.

'Idiot,' Jenna sighs. 'It was almost a nice moment.'

'We are amazing, though,' I say. 'They should be jealous.'

...

You know how buses normally have that tilting thing to help the elderly manage the step off the bus? Yeah, no tilting today. Either it's broken or the bus driver didn't think we needed it. But I stagger as my braced knee hits the ground with my weight on it. Daniel catches me, steadying me.

'Rude,' Jenna says, glaring at the bus driver.

He shrugs, because he literally doesn't care, and drives away.

'You okay?' Daniel asks. I suddenly realise how close he is. How he has one arm around my waist and the other has my hand. How his eyes aren't completely brown, like I thought, but they have flecks of amber in them, when you look closely. For one breath, I feel completely safe. In the next, I panic, jolting away. He doesn't let me go, though, keeping me upright as if I might fall without him.

'I'm fine,' I say, and my voice sounds stilted and strange to me. I pray it sounds normal to them.

He releases me slowly, just in case I still need him.

'What a prick,' Jenna says, ranting about the bus driver still. I wonder if she hasn't noticed the weird moment between Daniel and me, or if she really is just pissed at the driver. 'He didn't even apologise. You're wearing a brace! Isn't it policy, anyway, to lower the bus for passengers to get off?'

'Breathe, Jenna,' Daniel tells her, lazy half-smile playing across his features. Did he miss the moment? Was it all in my head? 'Turing's fine and we have places to be.' He pauses. 'Provided you're okay to walk?'

I test my knee a little then nod. 'Yep. Lead the way.'

'Seriously, though,' Jenna says as she falls into step beside me. 'I should write a complaint.'

'Jenna, breathe. It's fine,' I say, repeating Daniel's words. 'I have an invisible illness. I'm young. It's par for the course.'

'It's not invisible if you know where to look,' Daniel says.

'That's true,' Jenna agrees. 'He always seems to know when you're not okay. I'm learning, too, I think. I'm trying to.'

There's suddenly a lump in my throat and I look away from them. My eyes prick with tears.

'Thanks,' I manage, eventually. 'So, how far away is the cinema?'

'Subtle subject change,' Daniel whispers in my ear.

I almost shiver.

'Three blocks,' Jenna says.

'Did you know that the crowds for the pod races in Star Wars Episode 1 were actually half a million cotton buds dipped in paint and blown around by a fan,' I say.

'Did you know the line "he's a friend from work" in *Thor: Ragnarok* was actually suggested by a Make-A-Wish kid who was on set that day?' Daniel asks.

'Did you know that J.A.R.V.I.S. stands for "Just Another Rather Very Intelligent System"?' I say. 'Which is rather forced, in my opinion.'

'Very forced,' Jenna agrees. 'Given Jarvis was the name of Tony Stark's butler in the comics.'

Daniel and I stop walking and look at her.

'What?' she asks, looking nervous.

'You read comics?' Daniel asks.

'No,' she says. 'But Dad does. He used to read them as bedtime stories. Mum thought they were inappropriate fare for undeveloped minds but she supposed they weren't worse than misogynistic fairy tales that foster a belief that women need rescuing.'

'Wow,' Daniel says eventually.

'If you hadn't told me that your mother was a psychologist, this conversation would have solved that mystery,' I say.

'*Iron Man* is definitely better than *Sleeping Beauty*,' Daniel says.

We start walking again.

'It was fun to get a fact in, though,' Jenna admits. 'I don't know how you guys keep all that irrelevant shit in your brains.'

'I wish I could get it out,' Daniel moans. 'Turing broke me.'

'Dancing baby Groot took two years to create,' Jenna adds. 'That's it. I'm tapped out.'

'Hugh Jackman has played Wolverine for sixteen years. It's a world record,' I say.

'No shit,' Jenna replies. 'I'm going to tell that one to Dad later. He'll get a kick out of it.'

'You don't really talk about your father much,' I say. 'I thought maybe he wasn't around.'

'He's not,' Jenna says with a shrug. 'He's in Switzerland now. He got remarried last year and I got to go to the wedding. I'm also no longer an only child.'

'I'm sorry,' I say.

'Don't be,' Jenna replies. 'I get international holidays every summer, I speak to Dad all the time, and it's not like he was around much when he was here. Their marriage was very dysfunctional, and they're both happier.'

'Still,' Daniel says. 'It can be hard with parents.'

It's as much as I've ever heard Daniel say out loud about his family.

'It was harder when it happened. But it's been a few years. The new normal is okay.'

'Parents,' I say. 'Can't live with them, can't throw them off a cliff.'

'Well, if you ever find my sperm donor, feel free to test the cliff theory,' Daniel jokes.

'Well, I'm the odd one out,' I say. 'My parents are still together and mostly functional.' I try not to think about Dad sitting in the car after fighting with Mum. I try not to think about how the only real fights they have are about me. I don't want to 'Me Too' my problems, because it isn't the same.

'And you have Ivy,' Daniel says. 'She's the best. Being an only child can be boring sometimes.'

'I always thought I wanted a sibling. Then I met other kids and changed my mind,' Jenna says. 'Having a six-month-old baby brother in another country is just weird.'

'Ivy is the gold standard of siblings. I'm pretty sure they broke the mould when they made her,' I say, smiling proudly.

'I get why you're protective of her,' Daniel says.

'Which is why you shouldn't talk to her so much,' I sigh. 'You've got to stop pretending you want to date me. It's exhausting convincing my parents that she's wrong. And trying to convince her she's wrong is impossible now.' I look at Jenna. 'You could tell her he's just a teasing ass, right?'

Jenna laughs and Daniel sighs heavily.

'You're so mean. And boring,' he says. 'What are you going to do if I actually like you?'

'If she's smart, she'll run in the opposite direction,' Jenna replies, grinning. 'Wait, can you run? Want me to kick him in the shin to give you a head start?'

'Hey! Don't make me regret forcing you to be friends with us again,' Daniel complains. 'You're always ganging up on me.'

'Well, stop being an ass,' Jenna says.

...

Daniel brought the good milk bottles and candy corn. I buy him and Jenna frozen cokes. Jenna buys the popcorn. I sit between them with the giant box on my lap. The movie is good, but I keep slipping into my own thoughts.

'What are you going to do if I actually like you?' Daniel had asked.

Ivy had said something similar not that long ago, too.

When the whole hormone thing had started, I'd been too busy getting sick to think about boys or girls or whatever it was that I was into. I didn't even know that much about myself. And then, when I did think about it, all I could think was that no one was ever going to want Sick Girl to be their girlfriend.

But Daniel knew I was Sick Girl.

Did he actually like me? Or was he just being a teasing prick, like I originally thought?

At some point, I was probably going to have to figure out how I felt about it.

...

Dad was waiting for us outside the cinema. I tried not to cringe with embarrassment.

'Hi Dad,' I said, walking over to him. 'Jenna, Daniel, meet Brett Turing: father of the year.'

'Hi Mr Turing, nice to meet you,' Jenna said, smiling.

'Hello, Mr Turing,' Daniel said, a little awkwardly. I wondered if this was harder for him after his earlier 'sperm donor' comment.

'Nice to meet you both, you can call me Brett, though. I've heard a lot about you,' Dad says. He grins at me. 'From Ivy.'

I roll my eyes and Jenna snickers. Daniel looks increasingly awkward. I almost want to touch him, reassure him that it's okay.

'Dad,' I sigh.

'Alright,' he says. 'Do either of you need a ride home?'

'I'm walking to Mum's office,' Jenna says. 'It's just four blocks that way.' She points down the street.

'I'm … staying with my uncle this week,' Daniel says carefully. 'It's a bit out of the way. I'll make my own way there.'

I have a pretty strong suspicion that this means his mother is really not okay right now. I keep the thought to myself and decide to message him about it later. I'm also low-key annoyed because he knows things and he's not talked to me. I thought 'it doesn't matter' was over.

'Define out of the way,' Dad says.

'It's, uh, on a farm, about twenty minutes outside Launceston,' he says. 'It's fine. My cousin finishes work soon, or there's the buses.'

'Buses plural?' Dad asks.

'Dad,' I hiss. 'Enough.'

'It's fine,' Daniel says. He looks at me. 'It doesn't matter.' I think he's trying to tell me that I don't need to worry, or not to say anything.

'Well, if you're fine, we're fine,' I say, smiling. 'Let's get out of here, old man.'

'Bye!' Jenna says. She gives us a cheerful wave before heading off down the street.

Daniel lingers.

'We can give you a ride if you want,' Dad offers.

Daniel shakes his head and nods at my knee. 'Grace's paler than when the movie started and I'm pretty sure her knee is killing her. Get her home. I'm fine.'

I stare at him.

'Thank you,' Dad says, smiling as he revaluates Daniel. 'I appreciate you caring about her.'

Daniel shrugs. 'Message you later?' he says to me.

'Is posthumous marriage legal in France?' I reply.

He grins and I feel like he's the Daniel I know again for the first time since he saw Dad. 'I'm going to go with yes, then.'

'Fact checking is important,' I say.

'Bye, Turing. Stay weird. Say hi to Ivy for me. Mr Turing,' Daniel says, finishing with a nod to Dad. He turns and starts walking in the opposite direction to Jenna's.

'Ivy's right,' Dad says.

'About what?' I ask.

'He's a good guy. He cares about you a lot,' he says. 'And, you know, I'm pretty sure he has a crush on you.'

'Don't be ridiculous,' I say. 'He's just a flirt.'

'Grace, he sees you,' Dad says. There's something in his voice I haven't heard before, not really. It reminds me of the way that Mum smiles at him. His words twist in my chest, because Daniel does. He does see me. He knows me. 'Seeing someone like that, it's special. It doesn't happen often.'

'Did you see Mum?' I ask him.

He smiles clearly riding on some nostalgia. 'She saw me first, actually,' he says. 'She walked up to me one day, handed me a can of WD-40, and said someone who looked like me shouldn't ride a bicycle that sounded like that.'

I laugh, because it's just so typically Mum.

'Then I started seeing her. She gets so caught up in her head she skips meals. I can chart that woman's day by the state of her hair.'

Dad wraps an arm around my shoulders and steers me toward the car.

'Obviously, I'm your dad, so I want to say you aren't allowed to date until you're at least thirty, but I don't think I have to worry too much if you end up with a guy like that.'

'Maybe,' I say. 'Or maybe he's into Jenna. Or he's a serial killer and has you and Ivy completely fooled.'

It's a pretty lame attempt at deflection, but Dad plays along. I'm grateful. Because it suddenly seems like the whole world is making plans for me that I don't get a say in. It's ... too grown up. I'm sixteen. I'm not meant to be meeting the person who really sees me. I'm not meant to be being looked after because my body is a piece of shit. I'm meant to be giggling about cute guys and my biggest problem should be Mr Simmons.

Mostly, I'm okay with the way things are. It's not like I can change it, anyway.

But the dating thing? Daniel?

Daniel is too much to think about.

CHAPTER ELEVEN
Border Skirmish

For the first time since I arrived at Riverview High, I find myself waiting in front of Daniel's locker. I wish he would hurry up because I'm getting strange looks, and it is so much easier to deal with when he's there teasing me about fighting ninjas and helping me deflect. Jenna's called in sick, too, so I feel a little adrift without either of them.

I shift uncomfortably and lean back against the lockers, trying to balance my weight differently. I'm wearing the knee brace. There had been a minor argument about using the walking stick today, too, but the brace was the only concession I was willing to make right now. It's not first day at school with a walking stick bad. Without it, I knew my knee would sublux, and probably not even during sport. It nearly went last night when I got up from the couch. Which is why, I'm sure, I'm getting the looks.

'What have you done to yourself?' Liam asks.

I stare at him.

I really hate that question. It implies that I've made a mistake, or I'm somehow responsible for being in pain. I fight back the scowl and the sarcastic remark.

'Oh, nothing,' I say, attempting to be casual. 'It's just a –'

'Fashion statement?' Liam cuts me off. He's annoyed. 'God forbid you tell me the truth. I just want to know if you're okay.'

I sigh. 'I'm okay. My knee's just a little sore today. I have problems with it sometimes.'

'That's the knee you hurt during the Beep Test, isn't it?'

'Yeah,' I say. 'It's a bitch.'

Liam laughs. 'Do you need a hand?' He looks at the books in my arms meaningfully.

'Um ...'

'I mean, I know you're with Daniel –'

'I'm not with Daniel,' I say quickly. 'He just finds the rumours amusing.'

'Oh,' Liam says, and a different smile appears. 'Right.'

I look around awkwardly and press my lips together as I wait for him to say something.

'Well. If that's all?'

'Will you have lunch with me?' Liam asks.

I blink, surprised. 'What?'

'Will you have lunch with me?' he repeats. He ducks his head and smiles at me from under his lashes. He is so very pretty. I feel like a squid standing next to him.

'I ... why?' I ask. Because that's the bit I don't get. That, and the fact that I don't think he'd ask me if he knew my secret.

He does this half-smile that is kind of self-deprecating but he has to know how good it looks on him. 'Why do you think?'

'Grace?' Daniel says.

I turn to look at him. He looks nervous. I smile at him.

'Hey,' I say. 'I was waiting for you.'

Daniel looks from me to Liam and back again. 'I need to get into my locker.'

I move aside and try not to frown at his tone.

'Well?' Liam asks as he reaches out to touch my arm, drawing my attention back to him.

'Sorry, no. I don't think so,' I say. 'But thank you for asking.'

'Why not?' Liam asks, genuinely confused. That face, I think again, has probably never been told no before.

I shrug. 'I just don't think about you that way.'

'What?' Liam is incredulous now.

I bite back the reasons why I'll never be close to Liam. How he looks pretty but he's weak, like some kind of lacklustre Prince Charming. How he lacks the courage of his convictions. How he's always a bystander and never stands up for anyone. Even me.

'I don't think about you that way,' I repeat. 'Thank you for ...

asking me to have lunch with you. But we're just friends.'

'It's just lunch,' Liam tries. 'How do you know you don't want to be more if you don't spend time with me? Unless there's someone else you're interested in?'

'How do you know you want more?' I ask him. 'It is what it is. It's not about there being anyone else, it's about you and me. Daniel?'

Daniel is staring at me a little shocked. 'Yeah?' he asks.

'Shall we go?'

'Grace?' Liam says. 'Are you sure?' He looks at Daniel suspiciously. I can almost feel Liam asking me if it is because of Daniel.

'Friends?' I ask Liam.

He shakes his head. 'Yeah, whatever,' he says, and then walks off.

I pretend that I can't see half of our homeroom staring at me.

'How's your knee?' Daniel asks.

I sigh. 'Hurts like a bitch. But, you know, worth it for yesterday.'

'And your brain?' he asks.

'What?'

'Liam Granger just asked you out.'

'He didn't really ask me out. He asked to get to know me,' I reply, deliberately.

'Turing, don't be dense. It doesn't suit you.'

'Well, he didn't ask me out! He asked who he thinks I am out,' I say.

'That's the weirdest thing you've ever said. And you have said so many weird things.' He's looking at me like I'm an alien.

'He doesn't know I'm sick,' I say, lowering my voice. 'He wouldn't ask me if he knew.'

'So? Tell him,' Daniel says.

I frown. 'What's wrong?' I ask. 'You're not okay. Is – is it your family?'

He scoffs in disbelief. 'You tell me. How would you feel if you arrived at your locker to find Amber or Emmanuelle asking your best friend out?'

I'm confused, but I latch on to his words: 'You're my best friend, too.'

'Turing,' Daniel says, the warning edge to his voice intensifying. 'Come on. You aren't this stupid.'

'You're jealous,' I realise, eyes widening with surprise.

He scowls. 'Forget it,' he says, and then he turns on his heel and walks away.

'Wait!' I call after him. I try a couple of limping steps, but I can't catch up. So I stop and stand there, closing my eyes against the pain in my knee and the ache building in my stomach.

I'm left behind and stranded and alone.

It's everything that I always expected would happen, in the end. I'll be stuck in limbo while people my age grow up and get jobs and married and have kids. I'll be alone and they'll eventually forget about me. We'll have nothing in common anymore.

...

My eyes fly open at the sensation of someone taking my books out of my arms.

Daniel.

He came back for me.

Hope is the thing with feathers – Emily Dickinson.

'Come on,' he says. There's an apology in the hint of a smile he offers me. 'When the mummy of Ramses II was sent to France in the seventies he was issued a passport.'

'Okay?'

'His occupation was deceased king.' His smile widens a little.

'That's amazing,' I say. 'What a job description. I think I have new dream job.'

'You're so weird,' Daniel says. He inclines his head towards the classroom and waits. I limp forward, more slowly now I've irritated my knee by trying to catch up to him. I reach for my books and he takes a big step backwards and raises an eyebrow. 'Uh-huh,' he says.

I screw my face up in a scowling glare. 'Perkins.'

We face off for a moment and then I sigh in defeat.

'Kool-Aid was originally called Fruit Smack,' I offer.

He laughs, a short, unexpected sound given the tension laced between us. 'You never disappoint.'

'I try. But, are you okay? I was going to message you last night, but I got distracted,' I tell him.

His eyes flick to my knee, understanding. 'She's in hospital,' he mutters. 'It'll be fine. It's always fine.'

'Remember who you're talking to,' I say, bumping his shoulder with mine gently.

He smiles, but I can suddenly see the exhaustion pulling at him. 'It's shit and I hate it. The farm is hard work, the buses suck, and I miss her. But, she's not her right now anyway.'

'I wish I could help,' I say. 'But I'm here for you.'

'I know,' he replies. 'Even if you date Liam.'

'I'm not going to date Liam,' I say. 'He's boring and lacks grit. If life is a movie, he's the audience, you know?'

'Weirdly, I think I do,' Daniel says. 'But he looks like the leading guy.'

'Oh, he's pretty. But that's just what he looks like, not who he is. Just like my body isn't who I am.'

'Huh.'

We enter homeroom and I receive dirty looks from basically every girl in class. Clearly, news of the locker room scene has spread quickly. I exchange a look with Daniel who looks like he's about to laugh again. He looks at Liam like he's gloating. That's when I realise that I should probably accept the fact that Daniel likes me. Actually more-than-friends likes me. I'm normally way quicker on the uptake than this, but it still feels so improbable. I'm not a Real Girl, and Daniel knows it.

I also probably owe Ivy an apology. And, maybe one to Daniel as well. Maybe he's been trying to tell me this from the beginning and I never even thought that's what it could mean.

'Is it true?' Elsa comes over to ask me. 'You and Liam?'

'Um, I don't know?' I say.

'You turned him down?'

'Ah ... yes?'

'Why?!' Elsa exclaims. 'You said you weren't with Daniel? Are you a lesbian?'

'Why is that the most logical option?' I ask. 'Jenna said the same thing. I just don't like him like that. It happens.'

'You have eyes, right? He's an artist's dream,' she says.

I can't help the way my eyes find Daniel's profile. 'Maybe,' I say.

Elsa follows my gaze. 'Oh,' she says. 'Yeah, I see that.'

She's surprised. She's known Daniel her whole life, and maybe she missed the part where he got so damn sketchable.

'Right?' I sigh. 'I'm pissed I didn't draw him when I had the chance.'

Elsa pulls back and frowns at me. 'What do you mean? He's right there. You could still draw him.'

My hands tremble as I place them on the desk. I don't even know why I'm doing this, but it feels right. It feels like time. I trust Elsa, even though she truly has the shittiest taste in guys ever. Caleb, I mean, seriously. He's a bully and a jock. Heart wants what it wants, I guess.

'Your hands,' Elsa says, softly. She reaches out to touch them, but stops herself.

I pull them back and hide them on my lap. 'Yeah,' I say, nervously. 'It's new. I don't ...' I look around the room and then back to Elsa.

She nods. 'Of course,' she says. 'I'm so sorry.'

'So is everyone,' I say, smiling sadly.

'What happened?'

I hesitate. 'It's ... personal.'

Elsa chews her lip, thinking. 'I think maybe I get it now,' she says. 'You weren't just being a bitch the other week.'

I nod.

'Okay,' she says. 'But ... God, it feels so dramatic, but watch out for Emmy. She's not going to be happy Liam asked you out.'

I grin. 'I have to admit, pissing her off would almost be a reason to date him.'

Elsa laughs and goes back to her seat.

Daniel moves into Jenna's empty spot. 'Talking about me?' he asks.

'Indirectly. We were talking about art,' I say. 'You have a very drawable profile.'

'I can't tell if that's a compliment or not.'

I laugh but don't say anything. It's safer.

'Alright, 10W,' Miss Thompson says, calling us to attention. 'Let's get this show on the road!'

...

The next day, I can't get out of bed. A thunderstorm brewed above us, and my body is wrapped in barbed wire with it. Air pressure changes make me furious and powerless. I feel stranded. When the rain breaks, I know that I'll get relief. But there's nothing I can do before then.

Ivy promises that she'll tell Daniel and Jenna what's happening, and tell them not to message me. Because I can't face them today. I just can't. I put my phone on airplane mode.

Dad works from home. He brings me cups of tea and small servings of finger food. He does not ask me how I am.

It's a hippo day, I realise at around eleven thirty. See, most days, I get up and put on a good imitation of Grace Turing: Coping Edition. But every now and then, you've just got lean into the wallowing, like a hippo. It's a really shitty hand I've been dealt. I'd definitely need therapy if I pretended I was fine all the time. I can't even curl into a ball because it hurts too much. So I lay on my bed and stare at the ceiling. I watch cartoons on my phone. I hibernate like a bear. I barely speak.

Mum's the one who tries to coax me out for dinner. She sits on the edge of my bed and sighs with a smile that doesn't hide how sad she is for me.

'Well, Grace, sucks to be you today, doesn't it?'

I look at her and I find myself almost laughing despite myself. 'It really does.'

'But it's not all sucky. Ivy says Daniel and Jenna were asking after you. They aren't thrilled they haven't heard from you,' she says, twisting her long hair and letting it sit over her right shoulder. She never ties it up unless she's exercising, and it's movie star hair, really. She got it from her mother, who I only remember dimly as a little, old Malaysian lady who didn't speak much English anymore and was constantly, simultaneously, cooking and doing laundry.

'Do you miss your mother?' I ask her.

She frowns. 'How did we go from talking about you and your friends to my mother?'

'Your hair,' I say. 'You said you got it from her.'

Mum runs her hands through it again. 'Less than I used to,' she admits. 'But still almost every day. I don't think you ever grow out of missing your parents. Especially when you become a parent yourself.'

'I don't think I'll be a mother,' I say.

'You never know,' Mum says, she reaches for my hand but hesitates. 'Touch sensitive?'

'Sorry,' I nod. She pulls back. 'But I'm pretty sure about the kid thing. Genetics, you know?'

'Did I do that bad of a job?' Mum asks. I can tell she's hurt even though she's covering it with teasing.

'Mum, I love you. But even if I don't pass this hot mess onto my kid, what happens if I'm in this much pain with a two-month-old baby wanting me? I just couldn't do it,' I reply.

Mum sighs heavily. 'You know, your father always says you're growing up too fast, but I don't always see it. I do now.'

'A boy asked me out and I turned him down yesterday,' I say, throwing her a bone. 'Drama ensued.'

Mum laughs, first in shock, and then delight. 'Was it Daniel?'

'No, it was Liam.'

'Who's Liam?'

'He's the token hot guy,' I reply.

'And he asked you out?'

'No need to sound so surprised.'

'Well, of course I think you're wonder –'

'I was surprised, too,' I say. 'Despite my "exotic features", I'm not exactly the class hottie over here.'

'But you're so funny and interesting,' Mum says, then catches herself. 'Oh. Yeah, I hear it. I'll shut up. Why did you say no?'

'Well, there's now a rumour I'm a lesbian.'

'Are you a lesbian? It's, I mean, if you are, that's totally fine …'

'Mum. Breathe.'

'Are you?' she asks, her eyes wide. I think that she probably won't care if I say I am. Well, she will care, but she'll be okay with it. It's kind of nice to see.

'I don't think so,' I say. 'But who knows? I haven't really thought about it.'

'Okay. So why did you say no?'

'Because it's not about what he looks like, is it? It's a personality thing. And I don't like his. Liam is … nice, I guess. But he'll never speak up if someone is being mean. That, and he didn't know who he was really asking out. I don't think he'd be okay with Sick Girl for a prom date,' I explain.

Mum wrinkles her nose. 'Yeah, don't date him. He sounds boring.'

I laugh and sit up a little. 'Right? No one else seems to get it.'

'That's because when you're sixteen and a cute guy asks you out, your problems are over,' Mum says. 'Or at least, that's what those movies say, right?'

'They're stupid. But then, so are most sixteen-year-olds.'

'I hear Daniel isn't stupid,' Mum says, faking disinterest while looking at her nails. Something she only ever does when she's trying to be casual.

I roll my eyes. 'He isn't stupid,' I agree.

'Ivy loves him.'

'Ivy loves everyone.'

'She likes him better than most,' Mum argues. 'She says he's funny and kind and he really cares about you.'

I open my mouth to argue, but I can't. Those things are all accurate.

'And your father likes him, and I was pretty sure he was never going to like anyone either of you dated,' Mum continues. 'Respectful and considerate, were his words.'

'I –'

'Don't do that thing where you make a decision based on hypothetical situations,' Mum tells me.

'I don't –'

'You do,' she says. 'You always have. You didn't do ballet in grade three because your friend Julia would have been jealous. You decide you aren't going to enjoy something, and then you don't. And you're so convinced that everyone is going to treat you like a leper that you are keeping your health a secret. I'm not saying I don't do the same thing sometimes, Grace. Or even that it's a bad thing.'

I stare at her because I honestly didn't think she paid that much attention to me. Not in a dramatic not-caring way. Just that Mum always had work, and Dad, and Ivy was easier than me. She loves me because I'm her daughter – that's what I thought. But it turns out, she loves me for me, too.

'I love you, Mum.'

'I love you, too. I really want to give you a hug, though.'

'Please don't.'

'Only if you agree to come out for dinner. Your father made lasagne.'

'Blessed be,' I say. 'I'll be out in a minute.'

Mum gives me one last smile before she goes.

...

I turn my phone off airplane mode and am assaulted be a series of message tones. Five from Jenna, and sixteen from Daniel. So much for not messaging me today, I think to myself with dry amusement.

Jenna 8:45 am

> What do you mean you aren't at school the day after LIAM GRANGER ASKS YOU OUT

8:50 am

> Just saw Ivy. Are you okay?

8:51 am

> Obviously you aren't okay. I'm bad at this.

11:15 am

> I know Ivy said we shouldn't message you, but it is kind of weird that you haven't even read these messages. Also: Daniel is driving me insane rn. Pls come and save me from him.

3:20 pm

> I'm low key worried. Message me back pls.

6:02 pm

> Air pressure = bad pain day. I'm fine and will see you tomorrow.

6:02 pm

> Also Daniel driving you insane is basically him breathing. No help can be offered.

Daniel 8:50 am

> Ivy says you don't want to hear from me today which is clearly a lie. Strange, because she seems so honest...

8:51 am

> Srsly tho, I hope you're okay

11:10 am

> Mr Simmons gave the most epic sigh when he saw you were absent.

11:11 am

> It was long suffering not relief.

11:15 am

> Turing, Jenna is talking about horticulture. I need weird facts

1:22 pm

> Elsa is asking about you again. I told her you were fighting ninjas. She smiled. Did you break her? Should we be concerned that she's been body snatched?

1:40 pm

> You're not even reading my messages? That's cold, Turing

3:12 pm

vOn the first bus to the farm. Send weird facts.

4:13 pm

> I'm now on the second bus Turing

4:15 pm

> My worry level is escalating because radio silence

4:28 pm

> So you're going to be pissed but I just messaged Ivy to make sure you hadn't died. She said you were having a hippo pain day? You're gonna have to explain that one to me later.

4:29 pm

> In 2010 a Norwegian skier said he didn't win Olympic gold because he, and I quote, 'saw too much porn in the last fourteen days'.

4:40 pm

> Tongue prints are identical like fingerprints

5:12 pm

> At farm. Kangaroos have three vaginas

5:21 pm

> Some sadist in 17C Germany invented a cat piano that was played by driving nails into their tails. (I miss you)

I stared at those last three words for longer than I'd like to admit. So long, in fact, that Dad is yelling for me to get my ass to the dinner table.

6:06 pm

<   Air pressure = bad pain day. Hippo day = day for wallowing in how depressing my body is.

6:06 pm

<   Thank you for my weird facts. Not thank you for messaging Ivy. But I wasn't answering, so I guess it's fair.

'Grace! Now!' Dad shouts.
   'One minute!' I yell back.

6:07 pm

<   Hitler was (ironically) nominated for a Nobel Peace Prize. Lobsters taste with their feet. Some scientists once turned a live cat into a telephone. (I missed you too)

7:19 pm

>   I am now on a weird cat fact spiral. Thanks for that. Will you be at school tomorrow?

7:27 pm

<   I think so and you're welcome.

7:30 pm

>   Isaac Newton invented the cat flap because his cat, which I shit you not was called Spithead, kept opening the door and the light ruined his experiments. Night Turing.

7:32 pm

<   I think you win the cat fact off. Tesla's cat gave him an electric shock that inspired him to investigate electricity. But the dude wanted to marry a pigeon. So. Who knows what really motivated him? Night Perkins.

...

In hindsight, convincing everyone that I should be allowed to do sport the day after a bad pain day with my knee in a brace was probably not a great idea. But it was kind of an impressive feat.

'If you blow your knee out again I am not carrying you to the office,' Daniel mutters.

'Seriously, Grace. WTF?' Jenna adds. 'It's *dodgeball*. They are literally throwing balls at your knees. Are you insane?!'

'Dodgeball is the only thing I like about PE,' I reply.

'Do you like pain now? Have you become a masochist now?' Daniel asks.

A ball comes toward us and we scatter, only to regroup in a different corner.

'It'll be fine,' I say. I look up to find Mr Holt glaring at me. 'We're using the foam balls.' Which Mr Holt had dragged out of the sports utility cupboard when he gave in about me playing. Seriously, why did he think a bunch of kids in grade eleven should be allowed to peg each other with basketballs?

'Move!' Ryan says, shoving Jenna slightly to get out of the way. The kid is freaky fast. If we were in an American teen movie, he'd be fast because of running away from bullies. But he lives in my neighbourhood, and I see him running past our house sometimes with this ridiculously large and furry dog. I think he likes the running.

Jenna takes a ball to her knee and she gives me a pointed glare to communicate that this is exactly her point.

'Grace, please. Pick a different hill to die on,' Daniel says. 'This is stupid.'

'You're stupid,' I say.

He grabs my arm and yanks me out of the path of an oncoming ball.

'Hands off policy, Perkins,' Mr Holt snaps.

'Sorry,' Daniel says, rolling his eyes.

'I'm fine,' I say. 'Be cool.'

Then a foam ball hits me on the head. I take a staggering step backwards and curse, more out of shock than anything.

'Mackenzie, you're out. Hit the bench. You know headshots aren't allowed,' Holt yells.

'Sorry, Mr Holt. It was an accident,' Kenzi says, smirking at me.

Jenna is ranting at Kenzi, and I fight back a smile. Jenna could barely speak in class eight weeks ago, and now she's giving Kenzi hell.

Caleb takes the opportunity to pelt the ball at my feet and I trip over myself trying to avoid it, but Liam catches me.

'I've got you,' he says. 'You okay?'

'Hands off policy,' Daniel mutters. But his eye clocks my knee.

I step away from Liam. 'I'm good,' I say. I give Daniel a pointed 'calm down' look.

Liam takes the ball and throws it at Caleb. It's the closest thing to him standing up for another person that I've seen. He catches Caleb on the foot.

'Dodgeball was invented in Africa two hundred years ago,' I say. 'They threw rocks instead of balls, though.'

'Hardcore,' Daniel says. 'Ben Stiller hit his wife in the face with a ball during the shooting of *Dodgeball*, and broke three cameras.'

I snort a laugh.

That's when a bunch of things happen set to a white noise soundtrack:

Amber gives Emmy a nod, then throws the ball near her.

Emmy pantomimes dodging and uses it an excuse to push me to the ground. Hard.

Daniel yanks Emmy off me.

Jenna runs forward calling my name.

I realise my knee has subluxed and that I'm bleeding.

Graham is getting between Daniel and Emmy.

I dry retch from the pain.

I'm dimly aware of Mr Holt yelling for someone to go the office. He's touching my knee to check it so I dry retch some more.

Daniel tells Jenna to go get Ivy and Mr Holt tells her not to go.

Mr Holt is talking to me but I can't hear him. I can't hear anything until Daniel takes my hands in his, forcing eye contact.

'Turing,' he says, his eyes searching mine. 'Out of ten?'

I close my eyes, taking another breath against the pain.

'Her ankle doesn't look good,' Mr Holt mutters.

'Turing, stay with me,' Daniel says. 'Out of ten, come on, you can do this.'

I open my eyes again. 'I don't feel so good. Hurts.'

'I know,' Daniel says. He touches my cheek.

'What's wrong with her?' Emmy asks.

'What's wrong with you?' Elsa accuses. 'You did that on purpose.'

'You're pathetic,' Jenna adds.

'Grace,' Daniel says, bringing me back to him. 'Out of ten. Ivy said dry retching was an eight or nine. Is it just the knee?'

I shake my head. 'Hurts,' I say.

'Shit,' Jenna says.

'Turing, talk to us, Mr Holt says.

'Nine,' I say.

'Hospital time?' Daniel asks.

'What is going on?' Emmy asks again.

'Shut up,' Elsa snaps. 'Go away and be a bitch somewhere else.'

'Elsa, language,' Mr Holt says.

'She's the one who hurt Grace!'

'And she'll be punished for that. But unless you want to join her in detention, you'll calm down,' Mr Holt says.

'Can't think,' I say.

'Everyone go away,' Daniel says to them. 'She needs some space.'

'I need to put my knee back in,' I say.

'I'm not sure that's a good idea,' Mr Holt says. 'I think your ankle isn't in good shape. It might be sprained.'

I take a hand and cover my eyes to try and hide that I'm crying. I dry retch again.

'Are you going to be sick?' Mr Holt asks.

'Maybe,' Daniel says.

'I don't know,' I say. 'It just hurts.'

'I've got you', Daniel promises.

'Grace!'

I look up to see Mrs Easton running over to me.

'Hi, Mrs Easton,' Daniel says.

'How bad is it?' she asks Daniel.

'She says a nine. Her knee is definitely out, the blood is from her hands. Mr Holt said she might have sprained her ankle,' he says. 'She's super pale, though.'

'Should we try getting her to the office?' Mrs Easton asks.

'I'm not ready to move,' I say. I reach out and catch Mrs Easton's hand. 'Please don't make me?'

'Okay, sweetheart,' Mrs Eason says. She opens the first aid kit beside her and pulls out a roll of gauze. 'We're going to test your ankle first, then your knee. You ready?'

I nod and she carefully removes the shoe from my foot and tests the range of motion. I vomit a little in my mouth but swallow it back down.

'Where's the pain coming from?' Mrs Easton asks.

'Knee,' I say. 'It's moving my knee.'

'Okay. I'm going to strap your ankle, and then we'll look at the knee.'

'I'll go call her father,' Mr Holt says.

'No!' I say.

'Grace Turing,' Mrs Easton says. 'Don't be so ridiculous.'

'He'll panic,' I say. 'And ... and he wrote me a note to stop me doing sport.'

'For fu – eff's sake,' Daniel snaps. 'I told you not to do sport.'

'Do you have any idea how dangerous this was?' Mr Holt asks.

'And I think someone who's not Mr Holt should call,' I say, eyeing him.

'Christ,' Holt curses. He cuts his eyes to Mrs Easton.

'She does bring that out in people', she says, and I think it's the first time I've ever seen Holt smile.

'I feel attacked,' I say, my voice dreamy and distant. 'Is my pain not enough punishment?'

'No,' everyone says in unison.

My pout is ruined by the dry retch as Mrs Easton repositions my foot to strap it better.

'School policy –' Mr Holt begins.

'That's a great idea,' Mrs Easton says. 'Justin, go distract the other students. I'll call her father.'

He does what she says, and I stare a little in awe.

'But he's so grumpy,' I whisper.

'He's going through a divorce,' Mrs Easton confides.

'Mrs Easton is the best,' Daniel tells Jenna.

'Right?' I hiss as she shifts my knee.

'You're sweet,' Mrs Easton says. 'But don't tell anyone.'

'So, what's the plan?' Daniel asks. 'Should someone get Ivy?'

'No,' I say. 'I'm fine.'

'We're calling an ambulance and her father,' Mrs Easton says.

'But –'

'Grace Turing,' Mrs Easton cuts over me. 'No. If you want to keep your secret, you will follow school policy.' She gives me a look that promises she'll out me to the school that my condition might be worse than they think.

'You win,' I sigh. 'But I'm putting my knee back in.'

'I'm going to throw up,' Jenna says.

'I wanna watch,' Daniel says.

'I'm not sure about this,' Mrs Easton says.

'Trust me,' I say. 'But … do you want to step away?' I ask Jenna. 'It's bad, there's going to be an audible pop.' I undo the velcro strapping on my brace.

'Na fam,' Jenna says and backs away. 'Thank you for the warning. Love you, Grace.'

I shake my head and smile.

'Pain's coming down, then?' Daniel asks.

'Yeah. I think the shock made it worse. On three,' I say and brace my hands on my knee. I know that I should stand because the gravity can help. But there's no way I'm putting weight on my ankle. My knee is red and swelling.

'Maybe I shouldn't put it back in,' I say. I prod the edges of the swelling tenderly.

'Call the ambulance,' Daniel says. 'We'll move her to the side.'

I look at him dubiously.

Daniel takes my hands in his again. 'Grace, have I ever led you astray?' he asks me. 'I've got you.'

'And you're not dating him,' Mrs Easton sighs, shaking her head. 'What a wasted opportunity.'

We laugh a little. A silly moment that lightens the bleakness of the situation. We're all scared of my pain, scared of moving me. Scared of how badly I might be hurt.

'Do you need a hand moving her?'

We all look up to see Liam standing over us.

'And you are?' Mrs Easton asks. She's probably the only female in the entire school who doesn't know Liam Granger on sight.

'Liam,' he says, offering her a charming smile.

Mrs Easton raises an eyebrow at me.

I shrug.

'I think we'll be fine,' Daniel says.

'Two guys are better than one, surely,' Liam replies.

Daniel opens his mouth to argue again.

'That would be great,' I say. 'Thank you.'

'I'll head back to the office to make those calls,' Mrs Easton says.

'Thanks,' I say.

'How are we doing this?' Liam asks, crouching down. He's asking me, not Daniel. I kind of want to knock their heads together.

'We're going to stand me on my left leg, and then I'm going to gracefully hop.'

'Turing, you're hilarious,' Daniel deadpans.

'I –,' I open my mouth to argue but I cut myself off. It hurts too much to play this game with him. 'Need you on my right side,' I tell him, and I hate the small, vulnerable voice that comes out of me.

'I've got it,' Liam says. He's already on my right.

'No,' I say. 'I need Daniel on my right.' I need the person I trust most in the world outside of Ivy and Dad to be on the side that hurts. I know he'll protect me. I know it like I know Ivy is part of my soul and that my father will always fight for me.

'I've got you,' Daniel promises. 'Liam?'

'I've got it,' he agrees, moving to my left.

They place their arms around me, under my arms, and pull me upwards. I balance on one leg for a moment and try to fight the urge to dry retch again.

'God, Grace,' Liam says. His fingers trace the torn skin from my wrist to elbow. I hadn't even noticed it was a wound, really. He looked over at Emmy and shook his head. 'That girl needs to be medicated.'

'She needs to be charged with assault,' Daniel counters.

'How about we just get me to the bleachers and go from there?' I ask.

...

The verdict: minor contusions, sprained ankle, dislocated knee. Full dislocation. It's my first real dislocation and I'm weirdly proud of it.

'This is exactly why you shouldn't keep this shit a secret,' Dad yells from the tablet Mum is holding. 'If she'd known you were fragile then she wouldn't have pushed you!'

'Brett,' Mum says, her voice soft, swivelling the screen to face her. 'We're still in the hospital. Do you think we could wait until we get home?'

Mum turns it back around and Dad is glaring at me, then at Ivy who is holding my hand beside me – they'd let her in with Mum, thank God, because I really didn't want to do this with just Mum. Which is rude because no one ever glares at Ivy. 'And where was that boy you like so much?'

'He tried to send Jenna for her,' I pipe up. 'But Mr Holt wouldn't let her. And what could Ivy do, anyway? There was first aid, an ambulance, and Daniel nearly got in the damn thing with me.' Mrs Easton had won that battle of the wills.

'You're high on painkillers,' Mum tells me. 'You don't get a vote.'

'Hey!'

'I'm sorry,' Ivy says.

I shoot daggers at Dad. 'Come here, little sister,' I say. 'I need a hug.'

She hesitates, but in the end she carefully climbs up onto the hospital bed and rests her head on my shoulder.

'This isn't over,' Dad says. 'And you need to stop undermining me.' That last part is directed at Mum before he disconnects.

'Drama llama,' I sigh.

'He's right, Grace,' Mum says. She's got her battle face on. 'If that girl had known how fragile you were –'

'Can we stop calling me fragile?' I ask. 'I'm not a creepy, porcelain doll in some weird, old woman's house.'

'You are fragile!' Mum says, throwing her hands up in the air. 'You got knocked over and dislocated your knee!'

'Could have happened to anyone,' I say, kind of glad the mask is muffling the full effect of this rant from me.

'And the sprained ankle?'

'Okay, I'll admit, the double whammy was probably a me thing.' Ivy gives me a slight squeeze.

I almost open my mouth to tell her that it was deliberate. Emmanuelle Delancey shoved me to the ground because Liam asked me out. Elsa had warned me, but I thought it was, as she said, dramatic. And it wouldn't be this dramatic if it wasn't me, right?

'How are we doing, Grace?' a doctor asks as he swans into our cubicle.

'Fine,' I say. I hate the way doctors use the royal we so much. 'Can I go home?'

'Not yet,' he says, almost smirking at me from behind his mask. 'We need to fit you for a splint and organise a referral to a physio.'

'I have a physio,' I reply.

'Oh, okay. Who are they? Can you tell the nurse?' he asks.

'We will,' Mum says. 'Is there anything we need to know before we take her home?'

'Ah, yes. I'm looking at Grace's blood work, and I'm a bit concerned,' he says. His eyes track to Ivy, still curled against me, then to Mum. 'Maybe you'd like to come with me for a chat?'

'No way in hell,' I say. 'It's my body, you can tell me. I'm sixteen, which means that legally you don't even need to inform my mother if I ask you not to.'

'Grace,' Mum hisses.

'Are there things you keep from your parents?' the doctor asks.

'Chance'd be a fine thing,' I mutter, then I clear my throat before continuing. 'No. We're a team. Team Grace's body is a shitstorm. If you're looking at my white cells they're always high, and my iron is always low.'

'No. The incident you described shouldn't have caused quite so much damage, and I noted you had some autoimmune markers, so we tested your ANA levels. They were rather high, which indicates that you might, well, you probably have mixed connective tissue disorder.'

We stare at him.

He looks sorry.

We are not reassured.

'What does that mean?' I ask. 'Because bodies are literally made of connective tissue.'

'We'll need to do some scans and ultrasounds, and potentially a biopsy, to see what tissue is affected by this, but your knee points to this conclusion.'

'Look, Dr ... whoever,' I say, waving my hand.

'Dr Maddox,' he supplies.

'Right. Can you please explain what it will mean for my day-to-day life?'

'Well, it is closely related to autoimmune diseases, and it usually doesn't shorten lifespans. We'll need to monitor you regularly, and you'll be on a low dose NSAIDs to start with. If it worsens, we'll need to consider corticosteroids or immunosuppressants.'

'NSAIDs?' Mum asks.

'Anti-inflammatories that don't have steroids,' he explains. 'We need to be careful about tolerances as Grace is quite young and she'll need to be on these medications long term.'

'Right,' I say. 'Are you going to discharge me, or am I staying here while you do the tests?'

'You're very ... calm,' Dr Maddox says carefully.

I shrug. 'It is what it is. It's kind of nice to have a diagnosis, to be honest. I've been sick for a few years now. It'll kill me or it won't.'

'Well, I'd prefer you to stay in as I'm not sure how widespread it is. If it's in your lung tissue or we have to put you straight on immunosuppressants, I'd prefer to do it under supervision,' he says.

I can feel Ivy tightening her grip on me, hiding her face with her hair. I can feel the gown getting damp from her tears.

'I'll be fine,' I whisper to her.

'And if we take her home?' Mum asks. 'Grace hates hospitals.'

'Don't we all?' the doctor says, amused. 'But it will take longer to do the scans and diagnostic process as an outpatient. It's up to you.'

I take a deep breath.

'Can I have a minute?' I ask.

'Of course. I'll be back in about half an hour,' he says, and then leaves.

'You need to call Dad back,' I tell Mum.

'You need to stay,' Mum replies.

'No, you need to call Dad,' I repeat. 'We're going to do this by family meeting.'

'Grace –'

'Please,' I say. 'I'm ... I need him here, too.'

'Fine,' Mum says, and ducks out of the room to make the call.

'Are you scared?' Ivy asks.

Her face is tilted up and I wipe away her tears. Where my crying face looks ugly, she is a pretty crier.

'A little,' I admit. 'But mostly about school.'

'Gray-ay,' Ivy complains, pouting.

'Things were weird when I left,' I say. 'I don't want it to become a thing.'

'Screw them,' Ivy says. 'That bitch knocked you down. Serves her right if she thinks you're in bad shape.'

I sigh.

'High school is a problem,' I say. 'It's awkward.'

'Screw high school. You're Grace goddamn Turing. And who gives a shit about those people? You've got Daniel and Jenna,' Ivy says. 'They already know everything and they're still Team Grace.'

'When did you get so smart, little sister?' I say, pushing some hair behind her ear.

'I had to be to keep up with you,' she replies, and rests her head on my shoulder again.

Dad is eating Skittles when we call him back, which is not a good sign. Skittles mean he's super grumpy. If it were red liquorice or M&M's it would mean there was some salvaging this.

'You're staying in hospital,' he says. 'No arguments.'

'See? I told you,' Ivy says.

'I just ... it's awkward,' I say. 'School and injuries ...'

'You have a dislocated knee and a sprained ankle. No kid is going to school the next day with that,' Mum points out.

The truth is, Ivy's already convinced me. But I don't have to like it.

Dad empties the rest of the Skittles into his mouth.

Mum gives me a meaningful look.

'I'll stay in hospital,' I say. 'But I have conditions.'

'Okay,' Mum says, already ready for negotiation.

'Someone brings me my pillow,' I begin.

'Done.'

'When I say that I'm done, I get to go home, even if the tests aren't finished.'

'Maybe,' Mum says. 'We need doctor approval.'

'You're staying,' Dad says.

'It's not summer camp or punishment,' I say. 'I hate hospitals, I hate feeling trapped, and I'm doing this because the diagnostic process is easier. If it drags out, though ...'

'We can negotiate,' Mum agrees.

'Samara! Did I not just tell you to stop undercutting me?'

'I'm sorry,' Mum says. 'You're right.'

'But I'll allow it,' he says. 'But in exchange, you are compliant when they do tests.'

'Okay,' I agree.

'I'm serious,' he says. 'No hyperventilating to get your heart rate up and freak the nurses out.'

'Fine,' I say, smiling a little. 'I'll behave.'

'And you do schoolwork,' he says.

I sigh. 'Ugh, fine. But I get to keep my secret at school.'

'No!' Dad almost shouts at me. 'No f-reaking way.' He lowers his voice a little, remembering where we are. 'Not knowing got you injured.'

There's more truth to that than he thinks. I'm definitely not telling him about Emmy the Bitch. 'And now we have a new diagnosis to investigate,' I counter.

'Grace, so help me –'

'Just until after camp,' I say. 'It's in four weeks, and it's only three nights. I won't even be limping by then, and all the teachers will know. After that, I'll rent ad space in the newspaper if you want me to.'

'You're not going to camp unless they know,' Dad says. 'And that, my dear child, is final.'

'Dad! Come on! Please! I just ... let me be normal for a bit longer,' I say.

'He's right,' Ivy says, softly. 'Especially if this connective tissue thing is going to be an issue.'

'Traitor,' I sigh. 'Look, I know it's not ideal. I get that I should tell people. But I like it at Riverview High. I have friends. I joke with people. They treat me like I belong. Well, like I'm mostly normal, at least. A boy asked me out! I want just a little more of that before … before I'm Sick Girl again.'

'A super popular boy asked her out,' Ivy adds. 'Even my grade was talking about it.'

Dad glares at me, then off camera, then at Mum.

'This is your fault,' he says.

'How is it my fault?' Mum demands. 'We both agreed to let –'

'No, you said we should and I couldn't be the bad guy!'

'Brett, she's sixteen.'

'Exactly! She's our child, Samara. We can't let her make all these decisions that aren't good ones.'

'So we should wrap her in bubble wrap?'

'That's an unfair comparison. She's sick, Sam. She's our little girl and she's sick and we're letting her go into places where she could get hurt.'

'You let Ivy do anything she asks!'

'That's different.'

'Yeah, because she's younger,' Mum argues. 'You can't keep treating them so differently. The only reason you get away with it is that Grace loves Ivy so much she doesn't care.'

Ivy flinches and tries to hide by melting into my side.

'This is an argument to have later,' I say. They both swivel to glare at me and I look meaningfully at Ivy. They both look instantly sorry. 'But I understand why you're concerned. I'm concerned, too. And maybe it's a conversation to have after we find out if I have this connective tissue whatever. But it's what I want. It's all I want. I keep giving in and pretending I don't care that I can't even catch the bus on my own. I just want to be sixteen for a bit longer. I want people to know me before they find out I'm sick. I want a chance. I will take whatever precautions you want, but, please, at least consider letting me wait until after camp to drop the proverbial bomb.'

There is a long pause that stretches out between us.

'Hi family,' Dr Maddox says, swanning in around the curtain without even asking if he could come in. 'Have we made a decision?'

'She's staying,' Dad says. He gives me a hard look. 'I'll be there in an hour or so with your pillow and stuff.'

'Snakes?' I ask. If he's really mad at me, he'll say no.

'Of course,' he says, a hint of a smile. He's disconnected before I can respond, but I know he's going to think about what I said. I know he's on my team.

'All good?' Dr Maddox asks.

'Yeah,' I say, smiling. 'It is. So, am I emergency rooming it?'

'We'll get you transferred to the kids' ward,' Dr Maddox says. 'There should be a bed available in a couple of hours.'

'Great,' I say. I remember Emily the Nurse, suddenly, and I'm a lot more positive about this whole staying in hospital plan.

'I'll get it organised,' the doctor says before disappearing again.

'Do you want us to stay?' Mum asks, checking her watch.

'Dad'll be here soon,' I say. 'I'll see you tomorrow?'

'Okay, sweetheart,' Mum says, and presses a kiss to my forehead. 'I love you, you know? And you call me if you need anything.'

'I know,' I say, smiling back.

'You know we only want what's best for you,' she adds.

'I know,' I say again. 'But I'm a teenager. I'm meant to argue.'

Ivy squeezes me tight.

'Ouch,' I tease her. 'I'll see you tomorrow, too, okay?'

'I love you, Gray,' she says.

'I love you, too, little sister.'

She climbs off the bed and pauses. 'And message Daniel,' she says.

I roll my eyes. 'I will.'

'Good.' She signs our handshake and I sign it back.

When they're gone, I sit on the bed in chilled silence. I'd ask for a warmed up blanket next time I saw a nurse. Those things are great. So cosy. I leaned over the side of the bed to reach for my phone in my bag. The splint wasn't on yet, and I wasn't keen to move too much. One grunt of pain and I managed it, falling back onto the bed with relief and heavy breaths like I'd run a marathon. Just as I finish achieving this feat, the physio arrives with the splint. It's hard to shut the irritation down – if I was patient for five more minutes, my life would have been much easier. Patience, apparently, is not a virtue I have in any kind of decent supply.

Knee splinted and warm blanket received, I finally check my phone. It had been two hours since the incident and I didn't think my phone ever had more unread messages than it does right now. I even have a couple of friend requests from people with attached messages hoping I'm okay and telling me what a bitch Emmy is. Liam wants to know if there's anything he can do. Elsa hopes I'm okay and made a joke about ninjas. Jenna alternates between furious and worried, and I kind of want to give her a hug and tell her it's okay. Daniel, though …

1:02 pm
> What's the verdict? Is your knee okay?
1:10 pm
> Turing, I need updates
1:15 pm
> Ivy said you've dislocated your knee and sprained your ankle. I'm going to kill that faux French bitch. Stop making me message your sister for updates
1:35 pm
> I've done some research and it turns out the best way to hide a body is to bury it below a decoy corpse. Which gives us two options: Option one, we dig a ten-foot hole, bury the bitch, then drop an animal carcass two feet above her. Option two, we bury her underneath a coffin in a fresh grave.
1:36 pm
> Obviously you can't do the manual labour but that's not a deal breaker
1:55 pm
> Can I visit you? Home or hospital?
2:02 pm
> We've talked about radio silence Turing. Tell me you're okay

2:02 pm
> Hearing it from Ivy is not the same as hearing it from you
3:10 pm
> Liam said you messaged him back. But you didn't, right? You wouldn't talk to him and not me.

I am suddenly struck with the desire to tell him that I love him. Not like boyfriend-girlfriend love; eros or romantic love. Platonic friend love, maybe even pragma, that enduring love of a long-term relationship. I feel an odd sense of belonging to him, or with him. I'm still smiling at my phone when the orderly arrives to transfer me up to the kids' ward. I quickly send a message to Dad and then I reply to Daniel.

4:06 pm
< You're my first message. The biggest problem with your plan is that these messages are motive.
4:09 pm
> My biggest problem is always you, Turing
4:11 pm
< Rude. But I'll be in hospital for a while it seems. They're going to run some tests to see if I have a connective tissue disorder or something
4:13 pm
> I'm still going to find a way to kill Emmy. Christ, you can't just be normal, can you, Turing? You're so extra.
4:15 pm
< I'm no basic bitch - that's for sure
4:17 pm
> Can I visit you?
4:20 pm
< Aren't you still staying with your uncle on the farm a million miles away?
4:21 pm
> I'm visiting ma rn
4:22 pm
< Come on up then

I find myself almost excited to see Daniel, but nothing tops the joy when Emily leans in through the open doorway and says:

'Did I not tell you not to come back?'

I struggle to keep a straight face as I sigh heavily. 'It's impossible to get good help these days.'

'How's my favourite medical marvel?' she asks, coming to sit on the end of my bed.

'Just super,' I reply sarcastically. 'I'm having an amazing week.'

Emily laughs and shakes her head. 'Connective tissue, huh?'

I shrug. 'Apparently we need it to stay in humanoid form, but who knows, right?'

'I'd be lying if I said I didn't miss you,' Emily says. 'Still got the wifi password?'

'Yep,' I reply, holding up my phone. 'You are a goddess.'

'I'll be sure to tell my girlfriend that tonight when I get home. I wonder if it will get me control of the remote.'

'That's a low bar. You should try for a better deal. You're a goddess, after all.'

'Any visitors we should expect tonight?' Emily asks as she checks her watch. 'We've only got about another hour before the ward closes but, obviously, special cases can be made. They're a bit looser on restrictions up here.'

'Dad should be here in about half an hour, and Daniel –'

'Speak, and I shall appear!' Daniel says, stepping into the room, sweeping his arms dramatically.

'Isn't that the devil, usually?' I ask.

Daniel shrugs nonchalantly. 'Whatever floats your boat, Turing.'

'Well, I'm going to go and start rounds,' Emily says, raising a suggestive eyebrow.

'How's your mother?' I say at the same time Daniel says, 'So, how are we killing Emmanuelle?'

I roll my eyes at him.

'Mum's okay. She's getting let out on Monday. There's not enough weekend support in Launceston,' Daniel says. He's not meeting my eyes and I can't even lean forward to catch his hand because of my stupid leg.

'I'm glad she's getting out. Do you think she's ready?' I ask.

'She's never ready,' Daniel says, huffing empty laughter. 'But she'll be okay. She's much calmer and she's making sense more. She's back on the meds.'

'What's it like?' I ask. 'I mean, is it like a psychotic break, or ...'

'It's hard to explain. When she's up, she's the most fun person ever. Everything is a party, and she doesn't sleep, and she can't finish a thought before getting to the next one. We stay up late talking shit and making plans I know we'll never carry out. When she's down, it's impossible. She doesn't get out of bed and I'm so scared all the time,' Daniel says to the wall. 'She keeps going off her meds because she says they take the edge of the world. She loves her highs and lows.'

'I can understand that.'

'She was up this time, and I couldn't get her to come down. Uncle Blake came and ... I feel like I betray her every time, you know?'

'Hey. It's not on you. Or her. It just is what it is and you do the best that you can,' I say, I reach for him anyway, my hand extended out into the space between us. The movement must catch his eye, because he turns to look at me and takes my hand. It's rough and calloused from farm work, and his dark skin looks darker and richer next to the slight yellow tan of my Asian skin. He doesn't say anything, just holds my hand.

'I'm Team Daniel,' I say, the hint of a smile on my lips. 'Always.'

'Thank you,' he says, and he says it with the kind of weight sixteen-year-olds aren't meant to speak.

And maybe that's the thing about Daniel that connects with me: we're not just sixteen. We're involved in things that are so big and foreign to most people. We've had to grow up faster. Him because of his mother, and me because of my health.

He opens his mouth to say something else, but we're interrupted by my father's arrival.

'Grace. Daniel,' Dad says, his eyes going back and forth between us with a deliberate slowness. Daniel drops my hand and sits back.

'Hi, Mr Turing,' Daniel says. 'Well, I should go ...'

'Please, call me Brett,' Dad says, amused. 'Feel free to stay. I'm just dropping off toiletries and dinner.'

'No, no,' Daniel says, backing away from the bed, giving Dad a wide berth. 'I was dropping by for a quick hello on my home. I think Uncle Blake is probably ready to go.'

I'm trying not to laugh at the scene before me. It's suddenly a lot more amusing now I know Daniel probably has a crush on me. Dad's clearly enjoying the freak out

'I'll talk to you later?' I ask. 'I don't think I'm getting day leave for school.'

'You're damn right you're not,' Dad says. 'Seriously, Grace, you don't have to make everything more difficult.'

'But she's Grace Turing,' Daniel mutters without thinking. 'She's always making things complicated.'

'Rude,' I say, but Dad laughs. Daniel looks mildly horrified.

'She wanted to leave hospital against medical advice,' Dad tells him. 'Who gets told they need tests and says can I go home now?'

'I still can't believe she did PE today,' Daniel replies. 'She's got a knee brace, a note, and pain, and she still wants to play dodgeball!'

'Dodgeball, Grace? Seriously?' Dad asks. He presses the heel of his hand to his forehead and closes his eyes. 'You're going to send me into an early grave. What the hell were you thinking?'

'Okay, how about we have the "bitch about Grace" session somewhere else?' I ask. 'My leg hurts.'

'Because you were reckless,' Dad says.

'It's not entirely her f –,' Daniel begins.

'Of course, it's my fault,' I say, cutting him off and giving him a look that I hope he interprets correctly as shut the eff up. 'I was reckless, and like Jenna said, why am I playing a game where they literally throw balls at my knees?'

'Right,' Daniel says, looking suspicious, but he doesn't argue or say it was Emmy's fault. I know we're definitely having that conversation later. But as long as it isn't in front of my father, I'm good with it.

'I'm glad you know you were an idiot, but I'd feel much better if I thought you'd make different choices next time,' Dad sighs. 'You're impossible sometimes.'

'She's mostly impossible, but that's why I like her,' Daniel agrees. Then he realises what he said and looks mortified. 'I have to go. Bye Grace, bye Grace's Dad.' He bolts from the room, and we look after him for a minute.

'You know,' Dad says. 'I was dubious as first, but I think I like that kid.'

'I'll be sure to pass that message on,' I say dryly.

'You have my permission to date him.'

'Because that doesn't suck the romance out of it,' I say, rolling my eyes. 'Surely you should be telling me not to date him given how contrary I am? Reverse psychology and all that.'

Dad laughs. 'How do you know I'm not already using reverse psychology to get you not to date him?'

'Because you like him,' I say. 'And you like that he's angry at me for getting hurt.'

'You're going to do what you're going to do, Grace. I can argue and beg and plead, but you're always going to do what you're going to do. And despite your foolishness today, I trust you,' Dad says. 'You're a smart kid. Just don't ever get pregnant so I don't have to think about you having sex.'

'Gross. Thanks for that,' I say, curling my lip.

'Mission accomplished,' Dad says. 'Here are your snakes and I got you teriyaki chicken from that Japanese place you like with the unpronounceable name.'

'Thanks, Dad. I am ... I am sorry about today. I know it's the kind of thing that makes you want me to tell everyone about my health. But it was a stupid mistake which I obviously regret.'

Dad sighs and shakes his head. 'I understand you wanting to keep the secret, too. You're a teenager and no one likes being different.'

'You're allowed to worry. But camp is only three nights and if I can seem normal for three nights, maybe it won't matter as much when they find out I've been sick all along.'

'It's risky, Grace. Look what happened twenty-five minutes from our front door today. I'm scared for you. Let me think about it. I promise not to make a decision without you,' he says. 'But remember how hard this is for me, too.'

I press my lips together. I know how hard it is for him, or at least, I can empathise. He's watching someone he loves hurt and can do nothing about it. *But think about how much worse it is for me*, I want to argue. Instead, I smile and thank him. He kisses my forehead before he leaves and tells me that he'll see me tomorrow around lunch time. I want to argue that he shouldn't take time off work, but I know that I'll need him. When the pain meds wear off and I'm left alone, I'm going to google connective tissue disorders and freak myself out. I think he knows that, too.

'Love you, Dad,' I say as he's walking out of the room.

He pauses in the doorway and looks over his shoulder. He smiles a soft, warm smile that people usually give Ivy. 'I love you more,' he tells me. 'Good night.'

'Night,' I call after him.

...

I spend the next half an hour wondering how well I'd cope without him.

Wondering how Daniel copes with his mother.

Wondering how I'll cope if Daniel actually asks me out.

How I'll cope if I have the connective tissue thing.

I think that the future is meant to be full of promise, and we're supposed to be scared by the vastness of possibilities. I'm scared because the more I find out about my body, the narrower my world becomes.

CHAPTER TWELVE
Waiting Game

The thing about being in hospital for tests is that it is boring AF. I don't have my books or assignments yet, so it's mostly me and my phone and being stuck in bed because my leg is immobilised and I'm not meant to move without assistance until physio clears me. Which is stupid because if they'd released me yesterday I'd probably be at school today. A normal person would definitely be fine. Hand me a pair of crutches and let me figure it out.

'Grace, what are you doing?' Nick the Nurse asks from the doorway. He's Scottish and constantly exasperated. I managed to get a couple of doors down on my crutches earlier and saw him with one of the cancer kids, and he was actually quite sweet. So maybe he's just exasperated with me because I do things like get out of bed when I'm not supposed to. Like right now.

'Going to the bathroom?' I say innocently. I channel my inner Ivy. I widen my eyes and smile sweetly. I teeter slightly as I balance on one leg.

They thought taking the crutches away would stop me … it probably should have.

'Uh-huh,' he says. 'Get back on the bed. I'll get you a wheelchair.'

'I'm almost there,' I argue. 'Look. It's like, three hops. I'll be in the bathroom by the time you get back with the wheelchair.'

'Do you have any idea how much paperwork it is when you fall on your arse?' he asks.

'Uh, a form?'

'No, Grace. It's five forms. Especially when your patient has connective tissue problems, is a falls risk, has two lower limb injuries, and is hopping to the bathroom instead of hitting the call button.'

'When you say it like that it sounds like I'm a bad patient.'

I think he takes a moment of prayer. His eyes are closed and his face is turned upwards. I'm not sure if he's praying for strength or if he's praying for me to get smited. Smote? Smitten? I've got to google that later. He crosses the room and stands in front of me, taking my weight using his arms under mine.

'I'm helping you to the toilet because if I don't, I'm pretty sure you'll go without me,' Nick says. 'Not because I'm condoning your behaviour. And you'll stay there until I get back with a wheelchair or I'll ...'

'You'll what?' I ask, teasing him a little.

He scowls for a minute, and then he grins. 'I'll make sure you get the orange jelly.'

'Gross! That's the worst jelly!'

'I know. The jelly hierarchy in this hospital is red, green, then orange. The last hospital I worked at had grape jelly. It was amazing.'

'I want grape jelly now,' I sighed, taking another hop.

'I think there's red jelly in the fridge. That's the best I can do,' Nick replies.

I wince and he sighs.

'I know,' I say.

'Right. So, next time?'

'I'll press the buzzer,' I sigh. 'I'm due for pain meds, too.'

Nick's eyes flick to the clock and the whiteboard with my next doses on it. He frowns. 'You were due for pain meds an hour ago. Why didn't you buzz me?'

'Yeah, well. Chronic pain. You kind of just live with it,' I reply. 'Unless you have acute pain that is inflamed by movement. Which is my bad.'

He gives me a look that I'm pretty familiar with. It's not straight up pity, it's more a kind of sadness that people in my situation exist in the world. It makes me uncomfortable and I look away. Fortunately, we're in the bathroom now, so he steps back to let me balance on my own.

'Do you need help?' he asks, eyes skimming over my knee splint.

'I've got this,' I say confidently. 'It's not amateur hour.'

'No, it's "cause yourself more pain than necessary" hour,' he replies as he leaves.

I shimmy my PJ pants down over my hips, letting them gather at my knee and go about my business. When I'm done, I hesitate and contemplate waiting for Nick to get back. I could just stand up, adjust my clothing, and then perch back on the toilet to obediently wait for my nurse chariot. Or, I could add in washing my hands. So I do, even though I know Nick is going to give me another look of exasperation and there is red jelly in the balance.

Hospital priorities.

Nick sighs as expected and he wheels me back to bed, which feels ridiculous because the room is the size of a shoebox.

'Did you know that the first wheelchair built for a specific person was built in 1595?' I ask him. 'It was called an "invalid's chair".'

'I did not,' he says, a little confused.

'The Bath wheelchair is considered the first mass-produced wheelchair, and that was in the late 1700s, which is a bit sad given how many paraplegics would have been in the world.'

'How do you know this?' he asks.

'I was bored earlier,' I reply. 'I googled it.'

'Huh,' he says.

I'm kind of disappointed by his reaction, because Daniel had also been meh about it. Which was rude because I'm clearly starved for attention.

'I also like weird trivia.'

'Right.' Nick looks like he's wondering if he needs to back away slowly.

'Can I have some pain relief, please?' I ask before he runs off and calls for a psych eval.

'Of course,' he says and offers me a smile before he leaves.

...

'Alright, Grace Turing, what's your birth date?' Nick asks, accompanied by a registered nurse who I think is named Katy. I'm pretty sure she was on shift last time I graced this place with my presence.

'Back again? You know we don't have a punch card for a free coffee,' Katy jokes.

'November third, 2005,' I reply. 'I don't drink coffee.'

Katy looks uncomfortable as I level an empty stare at her.

'Uh,' she begins.

I grin. 'Sorry, couldn't help it. How are you?'

Katy gives a nervous laugh and glances at Nick for help, who just shrugs.

'I'm okay. I'll see you later,' Katy says before leaving.

'You're a little odd, aren't you, Grace?' Nick asks.

'Aren't we all?' I say as I swallow my oxycodone with a glass of water.

'I suppose we are,' Nick says, and smiles. 'I like birds.'

'Okay,' I say. 'That sounds relatively normal.'

'No, I'm a twitcher,' he says.

'Like, a gamer who streams?'

'No, a twitcher is a birdwatcher who travels long distances to complete their life list. I actually came to Australia to work mostly so I could observe some native birds.'

I stare at Nick.

Nick stares back.

'You know, that's not the craziest thing I've heard this week,' I say.

Nick snorts a laugh, and catches himself. 'What's the craziest thing you've heard this week?'

I consider being honest, but I really don't think Liam asking me out is going to make this birdwatching weirdo feel any better. I mean, I like birds, but this guy is next level.

'The longest time between two twins being born is eighty-seven days,' I say. Daniel had told me that one and gone on a long rant about being in labour and the freaky, alienness of childbirth.

'Damn,' Nick says. 'That's ... that's a long time.'

'Can you imagine?' I ask.

'I really cannot. That's going to haunt me. I'm going to call my mother tonight and tell her to be grateful she wasn't in labour longer.'

'Are you a twin?'

'Yeah. My brother was born twenty-seven minutes earlier than me.'

'Huh. And you just up and moved to another country? Sans twin?'

'Sean and I aren't very close,' Nick says. 'Everyone always asks if we're telepathic because we're identical. But he's a rugby player. We have almost nothing in common.'

'I can't imagine living in a different house from my sister, let alone a different country. She's kind of what keeps me going, you know?' I say. I try to picture it. Ivy, far away, in another time zone. There's an odd sense of panic as I realise that this could be my reality in five years when she goes to university. She's going to have a life far away from me, and I'm going to be stuck in limbo. I can't hold her back, but I also want to hold her back.

'I speak to my mother every day,' Nick says, as if he can soothe the crazy spiral my brain has begun. 'She's my best friend. Which I suppose is kind of a cliche for gay dudes everywhere, but it is what it is. She hit menopause and got sassy. It's great.'

I laugh a little for him, but my heart's not in it.

'The thing about life is, you usually end up okay,' he adds.

'I'm a sixteen-year-old girl with multiple chronic health issues that will probably shorten my lifespan and limit my career options. And I haven't eaten in ten hours because scans,' I say. 'I don't get hangry, I get hungry-sad. Hu-sad. But sure, it'll all end up okay.'

'I've changed my mind. You're not weird, you're kind of hardcore,' Nick says. 'And very smart.'

'Does this mean I get the red jelly?' I ask hopefully.

'After blood test and scan,' Nick promises.

'Ughhhh, how much longer?'

'In theory, forty minutes. In reality, however, it could be at least an hour.'

'Alright, leave me to my despair,' I sigh dramatically.

He laughs, and this time, I think it's genuine. I wonder if he'll tell his mother about me. I wonder if I'm becoming an anecdote he'll tell at parties. It's kind of a morbid thought, I suppose.

'Emily said you were a trick,' Nick says. 'I thought she meant you were trouble.'

'Oh, I'm definitely trouble. Ask literally anyone,' I grin.

'Yeah, but you're the fun kind of trouble. Except when you're trying to make me do paperwork. Which is my least favourite part of being a nurse,' Nick says.

'I promise to call you if I need to use the bathroom,' I say. It seems like a fair promise. I have been kind of difficult if I view my behaviour from his point of view. He leaves and I go back to staring at my phone and waiting for lunch so someone will message me.

It's a glamorous life.

...

Much to my surprise, when my phone rings at lunch time, post-scan, it's Daniel. I barely have time to get my apprehensive 'hello' out before he starts his rant.

'Turing, settle a disagreement for us. Jenna said you decided to say you were at an archaeological dig this time, Elsa wants to play up the ninjas again, and I think we should say you're actually a robot from the future and you're getting a firmware update.'

'Ninja zombies,' I hear Elsa call out.

'Curse of the Pharaohs, though,' Jenna tries. 'There are eleven deaths attributed to the first ten years after opening King Tut's tomb.'

'I do like the mummies,' I say. 'Which kind of zombies?'

'Turing! You're meant to be on my side. I'm your favourite, right?'

'Favouritism has nothing to do with good myth construction,' I reply, trying not to laugh at the whine in his voice.

'I told you she wouldn't go for the robot thing,' I hear Ivy say. 'She literally calls her body "the meat sack".'

'Ivy! Stop hanging out with Daniel, he's a bad influence.'

'He's not! He's funny,' Ivy says. 'And –'

'No ands!' I say, perhaps a little too quickly. 'Why aren't you with Lydia and Mei?'

There's a pause.

'Oh my god, the love triangle,' I say without thinking, and Jenna and Elsa's laughter proves me right.

'Gra-ay!' Ivy complains. 'It's not my fault!'

'I'm sorry,' I say, and I am. I hadn't meant to say it out loud. 'It's the drugs. My filter isn't functioning.'

'Your filter is never functioning,' Jenna teases. 'That's why we like you.'

'Are we lynching Nathan what's-his-face?' I ask.

'No! It's just ... awkward,' Ivy says. 'I'll see you tonight.'

I can't give her a hug and I can't smack Mei upside the head. 'Jenna? Can you do big sister duty for me?'

'I'll do my best,' Jenna promises. 'Ives, wait up! Let's chat.'

'Does this mean curses are out?' Elsa asks. 'I've been really excited for ninja zombies.'

'You're on making sure Daniel doesn't actually kill Emmy duty,' I say. 'So, sure. Ninja zombies it is.'

'Yes!' Elsa hisses. 'You owe me a Snickers.'

'Whatever,' Daniel says. 'I feel betrayed, Turing. And if you think I'm not still plotting her death, you're wrong. I may also add Nathan to my shit list.'

'I'm kind of on team killing-the-bitch, to be honest,' Elsa says. 'I mean, I'm clearly not part of the gang or anything, but pushing someone over because the guy you have a crush on likes them is some bullshit.'

'You have a dislocated knee and a sprained ankle, you can't ask me to just be okay with it,' Daniel adds.

There's something in his voice that makes my chest a little tight.

'It's my fault as much as hers. I shouldn't have been playing sport at all,' I say. 'And I'm fine. If I'm fine, you should be fine.' I can vaguely hear someone calling Elsa's name; I'm pretty sure it's Caleb.

'It's cute that you think it works that way,' Elsa says. 'Talk to you soon, okay?'

'Bye, Elsa,' I say. 'Daniel, I really am okay. You can take a chill pill.'

I hear a shuffling noise I assume means I'm being taken off loudspeaker.

'Grace, just stop it, okay? Have they done any tests yet?' he asks.

I sigh. 'Yeah, I'm going to need a transfusion if they take any-more blood. I had the lung CT earlier, too. There's still a couple more tests. I'm living in hope I get to go home tomorrow, but Nick says it's unlikely.'

'Who's Nick?'

'My nurse. Well, he was my nurse. He just got off shift. Did you know that serious bird watchers call themselves "twitchers"?'

'That doesn't sound like a group of drug addicts at all,' he replies. I feel the smile in his voice. I find myself laying back on my bed, getting comfortable.

'Right? He's a twin, too.'

'Did you tell him the thing about the labour?'

'Yep. He said he was going to tell his mother to be grateful it was only a twenty-seven-minute gap.'

'Still longer than the standard seventeen,' Daniel says.

There's a long pause, but it isn't uncomfortable.

'Tell me about Ivy's love triangle,' he says.

'It's pretty standard. Mei likes Nathan, Nathan likes Ivy, Ivy refuses to like the same guy her friend does but her friend is still jealous.'

'Look at the Turing sisters, breaking hearts,' he teases. 'Y'all should have come with a warning. You'll get a reputation.'

'The only reputation I have is that I'm a weird lesbian. And if anyone says a bad word about Ivy, they'll die under mysterious circumstances.'

Daniel barks out a laugh. 'Are you a lesbian?' His voice is a little too casual.

'Why does everyone ask that? I don't know what I am. I haven't really thought about it,' I say.

'You don't have to think about it, surely. You just … know,' Daniel says. 'Well, that's how it works for guys. You just kind of wake up one morning with a stiffy and figure it out based on whatever you were dreaming about.'

'Maybe,' I say. 'I don't know. I think when I was meant to start thinking about it my meat sack started failing. So I didn't really notice, I was too focussed on just making it through the day.'

'But surely you have an inkling,' Daniel says. 'Like, what about famous people? Would you rather see Chris Hemsworth or Scarlett Johansson topless?'

I snort a laugh. 'Aesthetically? It's a tough call.'

'Who do you want to see topless, then?'

I think about it. I open my mouth to say 'you', but I catch myself. I don't know if I'm teasing him or if I mean it. I think about his brown skin contrasted against the green grass of the oval. I think about the line of his jaw and the spread of his smile. I know I want to draw him, but is that all it is?

'Jesus, Grace, don't break something thinking about it,' Daniel jokes.

'Shut up.'

'Make me.'

'There used to be vomitoriums off the main dining halls in Ancient Rome so they could keep the party going.'

'That is disgusting. And an eating disorder.'

'No, my friend, that's culture.'

'Hey Grace,' Dad says from the doorway, startling me.

'Hey Dad.'

'I'll go,' Daniel says. 'I'm not sure if I'm visiting Ma tonight or not. If I do, I'll come up and say hi.'

'Okay. Talk to you later.'

'Who was that?' Dad asks when I hang up the phone.

'Daniel. Well, it was Daniel, Jenna, and Elsa to start with,' I say. 'They wanted to know what excuse they should give people who ask how I am.'

'What did you decide?' he asks, and I grin.

'I'm fighting ninja zombies. We nearly went with the curse of a pharaoh, and Daniel was lobbying for I'm a robot from the future.'

There's a pause before he laughs. 'Seriously?'

'Seriously. Daniel started it last time I was in hospital,' I say. 'Everyone kept asking him where I was and he couldn't tell the truth, so.'

'He's a good friend,' Dad says. 'Can you eat yet?'

'Yes, is there food?' I ask, leaning forward.

He hands me a plastic container that's still warm.

'Lasagne!' I exclaim. 'Dad of the Year.'

'I think the bar might be a bit low if all it takes is lasagne.'

That's when I click. 'This is a bribe,' I say.

'It is.'

'What am I being bribed for?'

'It's about camp,' Dad sighs.

I put the lid back on the container and push it away from me. I try not to make it really obvious that I have to swallow a mouthful of saliva.

'Your mother seems to think that you should be allowed to make your own mistakes. But we're both concerned about how much can go wrong. There is an option for one of us to go along as a parent chaperone,' he says.

'Please, God, no,' I say.

'I thought you'd say that. What happened to Dad of the Year?'

'It's camp! No one wants to be that one kid whose parents come along. It's embarrassing, even if they are as amazing as you.'

'Noted. However, we can't just send you off without backup, Grace.'

'Well, we can make sure I share a cabin with Jenna and Elsa,' I say. 'Daniel knows, too. Mrs Easton could be considered as a chaperone, and the teachers are aware of the disaster that is my body.'

'They aren't fully aware, though, are they? And I've already received a rather unpleasant phone call from Justin Holt.'

'He's generally unpleasant.'

'He made some very valid points,' Dad counters. 'A simple dodgeball accident has you in hospital! God forbid you dislocate your knee on a bushwalk!'

'I get it, okay? You don't trust me, or them, or anyone. Sending your invalid child off into the bush is justifiably concerning,' I snap. 'But you keep saying I should be allowed to be sixteen and then taking away everything that sixteen-year-olds do!'

'Grace!'

'What?'

'We're going to let you go to camp,' Dad says looking petulant like a teenager. 'If the school okays it. There will be conditions, though. Some of them are non-negotiable.'

I stare at him in shock. 'What?'

'You can go to camp. I can't promise you'll be able to keep your health a secret while you're away, but we'll negotiate,' Dad says. 'Though I'm getting a little sick of everyone ignoring my opinions.'

I awkwardly throw my arms around him and try not to wince as I shift my leg in the process. 'I love you, Dad. I'm sorry I'm so difficult.'

'It's not your fault, Gracie,' Dad says, stroking my hair.

'It's a little bit my fault.'

'Well, it's not your fault that you're sick. It's just shitty,' Dad sighs. 'You're amazing for not letting it keep you down. I don't agree with how you're coping, but I can't deny that it's working.' He leans out of the embrace to look at me. 'I'm so proud of you.'

I feel the hint of a blush threatening so I reach for the lasagne. 'I accept the lasagne bribe.'

'I had a feeling you might.'

...

Jenna visits me in the afternoon with a shopping bag full of homework. She'd been allowed to visit because Mum wasn't coming tonight, and I needed that homework.

'I should charge a delivery fee,' she says. 'That was frickin' heavy. Daniel says he had to go home but he'll visit tomorrow.'

'Thank you. I'll be sure to leave a good Yelp review,' I tease. 'Tell me about Ivy.'

'Hi, Jenna, how are you? Oh, I'm great, thanks, Grace.'

'Hi, Jenna, how are you?' I parrot obediently.

Jenna rolls her eyes. 'Like you care. Ivy's okay. It'll blow over in a week, you know how it is with kids that age. Her friend likes a guy and the guy likes Ivy and now the friend is upset because clearly Ivy cast a spell on the dude.'

'I do actually care about you,' I say even as I slump with relief a little that it's nothing. 'It's just Ivy.'

'Yeah, yeah, I know. In the land of Grace, it goes Ivy, then literally everyone else on the same level.'

'Actually, it goes Ivy, you and Daniel, literally everyone else. Well, Emmy, Holt, and Mr Simmons might be a step down,' I reason. 'So, how are you?'

'I'm okay. Mum is riding me about building positive friendships. Graham and Caleb were dickheads and pissed me off in French. Daniel is irritating the shit out of me because he misses you,' Jenna sighs.

'Daniel always irritates you. It hasn't got anything to do with me.'

'Grace, you're not that stupid,' Jenna says, an odd edge to her voice.

'You and Daniel,' I say, trying to choose my words carefully. 'Sometimes it kind of seems like you might –'

'Imma stop you there,' Jenna says, cutting me off. 'He's a friend but I'm never going to think about him like that. I thought I might, but … nope. Besides, he's so clearly into you it would be stupid to like him.'

I chew the inside of my lip. 'I started to wonder about that lately. I thought it was just Daniel being Daniel, but … I don't know.'

'Well, I do. What did you say to him at lunch? He was acting weird in comp sci.'

'I don't know,' I say, but I think I might. It must be transparent because Jenna just raises her eyebrows at me.

'Uh-huh. You do understand the point of being friends with a girl is to talk through your emotional process,' Jenna says.

'You sound like your mother,' I say, attempting deflection.

'You haven't met my mother,' she counters. 'But I know what you mean. And you know what I mean.'

'I do. We just had a weird moment about sexual preferences,' I admit. 'I never know what to say. I feel like everyone has figured themselves out except me.'

'Well, what's there to figure out? You just like who you like,' Jenna shrugs. 'I mean, maybe it's simpler for other people than it is for you, but there's not a rule that says you have to pick a label and wear it for the rest of your life. Mum's always crapping on about how sexuality is a spectrum and it's okay to be not just different, but also unique. It's like the fact I'm bi makes her weirdly proud.'

'I'm sick,' I say.

'I know.'

'No, I mean, I'm really sick. I'm going to spend the rest of my life sick. Dodging illness, waiting for the next cascade failure that puts me in hospital. It's not as easy as boy likes girl. I can't … I'm not easy. Dating me would be exhausting and complicated and –'

'Grace, we're teenagers. Dating's always going to be exhausting and complicated,' Jenna argues. 'And Daniel knows the score.'

'But –'

'The thing you need to figure out is not how to save him from you. It's if you want to take a chance on him. I mean, Daniel's actually a surprisingly good guy,' Jenna says. 'I was wrong about him.'

'Can we talk about something else?' I ask. 'I just feel a bit … lost.'

'Sure. Can I ask about your health?'

I groan. 'I guess. What do you want to know?'

'So, you're being kept for tests, right? But you're okay? You don't need knee surgery, or whatever?' Jenna asks.

I'm strangely proud of how casual she is. The last time she'd visited me in hospital, she'd barely spoken.

'Yeah, the doctor in DEM was curious about my knee dislocation given my history so he ran bloods for the antibody that can show my connective tissue might be weak,' I explain.

'DEM?'

'Department of Emergency Medicine,' I say.

'I thought it was the ER or A and E,' Jenna said.

'That's TV for you,' I say.

'What exactly is connective tissue? I feel like it's going to be something essential and your medical marvel level is increasing,' she says, half teasing. 'Should we invest in duct tape?'

'Maybe, lol. Muscles and some organs are connective tissue, bones and marrow, the shit that holds you together, basically. And your uterus is entirely connective tissue. They're trying to figure out if it is localised, or if it's in my organs. Lungs are the real worry,' I explain. 'But my chances of carrying a child to term are not as great as they were, and a second child less so.'

'Oh,' Jenna says. She looks so sad. 'How do you feel about that?'

'Honestly? I'm a bit apathetic. I mean, I get the whole desire to procreate thing, but it's never been on my bucket list. I kind of figured I'd be forever alone with the whole sick thing, anyway,' I say with a shrug. 'I think my father is more disappointed than I am. He wants grandkids.'

'Heir and a spare,' Jenna laughs.

'He also keeps ramping up his attempts to make me come out of the closet health-wise, so to speak.'

'I get that I'm your friend, and I'm clearly Team Grace, but I think he's right,' Jenna says.

I stare at her, surprised. 'You do remember how you reacted, right? And you kind of liked me as a person already,' I say.

'Yeah, but you're not doing anyone any favours by keeping it a secret. Look how upset Elsa was when she thought you were just being a bitch and blowing her off? I get that she doesn't know everything, but she's so on your team. Emmy wouldn't have done what she did,' Jenna reasons. 'I mean, she's still a bitch, obviously, but you probably wouldn't be in hospital right now.'

'But if she didn't push me over, we wouldn't have discovered the connective tissue thing,' I argue. I know it's a weak argument, but it's part of the speech I've been rehearsing for Dad if he ever found out.

'Which is great, but you still have a dislocated knee and sprained ankle,' Jenna points out. 'Wouldn't you rather not be in more pain and be able to, you know, walk?'

'It's not the point, Jenna. I just want to be normal,' I sigh.

'Grace, I love you, but there is nothing normal about you.'

'Hey!'

'I'm serious. It's a compliment.'

'Is it, though?'

'Yes,' Jenna laughs. 'You have the weird trivia thing, you get passionate about random things and you, like, light up. You make me see people differently, not just art, but real people. You're just so ... you know, *you*.'

I'm speechless and trying not to smile or blush.

'See, you can't even argue,' Jenna says. 'Which means I'm right. Because you'd argue that a brick wall was horizontal if you looked at it differently.'

'That's a weird analogy.'

'Because you're super weird.'

'You're weird, too. And you really need to stop playing chess. You're, like, really bad at it. The worst,' I say.

Jenna laughs and shakes her head. 'Grace, people suck. Teenagers suck. But you've got friends, real ones, who are going to stick by you. I'm not saying I don't understand why you wanted to keep it a secret when you came to Launceston, because I do.'

'It defines me when people know,' I say.

'It might have when we met you,' she agrees. 'But you've gotta trust us, too.'

'I'm scared.'

The words sit between us, taking up space in the silence. She reaches out and takes my hand.

'You're the bravest person I know, Grace Turing.'

I chew the inside of my lip.

'You can only be brave when you're smart enough to know there's something to be scared of,' she adds. 'And you're not alone.'

'I'm not ready yet,' I say. 'I know it's coming, though. I want to try to wait until after camp. If I can pull off being Grace: Real Girl for four days, maybe it'll be easier to accept that I'm different.'

Jenna sighs and lets go of my hand.

'I just don't want to be Sick Girl.'

'Grace, the fact you're sick is one of the least interesting things about you.'

'Excuse you, I'm a medical marvel. They'll write papers on me.'

'And you're still not just Sick Girl. You're Grace goddamned Turing. You take no shit and you always stand up for what you believe in,' Jenna says, like somehow she's making me a promise. I'm not sure what that promise is, but I don't think that matters because I know what she means.

'I'm really glad I met you,' I say. 'You're awesome.'

'Shut up.'

'I'm serious!'

'Yeah, well, I'm uncomfortable with compliments. I'm working on my self-esteem and acceptance.'

I raise my eyebrows.

'Shut up.'

'I didn't say anything!'

'You didn't say anything very loudly and eloquently.'

'You must be hearing things. Have you watched *Sex Education* yet?'

'Oh my god, that show is a documentary,' Jenna exclaims. 'I don't know if I should make Mum watch it or not.'

I laugh and she grins.

I think that I should probably apologise to my mother about being such a bitch when I found out we were moving. Turns out, Launceston is full of amazing people and coming here was the best thing that ever happened to me. Well, second best thing.

Nothing's better than getting Ivy as a sister.

CHAPTER THIRTEEN
Glue

When the results come back on hospital day three, the doctor wants to know if I want to wait for my parents to be here. He checks his watch when he says it. I'm sure he's got good intentions of coming back or making a phone call. But he's a doctor in a public hospital and everyone who has even been in hospital knows that he's going to be shit at the follow through.

'It's okay,' I say. 'I know the drill. Do you mind if I record the conversation on my phone?'

'That's a very clever strategy,' the doctor says, like I invented recording devices. I'm tired because no one sleeps in hospital, hungry because the food is bullshit, and sick of lugging my stupid leg around. So instead of politely nodding, I glare at him for being a condescending prick.

'Who's my nurse?' I ask.

He looks confused.

'I'd like my nurse to sit in,' I say. 'In case I have questions later.'

'Oh, of course. Let me check.'

I text Dad to let him know what's happening. He makes me promise to record it and get the doctor's phone number. He knows the drill, too. I can almost feel his anxiety through the phone and his desire to be here.

The doctor comes back with Lee-Ann the Worst Nurse. She's the nurse who made me wait to use the bathroom for fifteen minutes because she was having a conversation in the hallway. I could literally see her and heard snippets of words like 'beach' and 'weekend'.

'Not to be rude,' I say, 'but are Nick or Emily around?'

'Emily isn't your nurse,' Lee-Ann says. 'I am.'

'Oh, I know. I just trust Emily a lot. I'd feel more comfortable, especially if it's bad news. Is it bad news?' I ask, faking a smile.

'I'll go see if Emily is available,' the doctor says.

Lee-Ann scowls at me as my stomach twists. It's not going to be good news.

'I'm disappointed that you don't trust me,' Lee-Ann says. She reminds me of a high school cafeteria lady from an American TV show. She's tall, broad, and has a bad case of resting bitch face. In her case, she's actually a bit of a bitch, so I feel like the face suits her. I also don't think I've seen anyone so bad at applying lipstick wear it in public.

'There is a way we do things at the hospital to ensure that all patients receive the best possible care. Part of that is making sure nurses only see their assigned patients,' Lee-Ann says.

She sniffs imperiously.

She scowls.

She looks down her nose at me.

'I don't think it is fair for you to receive special treatment.'

'It's hardly special treatment,' Emily says, coming into the room. 'And all patients have the right to request reasonable allowances. I hardly think me being here for fifteen minutes is going to throw the entire ward into chaos. But if you're worried, feel free to check in on bed six – she's been a little grizzly this morning since her booster shot.'

I silently cheer for Emily.

Lee-Ann scowls and storms out.

'I'm sure she's a good nurse, but she's not a very nice person,' I whisper.

Emily laughs. 'You sure you want to do this without your Dad?'

'Yes. Hospital doctors. You take 'em when you can get 'em.'

'That's true.'

The doctor arrives and gives a satisfied nod at Emily before closing the door behind him.

'You've met Dr Maddox before, haven't you?' Emily clarifies.

I'm grateful because I knew I'd seen him, but I couldn't remember his name. 'Yes, last time I was here.'

He waits until I hit the record button on my phone to start talking.

'Right, so we've got the results of all the tests and you do have mixed connective tissue disorder. The good news is that it doesn't appear to be in your organs right now; we think it's localised to muscle weakness, particularly around your knee joints,' Dr Maddox begins. 'However, the numbers are high enough for concern.'

'So, it's okay now, but it's almost definitely going to spread,' I say slowly.

He nods. 'We'll be doing yearly echocardiograms and pulmonary function testing.'

'Pulmonary what?'

'Lung function,' he explains. 'We'll use spirometry to measure the flow of air, muscle strength, and the volume of your lungs. It's pretty simple, painless testing.'

'Okay. So you think there's a good chance it's going to spread to my heart and lungs.' I feel like my body is a puppet I'm controlling from a distance.

'It can happen, but it might not,' Dr Maddox says, clearly trying to pick his words carefully.

'Is it going to kill me?' I ask.

There's a pause.

'No,' Dr Maddox says, finally. 'It can complicate acute and pre-existing conditions, though.'

'Meaning?'

'Meaning that if you get pneumonia, for instance, it's a bit more dangerous than it would be for the average person,' Emily explains.

I raise my eyebrows.

'More complicated than it would be for you before,' she adds with a smile of acknowledgement.

'And my risk of dislocating things is obviously higher,' I say.

'It also increases the risk of fractures and breaks,' Dr Maddox says. 'And osteoporosis becomes a concern. Which is why we'll treat you with supplemental vitamin D and calcium shots, and start you on bisphosphonates for prevention.

'The other risk we'll be watching out for is atherosclerosis, which is where fatty deposits start blocking or narrowing arteries. We'll obviously scan using electrocardiography, but there are some lifestyle factors we're going to need to get on top of, like diet and your cholesterol levels. And you'll need to kick that cigarette habit.'

It's a joke he's trying to make, and he's smiling at me in apology. Emily touches my shoulder.

'Damn, I was working myself up to a pack a day,' I say with half a smile.

'Do you have any questions?' he asks.

There is so much new information in my head that I can't think. I've latched on to the stupidest things, like how osteoporosis is for old ladies, and vitamin D shots, and how Mum's cholesterol is always too high.

'Can you please give me your contact information in case I have questions, or my parents do?' I ask.

'Of course,' he says, and starts digging out a business card.

Emily squeezes my shoulder. 'You did great,' she whispers.

'Are there things I can't do?' I ask as he places the card on my table.

He sighs for me. 'Well, skydiving is out, obviously. So is scuba diving because of the pressure. I'd advise against full contact sports, but definitely look into braces for your joints if you're going to play sport. Especially your knees and there's a note in your file about some left wrist weakness that you should watch out for. Is there something in particular that you're thinking of?

'There's a school camp in just over a month in the bush. I want to go, but I know that my parents are a little worried about it,' I say, nervous. 'It kind of sounded like it might be okay?'

'I don't see any reason why you can't go, but you will need to take some sensible precautions. Obviously there will be first aid-qualified teachers there, but make sure you have braces and medication in case of emergencies, as well as a clear plan if something does go wrong. We don't have to wrap you up in cotton wool, but you do need to be aware of the risks, and so do your carers,' Dr Maddox says thoughtfully.

I take a deep breath and let it out slowly. Cautious relief. 'Thank you.'

He smiles at me again, and this time the sadness is unmistakable. He doesn't want to spend his day telling kids that they have problems. He knows that he's just told me something that will impact the rest of my life.

I'm genuinely sad for him.

'Call or email if you have any questions,' he says. 'You're a brave kid.'

Bravery is when you're smart enough to know it's scary.

'I'm lucky,' I reply.

'Lucky?' he asks, surprised.

Emily is surprised, too, I can feel her physically pulling away to look at me.

'Yeah. I mean, I got dealt the shittiest hand medically speaking; my body is a piece of crap. But I've got good people. I'm not alone, you know?' I feel like I'm not explaining it well and I'm kind of embarrassed. I'm pretty sure that what I just said could be used on one of those disability-fetishised inspiration porn memes.

'You can't say she doesn't have her priorities right,' Emily says, grinning.

I smile up at her.

'I really can't,' Dr Maddox agrees before heading out of the room.

'Are you really okay?' Emily asks as I turn the recording off.

'I am,' I say. 'It'll sink in later and I'll be less okay. The bigger problem is why you've decided to hate me and look after other people.' It's stupid deflection because I'm not ready to think about how my life keeps looking shorter and shittier.

'Hey, I asked for you,' she says. 'But I've got mad skills with blood tests in small kids, so I'm needed at the other end of the ward.'

'Fine,' I sigh dramatically. 'I'll just hang out with Lee-Ann. Should I bribe her?'

'With what?' Emily asks.

'I've won Nick over with weird bird facts,' I say. 'He didn't like me much at first.'

Emily laughs. 'Unless you've got homemade cookies, I think you're just going to have to be nice to Lee-Ann.'

'Ugh,' I complain and wrinkle my nose. 'Thank you for coming, though. I know I'm not your patient today and you didn't have to.'

'Hey, any time,' Emily says. 'I'm glad you felt like you could ask for me. Makes me feel like I'm a pretty good nurse.'

'You're a great nurse. You're Emily, Goddess of wifi, nurse of children,' I intone.

'The good news for you is that now the tests are done, you can probably go home,' Emily says.

'Oh, thank Jesus,' I say, leaning forward. 'I didn't think of that. Oh my god, get the doctor back! Ask when I can leave!'

'And here I thought we were friends,' Emily teases me as she leaves.

...

I sit in the quiet for a little while after she's gone, just processing. My phone dings after a few minutes, and I know it's Dad wanting an update. I know I should respond and email him the recording of the conversation. I've got doctor's permission to go on school camp, and I guess I should feel like that's a victory. But I don't, not really. Instead, I feel this strange kind of urgent desperation to do a million things before I can't do them anymore. I remember this episode of a television show from the nineties about a kid who, when he was reaching the last days of being able to use his legs, left his house of the middle of the night to plant a tree. To leave his mark. He mut have fallen over a hundred times, but he did it. I wonder what mark I can leave or the things I'll regret?

I think maybe I'm being a little dramatic, but my grandpa broke his ankle without even really tripping over anything because of his osteoporosis. I wonder if every subluxation will become a dislocation. I wonder if I'll stop breathing or die from pneumonia like some pre-1928 penicillin-less bitch. Maybe I'll have a heart attack instead.

I shake my head, as if to clear the thoughts. It's not productive, it's not useful, and it's not the point.

I update Dad and send the audio file to him and Mum.

I message Ivy to tell her I love her.

I message Jenna saying that I do not appreciate her bringing me the math homework, could she not have 'lost' it?

I message Daniel and tell him that in 2005 there was actually a study done on how teaspoons always disappear from kitchens.

When Lee-Ann comes in to say I can leave tomorrow or the next day I smile and thank her. She says I need to stay in to have the injections and they want to monitor side effects on the bisphosphonates for the first twenty-four hours for some reason or other.

Dad calls, and I spend five minutes reassuring him that I'm fine.

Ivy's worried about me and I tell her that I can now make it to the vending machine outside the ward on my crutches. Everything's fine and I have a red jelly hook up.

I soothe Mum over her list of reasons why she couldn't be here for me even though she wants to be.

'I know you're fine,' she says. 'You don't need me, but if I didn't have this deadline …'

'Of course,' I say. 'What you do is important and you're on a deadline. I understand. And, of course, I'm fine. This ain't my first rodeo.'

'You're amazing, Grace. How did you come out of me?'

'Gross, Mum. Go back to work.'

...

Jenna says both that class is quieter without me and that I'm too quiet. I remind her that I'm Grace goddamn Turing and imagine her laugh.

Daniel asks for more information about the teaspoon thing so I link him to 'The case of the disappearing teaspoons: longitudinal cohort study of the displacement of teaspoons in an Australian research institute' article.

He asks if I'm surviving hospital.

I tell him it's hard to get good service, today lunch was fifteen minutes late.

I'm fine, I'm fine, I'm fine.

I say the words over and over to everyone I love. I think that it's kind of ironic how I can't keep my connective tissue together but I'm the glue holding everyone I love together with will power and half truths.

I don't know if I'm strong enough to keep protecting the people I love from how broken I am.

CHAPTER FOURTEEN
Celebration

'Do you want to know why there are no more cowboys?' Daniel asks. He's chewing on a daisy he picked from the oval and smiling into the lunchtime sun two weeks after I escaped from hospital. I ache pretty badly today despite the new meds, and I want to feel as good and warm and relaxed as he looks.

'I feel like you're going to tell us no matter what I say,' Jenna sighs.

'Is this the segue into a weird fact or the beginning of a joke?' Elsa asks.

'There are still cowboys,' Caleb says.

We still don't like Caleb very much, but we all think Elsa is the sweetest, so we put up with him. Occasionally. I honestly don't know what Elsa sees in him. I mean, he does have these moments where he's kind of sweet to her. But he's also such a dick, calls alcohol 'the piss', and asked Jenna if she was on her 'rag' when she told him to stow his white privilege last week. Yeah. Classy guy. I wonder if I can figure out a way to ask Elsa what she sees in him without sounding disparaging.

'My money's on a weird fact,' Jenna says.

'Turing, are you listening?' Daniel asks, nudging my foot with his.

'Of course, I'm listening,' I reply, not looking up from my pencil smudging. My hands aren't shaking too bad today, despite the pain. I feel oddly desperate every day I can sketch.

'How's it going with the iPad?' Elsa asks. 'It's kind of fun, right?'

'It's not the same,' I sigh, looking up. My eyes cut to Daniel's profile automatically and I bring them back. 'It's okay, though. It smooths out the tremors and I'll be able to do some portraiture again, at least.'

'I'm glad,' she replies, smiling warmly.

I hadn't even thought about digital art until she'd told me. And Mum had brought an iPad and Apple pencil home the next day and called it an early birthday present. I flex my hands a little before going back to the tree I'm drawing.

'Excuse me,' Daniel says. 'I'm talking about cowboys?'

'What about them?' I ask.

'You're really ruining my moment, Turing,' Daniel complains. 'I spend all my time finding weird facts to impress you –'

'Weirdest mating ritual ever,' Jenna mutters, not for the first time. I think she's been talking to Ivy.

'– and you aren't even listening,' he finishes.

'The invention of barbed wire in the late 1800s,' I say, trying not to smile at my page. I know I've stolen his moment and I love it.

'What?' Caleb asks as Daniel makes a long noise of complaint.

'It's why there aren't any more cowboys,' Jenna says, grinning.

'How do you know?' Daniel asks. 'So unfair.'

'I'm just that good,' I tease him, finally looking up from my page.

His eyes dance with amusement despite his expression and it's easy to forget there's anyone except us sitting here.

'You're the worst,' he says.

'Don't lie,' I say. 'You love m–,' I stammer, realising what I'm saying. 'You all love me. You all wouldn't even be friends without me.'

Daniel's eyes change again, and they look darker somehow. I can almost feel the frisson between us.

'So true,' Jenna agrees, covering the awkwardness. 'But should I really be thanking you for that?'

'You should,' Elsa says. 'I do.'

'Aw!' Jenna says, reaching out a hand to Elsa, who takes it for a moment.

'If I get you a room, can I watch?' Caleb asks.

We all make disgusted noises.

'Whatever,' Caleb says, and gets up off the ground to jog over to the game of football being played.

The weird tension is back in the quiet after Caleb's departure. I wish it wasn't. I don't want to have this conversation with Daniel. I've spent the past two weeks since I got out of hospital successfully not having this conversation with Daniel. With any luck, I can keep not having this conversation until the end of term. I still don't know how I feel except that I know I want to keep Daniel in my squad. I'm scared of losing him and I don't know what to do to stop that.

...

'Well, I need to go to the ladies',' Jenna says, standing up.

'I'll go with you,' Elsa says, bolting to her feet.

'Why do girls go to the bathroom in packs? Peeing is not a group activity,' Daniel says.

'It's weird,' I agree.

'Uh-huh,' Jenna says, rolling her eyes. 'Come on, Els.'

'You're not going?' Daniel asks.

'It's not a group activity,' I say.

He looks at me.

I feel a blush begin so I look down at my tree.

'Turing?'

'Yeah?' I ask. I don't look up.

'You're being weird.'

'I'm always weird.'

'Grace.'

'You're being weird. You never call me 'Grace'.'

'Please,' he says.

I look up.

He looks at me.

'So. You know, then,' Daniel says. His stiffens like he's bracing himself for a hit.

'Know what?' I ask, wondering if there's still a chance to not have this conversation.

'Don't be dense,' he sighs. 'But, fine. If that's how you feel, it's how you feel.'

'It's not how I feel,' I say, my mouth working before my brain finishes thinking. 'I'm just ... it's just ... complicated.'

He rolls his eyes. 'We're teenagers, it's always complicated.'

'I don't think you understand what you're asking,' I say. 'It's not … it's not simple, like Caleb and Elsa. They like each other. They date. It's normal.'

'Please never equate me with Caleb,' Daniel replies with a grimace.

'You know what I mean,' I argue.

'I know what you mean,' he says. He sits up, cross-legged, and looks me in the eye.

It's serious time. My breathing shallows with it.

'I know you, Grace. I know you're thinking about how you're high maintenance and problematic and always getting sick. You're probably creating scenarios where you somehow manage to ruin my life because you end up in hospital.'

I want to argue, but I can't. He's right.

'But that stuff doesn't matter right now. And even if it does, I know the score. You're sick and you're going to stay sick and probably get sicker. But whether or not you want to acknowledge how I feel about you, it's going to scare the shit out of me and I'm going to be there for you anyway. Because you're my best friend. Because you're Grace Turing. Because you're the best person I've ever met. I'm not asking to put a ring on it, I'm asking you to consider going on a date with me,' he says.

'I'm scared,' I say. My voice is small and foreign.

'Why?' he asks. And he looks so genuinely surprised that I want to shake him.

'Because you're the best person I've ever met, too. Because I'm scared of losing you or scaring you off,' I reply. 'I'm scared because the more I think about it, the more sure I am that you're this weird anomaly in my asexual-aromantic world. I'm scared about what that means and I'm scared of losing your friendship and I'm scared that you'll regret me. Because you will eventually. I'm sure of it.'

'You're overthinking it,' Daniel says. 'But you're you, so, par for the course. I like the part where I'm an anomaly, though.'

'Thanks,' I say, dryly. I'm a little annoyed, truth be told. I'm sharing my anxieties and he's teasing me. Then again, he's kind of baring his truth here as well.

'You know, you haven't actually said it,' I say.

'Said what?' he asks, confused.

'How you feel about me. "You know, then" is hardly the declaration of love we'll tell our hypothetical grandkids about.'

He laughs, all the tension leaving, and I grin back.

'I love you, Grace Turing. You're such a dork.'

'Not like?' I ask, holding my breath.

'I passed like at least a fortnight ago. That whole dodgeball incident did something to me,' he confesses with a shrug. Like it doesn't matter that he loves me and I know it. There's no self-consciousness, not hiding, and no drama. Just Daniel Perkins.

I wait for the panic to race through me at his words.

I wait for the fear and stress and the doubt.

I wait for the urge to run.

It doesn't come.

Instead, I feel a kind of warmth pool in the heart of me and a stupid smile form.

'I love you, too, Daniel Perkins. I don't know what it means, yet, or if I want more than … whatever this is. But I do love you,' I say.

'And you'll think about it?' he asks, hope lighting in his eyes, his head tilted to inspect me.

'I'll think about it,' I say. It's not like I think about much else lately. Not that I'm going to tell him that.

'Thank you,' he says.

The quiet that comes is comfortable again, and I consider thanking him, too.

'Now, impress me, Turing,' he says, leaning back again. 'You knew the barbed wire one.'

'The first recorded use of the acronym OMG was in a letter to Winston Churchill in 1917.'

'There's music recorded specifically for cats.'

'You've gotta stop the cat fact spiral.'

'It's too late for me, Turing.'

'Dork. Uh … oh! Pablo Picasso used to carry around a gun loaded with blanks so he could shoot it at people who asked him what his art meant!' I say, snapping my fingers in excitement before doing finger guns.

'No,' Daniel says. 'That can't be true.'

'I shit you not,' I reply, grinning.

'Seriously? No way,' he says, shaking his head.

'It's true! You can google it,' I reply.

'What are we googling?' Jenna asks as she and Elsa sit down after their trip to the bathroom.

'Picasso used to carry a gun loaded with blanks to shoot people who asked what his art meant,' I say.

'Apparently, if we can believe her,' Daniel says.

'I've heard that one, actually,' Elsa says.

'See!' I say, victorious.

'Fake news,' Daniel says. 'It has to be.'

'Nope, it's legit,' Jenna says, holding up her phone.

Daniel takes it from her and reads for a bit.

'Well, fuck me,' Daniel says, flopping back on the grass. 'Art just got hardcore.'

'Van Gogh legit cut off his own ear, Dali owned an ocelot and stole pens, Jackson Pollock was a thug, and Banksy's whole thing is illegally painting political statements on public property. Art was always hardcore AF,' Elsa informs him.

'Why does everyone know more weird facts than I do?' Jenna complains.

'Because you actually study?' Daniel says.

'Because you use your brain for relevant information?' I say.

'Because you're not a trivia-obsessed freak like these two?' Elsa says.

'Your words sound like they should be complimentary, so why am I feeling offended?' Jenna says. 'You can make it up to me by coming out for my non-celebratory dinner after this stupid chess competition.'

'You haven't quit chess yet?' I ask. 'But you're so bad at it!'

'I know,' Jenna says, miserable. 'Mum's still trying to live vicariously through me. I wish she'd picked something like karate so even if I was bad I might get some street cred. There's no social capital in the ebony and ivory of war.'

'That is oddly poetic,' Elsa says. 'I'll check with my fam. The parental units can be weird about school nights. But there's no Caleb and it's chess, so, the odds are in our favour.'

'As long as we're not eating Mexican,' Daniel says. 'If I have one more dinner of nachos, I may actually turn into nachos. And no, you do not have permission to eat me if I turn into nachos.'

'There's a joke in there about nachos,' I say. 'Nacho problem?'

'What about you, Grace? I know your family can be a bit weird about you going out,' Jenna says.

'Oh, I, uh … I probably can't tonight,' I say.

'Why not?' Jenna asks.

Here's the thing: it's almost two pm on the day of, and I know that what I'm about to say is going to upset them. It just never came up in conversation and I didn't know how to bring it up. So, I close my eyes, brace myself, and mumble.

'What was that?' Daniel asks. 'Because it sounded like you used the word "birthday" and I know that's not possible.'

'Oh my god,' Jenna says. 'It's November third. How did we not know it was November third?'

'It, uh, didn't come up?' I say. 'It's cool. I don't really celebrate my birthday or anything. I mean, aside from my complete lack of friends, celebrating my existence feels kind of depressing.'

Daniel and Elsa look mortified and Jenna's face is covered by her hands.

'Sorry?' I add.

'I'm the worst friend ever,' Jenna says. 'You told me your birthday and I forgot.'

'Two months ago,' I point out. 'It's not like I told you last week.'

'And why didn't you tell us?' Elsa demands.

'Because I don't celebrate my birthday?'

'Screw you, what if *we* want to celebrate your birthday? Did we not just establish that we all love you?' Elsa says.

'What she said,' Daniel says pointing at Elsa. 'Wait. Why didn't *Ivy* tell me? She tells me all the important shit you don't.'

'Seriously, stop talking to my sister,' I say. 'And I told her that I would withdraw sister movie night for a month if she told you.'

'I'm honestly speechless,' Daniel says after a moment.

'Clearly, the only solution to this is that my non-celebratory chess dinner is now a birthday dinner for you and your family are coming,' Jenna decides in a rare moment of true assertiveness.

Her mother would be so proud.

'Done,' Elsa says.

'Done,' Daniel agrees.

'So, I don't get a say in this, or ...' I say, trailing off, but Daniel already has his mobile phone out.

'Hi Brett, Grace is fine,' Daniel says before Dad can get out the question. Because why else would he be calling my father?

Wait.

'What are you doing?' I demand. 'And when did you get his number?'

'Problem solving,' Daniel says to me before directing his attention back to the phone call. 'We've just discovered that it's Grace's birthday ... No, she didn't tell us ... Right? We're a bit confused, too. Jenna has a chess club meeting but we'd all like to go out for dinner after that if you would join us? ... Thanks. Yeah, it's ...' he gives Jenna a meaningful look.

'Six thirty at Sweet Duck,' she says.

Daniel relays the information to Dad. 'Yeah, I'll let her know,' he says before he disconnects.

'I feel vaguely violated,' I say. 'But I guess it's because friend-ship?'

'You wouldn't have felt violated if you acted like a normal human being having a birthday,' Elsa says, already messaging her parents for permission.

'Brett says to tell you that you were being a little inconsiderate and he's glad you have friends like us,' Daniel says.

'I feel like most teenagers don't have to worry about their friends constantly contacting family members.'

'I feel like you need to stop keeping secrets from us,' Elsa says. There's a pause.

'Well, more than, you know,' she finishes, lamely.

'Knowing doesn't make anything make more sense,' Jenna sighs. 'It's just a lot of words.'

'Hey! Getting those words was hard fucking work,' I argue. 'Sure, I'd like them to be better words that more people understood, but at least now there are treatment plans and medication. It's not perfect, but it's easier, I guess.'

'Can I know the words? Elsa asks.

'Atypical autoimmune disease, with fibromyalgia, rheumatoid arthritis, and mixed connective tissue disorder,' I parrot. 'My hand tremor is either a medication side effect or possibly part of the mixed connective tissue thing. Or both.'

'Well,' Elsa says. 'That is a lot of words. I know arthritis, and maybe fibro? That's a pain thing, right?'

'Yep,' I say. 'If only it were cancer.'

Elsa frowns. 'But cancer's the worst.'

'Cancer would be easier,' Daniel says for me. 'Everyone knows what cancer is when you say it. And, as Turing has disturbingly and jealously pointed out on more than one occasion, it comes with the benefit of an end: remission or death.'

'It's true. Instead I just get a faulty meat sack until someone euthanises me,' I say.

'That is a disturbing image,' Elsa says, curling her lip. 'Meat sack.' She shudders.

I grin and Daniel laughs while Jenna consoles Elsa.

Daniel and I have drama after lunch while Jenna and Elsa go to horticulture. Jenna helps me up off the ground, and I groan like an old lady. After we wave them off, Daniel and I walk through the school side by side, not speaking. I kind of want to fill the empty space with facts, and I'm about to say something about how tossing foxes used to be an actual sport people played when he speaks.

'You should have told me it was your birthday, Turing.'

'I didn't want to make a big thing of it. You don't get it. I'm not happy to be alive,' I say.

'Grace.' He stops short and grabs my wrist, turning me to him. There's more force than I think he planned because it hurts a little. 'You don't get to say that.'

'Uh, you don't get to make that call,' I say, frowning. 'I'll say what I want.'

'You think I don't understand, but I do. I understand that some days living must be excruciating and you want to give up. You're strong and brave and all that bullshit. But I've spent my entire life living with someone who, when they say shit like that, might actually mean they're going to do something about it,' he says. 'So, no, you don't get to tell me you aren't happy to be alive. Not when you being alive makes me so fucking happy.'

I stare at him.

He glares back.

'You're right,' I say. 'I amend my statement. I like being alive, I don't love living in a shitty meat sack.'

He lets go of my wrist.

I rub it.

He winces. 'Sorry. I didn't mean to –'

'It's fine,' I say. 'You didn't hurt me.'

'I did,' he sighs. 'Fuck.'

'It's fine,' I repeat. 'It doesn't matter.'

He glares again.

'It doesn't matter that you grabbed me a little too tight. It matters that you said what you said and I heard you,' I clarify. 'I will celebrate the ghost in the meat sack.'

'I will never see *Ghost in the Shell* in the same way again,' he says, looking a little happier.

'You do have a thing for ScarJo, huh?'

'No, that movie was a fucking travesty. The original anime is where it's at,' Daniel says. 'I mean, ScarJo can get it.'

'Of course,' I say.

'But you're the only girl for me,' he says, half teasing, and, I'm pretty sure, half serious. He grins and I laugh.

'Hello, poppets!' Ms Oakley welcomes us, clapping her hands delightedly. 'Today, we're casting for the end of year performance! It's *Grease*! Aren't you excited?'

'If I get cast as Danny I might do something I'll regret,' Daniel says.

'But you love getting called Danny,' I tease.

'No,' he says. 'Not like this. Please, God, not like this.' He's doing a decent imitation of a soldier on a battlefield losing his best friend in the trenches.

'The only thing you'll regret will be all that leather,' I say.

'I look good in leather,' he muses.

'I want to sing "Beauty School Dropout",' I say.

'I'm only going to be Danny if you're Sandy,' he says. 'I don't think I'm a good enough actor to pretend to actually like Kenzi or that bitch Emmanuelle.'

'Language, Mr Perkins,' Ms Oakley sighs. 'Keep the passion, lose the expletives.'

'Yes, Ms Oakley,' he says while I snicker behind my hand.

'Slut shaming is so 2001,' I whisper.

'Shut up, Turing.'

...

In a state of affairs that surprises literally no one, Ivy is the most excited person about dinner. If you could vibrate yourself to levitation, she'd be floating.

'You have friends! They love you! They care! I'm so excited! I love you so much, Gray, and now we get to celebrate your birthday with your fam!'

'Are we not her fam?' Mum asks.

'No, like, her friend family,' Ivy explains.

'Oh,' Mum says and looks at Dad with raised eyebrows to communicate the fact she does not understand teenagers anymore.

'It's not a big deal,' I say.

Everyone responds over each other to inform me that I'm incorrect.

...

When we get to Sweet Duck, I'm genuinely surprised to see Daniel's mother there. I've never met her before, and I kind of figured that's been a pretty deliberate move on Daniel's part. He wants to protect his mother from his peers, and he wants to protect me from his mother. When we were in hospital at the same time and I suggested going down to visit her, he just about lost his mind. But she's there, chatting away to Jenna's mother, the psychologist. Which, again, feels kind of major.

'Danny!' Ivy calls out, announcing us and waving.

'Ivy, my second favourite Turing,' Daniel replies, doing the pound and peace. Ivy returns it. Then nudges me so I do it as well.

I roll my eyes as we walk toward the table, but no one seems to care what I think.

'I've heard so much about you,' Daniel's mother says to Ivy. 'Danny says you're a real sweetheart.'

'She's basically the best person to ever exist,' I agree, smiling proudly.

Ivy rolls her eyes but she beams happily. She basically radiates happiness.

'Both our daughters are wonderful,' Mum says.

'Mum, you don't need to lie. No one's going to think you're a bad mother,' I say.

Mum sighs.

'I'm a problem child,' I say, grinning.

'Ain't that the truth,' Dad mutters.

We share a grin.

'And you're Grace,' Daniel's mother says with a different smile.

My eyes flick to him, and he shrugs. 'You're kind of a big deal.'

'Right. Because you were a friendless loner?' I tease.

Daniel gives me a look that communicates how I'm being dense again. 'Because you're Grace goddamn Turing.'

'Has Ivy got everyone saying that now?' Mum asks.

'It's accurate,' Daniel says. 'It's nice to see you again, Samara.'

'I need a drink,' Mum says. 'Brett?'

'Lemon, lime, and bitters,' he says. 'Would you like anything … I'm sorry, I don't know your name.'

'Lowanna,' she says with pride. 'And, no, thank you, I'm good with water.'

'What does it mean?' I ask. 'Your name.'

'Because I'm an Aboriginal woman my name has to mean something?' Lowanna asks, leaning forward like she's about to start a fight.

I kind of like her for it even though I'm a bit taken aback.

'Ma,' Daniel hisses.

'Grace,' Dad cautions.

'Names have meanings regardless of where you're from. I haven't met anyone called "Lowanna" before, and it sounds pretty,' I reply. 'My name, for instance, means "God's favour", which is a very good joke.'

Ivy snorts a laugh and tries to cover it.

Dad grinds his teeth a little.

'Grace is into trivia,' Daniel says. 'It's not a race thing.'

'I mean, it could be a race thing in her defence. Particularly because I'm part-Asian, and we're kind of into names with meanings,' I shrug.

'It's a name from Country,' Lowanna says, relaxing. 'It means "woman".'

'Where's Country for you?' I ask.

'I'm Palawa, Tasmanian,' she replies. 'Where are you from?'

'Victoria,' I say, grinning.

Lowanna grins back.

'Mum's Malay,' I say.

'We're a very multicultural friendship group given we're in Tasmania,' Jenna says. 'Which shows how progressive and interesting we are as developing individuals.'

Linda, Jenna's mother, gives an approving nod and Jenna catches my eye to show how she's trying not to laugh.

'How was chess?' I ask brightly.

Jenna scowls and Linda sighs.

'She moved down a rank, but we learned good lessons, didn't we?' Linda asks, patting Jenna's arm.

I swallow down hard on a sarcastic reply.

Mum comes back to the table and the parents start chatting away like old friends. Jenna and Ivy are talking about the love triangle that never was. And I'm trying not to look at Daniel. Daniel, on the other hand, is trying to make me look at him. In the end, he gets up and walks around the table to take the empty seat next to me.

'Turing,' he says.

'Perkins.'

'You're being weird again,' he says. 'Is it because of Ma?'

'I like her,' I say.

'I knew you would,' he says, dryly amused.

'I thought you were … hiding her, I guess?'

'I was. Am. Will continue to do so. But, I don't know. If anyone's going to get it, it's you guys. She's important to me.'

I reach out and touch his arm in support. 'I get it.'

'Here,' he says, shoving a shopping bag at me. 'It's not wrapped because you're a terrible friend who doesn't tell people it's your birthday.'

'Yes, can I get in on telling Grace she's the worst?' Jenna asks.

'Me too!' Elsa calls out, from a few chairs away. She's arrived alone, and I'm kind of grateful I don't have to meet more new people. 'Grace is the worst.'

'I'm getting mixed messages,' I tease them. 'I thought y'all loved me.'

'Open your stupid present,' Daniel says.

'Here,' Elsa says, putting a small box on the table in front of me.

'I didn't have time to get you a gift,' Jenna says. 'But I'll do it soon.'

'I think organising this is gift enough,' I tell her.

She rolls her eyes and I know I'm getting ignored.

'Presents,' Ivy says, bouncing a little. She loves presents, even when they're not for her. Which is further proof that she truly is the purest soul.

I open Elsa's first, because I kind of want to save Daniel's. If I could, I'd sneak away and open it in private, savouring the moment, because he loves me and knows me and he bought me a present. I'm probably putting way too much emotional weight on this, but no friends kind of means no presents, and Abbie Lightfoot wasn't really a present kind of person.

At first, I think they're just silver stud earrings, but they're not. They're artist palettes. I audibly gasp, and clutch them to my chest for a moment.

'Thank you,' I say, looking up at her.

She's grinning, proud of herself. 'I saw them two weeks ago and knew I wanted to get them for you. Aren't they the cutest?'

'They are,' I agree, looking at them again. 'They're perfect. Thank you.'

'You're welcome. Now stop keeping secrets,' Elsa says, giving my shoulder a quick squeeze before taking a seat across the table from us.

'Grace and her secrets,' Dad sighs.

'Exactly. Mr Turing, I assume?' Elsa asks.

'Brett,' he says. 'You must be Elsa.'

She beams at me. 'Yep.'

'Next present!' Ivy says.

I look at the shopping bag and then at Daniel, who might actually be the most nervous person I've ever seen in my life. And I saw Ivy battling stage fright and tears when she was ten and had to speak at assembly.

'Next present,' I say, opening the bag. My chest tightens in anticipation.

'It's stupid,' Daniel says, as if that's going to make it stop.

I flick my eyes up to him to offer a reassuring smile, but he's not looking at me. He's looking at the bag.

'I'm sure it's not,' Ivy says. 'You know Grace super well.'

I pull the first object out of the bag without really looking at it. It's a second-hand copy of a book entitled *The Book of General Ignorance*. I grin like an idiot.

'Yes. Perfect. I love it. Oh! You're most likely to get caught in a hailstorm in Western Highlands of Kenya? I love it,' I say, already flicking through it.

'Stop reading at the table,' Mum says, quite possibly automatically.

'But look at it,' I say, holding the book aloft. 'I'm gonna know so many weird things!'

'You already know too many weird things,' Dad says.

'You lucky to have a child so engaged with knowledge,' Linda Harrington says.

'It is definitely strange,' Lowanna agrees with my parents. 'Since Danny met Grace he's been saying the weirdest things.'

'Perfect gift for Grace,' Ivy says, rewarding Daniel with a grin.

'I try,' he says. 'Last minute and all that.'

'You did good,' I say. 'Thank you.'

'I feel like I should not thank you,' Jenna says. 'Because so many more weird facts.'

'You love them,' Daniel says.

'I really don't,' she replies.

'Keep going,' Elsa says. 'There's something else in the bag.'

The second thing in the bag is a picture frame. I pull it out, and my jaw actually drops in shock. It's a picture of Daniel, Jenna, and me sitting on the oval. We're laughing, probably at something I said, because my hands are in the air, Jenna is bent forward, and Daniel's head is thrown back.

'Where did you get this?' I ask.

'Liam,' he admits, looking away.

'It's the best present,' I say. I trace a finger over each of us.

'Can I get a copy?' Jenna asks.

'Sure,' Daniel says.

'How did you get it from Liam?' Elsa asks.

'He … we had a discussion,' Daniel says, awkwardly. 'About Grace.'

'Omg,' Elsa says, her eyes wide. 'Tell me everything.'

I blink, surprised. 'Your thirst for gossip always surprises me.'

'Oh, come on!' Jenna says. 'It's *Liam Granger*. It's A-grade goss.'

'Is this about the boy who asked Grace out?' Mum says, catching our conversation.

I close my eyes and wish to disappear. 'Can we not talk about this? As a birthday present to me.'

'Later,' Elsa says, pointing a finger at Daniel.

'I'm pro never talking about this again,' he mutters. 'But … I thought Turing would like it.'

'I love it,' I say. I smile at him until I'm pretty sure he'd blush if he could. He ducks his head.

'Good.'

'You guys are so cute,' Ivy sighs, dreamily. 'What should their couple name be?'

'How about you never, ever give me a couple name with someone ever?' I say. 'Because that shit is the worst.'

'Let her actually agree to go out with me first,' Daniel tells my sister. 'Then we'll talk. I have some thoughts.'

'Well, that solves that dilemma,' I say. 'I'm never going out with you.'

'You wound me, Turing,' he says, but he grins, because he knows I don't mean it.

'My money is still on it happening eventually,' Elsa says as if she has some secret knowledge.

'I wouldn't want to steal the world's most unlikely couple from you and Caleb,' I say.

'That would have been you and Liam,' Jenna muses.

'Christ,' I say.

'I think it'll happen at camp. All the good stuff happens at camp,' Elsa says. 'That's when Caleb and I –'

'Nope,' I interject, noticing Dad tracking this conversation with interest. 'Nothing happens at camp, right? It's very boring and safe.'

'Oh. Yeah. Of course,' Jenna says, enthusiastically. 'It's very educational.'

'Hardly any co-ed activities,' Daniel adds, smirking.

'I might seem pretty old to you, but I do remember being seventeen and on school camp,' Dad says. 'Why do you think I'm so nervous?'

'Oh, leave it be, Brett. Or I'll tell them about how you came into possession of the bike that features in the story of how we met,' Mum says, good-naturedly. She's clearly on her second glass of riesling.

'How did he get the bike?' Ivy asks. 'Surely he just bought it?'

'Oh, sweet thing,' Elsa says.

'Camp sounds great,' Dad says, changing the subject. 'But I'm still not sure. You're … not exactly a normal teenager.'

'There is no 'normal' teenager,' Linda says.

'Let them be kids,' Lowanna says. 'They're only young once. They need to write the stories they'll tell in old age.'

'I don't have time to waste,' I say, without thinking. 'I've got maybe ten to fifteen good years left.'

'Why?' Linda asks, confused.

No one speaks.

I look at Jenna, who shrugs. She hadn't told her mother. I don't know how I feel about that.

Mostly, everyone looks at the table sadly.

I've killed the mood, and I hate it.

'And this is why I don't like celebrating my birthday,' I say in the end. 'Sorry. I just … need some air.'

I stand quickly, only pausing to stabilise my chair before power walking out of the restaurant.

'Grace,' Dad calls after me.

'Leave her,' Mum says.

Ivy is the one who comes for me. She sits on the ground beside me, resting her back against the side of the restaurant.

'That could have gone better,' she says.

I laugh a little, chasing away the tears, and rest my head on hers.

'Sorry.'

'You don't need to be sorry,' Ivy says. 'It's your truth.'

'It's not my truth. It's *the* truth,' I say. 'It's the only truth. I'm going to get sicker, Ivy. I got this diagnosis, and there's all this relief and joy because it's a real thing. But, it's also kind of a life sentence.'

'It was already a life sentence, Gray.'

I pull back to look at her. Her beautiful face is serious and her eyes are dark. I reach up and push some imaginary hair behind her ear.

'But family is a life sentence, too,' she says. And friends. I mean, I basically had to pay Jenna to tackle Daniel so I could be the one to come out here.'

I huff a laugh.

'I'm serious,' she says. 'It was intense.'

'I love you, little sister. You're my favourite.'

'I know.'

'I just get scared.'

'I know that, too. I'm scared for you. We all are. It's why we're overprotective. I mean, Danny's great and all, but would I be friends with him if you weren't sick? I don't know.'

'You're growing up too fast. You're not meant to have this kind of insight until your twenties.'

'You're growing up too fast,' she says, and pokes her tongue out.

I laugh and she grins.

'Okay, I'm ready to go back in.'

'You were happy in there,' Ivy tells me as we stand up. 'Really happy. Those people make you happy. Do you think that might be enough? Having people who love you and make you happy?'

'Ivy, that's all that matters,' I say, hugging her close. 'All that matters is now. It's the only thing we get for sure.'

'You're so weird,' Ivy says, but she hugs me tight. 'Don't leave me, okay?'

Tears threaten to choke me again. 'I won't,' I say. 'I promise.'

I know it's a lie. I know it's not a promise anyone can make. I know that, in the end, she'll probably be the one to leave me first. But right now, walking into the restaurant with my arm around her shoulders, to a table full of people who are happy to see me, I mean it. I won't leave any of them, and no one can take them from me. I won't let them.

Later, when we're leaving, Daniel holds my hand. He does it like it's normal and not happening at the same time. He's saying goodbye to Elsa and I'm talking to Lowanna, and his hand finds mine. We linger together for a moment and when I turn to face him, he drops my hand.

'Couldn't resist,' he says.

'I thought you were okay with how things are?'

'I never said that. I said I'd live with it if it was. I never said I wouldn't try to convince you,' he replies, grinning. Challenging me.

I try to fight the smile, but I can't.

'Goodnight, Perkins,' I say.

'Night, Turing,' he replies. He winks. Of all the ridiculous things to do.

And I smile like an idiot in his direction.

'Didn't you say you'd never date him?' Ivy teases me.

'Shut up,' I say.

'If you have to date anyone, he's a good pick,' Dad reminds me.

'He's a good guy,' Mum agrees. 'He made tonight happen.'

'Guys, you're meant to be Team Grace, not Team Daniel,' I tell them. 'I'm meant to be your favourite.'

'You'd think that, wouldn't you?' Dad says, grinning.

'Happy birthday to me, everyone likes Daniel better!' I throw my hands up in irritation and defeat.

'No, we like you so much that we want the best things for you,' Mum corrects me.

'This is a mortifying conversation. Y'all are way too involved in my life. It's because I'm sick. Well, you don't get a vote! I get a vote. The only vote. And my vote is … I'm scared,' I say.

'That's normal,' Mum says. 'But you're seventeen now and it's twenty-first century Australia. We're not marrying you off in exchange for a goat. We're encouraging you to have fun with a nice boy who likes you and knows you.'

'That's kind of the point, though. He knows me. He should know better,' I say.

'You're worth it, Gracie,' Dad says, pressing a kiss to my forehead. 'And he's smart enough to know that. Now stop making me talk my baby girl into dating a teenage boy. Teenage boys terrify me now I'm a father to daughters.'

'What about Ivy? She had a love triangle the other week,' I say, trying to change the subject.

'Gray!' Ivy complains.

'If anyone touches Ivy, we kill them,' Dad says with a shrug.

'I found a good place to dump the body,' Mum says.

'I heard that we should bury them below a decoy corpse to avoid detection,' I add.

'Ha ha,' Ivy says, rolling her eyes. 'You're all so funny.'

'We're deadly serious,' I tell her. 'Ha! Get it?'

'Not funny, Gray.'

'I'm hilarious. But, I swear to god, the standards we have for you are crazy high. You're special.'

'You're special,' Ivy says, rolling her eyes.

'Can we set up a fake crime scene and I'll answer the door holding a chainsaw?' Dad asks.

'Yes! I have a great fake blood recipe,' I say, clapping my hands with glee.

'Mu-um! Tell them to stop it,' Ivy begs.

'Sorry, sweetness,' Mum says. 'But we're going to flip a coin to see who gets to hold the chainsaw.'

A week later, we have a meeting about me going on camp. Mr Holt and Mr Simmons have teamed up. I think about it like the Big Bad just got badder. I am disappointed to see that Miss Williams has joined them. Mrs Easton, Ms Oakley, and Mrs Connors are arguing for the affirmative. I'm sitting beside Dad facing the two lines down like some kind of impromptu courtroom.

'I just don't think it is practical to take Grace to camp with her health concerns,' Mr Simmons says.

'Look what happened with dodgeball,' Mr Holt says. 'She was in hospital for a week.'

'Four days,' I correct. 'And, technically, it wasn't about the injury.'

'You dislocated your knee and sprained your ankle.'

'Anyone can dislocate a knee!'

'Grace,' Dad says. 'Calm down.'

I scowl and fold my arms across my chest. He's right. I need to calm down.

'I'll be at camp with her. I have all of her medical information and a contact list, and I'm confident that I can provide enough care until help comes should that be required,' Mrs Easton says.

I smile at her, grateful.

'It's a good experience for her,' Ms Oakley says. 'Girls her age need experiences more than anything else. The world is her oyster!' She's trying to convince me that I'm well enough to play Sandy in *Grease*. I'm trying to convince her that I'm not. I think her logic is that if I'm well enough to go to camp, I'm well enough to be Sandy. I'm sorry, but I'm not playing around with dancing and my dodgy joints. I am not at all sad to have that excuse. But then she'll have to recast her leads because Daniel won't be Danny without me, which sounds like a her problem, but whatever.

'I'm concerned about the emotional safety of the other students,' Miss Williams says. 'What happens if she dislocates a knee in front of them?'

'I have,' I say. 'It was fine. Lots of support.'

'They're teenagers not five-year-olds,' Mrs Connors says. She's got a smudge of blue paint on her nose and I love it so much. 'They have enough emotional maturity to handle someone getting injured.'

'And what if one of them gives her a cold?' Mr Simmons argues. 'It's a forty-minute drive to the campsite from the hospital.'

I would not have put it past him to have actually timed it.

'I'm not going to die from a cold,' I say, rolling my eyes. 'And if I did, it would take more than twenty-four hours.'

'It's the principle of the thing,' Mr Simmons says.

'Any of them could get meningococcal,' Mrs Easton says.

'The legal implications of accepting responsibility for her health is the real issue,' Mr Holt says. 'The paperwork would be astronomical, and for what?'

'Maybe her legal right to inclusive education?' Dad says, glaring at him.

Mr Holt shifts uncomfortably under his gaze.

'Here, here,' Mrs Easton says. 'The fact that I'm going along is adequate precaution.'

'And what about if something happens at the school while you're gone? Maybe her father should come with us,' Mr Holt argues.

'Please, God no,' I mutter.

'I should lose out on paid employment because you fail to meet your obligations as an educator?' Dad asks. 'Do I need to give you a copy of the legislation and the mission statement as set out by the education department?'

'When did you read that?' I whisper.

'I didn't,' Dad mutters back. 'I'm guessing.'

'Baller move,' I reply.

'He's not wrong,' Ms Oakley says. 'We do have an obligation to Grace as a student to provide as normal an education as possible.'

'It's three days at a campsite with cabins. It's not a week of rock-climbing,' I say. 'I'll be careful. Make sure you put me in a room with Elsa and Jenna, because they know about my health concerns. I won't do an activity without at least one friend who knows what's up, and I won't play dodgeball.'

'What about the bushwalk?'

'It's a well-worn path, Justin, don't be so ridiculous,' Mrs Easton says. 'Grace, you won't go climbing over rocks in the river? You'll just stick to the path?'

There is absolutely nothing about my personality that should make Mrs Easton sound so sure that I'll behave myself.

'Of course,' I say. 'I'm not an idiot. I want to actually enjoy camp.'

Dad gives me a look that communicates his complete lack of confidence in my ability to take it easy.

Mr Simmons lets out a very heavy sigh and holds up his phone. 'We can't legally stop her from going.'

'See?' Dad says, more to me.

'So, I'll be careful and we'll have fun,' I say.

'Excellent,' Mrs Easton agrees.

'Hmph,' says Mr Holt.

'Wonderful,' Ms Oakley says, with a clap of satisfaction.

'I'll make sure the room assignments work,' Miss Williams says. 'I just want you to be safe, Grace.'

'I appreciate your concern,' I say, and attempt a smile so I don't seem so sarcastic.

'Let us know if you require any additional information,' Dad says, standing. 'Thank you for your time.'

...

'You're kind of awesome, Dad,' I say. 'I know you'd rather I not go, but I appreciate you being on my team.'

Dad sighs. 'It's not that I don't want you to go.'

'It's that you want me to be safe,' I finish for him.

'I love you and I'm scared for you.'

'I appreciate that. I'm scared, too. But, I've got to make memories, Dad.'

The truth of that hangs between us for a moment.

'It might not happen,' Dad says.

'Dad. It's a degenerative condition. It's going to happen.'

'But science is doing amazin –'

'Dad.'

'I know, Gracie. But you can't expect me to just take this lying down. You're my baby.'

'I'm seventeen.'

'You'll always be my baby,' he says, and holds my hand, squeezing it.

'I'm sorry I have a faulty meat sack,' I tell him, squeezing back. 'But you know I can't handle thinking about what ifs for a relatively rare condition.'

He takes his arm and puts it around my shoulders, holding me to him. 'You're worth it. Clearly there was just too much awesome contained in you so it's slowly eroding your health.'

I laugh and lean into him.

'Mission success!' I announce the following morning to Daniel, who's waiting at my locker.

He grins. 'That's what I'm talking about!'

I don't even think about it, I throw my arms around him.

'Right? I'm so excited.'

This is where I realise I'm hugging him.

He isn't hugging me back.

I begin to panic, and start to release him.

'Uh,' I say, but he cuts me off by hugging me back.

'I'm happy for you, Turing,' he says, his voice low, and for me.

I move to pull away, but he holds me in place.

'I don't –'

'Let me have this,' he says. 'Ten more seconds.'

I hug him back.

'Thanks,' I say.

'Any time,' he says, and I know he's grinning even though I can't see his face.

We start to separate when Elsa says, 'Oh, come on! I've got ten bucks riding on you two getting together at camp.'

I think I actually jump away from Daniel.

'You'll spook her,' Daniel says. 'She's still pretending it's not going to happen.'

'You know how, in books, when a guy is convinced of the inevitability of a relationship and it's considered romantic?' I ask.

'Yes,' Elsa says dreamily.

'It's actually presumptuous and creepy,' I say.

'You have no romance in your soul,' Elsa says, dramatically.

'Is that how you ended up with Caleb? Did he corner you and tell you that since you were his chosen mate, you should give in early and not fight it?' Daniel asks. 'Because I think Grace might be onto something here. Toxic masculinity, anyone?'

'You deserve each other,' Elsa says, but her cheeks pink a little.

'Should we hold an intervention?' I ask Daniel. 'I'm worried.'

'Eh, it's probably too late. They've been dating for a year. Which is basically married for ten years by high school standards.'

'Still, abusive relationships can affect anyone,' I muse.

'You think I'm abusing her?' Caleb demands.

Daniel and I flinch as we turn to look at him. He's bigger than I remember, and furious.

'It was mostly a joke,' Daniel says.

'Definitely a joke,' I agree. 'Elsa loves you, that's all that matters.'

'Relax, bae,' Elsa says.

'No, it's not okay. Don't go gaslighting her because you don't like me,' Caleb says, stepping forward.

Daniel shifts so he's just in front of me, as if he can physically protect me from a football player.

'I'm not going to lie, Caleb, I don't understand your relationship. You're not my favourite person. But you're good to Elsa, and she loves you. We were just joking around because she was teasing us about dating,' I explain.

'Wait, you *aren't* dating?' Caleb asks, surprised. 'Hey, Graham, I owe you ten bucks.'

'Oh my god, is everyone betting on this? Is everyone at Riverview High addicted to gambling?' I ask.

'To be fair, if you weren't such a martyr, we'd already be dating,' Daniel points out. 'Feel free to just accept defeat at any time.'

'We were literally just having this conversation,' I say. 'No.'

'Are you saying no because I called it defeat?'

'No! I'm saying no because I still don't think you know what you're asking!'

The ensuing silence indicates that I'd clearly shouted and that everyone was listening in.

'I know what I'm asking, Turing. Better than anyone,' Daniel says, his voice at a normal volume. 'And you know I do.'

'I ...' Okay, he's got me there. I do know. He's got his mother and he's been through a decent amount of medical shit with me in the past three months.

'What do I have to do to make you believe it?' he asks. 'Because I'm running out of ideas.'

'I'm running out of excuses,' I admit. And then close my eyes because I was not meant to say that bit out loud.

'So,' Daniel says, turning to Elsa and Caleb. 'Clearly we're a disaster and have no right to judge your relationship.'

'Why doesn't she think you know what you're asking?' Caleb asks. 'Is she in some weird cult? Because I'd definitely believe Grace could be in a cult.'

'I'm not in a cult,' I huff. 'And ... I'm going to be late for class.'

'It's homeroom,' Elsa calls out after me.

Daniel jogs to catch up to me, and steals my books from my arms.

'Can you not?' I ask.

'Shut up, Turing,' he says. 'I'm annoyed at you.'

'Then give me my books.'

'I'm not giving you anything.'

'Perkins, so help me –'

'So help you?' he says, stopping to glare at me.

I stammer.

'Oh, I know, I said it would be okay. Well, I was wrong. It turns out I'm human and this is fucking painful. And then you hug me and I think it's going okay and then we take thirty steps backward and my heart's not a fucking yoyo, Turing,' he rants at me. 'So just let me carry your stupid books because you have a faulty meat sack and I love you and it's literally all I can do for you.'

'Daniel?' I ask, my voice is small as I take in the hurt shining in his eyes. The frustration. The love.

'What?' he snaps. 'Because I'm going to need a good fifteen minu –'

I dart forward to press a kiss to his check, stopping him mid sentence. I pull back carefully, watching his expression. His jaw is slack and he's shocked speechless.

'Hey – hands off policy: ten-centimetre rule,' a teacher chastises us.

We ignore them.

'What. The. Actual. Fuck?' Daniel says.

I'm pretty sure you can fry an egg on my cheeks.

'I ... It's ... You win? Christ, this is awkward,' I say.

'Use your words,' he says. His voice is flat and he's still frozen in place and if I didn't know him like I do, I'd think he was angry. He's not angry. He's scared. He's scared I did this to shut him up or to thank him. He's scared that I'm about to say it's over.

I take a deep breath. 'Okay. Even though I have a faulty meat sack, my parents and sister are way too involved in my life, and I deal with everything using weird trivia like Amelia Earhart and Eleanor Roosevelt once sneaked out of a White House party, and went for a joyride in a stolen jet, do you want to, maybe –'

'Turing. Spit it out.'

'I'm getting there. You're not helping.'

'Grace,' he says with even more warning.

'I give up,' I say. 'This is too weird. Just give me my stupid books and ignore me.'

'Wait,' he says, stepping back from my reaching hands. 'Are you giving up as in you want to finally be my actual girlfriend, or are you giving up on this conversation?'

'Both!' I say, throwing my hands in the air. 'I'm not built for this.'

Daniel grins, wide. 'You're such a dork,' he says. 'My girlfriend, the dork.'

'I'm not ... can we not do the name thing yet?' I ask, pulling a face. 'It's weird.'

'Nope,' Daniel says, stepping around to walk beside me. 'You're my girlfriend. Maybe if you hadn't made me wait this long I'd consider it.' He slips an arm around my shoulders.

'Hands off!' the teacher calls again. 'If I catch you again, I'll report you.'

'Sorry,' we call back. I duck out from under his arm, but Daniel just grins happily.

'And I'm the dork,' I say, rolling my eyes. 'Oh god, Ivy's gonna flip out.'

'Let's find her at recess,' Daniel says.

'Uh, or we could do not that?' I suggest. 'We could do what we normally do.'

'The sooner I tell Ivy, the sooner you're unable to take it back,' Daniel wisely points out. 'I'm taking no chances with you, Turing.'

'You don't think this is some kind of manipulative toxic masculinity moment?' I ask. 'Weren't you just implying Caleb's behaviour was toxic?'

'It's not manipulation, it's desperation,' Daniel corrects me. 'You forget how well I know you.'

'Is this what a panic attack feels like?' I ask. 'Am I hyperventilating?'

'One litter of kittens can have multiple fathers. Cats don't usually have eyelashes. Cats have an extra organ that lets them "taste-scent" the air,' Daniel recites as we walk into homeroom.

'Thank you,' I say. 'That helped. Also, are we getting close to the end of the cat facts?'

'Maybe,' he says. 'Hey Jenna, guess what?'

Jenna opens her mouth to respond, but Daniel cuts her off. 'Turing finally agreed to date me.'

'Christ on a crutch,' I say. 'Stop.'

'Can't stop, won't stop,' he grins. 'I told you, I've got to hit a critical mass of dissemination so you can't take it back.'

'Finally,' Jenna says. 'Elsa owes me ten bucks.'

I thunk my head on my desk. 'I regret everything.'

'No take backs,' Daniel says.

'Don't be mean,' Jenna says. 'He's liked you forever and you've been dumb about it.'

'Thank you,' Daniel says. 'She has been dumb. She's finally wised up.'

'Please let class start soon,' I say.

'Hey, Elsa, guess what?' Daniel asks.

'What?'

'You owe Jenna ten bucks.'

'F'f's sake,' I say into my desk.

Elsa laughs. 'Do I get to take some credit for this finally happening?'

'Could you guys not have done this earlier so I'd get ten bucks from Graham?' Caleb asks.

'Could we all stop talking about this?' I ask, taking my head off the desk.

'No,' everyone says.

I drop my head back down and groan.

...

Ivy does an actual happy dance and squeals. Daniel joins her. I watch them and feel embarrassed and pleased and safe and happy and scared, all at once.

'I knew it,' Ivy says, hugging me.

'I didn't,' I say.

'Well, you aren't smart about people,' Ivy says. 'You're smart about other stuff.'

'I feel like I should be offended?' I say.

'Be whatever you like,' Daniel says. 'As long as you–'

'Stay your girlfriend?'

'Exactly. Look at us, already finishing each other's sentences.'

'You think you're being cute right now. But you're not. You're driving me insane. I want to run for the hills. When did you get so corny and weird? Is this entrapment? Did you catfish me?'

Ivy laughs and grins. 'He's stupid about you, Gray. Enjoy it.'

'I can't enjoy it because I'm too freaked out!'

'Okay, I'll calm down a little,' Daniel says. 'I think enough people know now that you won't change your mind.'

'She won't change her mind,' Ivy says, confidently. 'She's kind of stupid about you, too.'

'Tell me more,' Daniel says.

'Well, she's been trying to draw and sculpt you for weeks,' Ivy says.

I reach over and clamp my hand over her mouth. 'O-kay. That's enough. Go enjoy recess,' I say, dragging her away.

'Message me later,' Daniel calls out after her, doing the pound and peace.

Ivy mumbles through my hand, nods her head, and returns the gesture.

...

I release Ivy after making her swear on sister movie night to not tell Daniel about the art thing. Daniel is watching us, smiling. He's happy. I'm smiling back even though I try to fight it off. I'm happy, too.

'What finally won you over?' he asks when I make it back to where he was waiting.

'You said it hurt,' I reply. 'I didn't ... I was so focussed on hurting you in the future, on getting hurt by you when you left. I didn't think about the present.'

'You think I'm going to leave you?' Daniel asks. 'I mean, it's high school. I suppose it's a fair concern. But ... seriously?'

'You matter,' I say, meeting his eyes. It's hard and I want to hide. 'I'm scared of how much you matter. I know that ... I know that after high school, most people are going to leave Launceston. They're going to go to university and have jobs and live lives. And I think I probably won't have that.'

'Grace,' he says, his voice soft. His hand reaches out and takes mine. 'You think we're going to forget you?'

'I think we're going to have nothing in common,' I say.

'You think we have things in common now? With Jenna, who doesn't like trivia or art or drama? You think she'll just stop talking to you?'

'It's like we're cellmates in prison,' I reason. 'We'll get released and never talk to each other again. We'll exchange nods in the supermarket.'

'You're an idiot about people,' Daniel sighs. 'Jenna loves you because you're different, which is the same reason you love her. It's about your heart. Same thing with Elsa. If she goes off and becomes a journo, do you think your art will be the only thing you have in common?'

'I don't know,' I say. Because I don't.

He lets go of my hand. 'And what about me? There's an expiry date on our friendship?'

'I don't want there to be!' I argue.

'Well, there's not,' he says.

'We're seventeen,' I say. 'It's not a realistic promise.'

'We're not just seventeen,' Daniel says. 'I'm my mother's carer and I've had to grow up way too fast. So have you.'

'I know.'

'So, stop worrying so much. I'm hashtag Team Grace, ride or die.'

I smile. 'Ride or die,' I promise.

'Okay,' he says. 'Now, do you want to go look at some birds?'

'Yes, please.'

We walk side by side to the edge of the oval where Jenna and Elsa are waiting for us. I re-enact yesterday's meeting about camp. Jenna complains about her mother not letting her quit chess. Elsa confesses that we'd been right, Caleb had pulled a 'creepy vampire' on her but she kind of loves him for it. Nothing changes, really. Except that Daniel's feet touch mine when he sprawls out on the ground.

I want to stay in this weird bubble of friendship forever.

CHAPTER FIFTEEN
Camp

'So, here's my question,' Daniel says.

I look at him blearily. My insomnia decided to come calling last night, skin sensitivity is high enough that touching anything other than my bamboo cotton clothing is going to be painful, and it's seven thirty in the morning in the school car park. Dad is giving a lecture to Mrs Easton and Miss Williams off to the side, while Mr Simmons and Mr Holt seem to be talking to all the other parents wanting to make sure their precious snowflakes won't be forced to eat eggs because they don't like eggs.

'Turing?' Daniel says. He touches my hand gently. 'You with me?'

'Sorry,' I say with a slight flinch. 'Tired. Hurts.'

'Should you be here?' he sighs.

I glare at him with all the fury and righteous indignation I can muster. I fought to be here. I want to be here. I'm not going to not be here for anything short of a zombie apocalypse, and even then.

It's not a very good glare though, because Daniel just sighs again.

'I've already had this argument with Dad,' I tell him. 'I'm not having it with you as well.'

'It's an hour on a bus,' he reminds me. 'Jolting, noisy, packed with people.'

'I'm aware.'

'Am I allowed to worry about you? I have a question.'

He takes my hand properly when he says it. After that one day of mad proclamation and the doomed date, he's been careful with me. Not just physically, but emotionally, too.

'I don't think I have control over you worrying. But I appreciate that you asked. What was your question?'

'My question was, how do you think you're going to keep your spoonie secret on camp?' he says. 'Because you have medication the teachers have to give you, you'll get a pass on some activities, and you can't just fake it for a lesson or nap on the oval.'

'This would have been a conversation to have before the day of,' I reply, tired.

'It's Grace,' Jenna says, having finally sent her mother off. 'She's over-thought it and has a plan.'

'Right,' I agree. 'My plan is to tell everyone it's none of their goddamn business. It'll be fine.'

'And if it's not?' Daniel asks. 'I just want to be prepared.'

'Then it's not, but it won't happen,' I say. 'We'll cross that bridge when we get to it, but we're not going to get to it.'

'Wishful thinking,' Daniel mutters.

Jenna says something about being supportive that I don't quite hear because Dad is calling me over.

...

'I've gone through your medication schedule and your emergency contacts,' Dad says. 'I've given Mrs Easton the folder.' By folder, he meant the stupidly thick display folder with my medical history, allergies, recent hospital visits, and all of my medical professionals' contact information. He spent a week compiling it and called it the 'Bible of Grace'.

'Okay. It's going to be fine,' I tell Mrs Easton, holding back an eye roll.

She smiles at me. 'Of course,' she says, before wandering off to the next overly anxious parent.

'See, nothing to worry about,' I say to Dad.

He doesn't hold back his eye roll, but he hugs me gently. 'Please be okay,' he murmurs into my hair.

'I will,' I say into his shoulder. 'We've got this. It's only two nights.'

'I know, I'm being dramatic,' he says, releasing me.

'You're a good father,' I say, with a smile. 'Thank you for caring.'

'I feel like you're being sarcastic,' he says.

'I'm not.' I look up at him, as if seeing him for the first time. His round face, dimpled with acne scars, the nose, crooked from a football injury, his brown eyes that make me feel warm and safe. A mix of emotions play over his face before he gives me a tight nod.

'Behave yourself, take your meds, don't do anything stupid, and listen to your teachers. And Daniel,' Dad instructs.

'It's not the forties, Dad. He's not the boss of me,' I argue.

'Daniel?' Dad calls, and my traitorous boyfriend practically runs to stand at attention, awaiting instructions.

'Hi Brett,' Daniel says. 'I'm worried about her, too.'

'Can you not?' I ask. 'I'm fine.'

They look at me sceptically, as if to say that I'm clearly not fine, and then at each other.

'Don't let her tell you she can climb trees, rocks, or go off the path,' Dad says.

'No unsupervised adventures,' Daniel agrees. 'Stay on the path, take her meds on time, sleep on a bottom bunk, and no contact sports.'

'Exactly how much say do you have over her sleeping arrangements?' Dad asks, narrowing his eyes.

'Jenna,' Daniel says quickly. 'Jenna and Elsa will be in charge of that.'

'Right,' Dad says, his expression not changing.

'Dad, calm down,' I sigh. 'You've been drilling him on this for a week.'

'He's a seventeen-year-old boy who knows where you're sleeping.'

'First of all, he always knows where I sleep. He's also not a creepy stalker who watches me sleep.'

'Oh, it's not the sleeping that worries me.'

'Secondly,' I say, over the top of him. 'I barely have enough energy for school on a good day, so I don't exactly have the spoons for sex.'

'Grace!' Dad exclaims.

'Christ,' Daniel mutters, ducking his head.

'What?' I ask. 'I'm easing your mind.'

'You're not easing my mind,' Daniel says. 'I'd like to leave this conversation now, please.'

'Me too,' Dad says.

They share a grin before they remember that I used the word 'sex'.

'See you in a few days, Brett,' Daniel says, quickly, turning on his heel and power walking away.

'Look after her,' Dad says, but his voice is still weird.

I smile at him.

'I'm leaving,' Dad says. 'But not because you made it weird.'

'You're definitely leaving because I made it weird,' I say.

'You're going to be okay?' It should be a statement, but it sounds like a question.

'Dad, I swear on Netflix, I'm not going to do anything to endanger my meat sack. I make no promises about my meat sack behaving, though. It has a mind of its own.'

'I love you,' Dad says. But he means that he's worried and he knows we've done everything we can to make this as safe as possible. But he still wants me to change my mind and ask him to take me home.

'I love you, too,' I say.

He gives me one last hug that isn't as tight as he'd like because I'm a little tender.

'Don't have sex,' he says.

'Dad, I lack the energy. Besides, knowing me I'd end up with vaginismus or something so my first time is definitely going to be closer to emergency services than a forty-five-minute car ride.'

'I hear how you think that sounds reassuring, but it's not,' Dad says. 'Do I want to know what vaginismus is?'

'Probably not.'

'Bye, Grace. Be safe.'

'Love you, bye!'

. . .

'Elsa's not coming,' Jenna says when I get back to her. 'She's in vom-city, apparently.'

My first thought is not for my friend's welfare, it's that I'm glad Dad left before he heard this piece of information. My second thought is for her welfare.

'She okay?'

'Food poisoning,' Jenna says. 'Her whole family has it.'

'Gross.'

'Right?'

'What's gross?' Daniel asks. 'Jellybeans are shiny because they're coated in insect poop? Well, it's shellac made from insect poop, but still.'

'That is gross,' I say, grinning. 'Bees jizz so hard it makes their dicks explode.'

'You two are disgusting,' Jenna says, curling her lip. 'Seriously foul.'

'You love us,' I say.

'Not anymore,' she says.

'Tell me the gross thing,' Daniel says. 'Is it grosser than exploding dicks and insect poop?'

'We set the bar pretty high,' I say, proud of us. 'Elsa and her family have food poisoning.'

'Oh, gross,' Daniel says.

'Yep,' Jenna agrees. 'It also means our room assignments have to change.'

'Oh, no,' Daniel says. 'This could end badly.'

'It is a concern. Thank God Dad's already gone. Miss Williams won't screw me though, right? This is a lie to me situation, btw.'

'She definitely won't screw you,' Jenna says confidently.

'Last I heard, Mr Holt had the room assignments,' Daniel says.

'Well, fuck,' I say.

'You're screwed,' Jenna agrees.

'He loves Kenzi and Amber,' Daniel says. 'You're definitely ending up in a cabin with them.'

'Maybe I am too sick to be here,' I joke.

Daniel has the nerve to look hopeful, so I glare at him.

'Be supportive,' I say.

'Turing, I'm the most supportive. But –'

'Nope,' I cut him off.

'He has a –,' Jenna begins.

'Uh-uh.'

'I'd miss you if you weren't here,' Daniel says. 'Three days without you would suck.'

'Better,' I say, smiling.

'You guys,' Jenna says, overwhelmed by the cute.

Daniel grins and I pull a face.

A piercing whistle makes everyone flinch, but no one more than me.

'Line up,' Mr Holt shouts as Daniel hovers his arm around me, just in case I need him.

'Hands off policy, Perkins,' Mr Holt shouts, noticing us.

'Not actually touching her yet,' Daniel argues.

'Is this really how you want to start camp, because you don't have to get on this bus,' Holt replies.

Daniel obediently takes a step away from me. 'Only because you're already down one friend,' he says quietly.

'Thank you,' I reply.

'But later, you and I are going to have a conversation about spoons and sex,' he whispers.

'Christ,' I say, cheeks burning.

'So *now* you're embarrassed,' he teases me.

'Shut up.'

...

As predicted, Jenna and I end up sharing a room with Amber and Kenzi. Huon Pine Cabin has two rooms divided by a little foyer. The other room has Mrs Easton, Miss Williams, Emmy, and Riley who has a different homeroom but is always in trouble for her attitude. Emmy is disgusted by this arrangement, and so, truth be told, is everyone in our room.

It starts with who gets the top bunk. In a surprise twist, everyone seems to want the bottom bunks. TV had led me to believe the inverse was true. In the end, we negotiate a treaty wherein half of the room belongs to the losers (Jenna and me) and the other half belongs to the superior beings forced to share our oxygen (Amber and Kenzi). Jenna isn't a fan of heights, so Elsa was going to take the top bunk, leaving Jenna and me on the bottom. Originally, Riley was sharing our room as well, but we figured she seemed chill.

It continues with who gets to use the power points and when. It turns out, our side of the room has better mobile phone reception.

We're not even meant to have our phones (except me, I'm definitely meant to have mine on pain of death according to Mrs Easton). Anyway, we have to swap sides. Miss Williams sticks her head in the door to say ask if we're doing okay and remind us that were meant to be at the main hall in half an hour, I think Kenzi actually manufactures a couple of tears about the situation.

I'm basically ready to rage quit camp at this point. I keep lingering back in the hopes that Amber and Kenzi will piss off and I'll get to rub liniment into my neck and knees. Possibly convince Jenna to rub it into my shoulders as well. Ideally before I have to go to the main hall and spend the afternoon doing a scavenger hunt. But they don't seem keen to leave us alone with their stuff, which makes me think they're going to do something to *our* stuff. In the end, I remove the liniment as stealthily as possible and take it outside with me. I'd go to the toilet block to do it, but it takes me past the main hall, and I just know that Mr Simmons is not letting me get past him. He has this weird organisational tic, so he'd definitely keep me there until the initial muster was over. Instead, I hide in the irrigation ditch behind the cabin and self-apply.

'Turing, I've seen you do some weird shit in my time,' Daniel says when he finds me. 'But this is next level.'

I look up from massaging my knee to see him and Caleb standing over me.

'Hardly,' I reply, scowling. 'You've seen me massage my knee before.'

'Yeah, but not in a ditch. The ditch is new,' he grins.

'We're gonna be late,' Caleb says. 'Get your ass out of the ditch, Turing.'

'Only I get to call her Turing,' Daniel says.

Caleb shrugs. 'Whatever. I'm out.' He wanders off without looking back.

'You're weirder than I am,' I say. 'Who looks at their friend in a ditch and judges them?'

'Girlfriend,' Daniel corrects me. He's always correcting me. 'And I'm about to offer assistance.'

'Oh, god, could you do my shoulders?' I ask.

'You want me to rub your shoulders,' Daniel says, eyes widening.

'No, not like that. Medically. I want you to medically apply a medical treatment for my muscles,' I say, cheeks burning. 'Or if you could get Jenna, that would be great.'

Daniel jumps down into the ditch and crouches beside me. 'Is it bad?' he asks, extending his hand for the liniment.

I nod as I hand it to him. I shift so my back is to him and twist my ponytail into a bun.

I shiver at the coolness of the cream on his fingertips, and his touch is hesitant at first.

'You won't hurt me,' I say.

'Not what I'm thinking about,' he says, and there's a weird edge under the teasing tone.

The pressure increases and I make an involuntary noise of pleasure.

'Now I'm really not thinking about that,' he says. 'I can't do this if you make that sound.'

'Sorry,' I say. 'Think medical thoughts.' I press my lips together to keep in a moan.

'I do this for my mother sometimes,' he says.

'I can tell I'm not your first,' I tease.

'Grace,' he groans. 'Stop it.'

'What? That wasn't anything!'

'I'm done,' he says, moving back. 'Thank God.'

I turn around and accept the tube from him. 'I'll put this back and then go to the hall.'

'I'll wait for you,' he says.

...

I join him a few moments later. He keeps a ten-centimetre gap between us, and I feel like it's deliberate.

'You're late,' Mrs Easton says with a knowing smile.

I step close to her. 'Sniff,' I say.

She looks at me like I'm crazy but she does what I ask.

'Ah,' she says. 'You should have found me.' The overwhelming smell of Fisiocream was not subtle.

'You do remember the craziness of our cabin, right? It was easier to do it myself. Daniel just found me.'

'Okay, but ask next time,' she says. 'I'm pretty sure your boyfriend rubbing your bare shoulders would be enough to get you expelled given how much the staff love you.'

'I'm exiting this conversation,' Daniel says. 'This day is way too confronting.'

I snicker a little, amused. 'I kept my shirt on,' I tell Mrs Easton, because it seems relevant.

'He's sweet,' she says. 'I like him.'

'Everyone likes him,' I sigh.

'They really don't,' Mrs Easton says. 'Shit, I shouldn't have said that.'

'The important people with good taste,' I amend.

'Now that everyone is here,' Mr Simmons says, giving Mrs Easton and I a loaded glare. 'Let's get some housekeeping out of the way before the scavenger hunt.'

...

I hold the laminated scavenger sheet and pray that Liam doesn't kill himself going for the only gumnut we could find.

'This is a bad idea,' I say for the sixth time. 'I hate losing, but if we can't find one, I doubt anyone else can either.'

'Almost there,' Liam says. 'Can you boost me a little higher?'

'I can try,' Caleb says. Because, yes, Liam is on top of Caleb's shoulders.

'I found a pebble in the shape of a heart,' Jenna announces, victoriously.

'Fuck,' Liam says, and I close my eyes.

'Do I want to know?' I ask Jenna.

'Probably not,' Jenna says a little breathlessly.

I open my eyes.

Liam is bent over a bough, legs dangling. Caleb is looking up at him.

'A little to the left, mate, you got this,' Caleb says.

'Don't do it,' I say.

'I can't watch,' says Jenna.

'Wait. I think I can get it,' I say. 'If Caleb can boost me to that bough I'll be able to step around and reach it.'

'No,' Jenna says.

'I can't reach it,' Liam says. 'Give Grace's way a try.'

'Uh, I'm not sure that's the best idea. Grace is kind of … fragile,' Caleb says.

I wonder if Elsa has told him about me or if he's just picked up on the fragile vibe. God, I hate being told I'm fragile. Which is why I'm about to do something stupid. I approach the tree, considering the steps.

'I've got this,' I decide, tilting my head.

'Grace Turing, if you climb that tree, so help me God, I'm calling your father,' Daniel shouts from fifty metres away.

'Controlling much?' Liam shouts back. 'She can do what she wants.'

'Jenna, go get Mrs Easton,' Daniel says once he's jogged close enough.

'Dude, get back here,' Graham says. 'It's not your problem.'

'It's not your problem,' Liam agrees, smugly. 'Grace, you do what you want.'

'Turing, I love your fighting spirit. But if you climb that tree, you will not like the consequences,' Daniel warns.

'Grace, listen to him. Or I will go get Mrs Easton. Or Mr Holt. Do you want to hear what Mr Holt will say about you climbing a tree?' Jenna tries.

'Fine,' I snap and back off. 'Liam, once you get back down, I'll show you the path.'

'Thank you,' Daniel says, almost slumping in relief. 'Are you trying to kill me?'

'It's a tree,' I complain. 'It's not a rock face.'

'Turing,' Daniel groans.

'What?'

'Do you need the full lecture that your Dad made me memorise?' Jenna hisses. 'It's got a good section on the impact of your pain on the people who love you.'

'You're acting like she's made of glass,' Liam says, then he lands on the ground with an 'oof' of air escaping him.

'She might as well be,' Jenna mutters.

I glare at her.

'Daniel!' Emmy calls, emphasising the second half of his name in her stupid, fake accent. 'We need you.'

The three of us collectively wince.

'That's what I have to put up with when I'm not freaking out about you breaking your leg,' Daniel says.

'Fine,' I say. 'I hereby swear I will not climb a tree.'

'Thank you, Jesus,' Jenna says.

'Promise me, Turing,' Daniel says.

I roll my eyes.

'That would be cute if you hadn't already almost climbed that tree after swearing you wouldn't climb *anything*.'

'I promise,' I say. 'And I'm sorry. I'll remember I'm made of glass.'

'Thank you,' he says, still glaring at me before jogging back towards his group.

'Make out with your girlfriend later,' Graham shouts.

'He's kind of a dick to you,' Liam says. 'You can climb a tree if you want to climb a tree.'

'Liam, I'm not even sure how to begin to explain that he's right, I shouldn't be climbing trees,' I sigh.

'She really shouldn't,' Jenna agrees.

'Are you pregnant or something?' Liam asks.

I stare at him, horrified.

'I'm really not,' I manage over Jenna and Caleb's laughter.

...

Later, when Jenna and Liam are retrieving a feather, I ask Caleb why he thinks I shouldn't climb a tree.

'I'm not an idiot,' he says. 'I have eyes. Even if I only saw you massaging your knee this morning.'

'I know you're not an idiot,' I say. 'I just ... I'm used to keeping the secret. But I suppose Elsa told you?'

'She didn't, so don't say she did, okay? She's been really stressed about not telling me,' Caleb says. 'And I don't really know, I just, you know, guessed.'

'Okay,' I say.

'I actually like you, you know, as a person. So, I care or whatever,'

Caleb shrugs. 'You don't have to tell me if you don't want to, though.'

'Thanks,' I say. 'Maybe … later? I just … it's hard to explain,' I manage. I'm surprised to find I do actually trust Caleb. I've even started to like him, now I think about it.

'Whenever,' he shrugs. 'But maybe don't climb trees, or whatever. Elsa would probs kill me if I didn't stop you.'

'Noted,' I say, smiling.

Another ally.

It's getting easier to think about everyone knowing.

…

We come first in the scavenger hunt. Liam hugs me and I flinch.

'It's all thanks to you and the gumnut,' he says after I escape him.

'You did the hard work,' I say, deflecting. I can feel Daniel's glare without even looking in his direction.

'If you were with me, I'd let you climb a tree,' he says, his voice low.

'No, you really wouldn't,' Jenna tells him. 'You'd make her have a five-metre radius from climbable trees at all times.'

I laugh and Liam looks confused.

'Girls,' Caleb says, rolling his eyes as he claps a hand on Liam's shoulder.

I nod, and Caleb nods back.

…

I'm getting pretty ready to drag my fatigued ass out of bed to smother Kenzi with a pillow. I'll let Jenna take Amber out. Miss Williams came in at least fifteen minutes ago and said it was after one in the morning.

'Right? Like, you should definitely wear pastels. Think the Asian chick in "To All The Boys I've Ever Loved", but, you know, less cardigans,' Kenzi says.

'Oh, you're part Asian, you'll know her name, right, Grace?' Amber asks.

I do know her name. It's Lara-Jean. But not because I'm Asian: because I read books.

'No,' I say, flatly. 'Shut up and go to sleep.'

'Killjoy,' Amber says. 'You don't have to be a bitch about it.'

'Please go to sleep?' I try.

'We're going to sleep, oh my god,' Amber says. 'What was that guy's name? He was in the fake dating one, too.'

'Screw this,' I mutter and throw the sleeping bag off me. 'I need drugs.'

'Can I have some, too?' Jenna whispers.

'Girl, you know I'd say yes if I could,' I whisper back.

It takes an extra two diazepams to go to sleep. I pity Jenna, but out here in the wild, it's every girl for herself.

...

At some point between going to bed and our camp group coming off breakfast duty, something happened that has made everyone look at me like I'm a freak.

'She's got, like, six braces in her suitcase,' I overhear Graham say to Morgan. 'She's faking it for attention. You should have seen Daniel freak out about her climbing a tree. She's gaslighting him.'

I freeze and feel sick. Daniel sees me and lunges toward me, but I step backwards, back out the door.

'Grace,' Jenna says, chasing after me. 'It's okay. It's just bullshit from people who don't know anything.'

'It's only four braces,' I say, like that's important. I won't cry. I won't cry. I won't cry. I won't –

'Turing, you okay?' Daniel asks. 'I think Kenzi and Amber went through your bag this morning.'

'Shit,' I say.

'Who are we killing?' Caleb asks, joining us.

We all stare at him, taken away from the crisis swirling around me for a moment.

'What?' he says. 'Elsa would say it if she were here.'

'Thanks,' I say. 'I'm fine. It's all fine. It's just rumours. It'll die down. It's nothing. Nothing to worry about it. It doesn't matter.'

'Have you ever noticed that when someone says "it doesn't matter" it usually means it matters quite a lot?' Jenna asks.

Daniel and I exchange a look.

'It doesn't matter,' I repeat.

'Turi–'

'It doesn't matter,' I repeat, firmer.

Daniel nods. 'It doesn't matter,' he agrees.

'We're going back in there and we're going to ignore it, because it doesn't matter.'

'Prove it,' Daniel says.

My lips twitch into an involuntary smile. I know exactly what he wants from me, and I love him for it.

'Tasmania has the oldest trees in the world.'

'Nope. Not weird enough,' he says.

'Yeah, that was lame,' Jenna agrees.

'The Tasmanian devil is the largest carnivorous marsupial in the world,' I say.

'Even I know that's C-grade material,' Caleb says.

'Right? Clearly not okay and we should go get Mrs Easton. Maybe even call her father,' Daniel teases.

I scowl. 'I like Tasmania facts.'

'No one likes Tasmania facts,' Daniel says. 'You're such a mainlander sometimes.'

'You know the vacuum toilets on aeroplanes? There are cases of them legit sucking the rectum out of people,' I say.

Jenna gags.

'Oh my god,' Caleb says, horrified and excited. 'For real?'

'I shit you not,' I say. 'I don't screw around with my facts.'

'Clean your face,' Daniel advises, smiling a little as he accepts my fine-ness. 'You cry like a trainwreck.'

'Such romance,' Jenna teases, and he gives her the finger.

'It's true though,' Caleb says.

'You're going in there now, and you're not going to say anything,' I tell them.

'Okay,' Daniel says. He looks at Caleb, who shrugs.

'Thank you,' I say.

The boys go back inside, and Jenna hovers around me nervously as we walk to the toilet block.

'Those bitches,' Jenna rants. 'They keep us up all night, and then they go through our shit. They better be grateful you aren't reporting them.'

'It'll make it worse,' I say.

'Voice of experience?'

'Yeah. It'll die down by tomorrow.'

'And if it doesn't?'

'If it doesn't … I promised Dad I'd tell everyone when I got back from camp,' I say. 'So it'll either get worse or better.'

'I do not envy you,' Jenna says, shaking her head

...

In my head, I repeat those three magic words over and over: it doesn't matter, it doesn't matter, it doesn't matter.

If you do something sixty-six times, it becomes a habit.

If I say 'it doesn't matter' sixty-six times, will it be true?

CHAPTER SIXTEEN

Denouement

The morning is spent in our camp groups doing 'creative problem solving' activities, that were probably meant to be an obstacle course. And then I came along and Mr Holt sighed dramatically a lot while reworking his plans. How to get a team member over a thing without touching it. Feed a team member through a tyre. Some strange leapfrog challenge I didn't want anything to do with.

Liam keeps hovering over my shoulder, actioning all my ideas and not asking about the weird brace collection I have. Which I appreciate, but also don't appreciate. Because it's weird and a normal person who was my friend would just ask, right? But, no, not Liam. Liam has to avoid conflict and doesn't like hearing things that might upset him.

'You definitely made the right call on not dating him', Jenna whispers while we watch Caleb and Liam leapfrog over each other. They're trying to go twenty metres where each pair only touch the ground ten times or something.

'What?' I ask. 'Not dating who?'

'Liam, obviously. He's kind of boring once you get past the face.'

I laugh, because it's true, and she bumps me with her hip.

'It's good to hear you laugh,' she says. 'I was worried you'd ... I don't know.'

'I have you and Daniel, and apparently Caleb, so, I'm okay,' I say. 'Sure, invasion of privacy and weirdness is shit, but it could be worse.'

'How?'

'I could not have been allowed to come to camp at all?'

'Seriously? You're going to say that after being locked in a room with Amber and Kenzi overnight?'

'Yep. Gotta make those memories, son,' I grin.

'You're insane,' she says.

Despite the fact she's just complained, I realise that she looks good. I mean, clearly the bright red uniform doesn't suit her, it just makes her curves look fat. But she's wearing jeans and a purple t-shirt that actually fits her. She seems to be standing at her full height, too, instead of hunching like she did when I met her.

'So are you. All the best people are,' I say.

Jenna smiles, and then turns to tell Liam and Caleb that they need to get more air or it's not going to work. I lean back on the grass, enjoying the sun. I look around and watch the groups all doing different challenges. It's actually painful to watch Daniel's group attempt the bridge challenge. I catch Emmy trying to flirtatiously get passed through the suspended tyre. I see Ryan standing a little apart from his group, looking at something. I follow his eyes and see that it's Jenna. I think he can see the same thing I can, this different, happier Jenna. The beautiful Jenna, who isn't 'quite pretty if she'd lose some weight' like people say, but actually just pretty. I know that if I tell her, she won't believe me. But I hope she sees herself one day. I hope Ryan tells her, even though she'll freak out because he's shorter and skinnier.

...

Mrs Easton takes a seat beside me on the grass.

'Hey, Grace.'

'Hi, Mrs Easton. How goes camp counselling?'

She groans. 'This is why I didn't become a teacher. Give me back my spreadsheets.'

I laugh and she pulls a face.

'So, I've heard a rumour', she says.

'Ah,' I say. 'I had nothing to do with the huntsman in the girl's bathroom but I'm happy to take credit.'

Mrs Easton snorts a laugh. 'You're hilarious. No. About you and some questionable luggage items.'

'You found my weed?'

'Grace.'

I sigh. 'It's fine. It doesn't matter. Sure, I hate it, and I'd like to work out a revenge plot. But in the end, if I make a big deal out of this, it becomes a big deal. It's not worth it,' I say.

'Are you sure?' Mrs Easton asks. 'I've overheard some not very nice things about you, today. I nearly overstepped my professional boundaries.'

'It's nothing I haven't heard before,' I say. 'But you get it, right, why I wanted to keep it secret? Do you think the others will understand now?'

'Miss Williams definitely does,' Mrs Easton says. 'She couldn't believe how cruel they were.'

'Miss Williams needs to get woke,' I say. 'She's first year out, clearly. She's young enough to remember high school. I don't get it.'

'She's getting there,' Mrs Easton says. 'You're good for her. The gentlemen, however, think you brought this on yourself. And that you're depriving the grade of opportunities for personal development.'

'Blame the victim. And, I swear to God, it's not any disabled person's job to make other people better. It's such BS.'

'Right? Honestly. Some men really are stupid,' she sighs. 'Wait. I didn't say that. I said ... oh, I give up.'

I laugh. 'There's a reason you're my favourite,' I tell her.

'Well, you're my favourite, too,' she says. 'But you can't tell anyone said that.'

'Of course not,' I say. 'I think you said something about how much you're enjoying the company of all the girls in Huon Pine Cabin.'

'Absolutely,' Mrs Easton says, laying the sarcasm on thick. 'So, you don't want me to say anything?'

'Let it run its course,' I say. 'It'll get better, or it won't.'

'Okay. Good luck with the ... whatever this is,' Mrs Easton says, waving a hand at the leapfrogging.

'Thanks,' I say.

...

I sit between Jenna and Daniel at lunch and pretend I can't see or hear anything. Caleb was eating with the rest of the football jocks, but he gets up halfway through, and brings his food over to our table. We all look at him, confused.

'If I have to listen to one more person say how terrible Grace is as a person, I'm going to do something that will get me sent home,' he says. 'Which is tempting because it would be satisfying and I'd get to see Elsa. But I really don't need any more disciplinary shit on my record before TAFE.'

'You know, I don't think they check that,' Daniel says.

'Well, my father would kill me then,' Caleb replies.

'Ah, of course,' Daniel says.

I raise my eyebrows in a question.

'He's a cop,' Caleb says. 'He doesn't approve of me using my fists to solve my problems. But I feel like he should give me a pass for this one.'

'You know, you're actually quite sweet when you're not being a misogynistic asshole,' Jenna says, teasing.

'Elsa says the same thing,' Caleb sighs, not getting the joke.

'Thanks, anyway,' I say. 'But you don't have to defend me. I appreciate the support. But, really. It doesn't matter what they think.'

'Can I punch someone?' Daniel asks. 'Can I punch Liam, specifically?'

'If anyone punches Liam, it's going to be me,' I say. 'And I'm not punching him.'

'Dude likes you and he just lets them talk shit about you,' Caleb says with a mouth full of food. 'I don't get it.'

'I don't get why he likes me at all,' I say. 'We have literally nothing in common. I think I'm a novelty.'

'Uh, you're gorgeous?' Daniel says. 'Smart, funny.'

'You're confident. Confidence is sexy. Cosmo says so,' Jenna adds.

I roll my eyes. 'You're all idiots.'

'They're not wrong,' Caleb shrugs. 'You don't exactly wet my wick or anything –'

'Gross!' Jenna says.

'Stop talking,' Daniel says.

'Please don't,' I say.

'Whatever,' Caleb says.

'Chainsaws were invented to help with childbirth,' I say to change the subject.

'What the fuck?!' Caleb says.

'No!' Jenna says.

'That's metal AF. Childbirth is insane,' Daniel replies.

'Right? Blew my mind. It was my zombie apocalypse weapon of choice until I thought through the splatter,' I reply, grinning.

'I'm eating,' Jenna complains.

We all look down at the spaghetti bolognaise, and then up at each other.

'It's illegal to own just one guinea pig in Switzerland because it gets lonely?' Daniel says.

'In Queensland, you need to be a licensed magician to own a rabbit,' I say.

Caleb skewers a forkful of spag bol and shoves it in his mouth.

Jenna contemplates her food again.

I take a mouthful.

'Alright,' she says. 'The Switzerland thing was really cute.' She keeps eating.

Daniel and I share a grin. We're both still thinking about the chainsaw.

...

Jenna and I leave the bonfire early claiming tiredness. It's not a lie. We're stupidly tired. It's a good thing we do, too, because when we get back to the cabin, our bags have been emptied onto my bed. Jenna's conditioner has been squirted into her suitcase lining.

'Well,' she says. 'I'm going to kill them.'

'Grace? Do you want your night meds?' Mrs Easton asks. 'I for–'

I turn to look at her as she stares at the mess.

'Those bitches,' Mrs Easton says. 'Shit. No, I didn't say that.'

'Of course you didn't,' I say. 'And the cabin door wasn't locked.'

'Oh, come on,' Jenna says. 'Who else could it be?'

I think she might actually cry and I can't blame her.

'Literally anyone,' I say, shaking my head.

'Well, I know where to start,' Mrs Easton says, and then she turns on her heel and storms out of the cabin.

'Step one: let's fold the clothes,' I say. 'We'll set aside anything that smells weird or has random liquid on it.'

'This is bullshit,' Jenna says.

'It doesn't matter,' I say.

'It matters, Grace! Look at this mess? They've been spreading gossip about you, bullying you, and now they're invading our privacy to screw with us! It's not okay and it does matter. If it doesn't matter to you, fine, but it sure as shit matters a lot to me,' Jenna yells. She picks up a t-shirt and shakes it out, revealing a cascade of glitter.

I am silent for the most pregnant pause of all time. 'Oh, fuck me. It's the herpes of craft supplies. They've done it now.' I can literally feel myself start to snarl.

'Seriously, Grace? Glitter? That's what gets you mad? Freaking glitter!?'

'There's a line on this high school bullying bullshit. I know the line. Before Riverview, I had stolen pens and pencils, rumours, the last girl chosen for everything. At camp, someone always pulled some bullshit prank like vegemite under a door handle or replacing my shampoo with some gross smelling liquid. But, yeah, glitter is my line. Because glitter never goes away,' I reply, fuming. 'Pranks should be easily remedied.'

'I ... I didn't realise.'

'Well, you should have. Why the hell else would I keep this secret so hard?'

'What secret?'

We turn to see Amber and Kenzi in the doorway, Mrs Easton standing behind them.

'Like we'd tell you,' I snap. 'Are you responsible for this bullshit? Glitter, Mackenzie? Really?'

'It wasn't us,' Amber says.

But I can see the weakness in Kenzi's eyes. She shifts on her feet. I narrow my eyes.

'Girls,' Mrs Easton begins.

'No, I wanna hear this from them,' I interject. 'Because emptying the suitcases? Whatever. Conditioner? Look, a load of laundry and it's fine. But *glitter never goes away*. And Kenzi has art with me and she knows how much I hate it. So tell me, what made you think this was a good idea?'

'Learn to take a joke, Jesus,' Kenzi says, looking away.

I smirk, victoriously.

'Kenz!' Amber hisses. 'Shut up.'

'Too late,' I say.

'You're such a freak,' Amber says. 'Who even has all those weird brace things?'

'God forbid someone needs a brace for their legitimate medical condition,' Jenna snaps.

I spin and glare at her.

She stammers.

'I knew it. You *are* a freak,' Amber sneers while Kenzi is still looking at the ground.

'Girls!' Mrs Easton says. 'That's quite enough! Now, I'll take the girls to speak to Mr Simmons and Miss Williams. Could you two make sure nothing is missing or broken? Then, I think, Amber and Mackenzie will be able to clean up the mess they made.'

'We'll do it. I don't trust them. Any chance we can switch roommates? I mean, I know it's inconvenient, but ...' I gesture to the mess.

'I'll talk to the staff about it,' Mrs Easton says.

'Thanks.'

'I'm so sorry,' Jenna says when we're alone.

'It's not your fault. You were angry.'

'What are we going to do?' she asks, looking at the mess.

'Step one, we check the clothes. Then we check the cases. And the bedding. We prioritise tasks and we leave to tomorrow what can wait,' I say.

'How are you keeping your cool?' Jenna asks. 'I want to cry and throw up.'

'Crying and throwing up aren't going to change anything,' I sigh. 'But a nap would go a long way for me right now.'

...

Mrs Easton and Riley sleep in our room. I don't even care what the punishment is for the stupid bitches. I'm too tired by then. At least we got new roommates who valued sleep.

We are marshalled to the scraggly patch of grass in front of the main hall after breakfast to be drilled on appropriate bushwalk behaviour.

'We will walk to the waterfall from here. It is a three-and-a-half-hour walk, return. Make sure you have a full drink bottle and your morning snack. The teachers have sunscreen, first aid kits, and whistles to attract attention if anyone gets lost,' Mr Holt says.

'We also have these snazzy, hi-vis vests so you'll be able to see us through the trees,' Miss Williams says, trying for a joke. The students roll their eyes and Mr Holt glares at her for interrupting.

'Grace, a word,' Mr Holt says as we prepare to set off.

'Sure,' I say, and linger with him.

'You shouldn't go on this walk,' he says.

I raise my eyebrows. 'Why?'

'You know why,' he says, pointedly. 'Your ... connective ... thing.'

'Mixed connective tissue disorder?' I ask. 'You know, my managed condition that a licensed doctor said shouldn't interfere with a bushwalk?'

We stare each other down.

'Come on, Grace,' Mrs Easton says. 'Walk with me. I'm terrified of snakes.'

'It's Tasmania,' I reply, walking over to her. 'You should be scared.'

'Aren't they all poisonous?' Jenna asks.

'Venomous,' I correct. 'Copperheads, tiger snakes, and ... whip snakes?'

'White-lipped snakes,' Mrs Easton says, her voice full of dread. 'They'll all kill you.'

'Cheery thought,' I say.

'Try not to scare the kids, Merry,' Mr Holt says, overtaking us.

Mrs Easton scowls at his back.

'You're doing it again,' I say.

'Damn it,' she sighs. 'Only for you, Grace. I'm never going on camp again.'

We laugh.

'I didn't know your name was Merry,' Jenna says. 'It's nice.'

'It's Miranda, actually. Jim called me Merry once at a work thing and now they all do,' Mrs Easton says.

Daniel and I are walking together as we approach the waterfall. He holds my hand, guiding me over roots and stones that he thinks might be awkward. I think he's using it as an excuse to touch me, but he says he isn't. While he does enjoy touching me, I think he's actually terrified my father might rescind his approval. I think the approval actually means a lot to Daniel. He hasn't had a lot of people believe in him.

'I love the sound of waterfalls,' I say, smiling. 'I wonder how much longer it is until we get there.'

'It's white noise,' Daniel replies. 'I mean, it's pretty, but I don't get it. I'm a beach guy. Give me the sound of the ocean.'

'I'm a river person,' I say. 'I think everyone has their water, you know?'

'Is this a weird philosophical identity question? Like Harry Potter houses?'

'No, it's just a weird observation I've made.'

'You are full of weird observations,' Daniel says, teasing me.

There's a moment where I think he's going to kiss me. It's almost been like he's scared of touching me. He darts kisses on my cheek, gently on the back of my hand like a weirdo, and occasionally we'll find a hiding spot to kiss at school or if we've got a moment after dinner at my place. But his hands never wander, he never presses me or holds me with any force. I've been working my way up to a conversation about how I'm not actually made of glass and I'm going to scream if he doesn't commit to making out with me soon. But this ... this feels like a moment and everything is building. We're a moment away from the kind of kiss that happens in teen movies with a gorgeous backdrop.

'Grace, I ...'

I hold my breath, waiting, leaning.

His free hand grazes my cheek and begins to guide me clos –

'So I was, like, meh, and she lost her mind and, like, came at me,' Amber's voice threads clearly through the trees.

They were close, and the knowledge of it makes us spring apart.

My left foot lands on a twig, and the roll of my body and momentum brings my weight down on my right leg, hard.

Too hard.

I bite back a scream as I go down.

'Grace!' Daniel's shouts. It feels like he's at my side before I finish landing.

I choke on bile, swallowing it back down.

'Christ,' he mutters. 'Eight out of ten.'

'It's just the shock,' I say, my voice breathy. 'It's … it's fine.'

'Babe, I have eyes,' he says. He looks pointedly at my knee. 'Subluxation, right? You're pale as.'

I close my eyes to take a breath. 'When you're right, you're right.' I say it like it's a joke.

'Uh, what are you two doing?' Amber asks, judgmentally.

Daniel whirls around to glare at her. 'She's injured.'

'Right,' Amber scoffs. 'She's putting it on. You know that, right?'

'She's –'

I cut Daniel off by pulling on his trouser leg. 'She's not important. Get Mrs Easton. She shouldn't be too far ahead of us.'

'I'm not leaving you,' he says.

'Well, someone's going to have to,' I say. 'Because Holt's bringing up the rear, and I'm not dealing with him without Mrs Easton.'

'Fair,' Daniel says. He looks back over at the group. 'Liam, go for Mrs Easton.'

'I … uh … okay,' he says. 'Are you sure she's hurt, though? Like, she really needs first aid?'

'For God's sake,' Daniel shouts. 'Go!'

'Okay,' Liam says, looking dubious and mildly offended. But he goes.

'I'm going to put it back in,' I say, gently. 'But I'm not getting out of here without a brace or tape.'

'What's wrong with her?' Kenzi asks.

'Drama queen,' Emmy says, flipping her hair. 'She just wants attention.'

As if Emmy wasn't the OG drama queen.

'Shut up,' Daniel snaps at them. 'Are you sure?' he asks me. 'Remember last time?'

'I'm sure,' I say. 'It's not dislocated. It's the other knee, too.'

'Gotta make it even,' he teases me.

I smile. 'Something like that.'

'Grace! What happened?' Jenna rushes over to me.

'Subluxation,' I say. 'It's fine.'

'She needs her brace,' Daniel says.

'I'll go with Jenna,' Caleb says. 'We'll tell Mr Holt.'

'Thank you,' I say, and then they're gone, too. I look at the group of bitchy girls still watching the show. 'Any of you faint easy?' I ask.

'Why?' Emmy asks.

I grin, and brace myself to pop my knee back in. 'You're gonna hear a pop,' I say.

'Oh God,' Emmy says, horrified. Amber looks like she'll be sick.

I pop it in place quickly, grunting out an unavoidable sound of pain.

'What was that?' Kenzi asks.

'Her knee, dipshit,' Daniel says, rolling his eyes.

'This is exactly why I said you shouldn't go on the bushwalk,' Mr Holt shouts as he jogs towards us. 'You've got an autoimmune disease, the connective tissues thing, and dodgy joints!'

'Justin!' Mrs Easton says, chastising him as she arrives from the other direction with Liam on her heels.

'She's got what?' Amber asks.

Mr Holt looks like he might be sorry under the anger.

'Atypical autoimmune disease, mixed connective tissue disorder, joints that pop in and out of place, and a bunch of other chronic pain bullshit,' I say. 'Not that it's anyone's business but mine.' I nearly thank Mr Holt sarcastically but manage not to.

Epic restraint.

God, I'm tired and it hurts and I want a nap.

'She's not faking it,' Liam says, kind of in awe.

'No shit, Sherlock,' Daniel snaps.

'Language,' Mr Holt says.

Daniel rolls his eyes.

'I put it back in,' I tell Mrs Easton. 'And Caleb and Jenna went back for my knee brace. If you and Daniel don't mind missing out on the waterfall, I think we can make it back just the three of us when the brace is here.'

'Should you have done that?' Mr Holt asks.

'Yes,' I say, my voice flat.

'Doesn't it, you know, hurt?' Liam asks.

'Of course it hurts,' I say. 'Just … go be stupid elsewhere, please.'

'Grace!' Mr Holt snaps.

'Fine. Sorry. Whatever. Pain and manners don't exactly go hand in hand.'

'You're forgiven,' Liam says.

I raise my eyes skyward and pray that they all piss off. I'm tired, I'm achy, and my knee really frickin' hurts. I look at Mrs Easton. 'I don't suppose you have some good drugs in that fanny pack?'

'What do you want?' she asks, smiling. 'I've got a little bit of everything.'

'You like sounding like a drug dealer, don't you?' I tease.

She laughs. 'A little.'

'Could I get an oxycodone and a diazepam? Oh, actually, let's start with an anti-inflammatory and a diazepam. I mean, I'm definitely going to want the oxycodone before I start walking,' I say, thinking. 'But when you fill the paperwork out on this later it'll look like you did SOP.'

'I appreciate that. RockTape?' Mrs Easton asks, coming to sit next to me. She looks up before handing me the pills. 'You can all keep walking,' she says, giving a stern look to the teens watching us like we're on stage as I take my pills.

'Move it along,' Holt says, shooing them.

They go, but he stays.

I take the tape and scissors from Mrs Easton and start strapping my knee. I'm still gonna need that brace, but this will help, too.

'Justin, if you're going to say something unsupportive to a student who is in pain and coping very well with herself, you can go, too.'

'Don't undermine me in front of my students.'

'Well, don't be ... I apologise if you perceive that I'm doing that,' she says, picking her words carefully. 'I have this situation under control. I hear the falls can be very relaxing. Perhaps you'd like to go and shepherd the rest of the students?'

Mr Holt works his jaw as he glares at her, then at me, and finally at Daniel. 'Perkins, time to go,' he says.

'Uh, no,' Daniel says. 'Grace needs me.'

'Grace has Mrs Easton,' Mr Holt argues.

'He stays,' I say, firmly. 'I need him.'

Mr Holt looks sceptical.

'To be my crutch,' I add. 'I'm going to be a bit limpy.'

'Fine,' Mr Holt says. 'But don't leave them alone.' He directs that last part at Mrs Easton, who sighs.

'Yes, because Grace is definitely going to feel like getting it on with her knee in agony,' she replies, her voice dry as dust.

Mr Holt glares a bit longer and then stalks off in the direction of the falls.

'So, I have to ask,' Mrs Easton says when he's out of hearing range. 'You didn't do anything that would have made this happen, right? No climbing trees or anything?'

'No,' I say.

'Well,' Daniel says.

'No,' I say again.

Mrs Easton raises a single eyebrow.

'It was an accident,' I say. 'That's all.'

'Daniel?'

'Yes, Daniel, would you like to break down what happened?' I ask him, curious.

He blows out a sigh. 'You're so difficult, Turing.'

'I know,' I say.

'Okay, tell me,' Mrs Easton says. 'It can't be that bad and I'd rather know and lie about it.'

'We were almost having a moment,' I say. 'And then we heard Amber coming around the bed and we panicked and jumped apart – completely unnecessarily because we weren't doing anything wrong.'

'Right,' Mrs Easton says.

'We were holding hands,' Daniel explains. 'And ... that's all.'

'Yep,' I say.

'Right,' Mrs Easton says.

'I'm sensing some dubiousness,' I say.

'Christ,' Daniel says. 'I can't have this conversation.'

'Then stop making us have this conversation!'

'You're the one that had this conversation *in front of your father.*'

'Oh, hardly! I just said he didn't have to worry.'

'Okay!' Mrs Easton says, cutting over us. Daniel and I look at her, remembering her again.

'You know, I really need to figure out how to stop forgetting other people are around,' I sigh.

'While that's kind of romantic,' Mrs Easton says before Daniel can talk. 'You were just holding hands?'

'Yes,' I say.

'And you sprang apart, Grace stumbled, and here we are,' she finishes.

'Yes,' Daniel and I say together.

'Okay. Let's talk about literally anything else,' she says.

Daniel grins wickedly. 'Turing had an excellent fun fact yesterday at lunch.'

'I feel like I should be nervous,' Mrs Easton says.

'There are more libraries than McDonald's in America' I say quickly. I've been saving that one for a moment like this.

'The chainsaw was invented for childbirth,' Daniel says despite my valiant attempts at not subjecting Mrs Easton to that fact.

'Oh my lord,' she says. 'That can't possibly be true.'

'If Grace said it, you can bet your ass it is,' Daniel says. 'It's one of the things I love about her.'

'Shut up,' I say. 'Daniel told me that the shiny coating on jelly-beans was insect poo.'

'I've changed my mind,' Mrs Easton says. 'We're going to talk about normal stuff, like what you're doing for tonight's talent show.'

'Oh God,' I say. 'I'd forgotten about that. I was doing a thing with Elsa and Jenna. But Elsa's not here and I'm injured.'

'Mandatory,' Mrs Easton says. 'Apparently, if it's optional no one would do it.'

'Funny that,' Daniel says. 'I'm doing my amazing comedy routine. I tell a joke about a pig shit using a balloon as a prop.'

'Amazing,' Mrs Easton says dryly. 'I can't wait.'

...

Jenna and Caleb reach us almost an hour later, and I'm super impressed by their speed. Jenna is flushed bright red and panting. Caleb looks mildly out of breath. They throw all four braces at me.

'Didn't know which one,' Jenna gasps.

'Thank you,' I say and offer her my water bottle. She drinks most of the water left.

'You two can go on to the waterfall if you like,' Mrs Easton says.

'Can I not?' Jenna asks. 'I'm dead.'

'Do you need help getting back?' Caleb asks.

'I'm good, thanks bud,' I say.

He gives me a nod of acknowledgment and then jogs on toward the falls.

'You know, Elsa was right. Camp is magic,' Jenna says. 'Caleb's a human being here.'

...

We are overtaken by everyone on the way back. I get lots of looks and whispers. I'm sweaty, flushed, and exhausted. I'm in so much pain and I'm leaning heavily on Daniel. I think he presses a kiss to my hair on one of our breaks. I want to cry and have him hold me. He doesn't tell me I'm doing great or that I'm fine or to take my time. Instead, he launches into a comparative lecture on how, despite how shit *Die Hard 2* was, it should have stayed a Christmas franchise for sociological reasons. Mrs Easton interjects with her opinions, and Jenna tells them both they're nerds, but she's seen all the movies. I talk when I can, but I mostly let the words wash over me. Daniel makes it so that I don't have to talk or think or feel like I'm a problem. I've never loved him more than I do right now.

One day, I'll tell him that.

...

When we get back to the cabin, Jenna goes and refills my drink bottle. Daniel leaves after I promise I'm fine and Mrs Easton reminds him he shouldn't be at a girl's cabin.

'We've got free time to prepare for our talent show item,' she says when she gets back. 'I already checked, we have to do something.'

'I don't want to. I've been the centre of attention enough for one day. Maybe I just won't go to the hall.'

'Everyone's talking about it,' Jenna admits. 'But, it kind of gave me an idea. I mean, if you want to, you don't have to. I just thought that, maybe, it might kind of be a way to–'

'Jenna, I'm in pain and drugged up. Get to the point.'

'I know how you can control the narrative,' she says.

'What narrative?'

'The you-being-sick narrative,' Jenna says. 'No one knows what's going on and there's people saying you're dying or have cancer or something.'

'And?'

'And, I'll interview you,' she says. 'That's my idea. You help me write the questions, and I'll help you write the answers. You get to control the narrative and explain what you want to.'

I stare at Jenna. She's nervous and I'm looking at her again and realising that she's more, somehow. Smarter. Camp is magic. And, maybe time away from her mother's therapising everything and the constant failure of chess.

She curls in. 'It's just an idea,' she says.

'It's brilliant,' I say. 'Let's do it.'

...

Amber sings, she's actually pretty good. Then Emmanuelle sings 'La vie en Rose', which is torture. Daniel does his joke about the three scientists who stuck a cork in a pig's ass to see what would happen, which was kind of funny. Kenzi and Riley do some weird, vaguely sexual dance routine that gets the boys hollering. Caleb, Graham, and Liam re-enact a Kiwi drink-driving advertisement, which would have been funny if any of them had committed to acting. Morgan does magic tricks. He literally bought those weird interlinking rings and a pack of cards. Daniel leans over and whispers that he could own a rabbit in Queensland, and we get told off for laughing. Jenna and I are up last. When our names are called, Daniel gives us a thumbs up of encouragement and I've never been more nervous in my life as we wait for Mr Simmons to set up our chairs for the interview.

'We can still back out,' Jenna whispers. 'I can fake a diarrhea attack.'

'True friendship,' I say, smiling nervously. I feel strung tight like wires.

We take our seats on 'stage' and I take a really deep breath. Jenna waits for my nod before she starts.

'Good evening, ladies and gentlemen of Grade Ten,' she announces. 'Tonight, we have the distinct pleasure of interviewing our very own Grace Turing!' She forces a round of applause while I consider vomiting.

'Okay, Grace, let's start with an easy one: why did you move to Launceston?' Jenna asks, playing at being an announcer.

'My mother got a job working for a not-for-profit, and so our family moved here in August.'

I'm talking too fast and mumbling. I take a deep breath, trying to calm my nerves.

'You made a decision when you transferred to Riverview High,' Jenna says. 'Can you tell us about that?'

Another deep breath. I swallow thickly. I can do this. Daniel nods at me encouragingly.

'I made the decision to not tell anyone that I was sick. At the time, I had what was known as "some weird autoimmune thing",' I say doing the finger quotes. 'A lot of people accused me of faking it because I didn't have a diagnosis, because they didn't understand how hard it was to get diagnosed.'

'You said that that was your diagnosis then, what about now?' Jenna asks.

'I have an atypical autoimmune disease, which is basically doctor for we don't know which autoimmune disease you have, but you definitely have one. My symptoms are fibromyalgia – which is pain in my muscles and nerve pain, and fatigue problems. After the dodgeball knee-sprain incident,' I give Emmy a meaningful look, 'we discovered that I have mixed connective tissue disorder. The disease is mostly in muscle around my joints for now, which is why I dislocate easily, and have subluxations, which is where certain joints, like my knees, slip out of joint, but not all the way, before they pop back in. I can usually put them back in myself.' I pause and look around the room. I don't think anyone has had a more rapt audience than I do right now. You could hear the proverbial pin drop.

'So, what does that mean on a daily basis for you?' Jenna asks.

'Well, I'm always in pain. Always. You know that pain scale at the doctor where they ask you to rate your pain out of ten? I'm never lower than a five, but usually more like six,' I explain. 'Which is where you can never forget your pain is happening, and it can stop you doing certain things. I'm always exhausted, and sometimes battle insomnia on top of all this. I have to be careful about how much I do. There's this theory someone with lupus – which is another invisible autoimmune disease – made up to explain it to her friend. It's called "spoon theory", and basically if you think about spoons as energy, you get a limited number of spoons a day. If you're healthy, you can borrow spoons from tomorrow, and you have a lot of them. Me, I can't borrow from tomorrow. Getting up is a spoon, showering is a spoon, getting dressed is a spoon. If I've only got, say, ten spoons, I can use a third of them in the first hour of my day. So, I have to be careful.'

'I'm also kind of fragile,' I say, smiling at Liam. 'Which adds to the careful thing as well.'

'It sounds like it's a pretty constant thing for you everyday. Wouldn't it be easier if everyone knew so they could help you?' Jenna asks.

'We're teenagers, we're not exactly the most understanding social demographic,' I say. I get a laugh. 'Right? And, honestly, at my last school, I stopped being me. I was "Sick Girl". It sucked, because there's a lot about me that's not my sickness. I kind of hope that you guys have gotten to know me a bit over the past few months so that, now you know, I'll still be Weird Grace.'

'You're definitely weird,' Riley says, but she's smiling. 'I've never met anyone who knows so much weird shit.'

I grin at her. 'Right? I'm awesome. I'm also sick. They don't cancel each other out.'

Jenna smiles at me pleased that this is working, proud of me for keeping it together. I may have gotten teary a couple of times rehearsing it.

'What do you want people to know about how to help you?' Jenna asks.

'Don't?' I say. There's another laugh. 'Seriously, if I need help, I'll ask for it. Some people,' I glare at Daniel, 'like to force help on me. If I'm injured, you should get Mrs Easton, Ivy, or one of my close friends –'

'Or your boyfriend,' Daniel interjects.

'– who know what to do. I want to be as normal as possible for as long as possible. I mean, maybe remind me not to climb trees or do the Beep Test.'

Another laugh.

I breathe a little easier even though I know what Jenna's about to say.

'As you've worked to keep it a secret, it's clear that you don't want to spend all your time talking about it,' Jenna says.

'That's right,' I nod. 'Which is why if you have any questions ...'

'Now's the time,' Jenna finishes for me. 'Hands up, folks! This is a limited time offer. We hope our judges will forgive us if we go a little over time.'

Mr Simmons looks like he's a little pissed we've hijacked talent night, but Miss Williams and Mrs Easton scowl him into submission. I'm surprised to find Mr Holt looking at me in approval. That's never happened before.

'Liam, what's your question?' Jenna asks, carrying her fake microphone over to him in the crowd. He stands up beside her and good-naturedly speaks into it.

'Will you get better?' he asks.

'No,' I say. 'I'm chronically ill. Chronic means forever in this context.'

'So, will you die?' Liam asks.

Silence falls and breath is held.

'We'll all die,' I say. 'So, yes. But it's not like cancer – I'm not actively dying right now, no. I'll probably have a shorter life than you because I've got a shitty genetic hand, but I've got some good years left before the pain and the real mobility issues start.'

Liam sits down and Jenna walks over to Caleb.

'How do you cope if you're in that much pain all the time?' he asks, seeming genuinely impressed.

I laugh. 'I don't have a choice. I can live or I can curl up in a ball and wait for death.'

'Seriously,' he says, pushing.

'Seriously,' I reply. 'I have to be careful because I'm young and it's easy to get addicted to pain meds. But, yeah, it comes down to my choice. The power of positive thinking or whatever.'

'Why did you stop art?' Kenzi calls out.

'Just a moment, audience member,' Jenna says, stepping over people to hold the fake mic up to her mouth. Kenzi rolls her eyes but repeats her question.

I hold up my hands even though they're barely trembling. 'They aren't too bad today,' I say. 'The diazepam – that's a muscle relaxant – helped. But one of my many medications has a side effect of hand tremors. It's been –,' I cut myself off to look down, trying to stop myself crying. I shake my head and take a deep breath, looking at the ceiling before I level my gaze again. 'God, this is hard,' I say, still a little choked up. 'It's one of the hardest things I've had to accept. I love art, it saved me over and over as I lost other things I loved, like dancing and bushwalking and stuff. But –' I brush the traitorous tears away. 'But, the medication helps make my life more liveable. It's a trade off.'

Kenzi sits back down, looking so sad. God, everyone looks sad.

'Don't y'all start crying, or I'll cry,' I say.

They laugh a little, and some of them look away to gather themselves. I don't look at Daniel because I can't.

'Are there things that make it worse?' Morgan asks.

'Weather pressure changes – there's a reason your grandma's arthritis gets worse when it's about to rain,' I say. 'Lack of sleep. Doing too much the day before. And, you know, sometimes my body just decides to be a dick.'

More laughter.

'As a rule, ask permission before you touch me. Sometimes the pain gets so bad it hurts when I'm touched. And, maybe don't give me your cold or random stomach bug, because my immune system is backwards and it can get me really, seriously sick. COVID would be a death sentence, which may have played into the move, too. So, if you're sick and contagious, please, please stay home or the hell away from me.'

There's some nervous laughter but they're really thinking that one over. I'm glad, because, you know, not dying because of the flu would be awesome. Jenna offers Amber the invisible mic.

'Can we catch it?' Amber asks.

I'm gratified by the scoffing and glares she gets.

'No, you can't catch it,' I say. 'It's a random twist of genetic fate. The rest of my family are fine. It's just me.'

'Well, that's shit,' Caleb says.

'I'm grateful,' I say. 'I'd fall apart if Ivy, my sister, had to live like this, too.'

'Two more questions,' Mrs Easton says.

Jenna jumps over some people to get to Ryan. He looks at her before he looks at me. I swallow a smile.

'You kind of answered this question,' Ryan says. 'But it's degenerative, right? Like, you'll keep getting worse?'

'Yes,' I say. 'I don't know how fast. But, yes.'

Silence reigns supreme.

Ryan sits back down.

Jenna looks at me, waiting.

I take a deep breath. 'It's okay. I made peace with it a while ago. I mean, the connective tissue thing could be a bit of a bitch moving forward if it spreads to my lungs or heart. Childbirth could be a no-go zone, which, I never pictured kids, so, whatever.'

I'm going in the wrong direction, I can tell by Jenna's face.

'But,' I say. 'The other thing about all of that, is that it makes the present that much more valuable. Sure, I'm scared of the future. But I'm also spending time with amazing people who love me, I'm going on school camp, and making memories. I think I'm lucky, because most people our age, and even older, put things off because they can do it later, or in the future. And sometimes, they can't, and they've missed opportunities. I'm not going to do that. I can't afford to. I'm carpe-ing that diem, you know? And, you know, not thinking about the future as much as possible.'

Despite our previous agreement that she would not let Daniel ask a question in case I cried in public, Jenna hands him the fake mic. I glare at her, but she just shrugs it off.

'Anyone else have a question?' I ask before he can speak.

He raises an eyebrow.

Everyone seems really curious as to what he's going to say.

'Alright, ask away, Perkins,' I sigh.

'Thanks. So, my question is: what's the one thing you most want to do before you can't?'

I open my mouth to speak but close it again. I don't know. I smile at him and he smiles back, like he's figured something out that I haven't.

'You're scared a lot, right?' Daniel says. 'About people leaving you behind or feeling trapped in your body.'

'Yeah,' I say. 'It's … shit, quite frankly. It's kind of why I'm so now-focussed.'

'So, what don't you want to regret?' he asks again.

'Having a plan,' I say. 'I don't have one. A career plan or a five-year plan. I'm kind of scared to make one, because my health is pretty unpredictable. But I don't want to get five years in the future and realise I shoulda, coulda, woulda had one.'

'So make one,' he says, smirking. He's so damn pleased with himself.

I wrinkle my nose at him. 'Maybe,' I say. 'I'll try.'

'You're Grace goddamn Turing,' he replies. 'You can do anything. Right?'

There's actual applause as Daniel gestures around him for support.

'Hashtag Team Grace,' Jenna says over the clapping and there are shouts of agreement.

I cover my face with my hands, sad and happy and grateful and scared and excited and …

Jenna comes up and hugs me, leading me away and out the door into the cold, night air. I hiccough a crying laugh and hug her.

'Thank you,' I say. 'Thank you so, so frickin' much.'

'Anything for you, Grace,' Jenna says, hugging me back.

'You girls need a minute?' Mrs Easton asks from the doorway.

'Five,' I say, wiping my wet face.

'I'm so proud of you girls. That was amazing,' Mrs Easton tells us. 'Brave and honest. I wish I had half the gumption you two have.'

I gesture her into our hug, and she joins us.

'You're the best, Mrs Easton,' I say. 'I don't know if I've told you before, but you really, really are.'

She laughs and wipes tears from her cheeks before she goes back inside.

'You girls,' she says, shaking her head as she goes back in.

'Are you okay?' Jenna asks, searching my face. 'I know I said I wouldn't ask Daniel, but, you know, he's your boyfriend and I thought he deserved a chance to ask.'

'Ugh, I'd forgive you pretty much anything right now,' I say. 'Best suggestion ever.'

'I love you,' Jenna says. 'It went better than I expected.'

'What do you mean I wasn't going to be allowed a question?' Daniel demands, joining us.

'I had you,' Jenna laughed.

'You're amazing, Grace Turing. Seriously. You're ... how did someone like you ever decide to hang out with someone like me?' Daniel asks me.

'And that's my cue,' Jenna said, heading back inside.

'I love you, too,' I call after her.

'And me,' Daniel prompts.

'And you,' I agree, pressing a kiss to his cheek. 'And, in case it wasn't obvious, because you're equally amazing. You're ... you. I don't know. It's like ... everything I say here is going to sound corny and dumb.'

'So, be corny and dumb. I won't tell anyone,' Daniel says, snaking an arm around my waist and drawing me closer.

In the darkness, I feel like we could get away with so much more, but I don't want to push our luck.

'It feels like you're meant to be here with me,' I admit, hiding my face. 'Like, you're ... you're just ... you're obviously not perfect. But you might be perfect for me.'

'That was corny and dumb.'

I hit him and tell him to shut up, trying to move away.

He brings me back.

'I feel the same way,' he murmurs into my neck as he holds me in his arms. 'I didn't know I could feel this way before you.'

'You need to get back in here before Mr Simmons comes out,' Jenna calls out, interrupting us.

We spring apart and grin guiltily.

'I love both of you and this has been a weirdly great night,' I say.

'We love you, too,' Jenna says.

'My harem,' Daniel sighs and we laugh and hit him as we go back inside.

I don't think I've ever been this happy.

...

I think that, in the future, I'll look back on today and know that I lived. I'll know that I was happy and loved and felt invincible because of my people. I'll love them forever.

We do not win the talent show, which earns Mr Simmons a lot of booing. Amber wins with her amazing voice. Morgan the Magician comes in second, and Daniel takes third. Jenna and I get an honourable mention. We don't care about any of it, we know we were the fan favourites.

We know it worked.

...

We fall asleep more easily than we expected, the adrenaline burning off quickly and sending us to sleep.

...

We eat breakfast feeling more like a family than a group of students forced to spend time together. Ryan and Graham are having an animated conversation about God knows what, Riley and Kenzi are dancing together like idiots. Caleb and Daniel are discussing various television shows and their importance. I have a trail of people who come up to thank me for last night which feels condescending and annoying. Telling me that they're on my team which would be nice to believe in. Apologising for the fact I'm sick, which I hate, but also apologising for talking shit behind my back. I know that this is the weird camp high, and it will peter out the second we get back to town. Graham and Ryan will never have another conversation. Amber will go back to being a bitch to everyone. Emmy will probably still pelt dodgeballs at me. But I feel freer without my secret. I'm glad it's out. Dad's going to gloat, and I don't even care. I think it came out the right way at the right time.

'So, you were right,' Liam says, before we get on the bus.

'Of course I was,' I grin. 'What about?'

'I didn't know what I was asking,' he says. 'When I asked you out, I mean.'

'Yeah. I wasn't ready to tell you.'

'Well, I get it now,' he says.

There's an awkward pause.

'I get it,' I say. 'I didn't ... Daniel knew everything. I kind of wanted to save him from dating the mess that is me. It's still nice that you asked.'

He smiles. 'Thanks,' he says. 'It's not, I don't mean –'

'Liam, it's cool. We're good. Friends, right?' I ask.

He nods, grateful. 'Friends,' he agrees.

'Did he ask you out again? Because I'm getting ready to challenge him to fisticuffs or duelling pistols,' Daniel says, slinging an arm around my shoulders.

I roll my eyes. 'Duelling pistols would probably explode in your face. But no, he did not. He won't again.'

'Ah. I wondered ... never mind.'

'You wondered if he knew about me and asked me out if I'd say yes?'

'Yeah,' he says, looking away. 'I mean, he didn't kno–'

'Daniel, shut up. I love you. Liam was never competition,' I say, smiling at him. 'You're you. And he's a cardboard cut-out where a person could go.'

'I'd kiss you right now if we weren't in public,' he says. 'Hell, if Mr Simmons weren't actually about to yell at me about the hands-off policy.'

I laugh as Mr Simmons yells about the hands-off policy.

'Grace?' he says when I start to walk away.

'Yeah?' I ask, turning back to look at him.

'I love you, too,' he says.

I hate how dopey my grin is and how happy he looks.

'You guys are the cutest,' Jenna sighs.

'I miss Elsa,' Caleb says. 'And my bed.'

'Oh my god,' I say. 'I think I'm going to perform an actual marriage ceremony between me and my bed when we get back. Not even the weirdest marriage in history.'

'If you say Tesla and the pigeon I'm going to be really disappointed in you for repeating a fact,' Daniel says.

'When did I say that one?'

'After the katzenklavier; the cat organ with the nails in their tails,' Daniel says. 'No, I tell a lie. It was Newton and the cat flap.'

'That's right,' I say.

'You two deserve each other,' Ryan says, joining our group. He smiles nervously at Jenna who doesn't notice because she's ranting about cat cruelty.

'Have I done French marrying the dead?' I ask.

'Yes,' Daniel says. 'Are you feeling okay? Are you sick?'

'Shut up', I say.

'So weird,' Jenna sighs.

'Is it weird I've started to enjoy it?' Caleb asks.

'Yes,' Jenna says.

'One of us, one of us,' Daniel chants.

I laugh.

'There's a guy who married a Barbie doll,' Ryan says. 'And some women who married landmarks. Oh, and that Chinese dude who married a picture of himself.'

'One of us,' Daniel chants again.

'That's insane,' Caleb says.

'I think that's the point,' I reply.

'Another one,' Jenna says, disgusted.

'You can stay,' I tell Ryan.

He looks at Jenna and then away.

I wonder how long it will take her to notice. Daniel and Caleb haven't yet, but Elsa's going to see it in under thirty seconds. Maybe I'll talk to Jenna. Or Ryan. Or maybe it's none of my business.

'Get on the bus, Turing,' Daniel says. 'Unless you don't want to sit next to me.'

'That's an option?' I ask.

He rolls his eyes and I get on the bus.

CHAPTER SEVENTEEN
The Future

It's a week after camp and, as expected, everyone is back to normal. With the exception of Caleb, who is doing a pretty good job of not being a misogynistic prick, and Ryan, who has joined our group to moon over Jenna. Jenna remains oblivious, and Elsa keeps trying to draw me into betting over it. But I can't, because then I'd be a hypocrite and life's too short to be hypocritical. Besides, this unrequited BS is part of high school. Jenna will figure it out or she won't, and Ryan will tell her or he won't.

We're meant to be in the library this history block to research our modern Australian history assignments. Instead, we're in our homeroom staring at those paper tests where you colour in the bubbles.

'I know most of you already have plans for what you'll do after year ten, whether that's college or TAFE, but this test might help you broaden your horizons, or perhaps help you to consider a career you might not have thought of. You'll get the results next week,' Miss Williams says.

I'm seriously considering faking that I'm sick so I don't have to do this.

'You said you wanted a five-year plan,' Daniel whispers, sensing my fear.

'I don't know if I can do this,' I mutter.

'Sure you can,' he says. 'You're Grace goddamn Turing.'

Here's the thing: I haven't actually thought about a career. What's the point? Whatever I do, I'll probably be too sick by the time I get qualified to actually do it.

But, says the voice of reason, what if you're not?

What if I waste five years to eight years studying for something I can't do? I argue back.

'Grace, breathe,' Daniel says.

'Shut up,' I say.

'There should be no talking,' Miss Williams says, pointedly. 'No one else will see your answers or results. It's just for you. Cheating won't get you anywhere.'

People start filling out their forms and Miss Williams slowly makes her way down the back of the classroom to me.

'You okay?' she whispers.

'I'm fine,' I lie. 'I'm just ... the future, you know?'

She smiles at me sympathetically. 'It's just an experiment. Think about it philosophically.'

'Right,' I say. 'Pretend I'm not going to be in a wheelchair in five years and fill it out like I'm Grace Turing: Real Girl.'

'Something like that,' Miss Williams replies, clearly on shaky ground with the wheelchair comment.

I fill out the test as Grace Turing: Real Girl and I dread the results.

Everyone keeps talking about what they hope for. Jenna says it doesn't matter what the test says, she's going to TAFE. Her mother is going to kill her, but she wants to do cooking, which is science for hungry people, or hairdressing, which is science for people to feel beautiful. She has a little monologue about the importance of the small, everyday sciences that give people joy – it's kind of inspiring and I suddenly have more respect for hairdressers.

Daniel says he's thinking he wants to be a journalist or a lawyer – something about the truth mattering and unheard voices. It's hard to keep a leash on the heart eyes that threaten when he talks about it. There's passion in his eyes and a sense of honesty and urgency that he hardly ever lets out of the bag. I want to draw him and kiss him in equal measure.

Caleb decided to be a carpenter when he was five years old and has never wavered, even for a day. There's something undeniably admirable about that. He's so confident and safe. Elsa smiles at him like he's solving the mysteries of the world, and I kind of see how he's exactly what she needs. The feet on the ground to her head in the clouds.

Elsa says she's gone off the idea of journalism and is leaning towards sociology or something. She talks with her hands about understanding the world before we can change it. She's scattered and messy and honest. She's got pastel smudges on her fingertips and she's vaguely self-deprecating. Somehow, she's the most beautiful girl in the world for a minute, there: the sun glinting in her white-blonde hair and blue eyes sparkling.

Ryan is studying pure math. It's not even a debate and there's no explanation: 'I'm going to Monash and I'm studying pure mathematics.' Like the nerd he is. One day, I might ask him what pure mathematics actually is, because I genuinely do not know. We're supportive when we give him shit and he blushes, actually blushes. He's adorable, like a puppy. I hope Jenna can see him, really see him. Because even oblivious me can tell that Ryan's worth being really seen.

Daniel doesn't let anyone ask me what I want to do, and he doesn't ask me either. I'm grateful but it also kind of feels like another way I'm not like everyone else. Another layer of distance. Another piece of proof that I'll get left behind.

…

It's Tuesday, so I have art in the last period. I hang back to show Mrs Connors some of my digital art. She's been beyond amazing with letting me come back to art after everything, and working with me. She doesn't let anyone talk shit if I'm doing an independent study instead of some of the more detailed art projects. She's still teaching me and I'm learning. I remember the Tuesday afternoon when my hands wouldn't stop shaking. The day I thought my world ended. I thought I'd be saying goodbye to art.

'I really appreciate you, Mrs Connors,' I say as she flicks through the images making supportive noises.

She looks up, surprised. 'Sorry?'

I laugh. 'I appreciate you,' I repeat. 'You let me just … be.'

'Oh Grace,' she sighs. 'You're not meant to have favourites as a teacher, but you're special. Gifted. I'm glad you came back. There's a resilience that will serve you well as a person, and as an artist, in the years to come.'

I don't really know what to say to that.

'And the work you're doing here,' she says, showing me a sketch I'd done of a group of shops in town. 'I know it's not the same, but it's still yours. The colours, those lines. You're in this as much as you were in a pencil sketch.'

I think I might cry.

'What's wrong?' she asks, leaning forward to take my hand. 'Did I say something?'

'No, you didn't. I just … I'm scared,' I confess. 'I'm getting worse all the time. We're doing career quizzes and making plans for next year and study options. Everyone else seems to have it figured it out, and I … I'm just going to get sicker.'

'Grace Turing, that is nonsense,' she says firmly.

I'm surprised by her vehemence.

'Oh, you're getting worse with your health, that's a fact. But, that's not the only part of you. Look at this! Your art! Your knowledge of history is fascinating, and some of the facts you come out with, well, I've never met anyone like you, Grace, and I doubt I will again. You're one of a kind. Being sick doesn't mean you don't have a future,' she tells me, as if she's scolding me.

'I … I don't really have anything to say to that.'

'And no one knows what they want to do when they're seventeen,' she adds, softening. 'I thought I wanted to be a flight attendant. And then I studied tourism and marketing. I only found my way to this five years ago.'

She laughs at the surprise on my face.

'I'm happier than I've ever been, I'm facing down old age and retirement, and I finally figured myself out. Don't rush yourself, Grace. Have a little faith in you, in who you are.'

'I can't picture you as a flight attendant,' I say. 'Let alone as not an art teacher.'

'Exactly,' Mrs Connors says, patting my arm. She hands my iPad back to me. 'Now, away with you. I want to get home at a reasonable hour.'

'Thanks, Mrs Connors,' I say. 'You're … thanks. I have things to think about.'

'You always have things to think about,' she teases me.

...

There are these little routines that I used to have with my father. I don't really know when it stopped or changed. Maybe it was the move? But I think maybe it just kind of got lost in the mix of school and sickness. I used to take him out to the backyard, wrapped in blankets, and we'd talk while we stargazed. If I was upset or hurting, he'd make his special hot chocolate with real melted chocolate. Or, if I had bad news, we'd do this weird thing where we'd set it to a terrible cheerleader routine, and we'd laugh and laugh and laugh.

I know that I can tell Dad anything, no judgement. And I used to tell him everything, but now there's too much to protect him from. I don't tell him how sometimes I think about killing myself. I don't tell him how scared I am. When he loves me so much and looks after me so well, how can I tell him I'm not okay? I know he's noticed my withdrawal over the past two days, since the test. But he hasn't pushed. After talking to Mrs Connors, I realise that what I need most is some Dad wisdom.

I find him pretending he's awake and watching the news.

'Dad?' I say.

'I'm resting my eyes,' he's says, surging forward. 'Not sleeping.'

I bite my lip to suppress a laugh. 'Of course you weren't.'

'Thank you. Someone believes me,' he says, glaring in the direction of Mum.

'You were actually snoring, Brett,' she sighs. 'Get tested for sleep apnoea.'

'I do not have sleep apnoea.'

'You almost definitely have sleep apnoea.'

'Uh, I hate to interrupt,' I say. 'But, I was wondering if Dad wanted to stargaze with me?' I feel nervous and shift on my feet. My voice didn't sound quite right. 'It's weird, isn't it? We don't hav–'

'I would love to,' Dad says, launching him out of his recliner. 'Shall I make some hot chocolate?'

'That'd be nice,' I say, smiling. 'I'll get the blankets?'

'Meet you out there,' Dad says.

I watch him leave feeling really lucky to have him, and a little ashamed of how happy I'd made him.

'You're a good daughter,' Mum tells me, softly. 'He's missed this. He thought you got too old for him.'

'Do we ever really get too old for our parents?' I ask with a shrug.

'Very true,' Mum says. 'Everything okay? Stargazing and hot chocolate usually means you're upset.'

'I ... It's okay,' I decide. 'I just need to talk through something.'

'You don't have to tell me,' Mum cuts in.

'I know. It's not a secret, or anything. I just ...' I sigh.

'Boy trouble?'

'God no,' I say. 'Why would I talk to Dad about that? He'd flip out. I mean, he likes Daniel –'

'We all like Daniel, he's wonderful.'

'– but he's a dad and he "knows what teenage boys are like",' I finish, doing air quotes.

'Well, I'm glad things are going well with him,' Mum smiles.

I discover I have a stupid smile on my face and groan, rearranging my features back to normal. 'I'm just scared of the future,' I finally manage to say.

Mum's expression sobers. 'Ah.'

'Yeah.'

'Is there ... is there something that's happened?'

'A career quiz,' I say. 'I don't spend a lot of time thinking about the future.'

'Right.'

'As a self-protective measure.'

'I see that.'

'I think I need my dad.'

'Good call,' Mum says. 'You can talk to me anytime. But I have a feeling your father is the right parent to talk to. I have this monologue on jobs with few physical requirements and inclusive employment legislation on the tip of my tongue.'

'Mmm, please keep it there,' I say.

Mum laughs. 'Go get the blankets. He'll be out there buzzing with excitement. Your father is kind of a dork.'

'Yeah, but he's also Father of the Year, so.'

'He is at that,' Mum agrees.

...

Dad and I sit in our blanket burritos, cradling warm mugs in our hands as we look up at the sky.

'You know, the sky is better out here,' Dad says.

'We lived in the inner suburbs of a city. It was impossible to see the sky,' I remind him.

'Grace, just enjoy it.'

'Yes, Dad.'

'Yes, Dad, you're right and I'll enjoy the sky; or yes, Dad, you're an idiot but I still love you?'

'Little from column a, little from column b.'

'Rude,' he says, and bumps the shoulder of his blanket burrito into mine gently.

We sit in comfortable silence for a few minutes, and I know he's waiting for me to talk. He always waits until I'm ready.

'We did a career quiz at school the other day,' I say eventually.

'I see,' he says, and then he waits.

'I don't know what I want. I mean, I know what I want, but that's more like a wish than a real, tangible thing I can have,' I say, staring at the sky.

'Magic pill to make you better?' he asks, his voice smiling.

'Yep.'

'I want that, too, Gracie.'

'Thanks for not saying there might be one soon.'

'You're welcome. But, the career thing? You think no one will want you?'

I'm surprised at the speed a lump forms in my throat. I swallow thickly around it and try to hold back tears. Dad reaches over and holds my hand. Neither of us take our eyes off the stars. I rest my head on his shoulder.

'It's okay to cry,' he says gently. 'But you know that's not true, right?'

'Isn't it?' I ask. 'It's my – my biggest fear.' I'm sniffling as I try in vain not to actually cry.

'Grace, you're incredible. You are beautiful and brave, but you're also creative and intelligent. You can do anything you set your mind to, I'm sure of it.'

'But, I can't,' I interrupt, actually crying now. 'I can't do anything because the flesh bag is weak, no matter how willing the mind is.'

'What did you say to me when we moved to Launceston? I wanted you to take your walking stick to school and wear braces, and you wouldn't. What did you say?'

'I do what I want?'

'No, you said you were determined to be you. What changed?'

Everything, I want to say. Nothing, I think.

My brain ticks and turns, thinking it through and over and under.

'So, you can't be an astronaut. Who cares? What do you want to be, Grace? Not because you're meant to be the poster girl for invisible illness sufferers having jobs. Not because you want to be considered normal. Who do you want to be, because my daughter has never once been normal or easy in her life.'

I ugly cry as he awkwardly wraps me into his blanket burrito to hold me. He doesn't say 'there, there' or offer me a tissue or anything. He just holds me.

'When your hands started to tremor, you found ways around it,' he says when the sobbing ebbs. 'When they said you couldn't go to camp, you rallied and argued and went.'

'What if ... what if I'm useless?' I ask.

Dad pulls away to look at me. I wipe my face as I take in his frown of disapproval.

'Don't be ridiculous.'

'It's a legitimate question.'

'You are not useless, Grace, and you never will be. You have plenty to offer. Like your weird facts and your art and the way you care about people. If you wanted a pity party, you should have written that on the invitation,' Dad tells me. 'And freelancing is a very legitimate career choice these days, especially post-COVID.

Working from home and using contractors has caused a real shift in the job market.'

I laugh, because he's right. About the pity party. About the things I have to offer. They're small, but they're mine. They make up the parts of who I am. And I like who I am. I really, actually like who I am, I realise.

'Thanks, Dad,' I say, hugging him. 'You're the best.'

'You're welcome, I think? What did I say?' he asks, laughing a little.

'You reminded me I'm Grace goddamn Turing and I'm clever enough to figure it out. Whatever it'll be,' I say.

'I love you,' he says. 'You're gonna do something that makes me stupidly proud, aren't you?'

'Probably,' I tease him. 'But then, you get proud pretty easily so it's not exactly a high bar.'

'Disrespectful child,' he sighs, but he's happy and I'm happy and the hot chocolate is warm and the skies are bright.

It's a good night.

...

Daniel has had enough of my self-imposed distance by Thursday morning. He links his arm in mine and announces we're going to have a recess date to our friends.

'Gross,' I say. 'Recess date? When did you become that person? I thought Monday lunches were enough?'

He glares at me. 'Not up for debate, Turing. We need to talk.'

'Oh damn,' Jenna says. 'Are you breaking up? Because I'm telling you now, I'm keeping Grace in the divorce.'

'I call Daniel,' Caleb says and Elsa hits him.

'She wishes we're breaking up,' Daniel sighs. 'But she's not getting rid of me that easily.'

'Is there are an option where I don't get dragged off to have an ominous-sounding conversation that is probably actually a lecture?' I ask. 'I found some new *Die Hard* trivia?'

Daniel gives me a look that eloquently states that he is not impressed with my deflection.

I sigh.

'Thank you,' Daniel says. 'See you in math.'

I mouth 'save me' at Jenna and Elsa, but I don't mean it.

'Bye,' Ryan says awkwardly.

...

'So, what have I done?' I ask. 'Insulted your family? Developed halitosis? Invo–'

He cuts me off by pulling me into the narrow gap between the science block and the gym.

'They really should have just extended the science block,' I say. 'This gap is pointless. It's only good for –'

He cuts me off, but this time, he's kissing me. Lips gently pressed against mine, and for a second, I'm suspended in shock. One of his hands comes up, gently touches my face. It's the sensation of his fingertips that brings me into the moment. I lean into him, just a little, a hand on his shoulder, another on his hip. He breaks the kiss before it deepens into anything else, and presses his forehead to mine. It feels safe and intimate and I love the feeling of his hand on my cheek and hip. But it's also not enough and I want to press harder and deepen the kiss.

'This?' Daniel asks, teasing a little as he pulls away.

'I was going to say illicit transactions,' I reply, breathy and laughing. Also, low key annoyed. 'So, yes, I guess.'

He pulls back and leans against the science block. I miss him, but lean against the gym as his mirror.

'What's up?' he asks. 'Because this is getting ridiculous.'

I blink. 'I, uh … what? Can I have a clue?'

'The future thing is making you crazy, isn't it?' he asks.

'Yes. Or, it was,' I say. 'I'm …'

'Scared of being left behind?' Daniel asks, tilting his head to the side. Examining me. Reading the truth of me from my skin like he always has.

'Yes,' I admit.

'Scared of not being good enough?'

'No, I … maybe,' I allow, looking away.

'Don't know what to do because you're too focussed on the fact you have a degenerative autoimmune condition that's going to control your life eventually?'

I glare at him.

He waits for an answer.

'I love you,' I say. 'But you're being kind of ... intense right now.'

'I love you, which is why I'm being intense,' he replies. 'You're not meant to have all the answers when you're seventeen. I feel like you're my answer, which is terrifying and cliched. But you're not my answer. A person isn't an answer. Neither's a job. Which brings me back to you freaking out unnecessarily.'

'Hey! I'll decide what freak outs are necessary, thank you very much,' I argue.

'Turing.'

'Fine. I'm freaking out. It's dumb. I think ... I think I'm getting there, though. I get stuck on this image of me unable to move in agony. Of,' I take a deep breath and level my gaze. 'Of the day when I say goodbye and am euthanised. I don't know if it's next year or five years or fifteen. Odds aren't so great after fifteen.' I shrug, trying to make it seem like it matters less than it does.

'I fucking hate it when you talk about that,' he breathes out like I've hurt him. 'But I understand and respect your position.'

I reach out for him, take his hand. Our arms are almost extended completely with our backs against the buildings. My olive skin and his caramel tone. My small hand in his long fingers. Soft and paint-stained against calloused and scarred. Not quite opposites.

'Turing, I'm scared for you,' he says. When I look at him, his eyes are closed. 'I'm scared for me because of you.'

'Hey,' I say, tugging on his hand gently. He looks at me. 'It's okay to be scared. You'd be insane to not be. But ... that fear? That's what I'm wrestling with. I can do the present, the now. I can be with you and be at school, and love the moments, you know?'

'But what comes next is unknown,' Daniel finishes for me.

'Exactly.'

'So, what do you want me to do? How do I get my girlfriend back, because she's been checked out since that quiz,' he says. 'And I miss her.'

I blush. I must. He pulls on my hand and holds me against him when I stumble forwards.

'Sorry,' I say.

'You don't have to apologise. But you're forgiven.'

'Thanks so much.'

He laughs at my sarcasm and loosens his grip.

'Tell me what next,' he says, looking in my eyes.

'Kissing you?' I suggest.

He laughs and presses a kiss to my forehead.

'Not what I was suggesting.'

'After,' he says. 'Tell me.'

'I don't have answers!'

'Yeah, you do,' he says. 'You're just waiting for someone to provoke them out of you. Lucky for you, I'm an excellent provoker.'

I wrinkle my nose and step out of his embrace.

'Rude.'

'Accurate,' he quips.

'I think I'm going to study history, or maybe graphic design?' The words come out in one breath, a rush, all joined together. I'm not even sure they were intelligible.

Daniel grins, or, more accurately, smirks.

I scowl.

'Perfect,' he says. 'Grace Turing, historian. World War Two? Anthropology? Teaching? Researcher? You can write a textbook everyone can hate you for writing. Or graphic design, equally as good. You're an awesome designer.'

I open my mouth and close it, a little lost for words. 'You ... I ... How can you just ... know things so confidently?'

He laughs. 'I know *you*. I had a hunch. Jenna though you'd end up in social work or something for advocacy. But you don't want to be the poster girl for disability inspo porn. Elsa thought you'd do fine arts, which Caleb figured would be okay because no one ever makes money or does anything useful with an arts degree. Which caused an amazing argument I wish you could have seen.'

'Oh, great. So you're all talking about me behind my back!'

'Yeah, Caleb's a dick,' Daniel grins.

'Ugh!'

'You're not actually mad. You like that we care,' Daniel says.

'I'm mad! I'm allowed to be mad!'

'Fine, you're mad. But there's a group of people who love you, we're obviously going to talk about you.'

I want to argue, but I find the wind goes out of my sails while I stand there with my hands on my hips.

'History means research and weird facts,' Daniel says. 'You also don't need to be around people. You can do it from anywhere. Same with graphic design. Anywhere in the world at your own pace.'

'You spent way more time thinking about this than I did,' I say. 'I had vague ideas. You sound like you've picked out my career path.'

Daniel looks like he wants to say something, but can't. Or won't.

Internally, I smirk, because two can play the knowing game.

'You spent time researching this, didn't you?'

'Maybe.' He looks away.

'This matters to you.'

'It's about you,' he says, still not looking at me. 'Of course it matters to me.'

That's when it hits. I get it now.

He needs me to have a future. Because if I have a future, he can be in it. I'm not going to hide or leave earlier than I should. It matters because he wants me to have a life, a real life, even if it doesn't have him cast as the romantic lead. Because he thinks I deserve it. Because he loves me. Because he's Daniel Perkins. Boyfriend, asshole, knower of me.

I lick my lips, mouth dry, heart pounding.

I don't know how to tell him how much he means to me. How I understand how much I mean to him. How to describe the way my chest is full of him and my skin tingles with wanting him and my heart is beating harder because I didn't think anyone would ever love me like he says he does; like he shows me he does.

'We're seventeen,' I say.

'Ye-es?' Daniel says, looking at me, confused.

'You said you're not meant to have answers at seventeen,' I say.

'Yeah?'

'It's stupid and cliched.'

'I did just say that, yes.'

'Let's be stupid and cliched together,' I say.

There's a weird moment where I don't think he quite under-stands what I'm saying, and the he's grinning this ridiculously stupid, big grin.

'You're so frickin' weird, Turing.'

'Back at you, Perkins.'

He steps forward, gathering me into his arms and trapping me against the wall in a way that feels clichéd but is still amazing.

'I'm so glad I found you,' I say before he covers my mouth with his.

When we get to math, we're literally sixty seconds late and Mr Simmons gives us a warning. We're panting when we fall into our seats, still grinning.

'Do I want to know?' Jenna asks, smirking.

I laugh.

'I wish,' Daniel says.

'If the peanut gallery would quiet down,' Mr Simmons says, glaring at us. But, I don't care.

I don't care that we're in trouble or Mr Simmons is angry or that I'm out of breath. I don't care I'll pay for it later. Because for ten shining minutes, I was Grace Turing: Real Girl and it was glorious. I'm loved and known and real. No, I *am* Grace Turing: Real Girl. And the idiots in this room who love me have made it true.

I'm seventeen years old, and I don't have all the answers. I'm not meant to. But I've got some ideas. I've got Ivy and Dad and Mum. I've got friends who really are family. I've got Daniel Perkins, who is a multitude of things, and all of them perfect and better than I deserve or thought I'd ever get.

I've got a body working to betray me, ready to give out at any second. Maybe it kills me, maybe it doesn't. Maybe I'm in a wheelchair in a year and maybe my lungs give out in two, and maybe yoga really will help. (Okay, it won't. But punching people who suggest yoga ...). Maybe it ends things before they begin. But, maybe it doesn't.

Future, come at me.

My people and I are ready.

But, more than that: I'm Grace goddamn Turing, and what doesn't kill me better watch its back.

Acknowledgements

I begin with cliched and sincere thanks to my family.

To my husband, for being eternally patient (but only with me). If you are a writer, or have lived with one, you know what he endures.

To my perfect little sister, who read this book as I wrote it and demanded a new chapter each week: I'd do anything for you, always.

To my mother, for delivering us food each week for many reasons, the least of which is not that you wanted me to be able to use all the spoons I could to write (less thankful for the million and five times she said 'you should write a book' and would like to make it clear that I wrote a book in spite of that and not because of it).

And to my grandmother and step-father, who did not live long enough to see this happen but who would be so incredibly proud, I miss you both profoundly.

Especial thanks must also be given to my writing partner Freya Su, because I would not be publishing this book if she hadn't acted like success was a foregone conclusion. Meeting you during my first NaNoWriMo was magic and fate and all that good stuff. I hope we always do life connected to each other, regardless of distance and immune systems. Budding author Taleisha Lyall's incomparable belief in me gets a mention, and a shared adventure led me to Forty South's doorstep, and I couldn't be more grateful to have met Lucinda Sharp. Lucinda, thank you so much for seeing the importance of stories about young people living with chronic, incurable health conditions because it was a journey to find someone who did! Elizabeth Spiegel edited my book with such ease that I almost didn't notice it happening. And have you seen my cover? It's all due to Bianca Jagoe's creativity and brilliance – I cannot tell you what it means to have a fellow spoonie and local woman not just design it, but nail it.

AVERY MCDOUGALL (BEdS, GDipIM) has always loved stories and uses them as weapons in her fight with chronic illness. She lives in Tasmania with her beloved husband and a bunny-shaped destruction goddess.